BLACKFRIARS

BLACKFRIARS

BY

DEREK R MCDONOUGH

Dedication

I would like to thank my family for their endless patience during the writing of this novel. They have been my inspiration and have given me the energy to continue. Particularly I would like to thank Jonathan for his valued guidance.

My profound gratitude also goes to Victoria from Vicovers for her incredible artwork and wonderful imagination.

May I finally thank my dad, he taught me one very valuable lesson in life, if you want something bad enough, you'll always be able to dig deep and find it.

Prologue

April 1536

William ran as fast as he could. It was very late at night; the sky was inky black but no stars were visible. Heavy rain pelted William and it felt cold and hard on his face. The ground was soft and slippery under foot but he was too scared to stop running. He was too terrified to turn and look back, he knew that he needed to keep running and to be as far away from Newton House Abbey as he was able to be. Having just seen the Abbot brutally murdered, he was afraid that he would suffer the same torturous death. Not even God himself would stand by and allow another human to carry out such atrocities, he thought. William was 27 years old and had been a Dominican Order Monk with the English Province of the Order of Preachers for several years. He was tall at 5' 9" and was very slim. He had a slim face with a pale complexion but he had a strong jaw line and large eyes. He wore a gown with a hood that tied at the waistline and he wore leather sandals.

William began to question his faith, he chastised himself for this but his fear soon took a hold of him again and he returned to his thoughts of self-preservation. His gown became heavy as it absorbed more rain water and he felt that his sandals would surely not be able to withstand the conditions much longer. Still, he kept racing away from Newton House Abbey at the murder that was probably still occurring. He had to keep running and he had to warn all other members of the brotherhood, from the treachery that was unfolding because of the Act of Supremacy that Parliament had recently passed and approved. All monks, no matter their denomination were going to be in danger of persecution and they must be warned of the threat that the monarchy was unleashing upon them. The Act of Supremacy, passed in 1534 demanded an oath of loyalty from all English Subjects and many say, marked the beginning of English Reformation. Henry VIII was recognised as the head of the English Church and defender of the faith.

William ran faster and headed for Blackfriars Abbey in the far reaches of Northern Northumberland. It was many miles away and would take a number of days to cover. He clutched the royal parchments that had been delivered to his Abbey by the Monarchy and he kept running. The rain continued to pound into him until he suddenly lost his footing and slipped down a steep hillside. He rolled and skidded on the muddy hillside and finally came to rest against a small tree. His ribs were painful and his left leg ached above the knee. He still held the parchments but his chest felt like it would burst, he sucked in hard and the cold air tore at his lungs. He looked skyward and decided to find sanctuary for the night. He scuttled to his right, where he saw a small copse, he sat with his legs pulled in tight and pulled his wet hood over his head and face.

Act One – Injustice

Chapter One

Present Day

John Huggett was a man's man, at least that's what his friends would always say to him. And, in many ways, this was exactly what he had wanted to hear. Not that any of his, so called friends, would dare say anything else. You see, John Huggett was a bully. And not just any bully, but a dangerous one who had filled his niche and accomplished what he had set out to do. He had achieved success in his line of work and that had brought him power.

A tall man, he had an imposing stature and a large frame. In fact, he was quite over weight. This was probably the only thing in his life that he was unhappy about. He had battled for many years with his love for the wrong kinds of food but, more so his appetite for fine ales. Over the years, he had tried almost every diet available and even the odd spell of exercise. Nothing had seemed to work for him, but this was the one area of his life that he accepted he could do precious little about. He was 45 years old and looked every bit of it. His heavy frame was complimented by a thick head of dark brown hair which he tried to keep as neat as possible, and a small moustache which never looked wide enough for his large round face.

He would spend many evenings away from his wife Helen and their daughter Tabitha, in his local, the Red Lion. The pub was very small and cosy and it had an equally small clientele. This was largely down to its, 'off the beaten track' location, near the quiet, rural village of Lower Mittley. He had his favourite spot near the bar as this provided him with the ideal position to make him the natural centre of attention. He would captivate his unwilling, yet seemingly attentive audience on how he had made a killing that day thriving off the misfortune of another unsuspecting victim. His listeners, including the Landlord, all knew of course that somewhere, some poor soul was sat at home a couple of thousand pounds worse off, simply for being in the wrong place at the wrong time.

John Huggett owned a garage where he bought and sold used cars. He had built up his business, and his nest egg, by exploiting his rude and arrogant nature to its fullest extent. He had taken over the business from his father Ronald, after he had to retired from ill health. In the ten years that followed he had managed to destroy the reputation that his father had built up for being a fair man, with the after sales service to rival any garage within 100 miles. John had always been a bully, even since as long as his friends could remember. It was these tactics he employed most of all, and why not, bullying had always worked for him, so why should he change.

Robert Easton was driving along the busy A2321 road that led to his house, a little over 17 miles from his office. It always seemed a long journey, especially as he had to do it twice every day. In many ways, he didn't mind spending the 30 minutes or so that it took him. He would use the time wisely dreaming up new ideas and ways to get out of his present office job as an accountancy technician. He was reasonably happy but he wanted a job that would offer him more excitement. Robert had left the regular Army two years previously having served with the Parachute Regiment and latterly attached to 22 Squadron Special Air Service. Despite lacking the mental toughness to be able to pass the full SAS selection test, he served with the Regiment for two years as a member of their support staff, and whilst there he learned many of their skills and ways of working. When he left the SAS Regiment he felt that it was time he moved to a civilian job but he tried to cling to some of the excitement he needed in life and thought that he might find it in the Territorial Army as a part time reservist.

Robert was quite tall at 185 Centimetres and, altogether, he was a good man. He had short-cropped blonde hair, striking green eyes and a chiselled jaw line. He was in good shape, had remained unmarried and was quite a catch his envious mates at the TA would tell him. He thought perhaps that he hadn't found the right woman, but he was certainly not unattractive. He would spend every lunch-time in the gym which he had joined in town when it had opened several years earlier and sometimes he would run in the evenings. He would praise himself every time he beat his time on his favourite run. As he recovered from his exercise he would time his heart rate as it reduced, knowing that the quicker he recovered, the fitter he was.

Robert never really understood how he was still able to beat his fastest time. Surely he had to stop beating it eventually. After all he was 36 years old. He thought to himself that maybe he was gaining stamina as he got older, or perhaps he was just learning how to cut the odd corner and subconsciously trick himself.

Robert was also financially very astute. He had bought himself a large property when he had been in his early twenties following good advice from an older work colleague. He had been advised against this venture from several of his friends, especially having a mortgage on a property that was the limit to which his salary would extend. However, three years and one property market boom later, he had sold the house and once he had cleared the capital and settled his mortgage in full, he had realised a profit of more than forty thousand pounds. He moved into a studio apartment and banked his small fortune with a view to searching for another property as soon as possible. Housing repossessions were increasing rapidly following the property boom and Robert was in a good position having cash in the bank. Mortgages were more expensive so he decided to attend a property auction and gauge what sort of prices that repossessions would reach. Pleasantly surprised, Robert spent the next few weeks attending auctions until he found the ideal place. It was a large house with five bedrooms, however, this one needed work. With the help of a building society to set up a small mortgage and the forty thousand he had in the bank, he secured the property of his dreams and set about renovating it with every spare penny he could lay his hands on. He knew he couldn't sell the house within one year without incurring a large capital gains tax bill.

Over the next twelve months he turned a derelict house into a beautiful expensive family home. Again, he cleared his mortgage and saw another large sum transferred into his bank. A few years later, Robert had bought his own house outright and had over two hundred thousand pounds in savings. Content with his lot, he was now happy to live the life of a bachelor and was not short of friends.

He approached the junction where he had to turn left and drive the last 7 miles to his house. The traffic was heavy that night and Robert was not enjoying the journey. He had worked especially late that evening, helping to prepare his firm for their annual Quality Assurance audit from head office. He had felt out of sorts all day and he just wanted to be out of the traffic. He knew that if he turned right, he could turn off about one mile further up the road and take a really quiet drive home. It was approximately 3 miles longer, but it was February and already dark; he just wanted to be away from the noise and the headlights.

Robert approached the familiar old stone cottage on the corner immediately before the junction and he indicated right. He drove off up the road, looking for the small sign post that would point him towards Lower Mittley. It was to be a decision that would change his life forever.

It was about 9.45pm on a typical Tuesday evening and John Huggett was in good form in the Red Lion. He was surrounded by his usual drinking partners. Ray, a personal computer salesman, Phil, owner of a small local printing firm and Neville, a carpenter who had retired several years ago due to ill health.

Tonight, they were all joined by the landlord Peter Forton, who sometimes found himself unintentionally and reluctantly drawn into their conversation. Phil had been commenting on work to a proposed by-pass that was rumoured to be starting soon.

'How on earth do you expect me to believe that Phil?' John said sharply.

'It's only what I read in this morning's paper John.' Replied Phil, hoping that the attention would be drawn away from him.

'Everybody knows that the bloody by-pass doesn't stand a dog's chance! Besides, even if there *was* a miracle and it *was* passed, how the hell do you suppose they are going to negotiate that fuel pipeline?' John knew of no pipeline but he was hoping that they would back down now.

14

'What pipeline?' Enquired Ray with a tone that hinted his disbelief.

John Huggett had been faced with this type of situation many times in the past. He knew that he simply had to stick to his guns, apply a little subterfuge and his integrity would be once again restored.

'You know, that wretched thing they laid about 25 years ago.' Said John.

Neville looked puzzled.

'I don't recall any...'

'The thing's probably rusted away now.' John interrupted.

'Anyway, my point is, none of you need to worry. Besides, it is this that I wanted to show you'. John produced a small leather bound notebook from his pocket.

'Damn thing's been lying in my kitchen drawer at home for a while now, my uncle sent it to me and I've been meaning to show it to you all.' It's got a lot of nonsense in it about the Tudor Dynasty – my uncle is a bit of an academic and has been doing some research. I rarely see him these days; in fact, I haven't seen him for donkey's years. It looks like he may have been onto something though.'

John was afraid to admit his ignorance but he hoped that one of his friends may take an interest and offer to help him make sense of its contents. He was rescued by the telephone which rang behind the bar. Peter answered it in his usual calm voice.

'Good evening, the Red Lion.' There was a brief pause.

'Yes I'll just see if he's in.' Helen wondered why Peter always said that because she knew only too well that he could probably close his eyes and name everyone in the bar.

He passed the phone over to John who was into his second wind now.

'Sorry to interrupt John, think it's your other half.' The others looked relieved as he grabbed the receiver away from the landlord, as if he had been confiscating a catapult from a badly-behaved school child.

'Yes darling.' The others had often thought to themselves if he was in some way bullied at home, and that's why he avenged his wife's wrath on them.

'I am just finishing now dear, see you in about 15 minutes or so.' John was not bullied at home, although, he was afraid of her sometimes, and wanted to keep her happy.

Helen was the only child of Ronald and Edith Panter. Ronald was a farmer, he owned a small holding about 25 miles away. They were both in their seventies now but Ronald refused to give up work.

'Still, he's got one foot in the grave and the other on a roller skate.' John would often joke. He ended the phone call and he collected his sheep-skin coat from behind the door in the bar.

'Same time tomorrow night?' He said with an expectant tone in his voice, whilst pulling his coat over his shoulders.

Having received the reply that he anticipated, he opened the door and started off down the dimly lit lane that led to his home in a secluded avenue, about half a mile away. The fresh air had an immediate impact on him and he felt himself sway in the cold evening air. He felt assured that the half a dozen pints of Waverley Best Bitter and two double Whiskeys would keep him warm until he got home. He took his uncle's notebook out of his pocket and slowed down as he looked at it once more. He returned his attention to the blurred footpath and held the notebook in his hand as he walked.

Meanwhile, Robert's eyes were tired and sore. Spots of rain had started to appear on his windscreen and slowly crept their way upwards towards the roof of his car. He was about to turn on his wipers, but he remembered that he needed to replace the rubber blades. Over the last few days he had used his windscreen wipers on about four occasions and each time they smeared across the glass and left his visibility severely impaired.

Slowly the rain became harder and he realised that he was going to have to turn them on sooner rather than later. Nevertheless, he wished that he taken the time to change them. He pondered over the thought of driving faster in the hope that the rain may race its way up the windscreen faster.

His eyes became more strained and he lowered his head, moving it towards the windscreen thinking that this may improve his already limited visibility. Still, he knew it would be better to keep within the speed limits. He imagined the roads would be quite slippery now. He struggled to see the approaching right hand corner ahead but managed to negotiate it safely. He started to increase his speed out of the corner, back up to thirty miles per hour. He glanced down at the odometer and saw that he would have been only about 4 miles from home had he continued on his usual route.

When he looked up he tried to focus his eyes on the road again. The rain was hammering hard against the windscreen now and he found himself moving his head still further forwards.

Suddenly, he saw a shape standing in the road directly in front of him only about ten feet away. A pain shot down the centre of his body as he tried to swerve his car away to the opposite side of the road. He was only allowed a second to stamp his full weight on the brakes. Briefly, he saw the outline of a large man in front of him stagger, and to his horror, in the same direction that he was steering. As Robert's car struck the man, Robert felt the car shudder and he experienced the same pain shoot down his throat and into his stomach.

The man had appeared to be thrown to the right then Robert lost sight of him. He quickly stopped his car and switched on his hazard warning lights. He opened the door and felt the cool air hit his body. He was afraid to look down the road, not sure of what was going to confront him. He walked quickly towards the dark shape lying on a muddy grass verge; he felt a strange sensation in his legs at the thought of the horrific injuries he may have caused. He saw that the man was lying on his back, Robert reached the man and knelt down.

'Hello, can you hear me, can you feel any pain?'

The man did not respond. He reached out and grasped his arm. He gently shook the man but again but there was still no response.

He tried to recall his Army first aid training. He had the letters H R A B C in his head. Hazard, Response, Airway, Breathing and Circulation. He impressed himself at recalling this information, especially whilst under enormous pressure, and alone. He could see his Sergeant Major stood in the drill hall leaning across the "Resus Annie" doll. He satisfied himself that there was no hazard to himself or the patient and he had already deduced that the man was unresponsive.

Robert prepared himself for the worst as he carefully pushed back the man's forehead remembering that this would open the airway. He lowered his head towards the man's face, placed his right ear near the man's mouth and looked down over his chest. The pain he had felt, caused by the shock, immediately began to subside as he saw the man's chest moving up and down. He felt the warmth of the man's breath against the side of his face and at once Robert knew that he would be spared the last check, circulation.

The man was alive but Robert continued with his list of first aid priorities, before finally placing the man into the recovery position. As he rolled John Huggett towards him, he revealed a small leather bound notebook lying underneath him. Without giving it any thought he placed the book inside his own jacket pocket to protect it from the rain. He had other, more pressing concerns at the moment now and ran to his car to collect his mobile telephone, all the time praying that his telephone service provided him with a strong enough signal to make a call from this remote area. He picked up his telephone and was relieved to see four bars, denoting a strong signal.

He ran back to the man and hesitated for a second, trying to recall what number he needed for the emergency services. He was not convinced that it was 999 from a mobile telephone, nor that it was 112. Nevertheless, he had seen this number before when reading his telephone manual and decided that 112 was worth a try. He could see that rain was falling onto the leather cover of his mobile phone.

His cold fingers pressed the numbers and he heard a ringing tone, a woman's voice answered.

'Emergency services, which service do you require?'

Chapter Two

Helen Huggett sat in the back of the police car with her daughter by her side. The constable had called to her house a short time earlier and delivered the distressing news. Helen didn't show any real emotion during the journey to the hospital. Instead she appeared vacant and bewildered.

'Had your husband been out visiting at the time of the accident?' There was an empty pause. The driver wondered if he had been heard. He was about to repeat the question, but Helen replied.

'Yes he went down to the Red Lion to see his friends.' She held Tabitha's hand and tried to reassure her that her father was strong. 'What exactly is the extent of his injuries?' Helen enquired.

'I'm afraid I don't know Mrs Huggett,' replied the constable, trying to sound as sympathetic as he could. 'Unfortunately, I only started my shift a short time ago, and I've been told only to escort you straight to the Accident and Emergency Unit.'

The constable realised that he possibly could have conveyed this information in a slightly better way. However, he satisfied himself that she was entitled to know where her husband was, and she had to be informed sooner or later.

The police car drew up outside Accident and Emergency and all three walked into the hospital.

'I have been here several times this week, so please follow me and I will show you to A and E.' Again, he wondered if he might have been a little more tactful.

'Here we are now Mrs Huggett.' The constable asked Helen to take a seat in the relative's room and he approached the nurse's station. 'Hello, I'm PC Blackmore from Radley Street Police Station. I understand you had a Mr John Huggett admitted earlier this evening; I have his wife and daughter with me.'

He noticed the badge on the nurse's uniform, RGN Sally Radcliffe.

'Yes he came in only a short time ago, the Senior House Officer is still with him.' PC Blackmore knew that that could be a good sign. Had his injuries been life threatening then the Consultant would have been in attendance.

'Thank you, we'll take it from here. Where are Mrs Huggett and her daughter?' Nurse Radcliffe could see a woman in her early forties and a young girl through the horizontal blinds, sitting in the relative's room, but she wanted their identities confirmed by the young PC.

'They are sitting in that room there just down the corridor to the left.' The officer pointed expecting the nurse to help him out. The nurse walked off towards the relative's room.

'There was one more thing,' PC Blackmore added, before she was allowed to get too far down the corridor.

'DS Bretherton wanted to know when he could come in to see Mr Huggett, only he has several questions he needs to ask him.' The young PC posed the question as fairly as he possibly could. Even in the short time he had been in the job, he knew that the response was probably going to be negative, and he prepared himself for this.

'Oh, I'm afraid it's far too early to say yet. Can you get him to give us a call in the morning, we'll know much more about his injuries by then?' PC Blackmore allowed himself a wry smile before telling Helen that he would wait for as long as she needed and he continued down the corridor towards a row of seats along the wall at the entrance to the A and E unit.

The nurse approached the doorway of the relative's room. She caught a glimpse of Helen through the glass partition before she opened the door. She noticed her blonde hair that was styled in a bob, and worn just above her shoulder. She imagined that she would be very attractive when she was wearing make-up but understood that the events of this evening had probably taken their toll. Tabitha however, looked more like her father. She had thick brown hair that fell down her back, and a small round face.

'Hello, you must be Mrs Huggett.' Nurse Radcliffe then raised the pitch of her voice and crouched down to Tabitha's level.

'Hello, my name is Sally. And what's your name?'

'Tabitha.'

'That's a lovely name, how old are you Tabitha?'

'Nine.' Replied Tabitha, clearing her voice for the next round of questions. 'Well, I'm Nurse Radcliffe but you can call me Sally if you like.'

Helen started to shift in her seat and Sally recognised this as someone who wanted more information, and quickly. Sally stood up again.

'You will both be able to go through and see him in a few minutes. He is still unconscious but stable for the moment. And as far as we can see, he has no serious injuries.'

'Then why are you keeping him in Casualty?' Added Helen with an anxious tone in her voice.

'Well, we are waiting for him to regain consciousness and then we'll know much more.' Sally wasn't prepared to give any more information away at this stage. Her experience told her that she should wait now until the SHO had finished what he was doing and he could explain. Sally excused herself for the moment only to reappear a few seconds later.

'You can both come through now, please try not to be too alarmed by all the machines and tubes.'

They walked down the corridor following the nurse. There was a large amount of activity going on around them, people lying in beds behind half drawn curtains and hospital staff rushing past them. Helen and Tabitha however, were oblivious to this and followed Sally around a corner and through a set of double doors. John Huggett lay in a bed in the centre of the room. His head and neck were still supported by a brace that had been put in place by the paramedics at the scene of the accident. Sally explained that the heart monitor, attached to John by three wires, was there purely as an aid to the nurses and was not required because they suspected heart problems. Helen wanted to speak to him, but she could see that it was pointless, and asked if there was anything she could do at this stage. Sally explained that he was in good hands and that there was nothing more she could do now.

'Why don't you both return home for now and try to get some rest. You can both return first thing in the morning, when hopefully we should be able to give you all the information you need.' Helen nodded in agreement and walked off towards PC Blackmore who rose to his feet when he saw Helen and Tabitha approaching.

Robert Easton sipped at a cup of sweet tea in Radley Street Police Station. He had already provided a written statement, detailing the events leading up to the accident. A police sergeant was apologising to him for having to carry out the breath test earlier.

'You understand that it's purely routine, and once the SOCO has returned I will get someone to drive you home.' Robert looked puzzled,

'What or who is the SOCO?'

'He's the Scene of Crimes Officer; you know the guy you see with his tape measure out after a car accident. He's down at the scene now.'

Robert looked more puzzled, only this time he sat up straight in his seat.

'Am I in some kind of trouble?'

The sergeant inhaled, and was about to alleviate Robert's fears when he was interrupted by the door of the office opening. A constable stood in the doorway,

'SOCOs back sarge.' The sergeant stood up and excused himself.

'I'll only be a couple of minutes.' The sergeant said.

Robert sat alone in the sergeant's office. He equated his feeling to that of a man in the dock awaiting the verdict. He tried to reassure himself that he had nothing to worry about and he was sure he hadn't broken the law.

The sergeant returned as promised, he could almost sense Robert's fear lingering in the atmosphere. He wanted to put Robert out of his misery as soon as possible.

'Well, everything appears to be in order sir.'

'What do you mean?' Robert already felt some relief but he needed more reassurance.

'The SOCO has informed me that you were not in excess of the speed limit. I expect that you want to go home now. May I recommend that you leave your car here and I'll get someone to take you home?'

Robert was at ease now and he felt his confidence returning.

'I know that I wasn't speeding, but what makes you so sure now.'

'It's all very technical, it has something to do with the length of skid marks and the extent of the damage to the car. I'm afraid that's as far as my knowledge goes because I haven't done the course.' Robert thanked the sergeant for looking after him so well.

'Will I have to return here at a later date?' Robert thought he should make these enquiries now. His employers at Proctor's Accountants would be expecting him back in the morning for the audit.

'No Mr Easton, this will be the last time you need to come in. I will have one of my officers drive your vehicle back tonight. The damage is only superficial.'

Robert followed the constable through a back entrance of the station and they walked passed his car in the police yard. He briefly examined the damage to his car as they walked. This was the first time he had seen the dented grill and bonnet since the accident. He climbed into the police car and remembered the small leather bound note book that he had found. He took it from his pocket and looked at its cover once more. His thoughts returned to the poor man that he'd hit with his car and he hoped that he would make a full recovery. Not for his own selfish gain, but more that Robert felt genuine compassion for him. He glanced over his shoulder at his car once more as they drove him away.

Detective Sergeant Paul Bretherton drove into the small car park at the rear of the Red Lion in Lower Mittley. He asked himself why he was out in this weather in such a place. After more than 19 years with the Police he had hoped for more.

He had graduated from university with a two-one in Modern History. His parents had queried his decision to read History, especially as he had always expressed a special interest for joining the Police Force. They often asked him why the Police would be interested in a man with a degree in History. Paul knew of course, that it was not the subject that the Police would be interested in.

More that he had proven he was able to retain knowledge at this high level. During his probationary period, he was told that he would have a good career with the Police and could expect rapid promotion. He was once considered to be one of the chosen few in the Force with excellent prospects.

Nineteen years on and married with two children, he had realised that he was perhaps too good at what he did. Too good to be promoted and put into an office. However, despite these rare spells of bitterness, he enjoyed his job. He gained immense satisfaction from seeing every job he did, through to a full and successful conclusion.

He was not a tall man, at least when compared to his contemporaries. A little over five feet and nine inches, he had been one of the shortest and slimmest on his initial training course. He had now filled out slightly and his black hair had started to go grey at the sides, but he still congratulated himself on not looking bad for his forty years.

He climbed out of the car and hurried across the car park, through the rain towards the Red Lion's doorway. It was almost closing time but he still found five people drinking in the bar. A young couple sat in a quiet alcove near a cosy open fire and three men stood chatting to the barman.

Peter Forton looked surprised to see a customer arriving at this time. And one he had never set eyes on before.

'Good evening, what can I get you?'

'I'm sorry, I'm afraid I'm here on business. My name is DS Bretherton from Radley Street CID.' He spoke confidently whilst simultaneously displaying his warrant card in a small leather wallet.

'Do you know John Huggett?' He asked.

'Yes of course, he is one of my customers, he was in earlier tonight. Is everything OK, he's not in any trouble is he.' The four friends looked at one another wondering what the police would be wanting with John at this hour.

'Was he in here long, and did he have any alcohol?' DS Bretherton knew this line of questioning would provoke a defensive response and that was what he was looking for. He could add on a few drinks himself after the answer came.

'Only maybe three or four pints, and I think he had a couple of chasers too. But nothing too excessive,' replied Neville.

The four men were still curious and their question had still not been answered by the Detective.

'May we ask what has happened?' Repeated Peter.

31

'He was involved in an accident about an hour ago, he was run down by a car not far from here.'

'Oh god, is he badly hurt?' Asked Neville, whilst standing his drink on the bar.

'He is receiving treatment at hospital now, but I don't know his condition.' DS Bretherton took a note book from his pocket.

'May I take your names and an address where I can find you again should I need to? It's purely routine in these circumstances.' The three friends were happy to oblige and the detective replaced the note book in the inside pocket of his raincoat.

'Thank you; enjoy the rest of your evening.'

He opened the door and was followed by the young couple who had been sat listening to the conversation. DS Bretherton opened the door of his car and was stopped by the young man.

'Excuse me; I just thought you ought to know. About that man you were talking about earlier.'

'Yes.' Replied the detective.

The young man continued, 'he *was* drinking here tonight but I would say he had more to drink than they said.'

'Oh, thank you, that's most helpful, and your name is...?'

'Lamb, David Lamb. And if you ask me, that bastard got what was coming to him.'

DS Bretherton added his details to his note book.

'Why do you say that?' Paul Bretherton looked puzzled.

'Because he is the biggest crook around here, and I should know because I was stung when he sold me my first car.' DS Bretherton thanked the young man and his girlfriend and climbed into his car.

The nurse lifted up her fob watch and looked down to see it was 2.10am. She could hear John Huggett calling from the room where he had been moved, following his initial medical assessment. She walked quickly and found him in immense distress.

'Hello John, don't be frightened everything is OK. You have been in an accident and you are in hospital.' He looked up at the nurse sternly.

'You don't understand, I can't feel my legs. I am completely numb from the waist down, what the hell is going on, what's happened to me?'

Chapter Three

Neville Prevett climbed into his 10-year-old car. He had often thought of changing it, but since his retirement from Threapletons Cabinet Makers, he had different priorities. He couldn't understand why John Huggett had summoned him to hospital. He had been planning to go to hospital anyway to visit him with Ray and Phil, but they had wanted John to have time alone with his family, at least for two or three days. Especially, after the local radio had indicated he'd suffered appalling injuries.

Neville was feeling guilty that he hadn't visited sooner, but he placated himself that it was only 36 hours since the accident. However, he still felt that it would be wise to find some kind of excuse for his absence, despite how lame it may sound.

Neville was outwardly a rather timid and private man who led a fairly simple life with his wife Doreen. They had no children and that had been the subject of many heated discussions during their earlier married life. Now at 56, he acknowledged that he would never be a father and that suited him fine now.

He was a fairly small man with a narrow face and receding hairline. He had been retired now for almost three years with acute back pain. He had put it down to stooping over a work bench for the best part of 36 years but that had not stopped him from continuing with his hobby. He had been tinkering with old cars now for as long as he could remember. When he was in full employment he used to make a small amount of extra cash which always came in handy. Now his hobby had developed into a cottage industry and he had grown to rely on this additional income to supplement his small pension.

He drove passed the turning for the hospital car park. He knew that the car park there charged by the hour and that had always irritated him. He felt that the hospital had a kind of monopoly, as they knew their visitors always had more pressing things on their mind than a trivial parking fee. Neville knew of a free car park a further 500 yards down the road.

'I'm not paying anything I don't need to for that arrogant bastard,' he muttered to himself.

He arrived at the ward and he could almost feel his heart rate increase. He wasn't at all unnerved by hospitals, he was more apprehensive at how he would be received when he faced John and his new disability. He walked directly to the nurse's station and waited while the young Care Assistant finished her telephone call.

'I'm here to visit John Huggett, I'm a friend of his,' Neville tried to sound authoritative, hoping this would help prepare himself for his meeting.

The Care Assistant immediately responded.

'Yes of course, he is in a side room.' She turned to look at a large white board behind her and quickly scanned it.

'Now let's see, room twelve.' She said whilst turning back to face Neville.

'It's down there on the left,' she said pointing down the corridor. 'Would you like me to show you,' she enquired.

'No thanks, I'll find it.'

He opened the door of room twelve and was met at the door by a smartly dressed man who was just leaving. John spoke to the middle-aged man as he passed Neville in the doorway.

'Thank you Roger, you know what I want, let me know when it's all sorted out.'

Neville looked at John and immediately rushed to the side of his bed.

'I, I don't know what to say John.' Neville stammered.

'Well you can stop feeling sorry for me straight away,' John replied sharply. Neville was furious with himself for allowing John immediately to get the better of him.

'I have a proposition for you, and it means you're going to have to be on the ball, so pull yourself together and listen,' John continued.

Neville wanted to say that he was sorry about John's accident and that he couldn't possibly be of assistance to him, whatever the proposition.

'Of course John, I would be delighted to help you in any way I can.' Neville wondered why he would say such a thing, and thought that it would probably take a trained psychologist weeks to figure out.

'Good,' John replied. 'I want you to take over the reins at the garage while I am out of action. Don't worry, I don't want miracles just keep the place ticking over.'

Neville realised that there was still time to recover the situation.

'But how could I possibly step into your shoes John, it's true that I know the workings of an engine but I...'

'For heaven's sake man, I'm not asking you to take on the workload I had, all I want is for you to continue with a few repair jobs I have waiting and maybe the odd MOT that's all,' John interrupted.

Neville pondered for a moment and questioned himself over the legality of such a venture. John knew that he wielded powers of manipulation over Neville, but thought that he must strike now with the 'friend in need' approach.

'You see Neville, you're one of my oldest friends and the only guy I can trust with my livelihood. I have got so much to sort out.' John reached out, took hold of Neville's wrist.

'I have a legal matter which I will need all my energy to pursue.' John's voice changed to a more serious tone, and this was accompanied by a sinister facial expression, 'you understand what I mean, don't you?' Neville nodded.

Robert Easton arrived home from work and was greeted by a small pile of letters at his front door. He wasn't at all surprised to see at least three colourfully decorated envelopes containing the usual junk. He noticed one from his book club that, without doubt, would be offering him this month's editor's choice, should he not choose from the list provided.

What surprised Robert was a plain white envelope that bore his hand-written name and address. It caught his attention because of its resemblance to correspondence from his TA Regiment formally notifying him of a forthcoming training course. He was certainly not in the right frame of mind for another of those, especially following the events of earlier in the week. In fact, he was still trying to formulate an apology to Mr Huggett, and come up with the best way to deliver it without wanting to sound guilty, which of course, he knew he wasn't.

Robert opened the letter and glanced at its general content. It seemed rather short, but it was certainly to the point.

Dear Mr Easton,

I have been instructed by my client, Mr J Huggett, to inform you that, following the events of Tuesday 13th February, criminal proceedings are to be brought against you.

New evidence, not known to the police at the time of their initial investigation into an accident which occurred on the B4721, has since come to light. Please be advised that I will be submitting this fresh evidence to the Police.

In the meantime, you are further advised that you are to have no contact with my client, and all correspondence relating to this matter should be directed to me in the first instance.

Yours sincerely

Roger Towers

Robert had felt this sensation he had in his stomach before. Only this time it stayed there for some time. He wanted to tear up the letter but he felt he shouldn't. Despite his friendly and benevolent nature, he stared at it feeling angry and frustrated, yet at the same time he felt frightened and extremely vulnerable.

He looked at the note book again that he'd found and which lay on the table next to his mail. He had been planning to return it to John Huggett, along with the apology he'd wanted to make – now he was too angry and upset to think of anything.

John Huggett lay in bed in his side room of the orthopaedic ward discussing his circumstances with the duty doctor. In spite of his outward confidence, John had developed a deeply ingrained fear of spending the rest of his life trying to control those around him from a wheel chair. This was very unfamiliar territory for him, and it worried him enormously.

He wanted answers to questions that even he knew might be too difficult to provide.

'I want to know if I will be able to walk again doctor. What are my real chances?'

'The prognosis is not as bad as first feared Mr Huggett, your injuries, albeit severe, may indeed be operable.' The doctor spoke in a way that humbled him.

This man could be the one who saved him from his unbearable future. This was also unfamiliar territory for John, having someone to whom he was completely reliant upon.

The doctor continued his prognosis.

'You have suffered a complicated misalignment of two vertebrae. It is complicated because your spinal cord has become compressed and it is this misalignment that is causing your temporary paralysis.' John was happy for a moment for the doctor to continue.

'Please go on,' he said.

'It is operable, and there is a possibility that you could make a 90 - 95% recovery.'

'But what does that mean?' scowled John. The doctor unhooked John's care plan from the end of his bed and pored over his notes.

'We must carry out a full scan around the area of the injury. However, once that is complete, I see no reason why you can't be at home. You will need to wear a neck brace and you will also need to remain chair bound, of course. But I think there is sufficient undamaged cartilage and this will provide adequate additional support.'

John could feel his confidence growing again. For the first time since the accident he could almost see a light at the end of the tunnel, without it seeming like a train coming towards him.

'When can I have the scan doctor?' Eager to know when he could call Helen. 'Tomorrow morning should be OK,' said the doctor. 'That will allow us time to make the necessary arrangements prior to your discharge.'

'What arrangements?' The doctor appeared shocked at John Huggett's pointed reply.

'Nothing to worry about Mr Huggett, simple things like organising your scan, a suitable wheel chair and a few safety points for you and your wife, that's all.'

The doctor scribbled a few comments onto John's notes before excusing himself from the room. John's eyes narrowed and he looked stern as his thoughts returned to the man who had run him down.

Chapter Four

It was a cloudy afternoon, and fairly cold too, it was not raining but the roads had remained quite slippery from an earlier brief shower. Neville hated driving on wet roads, it had always been the source of an argument between himself and Doreen. He laughed out loud at the thought of Doreen who, had she been sitting next to him, would be nagging at his every over emphasised turn of the steering wheel. He carefully fed the steering wheel into each corner and wound his way along the road that led to John Huggett's garage.

He drove onto the forecourt and made a point of parking in front of the modest showroom window. He knew that John hated him doing this, because his car blocked the view of potential customers. He got out of the car, collecting the large set of keys that had been on the passenger seat. He had remembered Helen Huggett's instructions, the silver mortice key fitted the side door and the alarm deactivating code was 4721. Neville thought this was ironic to say the least as it was the number of the B Class road upon which the garage lay. Moreover, it was the road where John had met with his unfortunate accident.

Once inside the garage he continued to follow the directions he had been provided with, and proceeded into the office to locate the diary. Here he would find all the jobs that were programmed for the next few weeks.

Flicking through the pages he noticed the letters 'MOT' jump out at him several times. Again, he stopped to ponder over this and wondered about the implications of him signing one of John's MOT certificates. He remained content for now, knowing that John still held the keys for the small grey safe that occupied the corner of the office. He guessed that the certificates and the embossing stamp, bearing the limited company name "Huggett's Auto Repairs", were both safely locked in there. He decided not to bring up this subject with John just yet, fearing he would be given possession of them. He settled himself into the rather worn, large leather office chair and began familiarising himself with tomorrow's work that awaited him in the morning.

By the time Robert arrived at the police station he had fully rehearsed what he wanted to say. However, he was still frustrated and he felt he knew that his preparations were about to be wasted. He approached the counter and a young PC looked up from his paperwork.

'Can I help you sir.' The constable spoke assuredly.

'Yes I hope so; I would like to speak to someone in connection with an accident which occurred a few nights ago.'

'Yes of course sir, may I take a few details and I will see what I can do. Where did the accident take place?'

'It was on the Lower Mittley road, a man was run over.' Robert expected a line of questions now, about why he was interested in the accident?

'I think DS Bretherton was looking into that, would you like to take a seat and I will see if he is available to see you.'

Robert sat down and again thought over what he wanted to say. He kept reminding himself that he was not guilty of any crime, he had already proved that to the police on Tuesday night.

Robert could hear the buttons of a simplex lock being pushed on the other side of an adjoining door to the reception area. The door opened and Robert was greeted by the detective.

'Hello, I'm Paul Bretherton, I understand you wanted to see someone about a recent incident.'

'Yes, that's right. I was the driver of the car, and I have received a very disturbing letter.' Robert's face reddened and he started to perspire. Paul Bretherton could see that the man was very nervous and distressed.

'Please come through and we can talk somewhere a little more comfortable.' Robert thanked him and followed him into a corridor. Robert thought it ironic that they walked further into the familiar station, where he had previously been told he would never need return. Robert began to recount his story from the beginning but he was politely interrupted by the DS.

'I can see that this letter has upset you, how may I help you.' Paul explained that he had read Robert's statement and was fully acquainted with the facts. He continued, trying to ease Robert by telling him that he was fully aware of his co-operation earlier that week and he felt that he really had little to worry about. Robert produced the letter from his jacket pocket and handed it to DS Bretherton.

In the Red Lion, later that evening, things were almost back to normal. Only four people were drinking in the bar that night. A young couple sat in the alcove by the window and Ray and Phil, who chatted continuously about the events of the last few days. This had remained the main topic of conversation but Ray and Phil had explored almost every single permutation of how John could have ended up where he did. The door opened and Neville Prevett walked into the Red Lion. He had more of a spring in his step than usual and as he walked to the bar he pressed his hands together and wore a broad smile.

'Evening gentlemen, usual please Peter,' said Neville with an uncommon air of confidence in his voice. Peter Forton looked over the top of his half-rimmed spectacles as he poured Neville's pint of beer.

'You seem very pleased with yourself, have you finally sold that bloody car you've spent the last few months restoring.'

'No,' replied Neville. 'Although, it is something to do with cars.'

'Come on then,' said Phil, 'what is it you're so clearly bursting to tell us.' Neville related his news in detail, explaining John's wishes.

'So that will keep me busy for a good few weeks, and the extra cash will come in very handy I can tell you.' Ray was more curious to learn about John's progress as he knew Neville had been to see him.

'How is he anyway?'

'He's ok, well as ok as can be expected given the circumstances. Although I don't think he's completely with it yet, entrusting me with his pride and joy.'

'Perhaps the accident has affected him.' Interrupted Phil. 'Maybe it's caused him to mellow a little.'

'Yes this could be the beginning of a whole new type of conversation in future,' joked Peter.

The others felt guilty as they laughed at this comment. Neville wanted to continue with his briefing about his new responsibilities but he waited for a suitable break in the laughter. His growing confidence had allowed him to even embark in a little mockery of his new employer.

'Do you know the combination for the alarm in the garage is 4721?'

'No, but we do now,' said Ray. 'What's so special about that anyway,' said Phil wondering what the significance of the four-digit number actually was.

'It's the number of the road, isn't it?' There was a short silent pause before Neville continued with an enhanced pitch and expectant tone in his voice.

'The number of the road on which the garage lays, the same road where he almost met his maker!'

'Oh right, that is spooky that, don't you think Pete,' said Phil sarcastically.

Neville was about to respond when he was interrupted by the young man who reached across in front of him placing two half empty glasses on the bar. David Lamb glanced momentarily at Neville and said goodnight to the landlord before following his girlfriend out of the bar.

David Lamb waited at the passenger side of his car whilst his girlfriend opened the door from the driver's side. As he climbed into the car and adjusted himself in the seat, he rewarded himself a brief smile. Genie, his girlfriend of two years, sensed that a sinister plan was beginning to formulate in his head. Genie was a bright, but somewhat plain young woman who had done very well at school. She had decided not to continue into the Lower Sixth Form and commence her 'A' Levels, instead she had left at the earliest opportunity to work as a Librarian.

Her parents were disappointed with her, not only for her choice of career, but equally for her choice of boyfriend. David Lamb was a small young man and very slightly built. He always had untidy brown hair but it was his mysterious ways and deep set eyes that gave his potential 'in-laws' the impression that he always had something to hide. He had never been overly academic at school and this had frequently been reflected in his annual school reports. Nevertheless, when he left school he immediately found employment, albeit as a labourer at a local foundry.

Genie, mindful of David's dealings with John Huggett, decided that distraction would be the best course of action. Knowing his attention could be easily diverted she reminded him that they could stop in Leazes Woods on the way home. The positive reply came as expected, only this time he seemed a little less enthusiastic and preoccupied by other things. As they pulled out onto the road they passed Robert Easton who was waiting in his car to turn into the Red Lion's car park.

Robert was still too angry and frustrated to even consider preparing what he felt he needed to say inside the Red Lion. He had a deep routed feeling that he was doing the wrong thing and yet he knew he would regret not trying to do something. He also knew that he was probably on John Huggett's home ground and therefore, unlikely to walk away with any real results.

There were still a couple of hours to closing time but, Ray and Phil were already attempting to persuade Peter Forton to stay open late. Peter was considering the offer, he had to grasp every opportunity of business that came his way for such a small inn. Meanwhile, Neville was going over ways he felt he could improve the business, not that the others were listening.

As Robert approached the small porch that housed the beautifully ornate and old oak door, a thought occurred to him. Maybe if he applied a little common sense, use the intelligence he knew he possessed, maybe then he would achieve something. Robert entered the small bar, stopped briefly to scan the room, and slowly walked to where three men were chatting.

'Hi, good evening, may I have a large orange juice please?'

'Certainly,' replied the landlord. The three men next to Robert were chatting to each other, and Robert began to wonder if this was going to be worth his while. He was only guessing that John Huggett drank there. No, he must continue, he reminded himself exactly what this man was trying to do to him.

'It's cold out tonight,' Robert thought it good to start with small talk.

'Always the same down here,' replied Ray. 'The wind always whistles down this road, it's like a wind tunnel at times.' Robert laughed, happy that his corny line had been greeted by an equally corny reply.

'You're not from around here then,' said Peter. 'Only I haven't seen you in here before.'

'I don't live too far away, only a few miles down the road. I've been working rather late tonight and I was a little parched driving home.'

'I know if I'd had a long day, I would be mixing that orange with something a little stronger,' said Neville. 'Believe me I would love to, but I have to drive home tonight, and can't be too careful.'

'That's very responsible of you,' Peter responded. 'There was a nasty accident along here a few nights ago, a friend of ours was knocked over.' Robert couldn't believe his luck, the brief conversation had already been tuned to the topic he wished to talk about, and by someone else. What was more, he now knew that they were friends of John Huggett.

'Yes I heard about that, terrible business.'

'It was,' replied Neville. 'But we're hoping he will make a full recovery and hopefully, he will learn to walk on the footpath on his way home in future.' Robert thought about Neville's remark and quickly replied with a slightly light-hearted response.

'Oh I see, you mean he had a few tipples then.'

'Yes, at least he won't have felt the initial impact,' said Phil as he grinned, in Neville and Ray's direction.

Robert was nearing the end of his drink, and he felt that this initial meeting in the Red Lion had gone better than he even dared hope.

'Well, I must hit the road gents.' Ray made an attempt to persuade Robert to stay for one more. He thought the company of this new man might put Neville, who was busy repeating the alarm code gag, out of his stride.

'No thanks, but I may pop in again tomorrow night on my way home.' He placed his empty glass on the bar, thanked the Landlord and said goodnight to all four men.

'Thanks, maybe see you tomorrow night,' said Peter in anticipation.

The next morning, Neville woke especially early helped by two alarms. He wanted to get there with ample time ahead of his first job, scheduled for 9am. He was keen to make sure he was aware of the location of all his tools and the specialist equipment that he was going to need. Further, he was intent on satisfying himself that all this equipment was in a serviceable condition. Knowing John for as long as he had, he was half expecting to find some of the equipment not only unserviceable, but probably downright dangerous. This didn't worry him too much, as he was more a hands-on, spanner and screwdriver mechanic. As opposed to the modern, computerised technician whom he suspected would be hard pushed to know what a spanner looked like.

His first job arrived a little before 9am. He confirmed the minor repairs that were required with the young man and asked him to leave the keys. He briefly explained that he would be carrying out the repairs in John's absence, before instructing him to ring later that afternoon.

He thought to himself that a simple exhaust change would take him no more than a couple of hours and he was right. He set about the work and 90 minutes later he was wiping his hands on an oily rag congratulating himself on a successful job. A moment later the telephone in the office rang and he hurried through the back of the garage to answer it. He cleared his throat and answered the call.

'Good morning, Huggett's Autos.' The voice at the other end of the phone enquired about a vehicle he had saw in the local free newspaper.

Neville had not banked on having to sell John's cars from the forecourt but he saw this as an opportunity to impress John further.

'Yes, around 1pm this afternoon will be fine, I'll see you then…'

Neville replaced the receiver and began searching for the keys for the car, which he soon located in the desk drawer. He had plenty of time to make the car as presentable as possible, but wondered whether he should clear it with John first. He thought it best to telephone Helen first to check on John's condition, rather than just ring the hospital. Maybe she would give him the 'thumbs up' to go ahead and make the sale.

Neville heard the ringing tone and was surprised to hear John answer the phone.

'John, I wasn't expecting you, it's Neville, I was just ringing to see how you are?'

'I'm fine Neville,' replied John sharply. 'You're not ringing to say you've burnt the place down are you.' Neville felt annoyed at John's remark wondering how he always managed to make him feel this way.

'You know it's nothing like that John, it's good news actually.'

'Oh really, what's that then?'

'Well, I've just had a call about one of the cars on the forecourt. Someone wants to come and have a look at one of them this afternoon.'

'And you're asking my permission to go ahead with the sale?' interrupted John.

'All you have to do is look in the back of the diary alongside the car's registration. That will show you the car's lowest price.'

'So you're happy with me to go ahead with the sale.'

'Yes, just don't go below the lowest price, I'm sure you're capable of that Neville.'

'No problem John, I'll ring you later and let you know how I got on.' John simply replied 'OK,' before hanging up.

John had never really bothered himself about the pleasantries of saying goodbye properly. Nor was he particularly bothered how Neville got on, he had much more important things on his mind following his discharge from hospital.

One o'clock came all too soon for Neville, but he was content that he had prepared not only the vehicle but also himself sufficiently for the potential buyer. Neville led the man out onto the forecourt to allow him a closer inspection of the car. The man started the proceedings as they both walked towards the car.

'It's 5 years old, isn't it?'

'Yes, that's right.' Agreed Neville.

Neville expected the man to want a test drive at some point. The man however, satisfied himself with looking under the bonnet for now and walking around the vehicle. It wasn't until he had subjected Neville to a whole host of questions that he enquired about the possibility of a test drive.

'Yes of course, I will just run in and lock up the office as I'm on my own today.' Neville used this opportunity to check the price in the back of diary once more before he returned to his customer. He scanned the list briefly until he came to the red Vauxhall.

After the short drive along the B4721, the man turned the car around and headed back for the garage. He explained to Neville that he was happy about the car but would like to negotiate a price. By the time they had returned to the forecourt they had both decided on an acceptable deal. The man seemed happy with the price and Neville felt equally delighted that he had secured an additional £500.00 than the bottom price that John had initially set.

'I'll go straight round to the bank now.' The man said. 'I will be back in an hour with the cash if that's alright; it's only down the road?'

'That's great, yes, see you then.' Replied Neville feeling very pleased with himself.

He walked back towards the garage and decided that he had had a very good day and thought he should reward himself with a cup of tea whilst he waited for the man to return. He sank into the large office chair and sipped triumphantly on his sweet tea. With today's duties successfully concluded, he pored over the diary for tomorrows work.

The man returned a little over 40 minutes later and presented Neville with the cash which they both counted out onto the desk in John's office. Neville exchanged the money for the vehicle registration document and went about explaining the obligations of a new vehicle owner. Neville felt comfortable with this as he had done this many times before when selling his own vehicles.

When the man left, he decided that it would be professional of him to place a neat line through the vehicles details and he opened the rear of the diary. From previous entries, this appeared to be John's way of closing a sale. He scanned the list of cars for a second time that hour but this time he could not find the vehicle. He saw a red Vauxhall but that could not be it. Not for £800 more than he accepted. Then he returned to the top of the page and noticed what he had first saw an hour earlier. It was another red Vauxhall. He sensed a tightening inside his stomach; this was followed by a terrible sick feeling when he looked again nearer the bottom of the page. He confirmed that this was the vehicle that he had sold, that he had sold for £800 less than he should have.

Robert Easton drove along the B4721 from work towards the Red Lion. He noticed drops of rain, starting to race their way up his windscreen and he grinned at the irony of it. It had seemed like only yesterday that he wound his way up this road tired, after a difficult day at the office.

He had expected heavy rain after hearing a weather report earlier that afternoon, and it looked as though the forecast was going to be correct. He forced out another smile at the double irony of the Met Office only getting it right when it was bad news. For a second everything seemed to be fine in his life. Then it was as if his mind was searching for reasons to ruin this brief moment of happiness and he would once again be reminded of the challenge that awaited him.

This helped to make up his mind that he must return to the Red Lion again that evening. He was not about to allow this to get the better of him and, he must try anything he could to fight back. By now the rain had begun to pound his windscreen and he was relieved to have had new wiper blades fitted the same time as his repairs had been carried out. He gave a baleful glance to his left as he passed the garage then returned his stare to the road as he rounded the last bend that would lead to the Red Lion.

A few moments later he saw the blurred outline of the Pub through the rain and turned left into the car park. He felt a little more at ease than he had done 24 hours ago. He pressed his key fob to remotely lock his car and walked towards the door of the pub. He heard voices inside but one that rose above the others. When he opened the door, he saw a man sat in a wheel chair. He recognised him immediately, and froze to the spot. He couldn't continue into the pub as normal as he knew that would be foolish. He knew it would be equally foolish to walk straight back out of the door.

Despite his dilemma he identified that he would have to opt for the latter. He slapped his pockets to signify that he had forgotten something and muttered to himself before retreating hastily back outside. Once on the other side of the door he closed his eyes tightly and clenched his fists. He wasn't mad with himself but he was immensely frustrated to have found himself in such an awkward position.

He didn't know if John knew who he was or not but that was irrelevant. What bothered Robert was that he had to meet him sometime, probably in court, and he would certainly remember him then as the man who made a hasty exit from the pub. Furthermore, how would the court receive the news that he had been in the pub only the night before quizzing his friends about the accident. He returned to his car and sat in deep thought.

In the Red Lion John, had completely forgotten his brief interruption from the man at the door. Neville had hardly even noticed that the door had opened and was far more aggravated by John's vicious remarks.

'I leave you in charge for one day, just one bloody day, are you some kind of idiot?' John Huggett's stare was fixed in Neville's direction. Neville could feel the anger building up inside him, and to add to his annoyance, the pub was busier than it had been for more than two weeks. He didn't dare to look around the room but he guessed that at least a dozen or more people were witnessing his humiliation first hand.

He could sense that the confidence that had been growing inside him for the last couple of days was starting to ebb away. He needed to act now if he was to save any face at all. He started to perspire and he demonstrated visible signs that he was about to explode.

'Who the hell do you think you are Huggett?'

'I'm the man in a wheel chair who entrusted his livelihood to his so-called friend, only to be left nearly a grand out of pocket. And, all inside one day.' John replied with a calming tone to his voice, but his eyes remained firmly set on Neville.

Neville continued to shake, but did not respond. Instead he slammed the garage keys onto the bar and stormed out of the door and into the rain.

A short but empty silence hung in the atmosphere of the Red Lion before Peter Forton spoke.

'Don't you think you were a little too strong there John.'

'Are you asking me or telling me Peter? And do you consider £800 to be small change?' John did not wait for an answer, but reached for the keys from the bar.

He wheeled himself towards the door and Ray followed to help him open it. As he negotiated his chair through the door he stopped and turned.

'Good night gents, I am going to my garage to see if I can salvage anything from this whole bloody mess.'

'Can I walk you down there John,' enquired Ray. 'It's shocking weather out there tonight.'

'No thanks Ray, I think I need some air and I suspect I will need a clear head when I get there.' Ray sensed an element of compassionate humour in John's voice.

'OK John, mind how you go, will we see you tomorrow?'

'No doubt.' Replied John.

John heard the door close firmly behind him. He looked skywards at the weather, pulled up the collar on his jacket and started to wheel himself in the direction of his garage. He was only a few yards down the road when he heard a car pull out of the Red Lion's car park. It sped past him and its lights disappeared around a slight bend. He continued a few more yards before being forced to stop and turn around. He could sense that someone was close behind him, but he could see no one.

He continued along the narrow footpath that was flanked down one side by an overgrown hedgerow. Still he sensed a presence behind him only this time it was accompanied by a faint rustling. He turned to look back down the road and estimated that it was about 30 yards behind him.

He began to wheel his chair in the direction of the sound but as he drew nearer he could neither see nor hear anyone. This time he dismissed his fears and chastised himself for behaving like a schoolboy with an over active imagination, and wheeled himself back towards the garage.

As he travelled over the forecourt he stopped to reach inside his jacket for the garage keys. He went down by the side of the garage to the side entrance and stopped near the door. He held his keys at head height inspecting them in the poor light to try and locate the silver mortice key. Again, he sensed the presence of someone close and this, coupled by more rustling, unnerved him. He moved himself closer to the door and felt around with his cold, wet hands for the key hole but as he tried to put the key into the door – it swung open. He noticed that it had been forced and there was damage to the wooden door frame.

Aware that someone had broken in and had been in the garage, he was halfway through the narrow doorway when he saw a figure running towards him through the corner of his eye. He barely had time to turn his head before he was struck by the crushing blow of an iron bar to the rear of his head. He was propelled out of his wheelchair and onto the floor of his office. More blows rained down relentlessly on his head and neck. A large pool of blood formed around his head and in a matter of minutes, John Huggett lay dead.

Chapter Five

DS Bretherton was sat in his office and was going through some of the week's paper work. It required his comments before being sent to the Chief Superintendent for final closure.

This was the necessary part of his chosen career that he most disliked. He understood that it was an equally important part of the job and that the data he provided performed an important function in detective work. Nevertheless, he always left it until last.

He looked up through the glass partition, the Custody Sergeant who had been passing knocked briefly and popped his head around the doorframe.

'Take it you've heard about the suspicious death on the patch.' He spoke to Paul Bretherton quickly before making an attempt to leave as though he had more pressing business to attend to.

'No. Wait, what death?' Replied DS Bretherton.

'Uniform called it in about 20 minutes ago, a guy with head injuries has been found at the garage on the Lower Mittley road. The desk got a call from the dead man's wife in the early hours when he hadn't returned home.'

'Do you know what his name is yet?' Responded Paul, who was now clearly interested.

'Huggett I think. Why?'

Paul Bretherton didn't offer an immediate answer, but grabbed his coat and car keys from the desk. He had raced halfway down the corridor before he shouted his reply.

'Tell the DI I'm down at the scene.'

'I would, but he rang in sick. That's what I was about to tell you.' The Sergeant replied, unsure if his shouted words had been heard or not as DS Paul Bretherton had already disappeared through the door.

Paul Bretherton arrived at the Garage a short time later. He was greeted on the forecourt by two uniformed officers.

'Alright lads?' Asked Paul.

'Yes thanks Sarge, it's a bit of a mess in there I'm afraid.' Answered the taller one of the two young constables.

'OK, show me what we've got then!'

Paul Bretherton was led down the side of the garage and through the side door into the office. He saw John Huggett's body lying face down on the floor in front of his wheel chair.

'Any murder weapon?' He asked the constable who was standing behind him.

'No, at least nothing immediately obvious Sarge. Could have been any number of things lying around here.'

'Do you think he was definitely murdered then?' Asked the other PC who had now joined them at the side door.

'Ask yourself this.' Paul Bretherton paused briefly before he continued. 'The man has severe injuries to the rear of the head, caused by an immense blow that was so powerful, it launched him from his wheel chair. Yes, I believe he was murdered.' The detective tried to answer the constable's question without sounding flippant, but feared he probably failed in his attempt.

DS Bretherton instructed the two PCs to cordon off the garage, call for the duty coroner and organise the forensic team. He commenced a search around the garage for items that could potentially be a murder weapon. He began to formulate a picture in his mind of the previous evening's events that led to John Huggett's demise.

He tried to maintain his professionalism and concentrate on the facts in hand. He had always congratulated himself on his ability to focus, and not allow assumptions to cloud his judgement – these were among his greater qualities. However, on this occasion his mind kept returning to Robert Easton and his obvious motive. Still, the fact that the door to the office had clearly been forced and this was bothering Paul – it made no immediate sense. It would suggest that someone had perhaps broken into the garage and had been disturbed by Huggett.

Paul Bretherton had liked the man who had come to see him, but again, could another of his finer qualities, his usual excellent judge of character have tricked him? He was almost afraid to admit that sooner or later, despite the unusual evidence to the contrary, he would be arresting Robert Easton for the most malevolent of crimes.

With his preliminary investigation complete he returned to Radley Street to compile his initial findings. Although he was short of compelling evidence, he was not short of a murder victim or indeed a motive.

Then he remembered the young man who had stopped him in the car park of the Red Lion. Paul considered for a moment the intent, the motive and the obvious deeply rooted hatred that David Lamb held for John Huggett. Moreover, when compared to Robert Easton, David Lamb probably had more character weaknesses that would make him capable of such a crime. Of course, this initial assessment was being based on the brief conversation that he had a short time ago. Still, Lamb was high up his list of suspects and would be interviewed as a matter of priority.

Only one more hurdle remained for Paul - convincing the Chief Superintendent that he had sufficient experience to commence the case in the DIs absence.

This proved to be easy for Paul when thirty minutes later he was summoned to the Station's Senior Officer to be informed that he would be leading the investigation. Paul remained with the Chief Superintendent for an hour or so discussing the murder and his responsibilities. The decision to put him in charge had been made following the news that his immediate superior, the Detective Inspector, had been granted two week's sick leave.

Paul gathered the remaining CID Officers together and gave them the facts of the case as he knew them. The three Detective Constables that stood before him listened intently as he outlined the events leading up to the murder and he explained that the Chief Superintendent had instructed him to treat Easton as his main suspect.

Two of the DCs were young and relatively new to CID. Paul considered that under normal circumstances he would have paired up one of them with himself, and the other with DC Jim Craven, a more experienced man.

However, because of the importance of the investigation he felt that it would be better to team himself up with Jim, leaving the young DCs to do the more routine running around.

Jim Craven was what most of the Station would describe as a good solid copper. He was experienced and had served his time in uniform before being accepted into the plain clothed branch or 'Brethren' as his uniformed colleagues often joked. He was a family man and had been with the Force for twenty-one years, the last eleven with CID. Like Paul Bretherton, he had been overlooked for promotion and now accepted that he would probably retire as a DC. Nevertheless, he was immensely experienced, had a very pragmatic approach to detective work and it was those qualities that Paul Bretherton wanted most at the moment.

Paul Bretherton sent the two young DCs to their duties and he sat chatting to his most senior detective.

'Jim, the Chief Super thinks we've got enough on Easton to make an arrest. I'm not so sure though, I think we're going to need more.'

'Then there's Lamb.' Replied Jim.

'I know, and I would like to go and chat to our friend David Lamb. But first I think we should go down to the Red Lion.' Uttered Paul.

'Don't you think it's a bit early?' Jim laughed. Paul either didn't get the joke or chose to ignore it.

'We need to chat to the Landlord, maybe he saw or heard something, the garage is just along the road.'

DS Craven turned into the car park of the Red Lion and parked near the back door of the pub. Paul hadn't expected the pub to be open for business but he was pleased to find the door open. Both detectives walked through to the bar and were greeted by Peter Forton who stood cleaning glasses behind the bar.

'Hello again,' said Peter.

'Good morning, I see you remember me.' Paul remained straight faced as he gave his reply.

'Yes I remember, how can I help?' Peter spoke and displayed a puzzled expression.

'This is my colleague DC Craven; we need to ask you a few questions.'

'You're an inquisitive man,' laughed Peter. 'But, I will be delighted to help.' Paul was aware that the Landlord was a friend of Huggett and therefore needed to choose his next words carefully.

'I'm afraid I have some rather bad news. It concerns a Mr John Huggett.'

'Yes.' Replied Peter, looking rather worried.

'I'm afraid he died last night in his garage, and we are treating his death as suspicious.' Paul looked for a response in Peter Forton.

'Good god I, I can't believe it. How did it happen?'

Paul asked Peter to sit down, and he explained to him what he considered appropriate. Paul wanted to be as sincere as possible with Peter Forton. In his experience, it was important for him to form good relationships when carrying out an investigation. Being as open as possible, and making the interviewee aware that he was providing more information about the case than he ought, always formed a good basis from which to forge this relationship.

Peter responded accordingly, and began telling the DS about the confrontation in the Pub the previous evening between Neville and John. However, he was quick to dispel any thoughts that the Detective might have about Neville committing murder, describing him as a timid and very reserved individual. Still, Paul would be interviewing him as part of his initial enquiries.

Paul continued with his questions and asked about David Lamb. Peter answered, telling Paul Bretherton that although he did not know the lad well, he explained that he was in the pub with his girlfriend the previous evening.

Peter continued, trying to remember the remainder of his clientele and concluded that earlier in the evening a man paid a very brief visit who had been there the night before and had asked about John Huggett. He remembered him because he would not take any alcohol at all and said that he was on his way home. Additionally, he had thought it strange for a young man to stop, when so close to home. Paul asked him to provide a description of the man he saw with as much detail as possible. Peter described Robert Easton down to the last pimple.

The two detectives rose to their feet and thanked Peter Forton for his assistance. With three potential suspects, they knew the next few days were going to be extremely busy.

Neville Prevett rang Helen Huggett's door bell. She had asked him to see her to discuss the arrangements that would need to be made for him to take over responsibility for the running of the garage.

Neville had made Helen aware of his altercation with John during their earlier telephone call. There was no need for him to apologise, or offer any kind of explanation, despite the fact that he may be visited by the Police at any moment. Neville was an old friend of the family and Helen had swiftly made the decision to ask Neville to run the garage on her behalf.

Helen answered the door and before Neville was allowed to speak she told him that the Police were in the drawing room.

'They've been here about 5 minutes, they said they were here to offer their condolences but they probably want information as well. Whispered Helen as they both walked along the hallway.

'Helen I'm so sorry about John, I can't even begin to imagine how you must be feeling. And Tabitha too, how is she coping with all this?'

'My parents came down to collect her Neville, she is better off out of the way at the moment, especially when the police are going to be in and out over the next few days.' Replied Helen as she opened the door to the drawing room.

'Sergeant, this is a good friend of ours Neville Prevett. Neville this is the detective in charge of the investigation into John's death.' Helen could sense a little tension in the atmosphere as she continued to tell the detective that she had invited her old friend around to help. Paul shifted in his seat. He was aware that his body language suggested he was uneasy about seeing Neville Prevett in these circumstances.

'Hello again Mr Prevett, you must be very shocked to hear this distressing news?'

'I am indeed Sergeant,' replied Neville. 'I am doubly upset as John and I had a disagreement last night. Probably the first time we've ever had a cross word for one another, and now I just want to say to John how sorry I am. I'm very saddened.'

'That's perfectly understandable in these situations,' stated Paul. He felt that professionally, he was still on new territory. He knew that he could not question Prevett about the murder at the home of the victim's wife and now he must demonstrate total tact and diplomacy.

'You will obviously have much to talk over, so DC Craven and I will make ourselves scarce. I still may need to talk again with you Mr Prevett, purely as a matter of routine.'

'Yes of course, do you still have my details from when we first met,' said Neville.

'Yes I do, thanks. Mrs Huggett, thank you for your time and if there's anything we can do, you know where you can find me. We'll show ourselves out.'

The two detectives had no sooner closed the door of the car when the radio announced their call sign.

'Alpha Tango to three five receiving over,' came the announcement from Radley Street control room.

'Go ahead Dave.' Answered Jim craven. There was a short pause followed by the message.'

'Can you contact your office on the land line, apparently there've been some developments you need to know about.'

'Roger.' Jim ended the conversation with control. Paul instructed Jim to drive straight back as he had wanted to return to the Station anyway. He added that as far as he was concerned there appeared to be little point interviewing Prevett. Jim Craven concurred with his superior, stating that two people had provided positive character assessments of Prevett, albeit as long term friends.

'Anyway, let's see what the two lads have for us,' said Paul.

The two detectives entered the CID office where the two young detectives waited.

'What we got lads?' Asked Jim.

'We think we've got the murder weapon.'

'What?' Enquired Paul sceptically.

'We were making some initial enquiries at Easton's house but he wasn't there. However, this iron bar was though. We found it lying down the side of his house. Forensics' had a look at it and it's got the victim's blood and hair on it.'

'Good,' have forensic come up with anything else yet? Asked Paul.

'Yes, they gave the time of death between 9pm and midnight.'

'Is that the best they can do? Well that's not important at the moment. Let's see if we can get a match on the prints and get this wrapped up quickly.'

The other of the two young detectives spoke, adding that they had tried to contact Robert Easton but he hadn't shown up for work.

'We've tried his house and his neighbours too but no one has seen him all morning.'

DS Bretherton leant against the edge of a table. He spoke to the three men in a sombre manner telling them that they needed to find him urgently. He explained that he and Jim Craven would go to his house to find out anything they could. Meanwhile he told the others to go back to Robert Easton's office in town and get as much information as possible from his employers. DS Bretherton stressed however, that they were not to give too much away at this early stage.

Paul Bretherton climbed into the passenger side of the car and Jim drove them immediately to Robert Easton's house. When they arrived, they were surprised to see Robert Easton vacuuming the inside of his car.

'Hello again Mr Easton,' said Paul.

'What can I do for you Sergeant?'

'I need to ask your whereabouts last night between 9pm and midnight.' Stated Paul.

'I was here at home, why?' Said Robert.

DS Bretherton nodded to DC Craven.

'Robert Anthony Easton, I am arresting you on the suspicion of murder.' DC Craven continued with Robert Easton's rights as an arrested person before they escorted him to their car.

Chapter Six

Robert Easton sat in an interviewing room in Radley Street Police Station. He noticed that the room was clean and modern, almost clinical in fact and furnished with a single table with two chairs on both sides. At the end of the table was a recording device that was built into the wall.

He did not dare cast his mind back to the short time ago when he led a simple and normal existence. Now he sat in this unfriendly room afraid of the unknown. Occasionally, he would allow himself a brief moment of relief and remind himself that he was innocent, but this only served to make him angry. He wouldn't think of that again. He cast an eye at the recording machine, and the name it bore, 'Tapecast.' Does the man who thought of that name really know how lucky he was? He was probably sat at home with his family safe and secure.

He reprimanded himself for thinking such ridiculous thoughts. Now he had to be strong, he had to channel all his spare energy towards the incredible situation he found himself in.

He was spared further self-induced mental torture when the door suddenly opened. The two men who had called to his house a short time ago entered the room and sat down facing him.

'Interview with Robert Anthony Easton, DS Bretherton and DC Craven present.' Jim Craven delivered the well-rehearsed words that he knew were a legal requirement. He continued explaining to Robert Easton that whilst he was still under arrest, no formal charges had been brought against him. He would be held for a short time during which he would be formally interviewed and would be invited to make a statement. He was entitled to have a solicitor present and if he was unable to provide one then the duty brief would be appointed to act on his behalf.

The interview continued and Robert maintained his complete innocence throughout. DS Bretherton then tried a different angle in his questioning and put it to him that there was damning evidence against him. In that an iron bar, had been found on his premises with his finger prints on it. The iron bar had traces of John Huggett's blood on it as well as his hair. He tried to explain without sounding flippant.

'I found the bar near my car, and I picked it up to prevent me from running over it with my car. I assumed that children from my neighbourhood may have been playing with it and left it there. I can offer no other explanation.'

'You can see our problem Mr Easton, that the evidence against you is manifold. You had a strong motive, we have the weapon and you can provide no alibi as to your whereabouts at the time of the murder.' DS

Bretherton stated the facts to Robert Easton unsure of the response it would provoke.

'I do not wish to say anymore until I have spoken to a solicitor,' continued Robert. Robert Easton felt that his world was caving in around him and he was powerless to prevent it.

He was returned to his cell and awaited the brief that would be appointed to him. He looked around the tiled walls of the cell and at the steel door with the small inspection hatch. He wished that the door would open and for the detective to stand and tell him that there had been a huge mistake and they were sorry. Of course, this was unlikely and he knew all too well that the odds were stacked against him. He recalled all the other souls that had been released following miscarriages of justice in recent years. More so, the many years that they served behind bars before their eventual liberation. Then of course there were his friends at the office. What would they be thinking about him now? They surely knew that he was here and under suspicion for the most evil of crimes.

Robert Easton was spared more self-induced emotional torture when his cell door was opened. The Custody Sergeant explained to him that the solicitor appointed to him was in the building and would be with him in a few moments.

When the solicitor arrived at the cell he introduced himself as James Wilbert and asked if he may sit down.

Robert studied the man that sat before him. He was young, may be in his late twenties, but he looked distinguished. Robert imagined that in the legal profession, he would be regarded as Junior Counsel. Still, he impressed Robert, not only with his immaculate appearance but also in the way he spoke.

'We have much to get through Mr Easton, so if we're to win this I suggest we get to work right away.' Robert was further impressed by his down to earth and straight forward attitude. He took encouragement from his positive comments.

'OK.' Said Robert. 'I'm all yours, I'm completely innocent and ready to help you prove that. Ask me what you need to.' Robert was equally as straight forward with his reply and was keen to help, although he found it difficult to demonstrate the same optimism.

Robert's counsel continued with his questions until he was satisfied that he had the makings of his case against the crown. James Wilbert knew of course that the evidence against him was strong and that much work lay ahead of them both.

When the solicitor left the cell, Robert returned to his own thoughts. He tried to recall anything that may be of assistance to his brief in support of his weak defence.

Meanwhile in another part of Radley Street Station, Robert's fate was being sealed. DS Bretherton, DC

80

Craven and the Chief Superintendent sat discussing the main points of the case.

'I think that we've got more than enough on Easton and I want him charged.' The two-detectives listened to their superior officer and although doubts remained in DS Bretherton's mind, he knew that it would be futile to argue with such solid evidence.

The Chief Superintendent reminded them that crimes of this nature were rare on their patch and that he would be seeking an early trial. He explained that it would be pertinent under the circumstances to have this particular case concluded quickly, adding that it would put the Station in a particularly good light with the local community. Paul Bretherton knew differently and gave DC Craven a look that said it would be viewed favourably at Division where the Assistant Chief Constables appointment remained vacant.

DS Bretherton and DC Craven walked down the stairs of the Station and prepared to give Robert Easton the worst news possible and formally charge him for the murder of John Huggett. They entered Robert's cell and DC Craven delivered the news he'd been dreading.

'Robert Anthony Easton I am charging you with the murder of John Huggett.' Robert didn't speak. Instead he sat in disbelief and tried to make sense of what was happening to him.

He was transferred to a nearby remand centre the same day. The police had made an application to have him remanded in custody until the trial and he was advised to prepare to be in custody until the trial.

Robert was told that he would be expected to appear in court to enter a plea. This was a procedure required by law and whilst he was told it was mandatory, he was advised that it may only take a few moments. He would be accompanied by his formal legal representative, Mr Matthew Silkin QC. The visit to the court was indeed brief and Robert was in attendance with his counsel. The other members of the court that were present were the judge, clerk, usher, and a number of people who had gathered in the public gallery.

The judge, who had been appointed, was a tall and very slim man. Robert guessed that he was in his late sixties and he spoke in a very eloquent and distinguished way. He asked Robert to confirm his name and address and this would be Robert's only part in these proceedings. The judge then turned to My Silkin and asked him if he was ready to enter a plea.

'I am my Lord. Said Mr Silkin. 'My client is not guilty my Lord.'

The judge asked the Clerk to record the plea and then he said that a date would be set for the trial and a jury would be appointed.

Mr Silkin had already briefed Robert that it would be unlikely for him to be granted bail but he would try to secure it for him anyway. He would present a robust case given his previous clean record and military service.

Mr Silkin made his plea to the Judge and delivered a strong case for bail. However, as he'd warned, the judge would not be moved and he outlined that given the seriousness of the case, a date would be set for two weeks on Monday and he asked Robert to be detained in custody until the trial.

Robert was taken down to a waiting cell where Mr Silkin briefed him what would happen in the next two weeks. He would be taken to a remand centre where he would remain while Mr Silkin and his junior counsel, James Wilbert, would build their case for his defence. Mr Silkin also advised that there would be occasion for him to visit Robert and he would need to prepare a number of statements as part of the defence.

Mr Silkin rose from his seat and offered his hand to Robert. Robert rose and shook hands with Mr Silkin and he left the room. The two detention officers escorted Robert to the waiting van and he was driven from the court in custody.

He spent the next few days alone with his thoughts. He went over the events leading to his arrest again and again trying to add something laudable that might help his cause. He pondered that there must be a reason for all of this, a reason why he was in this invidious position.

The next few weeks passed all too quickly for Robert. His solicitor would be acting as junior counsel to Mr Matthew Silkin QC. An experienced trial lawyer who on balance, had a respectable success rate winning approximately half of his cases. Some of his colleagues had disagreed over the years as to his success but Matthew Silkin remained happy for them to squabble, knowing that his record would be far greater had he been more selective with his clients.

James Wilbert sat in a side room adjacent to Mr Silkin's chambers having been requested to discuss final details of the impending case. Matthew Silkin had visited Robert Easton on two previous occasions and now required the presence of James to tie up any remaining loose ends.

A legal secretary opened an adjoining door and told James that he may go in. He hesitated for a moment and knocked once before opening the door. He remembered the first time he had been chastised for daring to enter the chambers of a senior member of the bar without knocking first, despite being invited to proceed in by the man's secretary.

This was the first time he had met Mr Silkin, but he had read articles written by him in legal journals. As he walked across the large room towards the vacant chair, he was already putting labels on him trying to determine the man's character from the way he looked and the way he positioned himself at his desk.

He was however, pleased to find that Matthew Silkin was a very pleasant man and most affable. Matthew Silkin was 56 years old and spoke very softly with a down to earth Yorkshire accent.

'Sit down lad,' he instructed. James guessed that he wouldn't be a tall man, maybe five - seven but he had a friendly face.

'Thank you sir.' Replied James.

'We'll have less of the sir, Mr Wilbert. I don't mind politeness but I don't want you thinking that I don't work for a living. Call me Matthew.' James smiled at Matthew's comments, surprised to find a man of his standing with such a friendly and approachable nature.

'Now lad, what are your thoughts about our Mr Easton. Do you think he's guilty?' Enquired Matthew.

'I believe that he's an honest man who has led a crime free life.' Stated James.

'Until now you mean?'

'I'm not sure I understand you Matthew.'

'You haven't answered my question James. Do you believe this honest man who has led a crime free life to be guilty of premeditated murder?' Repeated Matthew.

James bowed to his superior's experience and tenacity. He hesitated for a moment before offering a reply.

'In my humble opinion I believe that any man, given the right or should I say wrong circumstances, is capable of murder. And with the amount of evidence against him, it is difficult to think otherwise. But if you were to ask me if I thought that he was, beyond reasonable doubt guilty, then I would have to say no.'

Matthew smiled and wondered if the young solicitor ever considered a career in politics.

'Well we'll see, won't we lad?' He said.

The first day of the trial brought a small crowd to the main entrance of the Court. Matthew Silkin QC, walked past the bystanders closely followed by James Wilbert. James carried a box file under one arm and a brief case in his other hand.

Meanwhile, Robert Easton arrived at the Crown Court in the Prisoner Transfer Vehicle; it came to a stop and the driver waited for the gate to fully open. Traffic waited for the vehicle to make the right turn into the court. Once fully inside, the gates closed and the bystanders who had watched its brake lights, gradually lost sight of the vehicle,

In a side room adjoining the court, the Jury had gathered and were being briefed on the proceedings and their duties by the Clerk of the Court. The jury, comprising eight women and four men had been selected by due process and now would wait to be called into the court.

Robert sat in a separate area that was not accessible by the jury, members of the gallery or indeed, the wider general public. He was flanked by two crown court guards who would be escorting Robert into the court when it came into session. Robert didn't have to wait too long before he was asked to stand and he was escorted into the dock by both guards. The guards told him to sit and that he would be expected to stand when the Judge entered and left the court room.

This was an unusual experience for Robert and he found it difficult to take in everything that was going on around him. He scanned around the room at the different people and the roles that each would play throughout the proceedings. The Clerk, the Counsels for the defence and the prosecution, the Jury and of the course the Gallery that would play no part, other than to witness the drama that was about to unfold.

The court room felt exceptionally formal to Robert. Furnished throughout in light oak, all the chairs and tables matched the wood panelling and this was all complimented by blue-flecked carpeting. The Bar that would accommodate the judge was raised above the rows of seats that were laid out in two rows that faced the bar. The judge's seat was a large leather chair and the Royal Coat of Arms Crest, that adorns every court room in England and Wales, was attached to the wall behind where the judge would soon be sitting.

To Robert's right were two rows of six seats where the Jury would be sitting. Immediately to his front was the prosecution and defence counsels who were sat along the same row. Behind them sat two junior court officials and to the left was a booth and table where a further two court officials were located. Above the booth was the public gallery that had three tiers of seats. Robert attention was drawn to the final row of seats in the gallery that was being filled and this caught his eye.

At that moment, a door to his right opened and the jury filed into the court led by the court usher and they were shown to their seats for the first time. A lady wearing a judicial wig was sat at the front of the court, directly in front of the judge's seat facing Robert. She had a computer screen and keyboard and had been typing since Robert's arrival. On her desk was a digital clock showing the time in glowing red digits and this was also facing Robert and both the Defence and Prosecution teams.

Robert sat in the dock which was surrounded by toughened safety glass which spread the full width of the dock at the rear of the court room. The glass in front of Robert contained gaps at regular intervals so that he would be able to hear the proceedings. Robert looked around again and tried to absorb all the activities that were going on around him.

Another door opened and this time the court usher appeared, followed by the judge. All those present in the court stood as Mr Justice Fielding QC took his seat ready to commence proceedings. His opening statement was brief and mainly comprised instructions to the jury. He was followed by the Prosecution and Defence counsels who made their opening statements respectively.

The trial commenced with the Prosecution making its case. The Prosecution team was led by Mr Warren Hinds QC, a senior Barrister who had been in the profession for many years. He was an extremely distinguished gentleman, 53 years old with grey hair and a beard. Mr Hinds was a respected Barrister and revered by those in the legal profession as a legal expert and one who could be relied upon to always present lucid, well-balanced arguments. This was something that Mr Silkin had discussed with James Wilbert and that they would need to be well-prepared come the trial.

Mr Hinds' first witness was the Coroner who had carried out the post-mortem on John Huggett. Dr Finlay Robinson, was a well-spoken man and Robert guessed that he would be approximately in his mid to late forties. Mr Hinds asked the Doctor to go through his findings and to describe accurately each wound that he found on the deceased.

The Judge addressed the members of the jury and he advised them that this may involve some unpleasant descriptions of the victim's injuries and there would be graphic illustrations of the wounds shown to them in the report of which they all had a copy. The object of this exercise would be to find the exact cause of death and possibly match which wound it was that caused the victim to die.

'Members of the Jury, please can you turn to page 4 of your report and look at the left hand graphic. Dr Robinson, please can you describe your findings to the members of the jury.' Asked Mr Hinds.

'Yes, the wound in the left-hand graphic was 181 centimetres from the heel. It was most probably caused by a heavy instrument that would be approximately 2 centimetres in diameter. The blow to the back of the victim's head would have been caused by a sweeping motion and would have impacted with a great deal of force. The force of the blow caused a defect to the occiput and damaged the sub-cutaneous tissue.' The doctor gave a full account of the wound and the damage caused.

'Thank you doctor.' Replied Mr Hinds. 'If I may stop you there, for the benefit of the members of the jury, can you explain the term occiput?'

'Yes this is rear part of the skull that sits immediately above the cavity that contains the brain stem.' Replied Dr Robinson.

'In your opinion, can you confirm if it is possible for this wound to be the result of the blow to the head that propelled the victim from his wheelchair and onto the floor?' Asked Mr Hinds.

'Yes indeed. The force of this blow was so severe that it is probably this blow that caused him to be catapulted from his chair. It is without doubt that this blow was the one delivered with the most force.'

'Thank you. Members of the jury, please can you now look at the right hand graphic. Dr Robinson, this wound is described as being on the right-hand side of the skull and is 183 centimetres above the heel. Can you describe this wound please?' Asked Mr Hinds looking up from his notes.

'This wound was caused by a slightly less severe blow and was also caused by a heavy instrument of similar size to that described a moment ago!' Said the doctor.

'Thank you. Sorry to interrupt you once more. Can you state categorically that the weapon used causing this wound to be the same?' Asked Mr Hinds.

'I cannot say for certain, however, I can say that it is highly likely.' Replied the doctor.

'Thank you, please continue.' Instructed Mr Hinds.

'This wound whilst not as severe as the first, nevertheless impacted with a large amount of force and also caused significant damage to the sub-cutaneous tissue on the victim. The instrument had impacted to the victim's temple. This is the lateral region at the side of forehead above what is clinically known as the zygomatic arch.' Continued Dr Robinson.

Dr Robinson and Mr Hinds went through every wound in extreme detail and the jury were assisted throughout with the graphics in the report. At the end of hearing about all seven wounds on John Huggett's head, Mr Hinds pressed the doctor to ascertain which, if any of them was the fatal blow and what was the cause of death.

Dr Robinson described the second as being the most likely to have been the fatal blow and that the victim died of a massive cranial haemorrhage. At this point, Mr Hinds asked for the weapon that had been recorded as an exhibit to be produced.

'My lord, if I may, I would like to produced Exhibit A and have the members of the jury view the weapon.' The Judge nodded in approval at Mr Hinds' request.

'I'm very much obliged my lord.' Replied Mr Hinds.

The weapon was produced in a light weight card board box with a window panel in the top so that the weapon could be seen. First it was passed to the coroner and then to the judge before being passed to the jury by a member of the court.

'Members of the jury, you will notice that the weapon that has been recorded as an exhibit is boxed. This is merely for your protection because of contaminants and scientific chemicals used in forensic processes.' The judge explained to the jury.

It was also pointed out that this was the first time Dr Robinson had seen the suspected murder weapon. When asked about whether it would, in his opinion, be consistent with the wounds on the victim, he said that it definitely would.

For two more days, the court heard from Mr Hinds' prosecution team how Robert Easton had avenged his own justice on the man who was preparing to ruin him. They heard how the intelligent Robert Easton had used his military training to plan the brutal attack on John Huggett. How he had disappeared on the morning prior to his arrest, deprived a young girl of her loving father then lied to cover up his appalling actions. At the end of the final court session for that day, Mr Hinds QC concluded his case for the prosecution.

The judge addressed the court and declared that the session would close for the day and that the defence should prepare to make its case the next morning. Robert felt bewildered and abandoned by the judicial system. Whilst he had not heard Mr Silkin present the case for his defence yet, it had seemed to him that the odds were firmly stacked against him.

Robert did not sleep well that night and his thoughts were of a condemned man and he felt that hope was abandoning him too.

The next morning Robert was awoken and returned to the Crown Court where he'd heard his life taken apart by the counsel for the prosecution. His life and future were now firmly in the hands of Mr Silkin and his junior counsel, James Wilbert. As with the previous days of his trial, people gradually entered the court and finally the judge entered the court and the court stood while he entered and took his seat.

With the court in formal session, Mr Silkin stood and asked the judge if he may proceed. He addressed the members of the jury, repeating his opening remarks that he'd made at the beginning of the trial describing Robert

Easton as a hard-working, former military man with no previous convictions for any crime at all.

He went on to outline that at no point in his military career, despite being attached to the Special Air Service, had he had occasion to kill another human being or even commit any act of violence whilst in combat. In the previous few days Mr Silkin and James Wilbert had listened to the prosecution making their case. Aware of the massive amounts of evidence against their client, they knew they had to act quickly.

Mr Silkin would be aiming to demonstrate that all the evidence against him was wholly circumstantial and furthermore, he would be arguing that his client's character was exemplary and completely beyond reproach. He and James Wilbert had agreed that this may be an important component of their case for the defence and proving that Robert Easton was incapable of a crime like this, would be crucial.

In addition, they would be hinging much of their case on the term 'beyond reasonable doubt.' Whilst Mr Silkin was aware that, once the case for the defence was completed, the judge would explain its full meaning to the jury. He was keen to use this term as part of their tactics and he felt that were he to outline it now, the judge's explanation of it may emphasise its importance to the jury and make them focus on it a little more during their deliberations.

Mr Silkin opened his case file, turned to the page he needed and rose to his feet

'Your lordship, the defence would like to call Detective Sergeant Paul Bretherton to the witness box.' Said Mr Silkin.

DS Bretherton took his place; he was handed the bible and asked by the Clerk of the Court to read from the card.

'I swear by almighty god that the evidence I give, will be the truth, the whole truth and nothing but the truth.'

'Thank you for appearing in court today Sergeant Bretherton.' Said Mr Silkin. 'For the benefit of the court and members of the jury, please can you explain to us your part in the investigation?'

'Yes. I was appointed to lead the investigation into the victim's murder by my superior officer.' Answered Paul Bretherton.

'This is a high-profile case sergeant and one that would normally be led by a Detective Inspector at the least. Can you explain to the court why you were appointed to lead the investigation?' Mr Silkin was very direct in his line of questioning and he was aware that this may vex the experienced detective sergeant.

Paul was a little irritated by the attempt to discredit him but he was largely unfazed by this and he was experienced to know that this was simply a tactic to unsettle him.

'Yes my immediate superior was not available when the call came into the station about the murder and my chief superintendent felt that I would be capable of handling the case in my detective inspector's absence.' Paul was equally direct in his response to Matthew Silkin's question.

'Can you tell the court who assisted you in your investigation?'

'Yes I was assisted by my detective constable; he is a senior detective with more than...'

'Sergeant, I did not ask for a full resume of your team, only who assisted you. Please can you just answer my questions?'

Paul Bretherton was now indeed vexed by Mr Silkin's comments but he chose not to say any more. His experience told him that on these occasions, it is best to counter this line of questioning with calmness.

'My senior detective constable, two junior detectives and a number of uniformed police officers who were used throughout the investigation.' DS Bretherton gave the answer that was asked of him in clear and basic terms.

'Thank you. Can you describe to the court what you found when you first arrived at the scene?' Matthew Silkin was keen to establish the full scene in order that the jury may be able to build up a full picture in their mind of what the scene looked like and where the key areas such as buildings, walls and hedgerows were situated.

The jury had access to most of the information in their case reports and like with the prosecution, the defence team had prepared documents containing graphic images which were contained in the report.

'Yes, I arrived at the scene and it was late at night and therefore dark.'

'Was anyone at the scene when you arrived?'

'Yes there were two uniformed officers at the scene who had been protecting the evidence awaiting my and the forensic team's arrival.'

'Thank you. Please can you describe to the court what you found when you entered the victim's office?'

'Yes, the victim was on the floor inside the doorway.'

'Can you explain to the court where the victim's wheel chair was situated?'

'Yes it was positioned near the doorway to his office.'

'Can you therefore deduce, that the victim was struck from behind and thrown from his chair?' Asked Mr Silkin.

'The wheelchair had been moved slightly by my officers, but they moved the chair in order to get access to Mr Huggett. They were the first to find the victim having received a call from his wife that he had not returned home as expected. To answer your original question, yes it was my conclusion that he had been struck from behind and the force of the initial blow catapulted him onto the floor.'

'I imagine it would take quite some force to throw a large man from a wheelchair.'

'Yes I agree, it would.' Replied DS Bretherton.

'Would you also agree therefore, that to generate the force required, one would have to take a large swing with a wide arc?'

'Yes I would say so.' Answered the detective.

'In your opinion, would you say that it was possible for someone to take a large swing if they were standing at right-hand side of the doorway as you look at it from outside the building.' Asked Mr Silkin.

'I'm not entirely sure I understand your question.'

'Let me put it to you in a different way.'

Mr Silkin turned to the jury and ask them to turn to page eight of their report.

'You will notice from the left hand graphic that the area to the right of the doorway, which leads to the rear of the building has a narrow pathway. In your opinion detective, wouldn't you naturally assume that an attacker would not choose this side of the doorway to carry out the attack?'

'I think one would be correct in making that assumption.' Replied DS Bretherton.

'Unless of course, that the attacker was left handed. In which case, surely the natural place to carry out the attack would have been from that side of the doorway. Would you agree with that detective?'

'Yes I suppose I would have to agree.' Paul Bretherton began to wonder where the experienced barrister was going with his line of questioning.

'My lord, if it pleases the court, I would like to present to the court a short video clip of the defendant which was taken by one of his colleagues at a family's fun day last year.' Said Mr Silkin, directing his question to the judge.

'Is it relevant to the case? And can it be corroborated? Asked the judge.

'It can indeed my lord. I have been able to have the clip verified and validated as being taken in the early part of the summer last year by a number of my client's work colleagues.'

The judge nodded his approval and the monitors were turned on.

'I'm very much obliged my lord. Please play the tape.' Said Matthew Silkin to the Clerk.

The clip showed Robert Easton and a number of his work colleagues and friends playing cricket at a family's fun afternoon one weekend about year previously. Robert was shown batting using a left-handed batting style. The clip played for a little over one minute and Robert was visible to the court playing a number of batting strokes, all left-handed.

'Thank you.' Said Mr Silkin. 'Members of the jury you will notice that my client has a very fine batting stroke. However, you will also notice that he is naturally left-handed player. Do you find that odd detective?'

'I'm not sure I understand.' Said DS Bretherton, who shifted uncomfortably in the Witness Stand.

'Let me put it another way detective.' Don't you find it puzzling, that a clearly left-handed man, would choose the place to murder his victim here which would mean positioning himself in such a way that he had no other option but to make his first blow, arguably his most important blow, in a right-handed way?' Matthew Silkin ended his long sentence with a slightly raised voice and in a pointed way.

Paul Bretherton was about to offer a response but Matthew Silkin leapt to interrupt him.

'No. Because Robert Easton was not present at the victim's garage that evening and he did not carry out the attack, did he?' Mr Silkin remained equally loud and pointed in his closing comments. 'I have no further questions my lord.'

Matthew Silkin continued with his defence over that day and the whole of the next.

The court also heard the laudatory comments from a number of character witnesses; and why the previously described, intelligent Robert Easton, would have left the murder weapon at his own front door.

At the end of Mr Silkin's defence the judge announced that the session would close for the day. He stated that the next session would comprise a brief concluding statement from each of the defence and prosecution counsels and then the Judge would deliver his own concluding statement.

The next morning brought a larger than usual public gallery. Robert sat at the back of the court in the dock flanked by the same two guards that had been present throughout the trial. Following the concluding statements from the Mr Hinds and Mr Silkin, the judge delivered his comments. As Matthew Silkin had wagered, the judge emphasised the term 'beyond reasonable doubt' and that they should use this as the basis for their deliberations. He reminded the Jury of their hefty responsibilities and that they should retire and return when a unanimous verdict had been reached.

It was late in the afternoon of the second day of their deliberations when the Jury filed back into court. Mr Justice Fielding asked the Foreman of the Jury to answer the following question yes or no.

'Have you reached a verdict of which you are all in agreement?' Asked the judge.

'Yes.' Said the Foreman.

'The defendant has been charged with the murder of John Huggett. Do you find him guilty or not guilty?'

'Guilty.'

Robert was numb with the sound of the verdict. He was oblivious to everything that was going on around him. He didn't hear the gasps from the gallery and the shouts of support for the justice system that was now interrupting the proceedings. He didn't hear the judge's request to rise and was helped to his feet by a guard.

'Robert Anthony Easton, you have been found guilty of murder. Yours was a deliberate and heinous crime which was consciously planned and carried out with contemptible malice. It is my duty to impose the maximum possible punishment for this crime. Sometimes a later date would be set for sentencing but in this case I feel obliged to deliver this today. Do you have anything to say before I pass sentence?'

'Yes your honour, I am innocent and shall fight to prove it and clear my name.' Robert wished he could put his words more eloquently but he was too devastated and could not search for the words he wanted.

'The crime of murder carries with it a sentence of life imprisonment. You will go to prison for life, take him down.'

Robert could feel his legs weaken and he almost stumbled out of the dock. He was taken to a side room where he sat with a uniformed police officer inside the door and one outside. He was advised that he must wait with the officers until the paperwork was raised for his release into police custody. He was joined by James Wilbert soon afterwards. Robert was pleased to see him and needed to protest his innocence.

'How could this have happened, I'm innocent.' Said Robert.

'Robert I firmly believe that the Jury have got this one wrong. I don't know what else to say to you at the moment. I have already spoken to Mr Silkin and we plan to make an application for a formal Appeal. But you should understand that this is a long process and may take time.'

'That is something that I have more than enough of now.' Said Robert dejectedly.

The other officer entered the room and told Robert that everything was complete. He was handcuffed and taken down a corridor and into the enclosed yard to a waiting Prisoner Transfer Vehicle.

Act Two – Secrets Below

Chapter Seven

Three Years previously

Cornelius Galbraith came from a reasonably affluent family. He was 6 feet tall and athletically built. His mousy brown hair was always kept neatly trimmed and at 33, he had maintained his healthy complexion through a combination of modern diet and regular exercise. Cornelius had come through the educational system in what many would consider to be the standard way. He had attained straight 'A's in his GCSEs followed by equal success in his A levels and he excelled in Mathematics. Accepted into Corpus Christi College, Cambridge University, he studied Economics and business, graduating with a first-class Batchelor Degree.

At twenty one, Cornelius' family had tried to persuade him to expand his academic portfolio by studying for his Masters and hopefully a PhD. Funding was never going to be any real difficulty as his parents had prepared for this, but for the young Cornelius, the cut and thrust of the financial world held so many more attractive and exciting opportunities. In the same way that funding was never going to be an issue, finding work was going to be an equally routine exercise. Life-long friends of Robert Phipps, Cornelius' parents secured him a graduate position at Johnson and Phipps as a Commodities Broker in the City.

During his first year in the Company, Cornelius would complete his apprenticeship with Johnson and Phipps doing the 'round robin' as the middle management called it, shadowing specially selected representatives from each of the company's main four departments to learn the entire history, current policies and future vision of the organisation. Being based in the financial district of the city suited Cornelius, he lived the life and fitted in well with the London social scene with which he was now associated.

Sally Thompson was a naturally very attractive young woman. She had long light-coloured hair which was not quite light enough to be adequately described as blonde. She was 5 feet 8 inches tall and quite slimly built. Similar to Cornelius, Sally had negotiated her way through the educational system in a conventional way. She performed equally well in her GCSEs and A Levels, and had progressed to read languages at Reading University, majoring in French. Her studies took her to France on several occasions; she was fortunate that her parents owned a small property in the Lille area of Northern France that she would use as often as she could. Sally would visit with her friends and they would purposefully not allow any English language to be spoken, finding that spending time in her parent's holiday home massively expanded her conversational vocabulary.

Classified on the Interagency Language Roundtable as Level 4, meant that she held full professional proficiency and what was commonly known as fluent. Her skills helped her into an investment company that had offices in France and her duties required her to conduct frequent visits to the Opera area of Paris. With her company having offices in London, this was where Sally was based and it also gave her the opportunity to exploit the social scene in West London.

Sally had met Cornelius in a crowded bar early one Friday evening in Kensington. The same age, they had enjoyed the company of one another's groups and agreed to meet again. Over the following few months they had become inseparable and moved into Cornelius' apartment in the South Kensington area of the City. They continued to grow together, developing their love and friendship and found that they both shared so many interests. Both had a love for fine wines, although Sally came to accept that it was Cornelius who had a natural talent in this field. Both shared a love of the cinema too and would visit whenever they had a spare moment in their busy professional and social lives.

They were married at St Cuthbert's Church in Aylesbury Buckinghamshire but remained in the City for a number of years enjoying their close circle of friends and all the trappings that their healthy salaries brought.

By the time they were 33 years old, they not only owned two very desirable apartments, one in London and another in an affluent area of Paris. They had also acquired an extremely healthy portfolio of stocks and bonds worth several hundred thousand pounds. Both Cornelius and Sally were very much in love and whilst they enjoyed their lifestyle, they felt that they were ready to begin a family. However, both agreed that London was not where they wanted to raise a young family.

They spent many weeks discussing it with their wider family, friends and between themselves however, they remained undecided between the two most attractive options, Scotland and Northumberland. Both held so many reasons that attracted them greatly but their decision was made easy when Cornelius was offered a senior position in a new office that Johnson and Phipps were opening in the North East of England. Flights to and from the City were easily accessible and they could be within easy reach of their friends when they had settled. Sally's decision to provide her employers with one month's notice was an easy one to make and with only six weeks before he was required at his new offices, Cornelius and Sally began their exciting hunt for properties.

Deciding to rent for the first 6 months would be sensible they thought, and whilst trying to start a family, they both settled into modest rented accommodation which they used as a base to explore for properties with potential. Cornelius and Sally had agreed on searching for a dwelling that would give them space, some degree of peace but they were not afraid of DIY work, should a suitable property present itself. With a number of potential homes provided by a local estate agent, Cornelius and Sally pored over the list and made arrangements for their first series of viewings. None of the first 3 listings met with either of their approval. They were either too near the local town, too far away or just didn't have the instant appeal that one looks for in a potential home to raise children. The fourth property, which was their first to view the following day, seemed to have them more excited and they examined the associated documentation a number of times the night before they were scheduled to see it.

Cornelius and Sally Galbraith turned off the main road and drove up the short drive way to Blackfriars House. The estate agent was already there and she had been waiting for their arrival. The agents were not optimistic that the property would be sold, nonetheless, it was the dwelling that they'd had listed for the longest period and had been advertised for as long as anyone in the office could remember. It was important to them that they send a suitable representative and that she was well-briefed on the property's virtues. Elizabeth had been with the company for a little over two years, she was dressed smartly and had also spent the previous evening poring over the documents associated to Blackfriars.

As a Grade 2 listed building, it had deterred a number of potential investors. Families too were usually put off by the amount of work that the building required, given that some of the local authority's demands were difficult to negotiate at best and barely insurmountable at worst, certainly without significant financial investment. Blackfriars had stood for over 500 years and had been the dwelling place for the Dominican Monks from Blackfriars Abbey.

'My god will you just look at this place' Cornelius' tone gave away his enthusiasm and he searched for an equally enthusiastic response from Sally.

'It looks absolutely incredible, I love it', replied Sally. 'I don't think there's any doubt that it's a fixer upper, but would you just look at it'.

'Sal, I'm not sure about you but this is exactly what I was looking for', continued Cornelius.

'I'm with you on this one, it is simply exuding character, don't you think? Sally was direct in her statement and it was clear that they were both of the same opinion that they liked what they saw. However, Cornelius reminded Sally that they still hadn't seen inside the property and they shouldn't give away their excitement to the Estate Agent.

Blackfriars was a large and imposing, double-fronted house. Its red brick walls had stood the test of time and despite it lacking symmetry with its bowed walls, it looked solid and well-built. The arched windows had white frames which complimented the building's weathered features. It had Tudor fascias all around the first floor and tall chimneys at both gable ends. The roof was tiled in slate and although it had patches of moss it looked like it had been fully replaced in the last few years and appeared be in a good state of repair.

Sally and Cornelius could see Elizabeth standing by the large oak door that was adorned with black iron door furniture. Elizabeth greeted them and they exchanged some pleasantries about the unusually mild weather that they'd experienced in recent days and Elizabeth concluded that it was a lovely day to be out viewing homes. A warm breeze of wind brushed passed them all that brought the smell of the small apple orchard that was established to the left of the building.

Eager to commence the viewing, Cornelius asked Elizabeth if they could go inside. Elizabeth had already unlocked the door and politely asked them if they would like to proceed in first. Sally had expected the door to creak and grown as she opened it but it opened without a sound. As they entered Blackfriars for the first time they were immediately struck by the oak panelling on the walls of the entrance hall. There was a faint smell of dust that had been disturbed when the door was opened and Cornelius associated the smell to exactly that of an old building that had stood empty for a long period. The floor was solid stone and was a little uneven in places. The entrance hall extended out in front of them into a large vestibule that contained a wide stair case in the centre that wound to the left.

The oak panelling continued around the entire vestibule and there were five large panelled doors, one to their right, two to their left and one at both sides of the staircase to the rear. There was a large red rug at the foot of the staircase that looked quite worn but equally comforting.

Sally was already forming mental images of how she would like her entrance hall to look when her friends would arrive for their first visit. She had vivid pictures in her mind transforming it into a warm and friendly place. She could visualise it holding on to its history but having modern luxuries such as beautiful red carpeting and new lights that would bring out its age and hidden beauty. Cornelius watched Sally looking up and around and knew exactly what she was doing. He smiled because he had been doing the same and he wondered if their imagination had any similarities.

Elizabeth was keen to press on with her tour, not because she wanted to end it quickly, but because she knew the property had far more to offer. She sensed that Sally and Cornelius were pleased with what they saw and she wanted to build on their obvious enthusiasm by showing them the more attractive parts of the house.

She guided them through the first door to the left and into a large room that had two large windows on the wall to the left that looked out to the front of the house. There was a further window on the wall at the back of the room which gave views of the orchard. A large open fire place stood against the back wall to the right of the window and there was another door was to their right. Elizabeth explained that this was the lounge and was one of two large rooms at the front of the house. She continued that this room was connected to the dining room by the second door. Cornelius and Sally walked to the centre of the room taking in its size and they commented to Elizabeth about the vast amount of light that the three windows allowed in.

Cornelius was immediately struck by the large fireplace and imagined a large wood burning stove with lights inside the fireplace that would illuminate horse brasses that adorned the rear wall behind the wood burner. Sally was busy forming more mental images of how her own décor would bring to life the room's warmth and homely features.

Elizabeth showed them through the door to the dining room that had an enormous dinner table in the centre of the room. Elizabeth explained that the beautiful oak table would be included in the sale. Cornelius could see that the table was old and required a little attention but he was excited at the prospect of having it restored to its former condition and having new chairs to surround it at meal times. The dining room was the same length as the adjoining lounge and whilst it was a little narrower, it was still a large room that would accommodate eight of their friends for dinner without difficulty. The dining room had three doors to it, one to the lounge, one to the entrance hall and a further door that led to the kitchen.

Elizabeth continued with the tour and escorted them through to the large kitchen. This was in need of modernisation but both Cornelius and Sally had expected nothing less. Properties of this type normally required some degree of work to bring them up to modern standards. Sally was quite happy that the kitchen required updating, this would be reflected in the price and they would be able to put their personal stamp on the design. There was another room attached to the kitchen that Elizabeth outlined had probably been used in the past as a storage room for food and supplies but was now used as a utility room. It had one quite interesting feature however, a large trapdoor in the floor that led down to the cellar.

Cornelius was keen to view the cellar but Elizabeth suggested they view the remaining rooms downstairs and the 4 large bedrooms and bathroom upstairs before going into the cellar. Elizabeth finished the tour of the interior of the rooms for Cornelius and Sally and then asked Cornelius if he would like to return to the utility room and view the cellar.

Cornelius hooked his forefinger through the large brass hook on the trapdoor and heaved the large heavy door open. A flight of steps led down into the dark, cold cellar and Cornelius offered to lead the way. Elizabeth switched on the lights to the cellar from the bank of switches in the utility room and both Sally and Elizabeth followed Cornelius down the stone steps. The cellar was cold and the lighting was only just adequate. Cornelius sensed that it was a little dusty but there was a dry smell that pleased him and it suggested to him that there appeared to be no damp at all. However, he wanted more information about this and asked Elizabeth about damp proofing.

'The property has recently been checked for damp and it has been given a clean bill of health', Elizabeth confirmed.

'Thanks that what I was expecting, it seems dry down here which is an excellent sign. Although, we would still like this checked and we would be having a full survey completed. If, of course, we would be making an offer.' Cornelius joked.

'Can you tell us anything about the current owners?' Sally enquired.

'Yes indeed, they have been living overseas in the United States, they are a retired couple who have moved to Florida for the sunshine. The property has been empty for a few months now. It has been on the market for longer than that but the couple wanted to waste no more time and left it in our hands.' Elizabeth gave a full and frank response. She was mindful that there was no point in being secretive about its length of time on the market, this information was freely available to any potential buyer.

Sally and Cornelius were satisfied with Elizabeth's answer and it confirmed to them that there was a genuine reason for sale.

Inside the cellar there were four rows of large wooden racks that stretched the length of the cellar and went from floor to ceiling. Cornelius joked that the owners clearly had a taste for wine but was disappointed that they hadn't left any behind. Still, Cornelius was delighted with the cellar and imagined it loaded with fine wines that he could exhibit and share with his friends. Sally was equally pleased that the wine racks were there and she knew that Cornelius thought of himself as a connoisseur, and quite rightly. She had always been impressed at his ability to describe a fine wine to Sally and their friends from its colour, texture and bouquet.

'I was wondering about the lower, sub-surface works, can you tell me about the services to the property Elizabeth?' Enquired Cornelius.

'Yes the electricity comes in a standard way from the grid but the drainage system leads out to a septic tank at the rear of the garden. It's a little too far from the beaten track to have ever been linked to the main sewerage system.' Elizabeth explained.

'That's fine, I was wondering what lay beneath us that's all – you see Sally and I are keen film fans and have always wanted to have our very own private cinema. This place seems to lend itself perfectly to that.' Cornelius knew that Sally had dreamed of this too and he was hoping to provoke a response from her.

'Darling that's a beautiful idea, you know I've wanted one for ages, but what about the wine cellar?' replied Sally.

'It's ok honey, I would like to keep that too. I was thinking more along the lines of going through one of the cellar end walls and then digging down into a subsurface level to make a home cinema. Just big enough for you and I, and maybe a few friends. What do you think?' Cornelius once again looked for a response in Sally.

'Darling you never cease to amaze me; I think it would be a wonderful idea.' Replied Sally.

'I can't see any real issues with that.' Interrupted Elizabeth. 'The house dates back several hundred years but any drainage works that have been added since will all be listed in the drawings and will have been retained with the deeds. Providing you avoid all those, and you get a thorough structural survey, you can probably go down as far as you want.' Continued Elizabeth.

'Well I think I've seen all I need of the inside of the property, what about you honey.' Asked Cornelius.

'Yes I'm content we've seen everything, could we perhaps have a quick look around the gardens?' Sally asked, expecting a positive reply.

'Of course, I'll lead the way. Be careful of the steps on your way up.'

Cornelius closed the trapdoor and Elizabeth pointed to a door at the rear of the utility room that would lead them out of the house and into the gardens at the rear. The gardens were fully walled and Cornelius reckoned the rear wall must have reached back about 50 metres. At the end of the garden stood a very old looking set of out buildings that probably dated back with the original property or some point very soon after. They were made from exactly the same bricks as the house and Cornelius wondered if the buildings had been used for keeping livestock in the past and asked Elizabeth about them.

'The outbuildings as far as I can see from the literature do indeed date back to around the time of the original dwelling. However, I think the owners have used them as a workshop and as a storage area for garden tools and equipment.

The gardens didn't require that much effort to restore them back to their best thought Sally and imagined that the previous owners had taken pride in keeping them in beautiful order. There was a full lawn that despite being in need of cutting, looked like it had quality turf. There were a series of bushes and other shrubbery that blended beautifully, complementing the ancient walls that surrounded the garden perfectly. Cornelius and Sally gained a better view of the orchard which stood to one side of the house and which led in neat rows all the way the front.

Cornelius, Sally and Elizabeth walked through the orchard along an adjacent stone path and back to their car. Cornelius and Sally both shook hands with Elizabeth and said they would be in touch. As they drove away with Blackfriars House to their rear, they looked at one another and smiled broadly. They didn't need to speak to one another and both knew they had found their new home.

The following evening, Elizabeth telephoned them and said that she'd spoken with the owners. Both Sally and Cornelius shared the telephone ear piece, closing in together to listen to her. She apologised for not getting back to them sooner but she'd had to wait for them to consider the offer that they'd made and, of course, there was the five-hour difference in time from the United States.

'I'm delighted to tell you that your offer has been accepted.' Elizabeth told Cornelius.

Cornelius gripped Sally's hand tightly on hearing the news.

'Thank you for contacting us Elizabeth, that's wonderful. We'll get our solicitors straight onto it and they'll be in touch with you tomorrow.' Replied Cornelius.

Sally and Cornelius hugged each other tightly then Sally went into their kitchen and poured two glasses of Cornelius' favourite red wine.

Cornelius look at Sally and said, 'We've done it.'

Chapter Eight

Cornelius and Sally rose early on the day of their intended move. They had switched all the central heating off the previous evening and huddled together through the night. Cornelius felt the cold immediately as he climbed out of bed. Sally too felt the cold air cling to her when Cornelius had pulled back the bed covers.

Breakfast for them both was cereal and toast, simple but effective they thought with their long day ahead of them. The removals company that they'd arranged had been suggested to them by the estate agents and Cornelius had told Elizabeth at the agency office that he was happy with their recommendation as they seemed to be a reputable and long-established firm. As promised the removal company arrived at 8am sharp and had prepared the removal vehicle for loading by the time they had knocked. For days, Sally had carefully packed her beloved Spode porcelain tableware that she had collected for a number of years. Cornelius had been busy wrapping the lesser valuable possessions and placing them all neatly into the boxes that had been provided by the removal company several days before. Keen to arrive at their new home, they assisted the removal men where they could, so as to hasten their departure and they were done in a matter of 2 hours.

In possession of the keys to Blackfriars, Cornelius and Sally went ahead of the removal vehicle and were excited at the prospect of seeing Blackfriars House again. Turning into the driveway seemed a new experience for Cornelius. Despite having been there on a number of occasions now, during the survey and numerous other times with the carpet and kitchen fitters, this time he felt an overwhelming sense of belonging and that they had finally arrived home. Over the past few weeks, Sally and Cornelius had managed to realise their vision of Blackfriars and had restored the property in their eyes to that of a warm and loving home that was fit enough to bring their children into the World and to give them a loving place that they could all call home forever.

Sally had the kitchen of her dreams with newly fitted units and a number of modern utilities and appliances. The house had been decorated in warm colours and fitted with new carpets and lighting systems. The drapes had been carefully manufactured by a local retailer to Sally's precise designs and were hanging in their designated places. The building had been weather sealed and the exterior had been prepared by a local landscaping company to give them a head start when tending the established gardens. Cornelius was delighted with his contribution to the house – the fireplace had been redesigned and was capable of being brought to life with interior lighting that illuminated the rear wall of the fireplace that was adorned with horse brasses as he'd imagined. Sally too was completely satisfied with her attempt to make the vestibule into a warm and inviting entrance. She was pleased that she had retained the oak wall panelling but this was now complemented by wall lights and floor mounted up-lights that had been installed to give the entrance a more imaginative way to welcome future guests. The carpet was deep red which lended itself perfectly to the panelling and wide regal staircase.

Life was good for Sally and Cornelius, their dream home was almost complete, all that was missing now was their few items of furniture that they'd wished to keep and of course their clothing and many other items of art work and small collection of wines that Cornelius had carefully packed and crated himself. When the furniture arrived a short time later, they were happy to assist the removal men and the off load was completed, this time a little under the 2 hours that it had taken them to load. Sally and Cornelius spent the remainder of the day unpacking and placing things into their pre-planned places. Of course, they knew that there was other work that remained for them in the coming days and weeks. They had received the plans of the sub-surface works to the property and they had the green-light from the structural engineer, signalling that work could commence on their underground cinema as soon as they chose to. Cornelius and Sally were both deeply enthusiastic about starting their project and saw no reason to delay, now that they'd had the go-ahead.

The engineer had said they were to knock through an archway that had been pre-marked out by the builder through the cellar wall that was situated at the orchard end of Blackfriars. This would lead them into a small entrance foyer and then down into their small cinema. They had decided to complete this work themselves, not because they needed to save cash, more that they wanted to say to their friends that they had started the project, and that Sally would end it by adding their personal design and décor to it.

Several days went by with Sally and Cornelius making finishing touches to their new home. Cornelius made a start on their garden to restore it to its former beauty. The grass was now trimmed, weeded and edged. The bushes and other shrubbery were delicately manicured and the orchard was cleared of weeds and other unwanted foliage. There was no doubt, Blackfriars was in excellent shape, it was a desirable residence in any estate agent's books and it held so many interesting features. Only the home cinema remained on their 'to do list' and when it had been added to the property, it would complete the transformation to make this Sally's and Cornelius' perfect home.

Early one evening - Cornelius walked into the cellar, lay down the 14-pound sledge hammer, the pick axe, the polythene to collect the rubble and broken masonry and the small pile of work clothing and protective equipment he would require to start the work. He told Sally that he would strike the first blow the following evening after dinner.

Cornelius sat down during dinner the following evening and had tried to outline his day to Sally, but it had been rather uneventful. Normally Cornelius would allow himself a little space from his main course for a small dessert but today he devoured his main course and said to Sally, that he wanted to make a start in the cellar.

Sally was keen to be able to offer her help. 'Can we wait until we've done the dishes and I will come down too? I want to see you strike the first blow.'

'No chance, let's load the dishwasher and get down there now.' Replied Cornelius with an excitement in his voice.

Sally and Cornelius rushed to get the dishes into their newly installed appliance and hurried to the cellar trap door that Cornelius had already opened before dinner. He donned his protective overalls, and pulled the goggles down over his forehead onto his eyes.

'Here we go Sal honey.' Said Cornelius.

'Give it what for, you're my hero.' Joked Sally.

Cornelius picked up the sledge hammer holding at the end of the handle with his left hand and with his right hand near the hammer end, he swung it from behind him like a baseball bat and unleashed the first blow into the cellar wall. A huge lump of old plaster fell to the floor, revealing bricks underneath. After several more blows Cornelius had made significant progress, making a rather large hole in the wall but he joked with Sally that this was going to be a much longer affair than he'd anticipated. Still, Cornelius was not going to be deterred and he wanted to press on before the builder would take over. In a little more than two hours, Cornelius had carefully removed the whole section of plaster and brick work to the guiding line and was deep into the earth at the rear.

He wanted to keep going until he'd reached the end of the stone floor that he'd unveiled beyond the expected foundations. He continued until he was tired and both he and Sally decided they would continue tomorrow.

'Sal, I'm really pleased with how it has gone tonight, but I'm a little puzzled by the stones that I've uncovered. It appears to be a carefully laid floor but the deeds suggest that I should be well clear of the building's foundations by now and we should be finding nothing but earth.' Stated Cornelius.

'I shouldn't worry darling, it's probably just pieces of rubble and old stones from when the place was built. Let's get some sleep and see what tomorrow brings.' Replied Sally.

'Yes you're right, I'm bloody exhausted.' Said Cornelius as he turned over and turned off his bedside light. Cornelius, lay awake for a few more moments wondering about the floor he'd revealed, then drifted off to sleep.

The following evening Cornelius arrived home with the same eagerness that had been with him the previous night. He kissed Sally and asked how her day had gone.

'I've been busy today.' Replied Sally.

'Really, what you been up to then?' Asked Cornelius.

'Why don't you go down into the cellar and see?' Sally led Cornelius down into the cellar and showed Cornelius what she'd done that day.

Cornelius was delighted, if not a little surprised by her progress that day.

'Wow, you have been busy darling.' Cornelius told Sally.

Sally had painstakingly removed all the excess earth from the floor and with the dexterity of a seasoned palaeontologist, she'd brushed all the stone work in the floor, revealing some interesting features.

'This is definitely a stone floor but it really shouldn't be here.' Cornelius looked puzzled and his tone changed to one that was much more serious. 'I think we should keep digging to see just how far it goes.'

Cornelius skipped his dessert that evening, and he only ate half of the dinner that Sally had prepared for him. He wanted to get straight back to the cellar and to continue with his digging. He continued excavating for another two hours that night before Sally tempted him away with a bottle of his favourite wine. He hadn't prepared to go this far in and by now he should have stopped and started to dig down. Cornelius told Sally that he would need to obtain some ceiling supports if he went much further. He decided he would buy some at the weekend because he was keen to know how far the stone floor was going to extend. He had already gone in about five feet and if he went any further, it may become unstable. Tomorrow was his last day at work for the weekend and he told Sally he would buy the supports on his way home.

'I think we should go about another two feet, and if we've still got stone floor after that, we'll just stop and get the builders in, what do you think?'

Cornelius remained confused by the stone floor and why it was there. He was beginning to wonder if it was just part of the foundations or possibly from another component of the building that may have been demolished at some point in the past. Either way, he knew he would need to stop at some point soon.

'I think we have gone far enough already darling but let's just give it a couple more feet tomorrow, after that I think it's time to hand over to the experts.' Sally wanted to just stop the dig now but she wanted to placate Cornelius.

The following evening Cornelius arrived home and was about 45 minutes later than normal. He explained that he'd stopped at the local DIY store to pick up the supports. He removed four telescopic metal supports from the rear of his 4 x 4, along with four thick planks of wood.

'I'm going to use these to go across the ceiling in between the supports. We may as well get them in place now, it can't do any harm. I will start digging after dinner but I promise this will be my last shift.'

Cornelius had known Sally long enough now to know that she felt he should be stopping now and he should be getting the builders in as they'd planned.

After another rushed meal, Cornelius excused himself from the large dinner table and he headed back into the cellar. Sally said that she would join him in a short time after she'd finished eating. She was not angry with him for rushing his evening meal. She was pleased that he was excited about the cinema project and he had that glint in his eye showing his excitement which she loved in him.

Cornelius had been eager to begin that evening and by the time Sally arrived he was already making good progress.

'More floor darling?' Asked Sally.

'Yes, but I seem to have hit a wall now.' Cornelius joked.

Two stones were at head height and were preventing him from going any further. Cornelius started to remove the earth from around the large stones with his hand trowel. This only served to reveal more stones surrounding the first two. He continued with his trowel, removing loose earth and still more stones became unveiled.

Cornelius stopped and took a step back. 'Sal, you know what I said a moment ago about me hitting a wall?'

'Yes.' Replied Sally.

She too had noticed that Cornelius had indeed discovered a wall. The stones were arranged in an overlapping method and they both immediately knew that this was a wall and it had been put there by design.

'This must have been added after the property was built. This is a stone wall and the house is made of brick. What the hell was someone doing building a wall under a house?' Exclaimed Cornelius.

'Perhaps they were building a home cinema.' Sally replied with a wry smile.

Cornelius laughed. More at himself than anything else. Still, he wanted to reveal more and he started clearing more earth away from around the stones. With the ceiling supports now firmly in place he asked Sally to stand back a little as he tried to dislodge a stone from the wall. He swung the sledge hammer, impacting the centre of a stone.

Instead of a dull thud, the impact returned a hollow sound that echoed behind the wall. Cornelius and Sally looked at one another and Cornelius swung again at the wall but this time only lightly and in a different place.

He repeated this action several times. Each time there was the same hollow sound.

Once again, Cornelius stepped back. Only this time he swore, something that Sally didn't often hear from Cornelius, unless he needed to emphasise something quite extraordinary.

'Holy hell!' Cornelius said. 'There's a room behind it.' He continued.

Both were eager to know what was behind and Cornelius started to dig at the mortar surrounding the first stone he'd struck. He wanted to remove the stone carefully so as not to cause the wall the collapse. He hammered and scraped with his trowel for a little while, but Sally who had disappeared, returned and tapped him on the shoulder. She handed Cornelius a small lump hammer and a stone chisel.

Cornelius kissed Sally on the cheek. 'You're perfect, aren't you? Cornelius said.

'I do my best.' She replied, smiling.

Cornelius made much more progress with the more appropriate tools and it wasn't long before he was able to grab the first stone with his hands. It was quite large and heavy but he was able to get a good purchase on it and move it from side to side until he was able to pull it free. Cornelius placed the stone on the floor and looked inside the hole he'd just made.

'Can you see anything?' Sally said.

'No, not a thing. Can you grab a torch from upstairs while I remove a couple more stones?' Replied Cornelius, who was now excited at what lay in the expanse behind the wall.

Sally raced up the stone steps into the utility room. She knew where two rather sturdy torches had been stored following the move a short time ago. She searched in the cupboard for them whilst listening to Cornelius' blows against the wall beneath her downstairs in the cellar. Every time he struck the wall it echoed throughout the house. Sally found the two large torches after a short time and she hurried back down the steps into the cellar.

When she reached Cornelius, he had removed another large stone from the old wall. Sally handed him one of the torches and they both peered into the hole that Cornelius had made. Cornelius was standing to the right of Sally and he was able to view into the empty expanse towards the left of the hidden expanse and Sally had a view of the right.

'I can see another wall.' Exclaimed Cornelius.

'Same this side.' Said Sally.

'It must be another room.' Cornelius was excited at the prospect of finding this and wondered to himself how old it might be.

'I'm not entirely sure it's a room darling. Take a look down.'

Cornelius looked towards the floor of the hidden room but it disappeared out of their sight.

'I don't believe it. There's a flight of steps leading down somewhere.' Cornelius said.

'Down where?' Sally asked, looking at Cornelius.

'Honey, I haven't the faintest idea, but we're sure going to find out.' Cornelius picked up his lump hammer and chisel again.

Cornelius began to hammer into the old mortar between more stones. He pointed out to Sally that they must be careful not to remove the higher stones. He thought it best to make a small arched entrance to give it as much strength as possible. He continued for about another thirty minutes or so until he'd made an entrance way that was big enough for them to climb through, albeit whilst crouching down.

Cornelius was keen to enter into the empty darkness and see what secrets it held. However, he was mindful that Sally would not want to venture in whilst wearing clean clothes. He asked her if she would like to change first and Sally agreed to get into her decorating clothes. She also wanted to put something warmer on too; she could sense from the darkness that it was much cooler in there and a little damp too. Cornelius continued to scan the other side of the wall whilst waiting for Sally to return. He could see that the stone steps leading downwards perhaps went down another ten to fifteen feet and it was difficult to see anything passed this point.

It wasn't long before Sally returned. Cornelius was surprised when he saw her dressed for a winter storm. He joked with her that they wouldn't be going on to the Arctic but they both laughed at Cornelius' comment as they both knew that Sally felt the cold easily.

Cornelius would normally have insisted that Sally went first. He was normally polite in this way but this time he was not going to risk harm to her and he took the bold step. He reached over a small one foot high lip and crouched down to step through the hole he'd made. Sally followed immediately after and they both shone their torches into the empty expanse. It was cold and Sally's suspicions had been right. It was indeed a little damp and they could smell the moisture in the atmosphere. The room they stood in was approximately eight feet wide and a little over six feet high. The stone steps that lay before them were fashioned into a crudely designed staircase. The walls inside the room were also very basic and quite uneven. They were not straight and were bowed in places. Nevertheless, Cornelius was pleased that the walls seemed sufficiently robust to give the room they were in some stability and they both felt safe. The stone steps looked as uneven as the walls but Cornelius was assured they would be safe to walk upon.

Cornelius took the lead and ventured down the stone steps and into the empty darkness, His torchlight darted from side to side, illuminating different parts of the steps as he descended. Sally was close behind and quickly calculated that there were fifteen steps that led them downwards. At the bottom of the steps there was a flat area that was also paved with stone and the walls seemed straighter and more stable. There appeared to be a corner at the bottom of the steps that turned approximately forty-five degrees to the right. Cornelius and sally arrived at the bottom of the steps and turned to look up towards the hole that led back into the cellar. Turning back, they shone their torches ahead of them and looked at one another.

'My god it's a tunnel.' Said Cornelius, shining his torch into the darkness.

'How far do you think it goes darling?' Sally replied.

'I've no idea, but what do you say we find out.' Cornelius hoped that Sally would want to explore further into the tunnel with him.

'I'm not sure that's a good idea Cornelius. We don't know what's down here or how safe it is. Can't we go back inside the house?' Sally was hoping that Cornelius would see sense and give up on their exploration of the tunnel. At least for tonight until they could get some proper equipment and lighting.

Cornelius knew that Sally was right but he tried to coerce Sally into venturing just a few more feet inside to see if it yielded any clues as to its reason for being there. Sally reluctantly agreed and once again they shone their torches further into the tunnel. It was not straight, Cornelius and Sally could see that it bent around another corner, this time to the left about thirty metres away. The tunnel had a stone floor that extended as far they could see. However, the walls were not made entirely of stone. Most sections were in stone and these extended up and over the arched ceilings. The remaining sections of the walls were comprised of thick wooden supports that extended from floor to ceiling and overhead.

Cornelius and Sally were completely amazed by their discovery but they had no idea why such a structure would be hidden beneath their house and garden. Nor did they know how exactly how far the tunnel travelled. They didn't know if it would stop around the next corner or extend for miles. What was important now was that they got back to the safety of Blackfriars and continue their exploration the following evening.

Cornelius and Sally were about to turn around and head back to the cellar when Sally noticed a darker section of the wall about ten metres further into the tunnel. She pointed it out to Cornelius and shone her torch directly at this section of wall. As they approached they could see that the darker piece of wall was in fact a recess that had been built into the wall. This too was lined with stone. Cornelius pointed his torch directly inside the recess and noticed a rather dusty parchment folder inside. It was made from leather and was clearly extremely old. It was approximately six inches wide and ten inches long and it was tied and knotted with a leather strap.

'Let's take it inside, shall we?' Cornelius said to Sally.

They both turned and headed back to the cellar. Cornelius held the folder close to him and they climbed back through the hole into the cellar. Sally expressed her concern to Cornelius that they should seal the hole again, at least for tonight.

'What if the tunnel leads somewhere, I don't feel safe. It's like leaving our back door open all night don't you think?' Sally said.

'I doubt it Sal, this leather folder has been there for years and if anyone had been in the tunnel recently, they would surely have found this by now.' Cornelius replied.

Cornelius' comments assured Sally and they returned upstairs to their dining room. Eager to examine the parchment folder, they placed it on the table and both took seats next to it.

Chapter Nine

Cornelius and Sally stared at the leather folder in front of them. Cornelius carefully untied the leather strap. The strap and folder were moderately supple and opened without any difficulty. Inside, Cornelius and Sally could see documents that had been written in manuscript but were noticeably completed in another period in time.

The words were sloping and gave the impression that they were in neat diagonal rows that appeared symmetrically across the page. Some letters extended into the row below and were finished with long sweeping tails. There were two pages inside the folder which they briefly scanned. They were immediately drawn to the top of the first document which had a date informing Cornelius and Sally that it was written on 21st October 1541.

They tried to read through the documents but the obvious older style of writing made it difficult to understand. Cornelius' initial assessment was that this was old English which had twenty-four letters in the alphabet, and he had expected to see such an old document written in Latin. They decided to transcribe the words as they appeared in the old parchment onto fresh paper, leaving gaps when they were unsure of a particular word or phrase. They worked late into the evening and decided to carry out further research on this style of writing the following day.

Cornelius' and Sally's work so far that evening had yielded some interesting results and they were surprised by what they had learned from the documents in the leather folder. Their initial research that evening had suggested that the folder was probably dyed sheep leather. This was commonly used in those times and would be why the documents had been protected so well for over four hundred and fifty years. Once they'd translated as much of the parchment as they could, they scanned their transcription to see if they could make any sense of it. They tried to fill in the gaps and they were left with their finished transcript. They believe this to be the words as intended.

It read:

21st October 1541

This is William and I am a Dominican Monk from the Order of Preachers. I live in God's gracious care and serve him at Blackfriars Abbey. I am fortunate to have been allowed to join my brothers here. I was granted sanctuary here following my woes at Newton house. Several days' travel led me to my brothers here and I brought them an important message.

We must strive to serve god and our humble community. This parchment is one of many that I have left as a message of my brothers' and my oppression. It remains here in our passage of escape that was built by our hands so that if we must escape, we can to continue god's work. I have left other parchments in the tunnel but they are more difficult to locate than this one.

Do not be deterred in your quest, god will grant you the strength you will need to continue and you will learn about me and about my brothers' lives. There are secrets here and treasures too unimaginable to understand.

Our struggles had been with the Tudor Monarchy and the recent Act of Supremacy which granted powers to the King Henry declaring him as defender of the faith. My brothers at Newton house were not profitable enough to maintain status and now Blackfriars is at risk after recent terrible events.

For the reader of this parchment, go in peace my friend. I will ask that god guides you and keeps you safe.

William.

Cornelius and Sally were more excited than shocked but they were equally moved by William's words. To have found what appeared to be the diary of a Monk, who lived at their home centuries ago, was truly incredible. Cornelius suggested to Sally that they open a bottle of wine and then sit down to discuss their uniquely astounding find. Thoughts raced around their minds about what they should do next. Cornelius wondered who the king would have been. Sally smiled and recalled her interest in the monarchy from her history lessons at school. She quickly pointed out that Henry VIII sat on the throne for many years from 1509 until he died in 1547 so it must have been him to whom William was referring.

Sally wondered about contacting the church to outline their findings, then there was the council.

'Would the council need to know about a tunnel we'd discovered?' Sally had so many questions.

'Sal, it is just a hole in the ground, albeit with some ancient pieces of paper in it.' Cornelius wanted them to remain more grounded about their find and suggested to Sally that they should keep this to themselves for now, until they knew the true extent of their findings.

Cornelius and Sally both agreed and decided that tomorrow they would go deeper into the tunnel. They would make a list of things they should do and what they would need. They would also try to find out more information about William and then went over the parchments repeatedly that evening. They wondered what William meant when he had written that he'd left other parchments in the tunnel and that they would be more difficult to locate. Why wouldn't he just leave them all in one place, and why would he wish to make it more difficult for them to be found? These were all questions that puzzled them but it also stimulated Cornelius and Sally leaving them intoxicated by their excitement and wanting more information.

However, Sally and Cornelius were content that they had time in their arsenal and would not rush anything. The following morning was Saturday and Sally and Cornelius used this as an opportunity to pay another visit to their local DIY store. They wanted to obtain a small selection of rechargeable portable lighting units that they could use in the tunnel. Cornelius had also suggested that more roof supports would be useful as they had no idea just how safe the structure was and he was not about to take any chances with their lives.

Later in the morning, they returned to the cellar with their lighting units and additional supports. Once again, they ventured into the tunnel and secured the supports in place where there was no stonework and turned on their portable lighting system. These were powerful devices that could be positioned anywhere they chose. The tunnel took on a whole new presence and the additional lights illuminated parts of the tunnel that they'd not seen the day before. The stonework whilst still looking rather crudely fashioned, appeared neater than they remembered.

They voyaged further than the day before and, curious as to what lay ahead, headed for the second corner. Cornelius scanned the wall and ceiling, all the time probing for signs of weakness. Despite being aware now that the tunnel had been in place for almost five centuries, there was no telling if their presence had made the structure unstable.

Cornelius and Sally reached the second turning point of the tunnel and positioned one of the lights to illuminate what lay ahead. It was much straighter than the previous sections and extended much further than they'd dared imagine. Cornelius gulped and found the length of the structure difficult to fathom. It was at least half a mile long and might have been longer but the lighting was not strong enough for them to see further. The floor was paved entirely in stone, as were the walls and ceiling.

Cornelius and Sally were puzzled why a group of monks would go to all the trouble of paving an entire tunnel, if it was only there as a means of escape. Of course, they would want to find their structure intact when they needed it but it seemed that they had made this structure to withstand the test of time. Cornelius wondered if the sections near the entrance that were not supported by stone, were there as means to collapse the tunnel in the event they were being chased. This made sense to Sally and she agreed with Cornelius that this was probably the case.

Treading carefully, they continued into the tunnel all the time scanning the walls for signs of structural defects but as they moved forward, they grew more confident in the tunnel's structural integrity.

As they progressed a little further Sally noticed a small 'W' that had been crudely indented into one the stones.

'Honey, will you take a look at this? Are you thinking what I'm thinking?' Sally looked at Cornelius and waited for a response.

'Yes I am. Let's mark it with the light so we don't lose sight of it, we can return with the hammer and chisel. By the way, your eyesight is quite incredible.' Cornelius gave Sally the reply she expected and took hold of her hand. His joke about her eyesight alluded to the size of the letter 'W' which was no larger than the face of a small wristwatch.

They returned together a short time later and Cornelius started to chisel carefully at the mortar. The stone was at head height and he was careful with his blows so as not to cause any collapse. Nevertheless, his hammering echoed all the way through the tunnel and he weakened his blows so they were more like taps. The mortar gave in easily and crumbled with each strike of the hammer and chisel. Once he had removed the excess debris from around the stone, Cornelius used the builder's chisel to prise the stone free and he pulled it clear of the wall.

He reached into the recess that he had just made. He couldn't feel anything inside and so examined the recess with his hand-held torch. Further back he could see another leather folder that protruded out of a second, internal recess. He reached in further, meaning he was at full stretch and grasped the folder. He removed it from the recess and blew a large amount of dust from it. Cornelius told Sally that they should back track slowly on their return. He felt it necessary to check for other letter 'W's that they might have missed on their way in.

They scanned each wall in detail but, finding no others, they returned to the cellar and proceeded back into the main house to examine their findings.

Cornelius and Sally were both as excited as the first time they'd found William's documents and wondered if this find would reveal any further evidence about him and his life. The parchment folder was similar to the last and appeared to be made from similar material. Cornelius unhooked the delicate leather strap and Sally watched, her eyes fixed firmly on the folder.

Cornelius carefully peeled back the cover of the folder revealing another parchment. This time there was only a single document inside but they both immediately recognised the familiar hand writing of William and felt like they were reading a letter from a friend. William was less formal in his writing this time and they both warmed to him.

'It's difficult to imagine that William has been dead for all these centuries and is laying at rest, probably not far from here.' Sally's words struck a chord with Cornelius.

'Yes, it's incredible.' Replied Cornelius. 'And here we are reading his words that he wrote all those centuries ago. It feels like he was writing to us personally, don't you think?'

Sally nodded. A lump formed in her throat and for the first time she began to see William as a person and not as just an entity from the past. She tried to visualise him and she formed mental images of him in his daily routine and walking through the rooms in the house that was now her home.

William's original parchments would be kept safely together in a box that Sally had used to move her precious Spode tableware a short time ago. They began to transcribe William's comments onto another sheet of paper as before.

5ᵗʰ November 1541

Dear Friends, this my second letter but I prefer now to refer to them as instructions to you. I offer you my apologies that this time my instructions to you were more difficult to locate. I am pleased that you have discovered this parchment, now that you have found the key to locating them, it will become easier for you.

My instructions to you now are to keep moving ahead. You may have already found that the tunnel is many miles long and it goes deeper as it grows longer. It has an end which I have told you is intended as our means of escape. Since then it has been made more permanent and it has been clad in stone to protect the treasures that lie within.

Please do not view my instructions as riddles to confuse you. See them as challenges to test your faith and resolve. See them as a way to prove your worth in learning about us so as not to judge myself and my brothers if you find the treasures that we have interred in this safe place.

Go now and continue with your quest. I will ask god that he continues to guide you and keep you safe.

William

Cornelius finished reading the transcript to Sally and, silently, they looked at one another. Cornelius remained silent because his mind raced with thoughts of excitement and exploration. Sally was silent because she didn't want Cornelius to know that the lump in her throat was now a little bigger.

Sally composed herself and offered a response to Cornelius' reading.

'Darling this is unbelievable, what do you think it means?' Sally's voice still wavered a little.

'I'm really not sure. I have more questions than answers at the moment. There's one thing I'm sure of though, I can't wait to find the next parchment. What do you think these treasures are that he's talking about? And why do we have to go through this bloody process of learning about him so as not to judge them?' Cornelius had more questions but saved them for now.

'I don't know for certain, but don't you think it's wonderful that we are being led by William and we are learning about him?' Sally's words were delivered softly but Cornelius felt he was being mildly berated.

'I suppose you're right. It's true though, I feel that we are building a relationship with William and whatever it is he's doing, he's captured our imagination. He's actually a really intelligent bloke?' Cornelius' words pleased Sally and the lump in her throat grew.

Cornelius and Sally decided to eat then agreed that they would go straight back to into the tunnel. They were now hungry for food but they were both ravenous and greedy for more information about William. Sally prepared a small snack for them both and they exchanged views on what William had hidden.

'Why has he gone to these lengths to hide the parchments in the tunnel? Why didn't he just leave one big set of documents telling the whole story with a map to the treasures?' Cornelius voiced more of his unanswered questions.

His comments vexed Sally a little and this time she outwardly berated him for being a little shallow.

'Can't you see that William is trying to get us to understand him and know more about him before he wants us to continue? You said it yourself, we are going through a process so that we don't judge him or his friends and I think he is even more intelligent that you are giving him credit for.' Sally finished her statement and the lump in her throat had now completely flattened.

Cornelius knew that Sally was right. He reached out and grasped her hand.

'Of course honey, I'm sorry. Let's finish up here and get back down stairs.' Cornelius had an impassioned tone in his voice and he knew that his apology would have been fully accepted.

They both finished their snack and put their warm clothes back on. However, this time Cornelius insisted they wear the hard hats that he'd bought for them earlier. He placed one of the hats onto Sally's head and adjusted the strap for her to ensure it fitted snuggly.

'I feel like a miner.' Joked Sally.

'You look like a miner.' Replied Cornelius.

They both continued to joke about one another's appearance and headed for the cellar. They climbed through the small entrance into the tunnel and switched their portable lighting units on. They felt more at ease this time. Cornelius' caution had now abated and he felt that the tunnel was much stronger and safer than he'd first calculated. He and Sally walked a little quicker than the last time and they reached the hole in the wall where the second parchment was hidden in only a few moments. All thoughts of their home cinema were now cast into the back of their minds and they continued into the tunnel. They walked more slowly now, scanning both walls for William's mark.

Cornelius and Sally looked up and down the full height of the wall but concentrated more on the wall around head height. They had found the other two recesses at this level and felt that William would have located them all in the same way. Cornelius remembered William had said that it would be easier to locate them from now and wondered if William would be kind enough to do this small thing for him. Cornelius smiled to himself for thinking this.

They walked slowly for another fifty feet or so and were starting to become anxious that they might have missed one of William's marks. They slowed their pace and scanned in more detail. Sally was looking closely at the left wall and Cornelius the right. They continued walking, holding their powerful torches that supplemented the lighting units more than adequately.

Cornelius suddenly stopped and could see William's mark – at head height. Cornelius smiled again.

'Found one.' Said Cornelius.

Sally turned and came to Cornelius' side to see for herself.

'I think we should work out a way to mark these. What do you think?' Sally looked for a nod of agreement from Cornelius.

'I agree.' He replied. 'I think I might take another trip to the DIY store and see if I can find something suitable. I might see if there's a better way of lighting the tunnel too, especially if it's several miles long.' Continued Cornelius.

They marked the stone and made their way back out of the tunnel. This time Sally went with Cornelius to the DIY store. She felt that she'd been inside Blackfriars for too long and craved human interaction. They returned a short time later with some fluorescent markers and more of the rechargeable lighting units.

Once again they climbed back into their protective clothing and headed into the tunnel. Cornelius held the hammer and chisel, one in each hand. They arrived back at the spot they'd left and Cornelius started to remove the mortar.

After the stone, had been removed he checked inside with his torch and another parchment was visible inside another internal recess. They replaced the stone and quickly returned to Blackfriars to transcribe William's third set of instructions.

25th November 1541

Greetings to my friends. You have found my third set of instructions. It is a number of days since my last writings and my brothers and I have been busy completing another section of the tunnel with stone. The people from the village have been a great help to us and bring us stone for the tunnel. They have reason to help us and they are aware of the tunnel's importance.

Yesterday we received a message that another monastery was attacked and burned to the ground.

The Monastery was merely 35 miles or so from us here. This is indeed nearby and possibly less than one day's travel by the King's men on horseback. We are not aware of the fate of our beloved brothers – but we fear for their lives as the King's men may be seeking retribution. We are living in fear now as are the local villagers. We support one another and we are growing more afraid that the good people of the village will be implicated if we are visited by representatives of the Tudor Monarchy.

I have brought readings with me from Newton House Abbey where my Abbot was brutally slain along with my brothers there 3 years ago. I managed to make my escape and travel here to Blackfriars.

We continue with our work and we hope that one day the treasures will be found and the truth will be known about the Tudor Monarchy.

Your friend William

'What the heck is that all about?' Said Cornelius looking directly at Sally.

'It sounds like something more sinister is was happening at Blackfriars. Darling I think we should get someone's assistance?' Replied Sally.

'What sort of assistance were you thinking about honey?' Sally thought that Cornelius' question came across a little pointed.

'I think we should get someone's expert opinion of what might have been happening here. I was thinking that we could perhaps speak with a local historian who may be able to understand this more. Perhaps he might be able to help us in the tunnel too?' Cornelius was not convinced that Sally's recommendation was the right course of action.

'Why don't we come to a compromise? Let's find a historian and see what information we can get. I was just a little reluctant because we really don't know what's down there yet.' Cornelius hoped that he might get Sally to agree with him.

'Perhaps you're right darling. Who do you think we should find?' Sally asked.

'I was wondering about getting in touch with the history department at a good University.' Cornelius raised his eyebrows at Sally in the hope that she might know what he was talking about.

'You're thinking about Cambridge, aren't you? Sally knew that Cornelius still maintained links through the

Alumni at Corpus Christie and felt that he wanted to speak to them first.

Cornelius' thoughts were to contact the university's faculty of history. He knew that there would be someone who could assist. At the very least they would be directed to someone who could probably point them in the right direction.

Cornelius rang the Faculty on Monday. He asked to speak with the faculty's administration office and he was put through by the switch board. From his office, he spoke with one of the administration officers. His request was simple; he was trying to locate someone from the faculty who had knowledge of the Tudor Monarchy and who might be interested in some interesting information.

The administration officer said she was delighted to assist. She recommended that he contact Professor Stephen Montrose. She explained to Cornelius that he was a former senior researcher from the University but had taken retirement unexpectedly. She explained that he had been carrying out some extensive research into the Tudors. She outlined that he had been working on a paper at the time of his retirement and remembered chatting to him about it. She provided Cornelius with a contact number for him but wasn't sure if he would be willing to discuss it with him. She continued to say that the professor had acted very oddly in the last few days of his work at Cambridge and left rather quickly. Cornelius thanked the lady for her assistance and said he'd contact Professor Montrose as soon as he could.

Cornelius wasted no time in contacting Professor Montrose and rang him immediately after speaking to the administration officer. The telephone rang three times and heard a man's voice answer.

'Hello good morning.' Professor Montrose spoke in a very distinguished manner.

'Good morning, I am trying to get in touch with Professor Stephen Montrose.' Replied Cornelius.

'Speaking.' Said the professor.

'Hello, good morning, my name is Cornelius Galbraith. I am a former student from Corpus Christie, my wife and I have stumbled across some interesting information after moving into our new house.' Cornelius didn't go into any further detail just yet.

'How might I assist?' Asked the professor.

'Well, it's a little unusual but I was told by Cambridge that you had been writing a paper on the Tudor's, and this is why I've got in touch. My wife and I have recently moved to Northumberland and we have come into possession of some very old documents written by a Dominican Monk in 1541 and while he has not exactly given away any information, I believe there may be other documents that contain interesting information regarding the Tudor Monarchy.' Cornelius waited for a response from the professor.

'I'm delighted to hear that but if there is no information I really don't understand how I can help.' The professor seemed a little cold in his response.

'The documents written by the monk talk about unimaginable hidden treasures. His writings refer to the Tudor Monarchy and I wonder if Henry VIII might be connected in some way?' Cornelius gave away more information that he'd wanted but hoped that this may be enough to get the professor's attention.

'Listen to me young man, I'm not entirely sure what it is you've stumbled upon. But know this, please enjoy your findings but leave it at that.' The professor's comments were direct if nothing else.

'I don't understand, I'm sorry if I have offended you in some way, I was hoping that I might be able to add to your research.' Cornelius hoped that this might help him gain some ground.

'Thank you but there is no research any more. I ceased it some time ago and I would recommend you do the same.' The professor's response was even more direct this time.

Cornelius thanks the professor for his time and apologised for having contacted him. He gave him his telephone number for Blackfriars and asked him that if he changed his mind he would be delighted to hear from him. When Cornelius returned home that evening he told Sally about the cold response he'd received from Professor Montrose.

'I don't understand why he was so cold and unresponsive. He sounded a little aloof and I think I might have struck a raw nerve.' Cornelius went on to describe the remaining telephone conversation he'd had with the professor.

'Perhaps he just wanted to give it all up and have a happy retirement?' Sally offered an explanation.

'No, there was something…, oh I don't know, let's say not quite right about his remarks.' Cornelius emphasised.

They both sat down to eat and they discussed the events of the day. They decided that they would venture into the tunnel again that evening after dinner, and that perhaps they would try to locate a different historian the following day.

They both chatted and exchanged views on what William's next parchment might reveal. They discussed their excitement and the events of the last few days that had seemed to take over their lives. Their conversation was interrupted by the telephone and Cornelius rose from the dining table and answered it.

'Hello.'

'Hello is this Cornelius?' Cornelius recognised Professor Montrose's distinguished tones from earlier.

'Yes, hello professor, it's good to hear from you.' Cornelius said nothing more and wondered what the professor would have to say following his earlier cold comments.

'I have thought hard since you contacted me this morning. I want to help you but I will only meet you in a public place and I will say when and where. These are my terms and they are not up for negotiation.' The professor spoke as directly as he had done earlier that morning.

Cornelius felt a shiver run through him and he was shaken by the professor's words.

'Yes of course, I agree with your terms. Where would you like to meet?' Said Cornelius.

'I'll be in touch.' The professor's response was short and Cornelius heard the professor hanging up.

Chapter Ten

Sally and Cornelius discussed Professor Montrose's comments. Concerned by his behaviour, Cornelius explored the many possibilities that would cause a respected academic to act in such an obtuse way. Was it that he was simply rather rude or had he other more pressing things on his mind? Whatever the cause, Cornelius was certain that the professor wouldn't have called him if he hadn't thought it was important. Sally was more intrigued that Cornelius had said the professor told him that he'd be in touch and then hung up. Sally considered this and concluded that the professor perhaps didn't trust them.

'Shall we just take another trip into the tunnel? Perhaps William can answer some of our questions for us.' Cornelius tried to inject some humour into the tense atmosphere that was growing.

'Yes darling, let's see what he's got to say. I'm sure he's bursting to tell us something important.' Sally followed Cornelius adding some light humour to the situation. 'Come on, let's grab our miner's helmets and get walking.'

Sally and Cornelius entered the tunnel again and turned on the powerful portable lighting systems. They started to walk into the tunnel and knew that it would only be a minute or two before they reached that last marker they'd found. They arrived at the fluorescent tag and commenced scanning the walls again. They both felt more at ease now that they were back in the tunnel; their excitement at finding William's next set of instructions overtook their earlier concerns and they focussed their efforts on looking for another of William's signs.

They continued walking for at least another twenty minutes or so. The tunnel continued to descend a little more and they felt they must be quite deep now. As before they wondered whether they'd missed one of William's marked stones, but they agreed to press on. Another ten minutes passed by and Cornelius stopped.

'Eureka. Found one.' Cornelius' claim came with some relief in his tone.

'At last, I thought we'd never find one. We must have walked well over a mile' Sally's reply was delivered with similar relief.

Sally was correct; they were now over one and half miles into the tunnel. It had remained reasonably straight over the last mile, but it had some slight bends. This was largely representative of the whole distance that they'd covered so far and the slight bends always prevented them from being able to see too far ahead. Cornelius started to break into the mortar with his chisel. Sally pointed her torch at the wall where Cornelius was working to provide him with some assistance. This had become a familiar exercise for Cornelius now and he knew how hard to hit the chisel and how to remove stone a little quicker each time.

After removing the stone, Cornelius pointed his torch into the recess behind where the stone had sat and could see another of William's folders. Sally tagged the stone after Cornelius had replaced it and they both set off on the long walk back to Blackfriars. They were tired now; with William's fourth parchment located, their thoughts returned to Professor Montrose and to his odd behaviour earlier that evening.

Back at Blackfriars, Sally and Cornelius took off their warm clothes, closed the hatch to the cellar in the Utility room and returned to their dining room to examine their latest haul. The leather folder was similar to the first three in terms of its size and material but this one felt a little heavier. Cornelius carefully opened the folder revealing another parchment that they both immediately recognised as William's. However, the folder also contained a small drawing that was enclosed in a wooden frame. The drawing was quite intricate in detail and of reasonably good quality. It was a portrait of a man, illustrating his head and shoulders.

'Goodness, look at the detail in this.' Said Cornelius, handing the drawing to Sally who carefully held it in the palm of her hand.

'It's remarkable.' Sally replied. 'I wonder if it's a portrait of William. What do you think?' Sally hoped the drawing was that of their friend.

The picture was of a man with a slim face and large eyes. He had short hair and a weathered complexion. The paper had an uneven surface but was of sufficient quality to illustrate the man displaying a serious expression. The garment he wore wasn't shown but the drawing depicted a hood that was visible behind his shoulders.

Cornelius and Sally commenced their fourth transcription which Cornelius translated onto fresh paper as before.

21st January 1542

Hello my friends. As you can see we have progressed well with our masonry work. I am glad you have found my fourth instructions and you will see that I am using these parchments to inform you of our progress as we proceed.

I have included a portrait of myself and this was drawn by one of my brothers. He has natural artistic talent and has captured my features very well.

My friends, we are deep into the tunnel now but there is still significant distance to travel before the end. I have told you briefly of treasures that lie within this place, they are unusual treasures, but as I have said before, they hold unimaginable value.

Please continue with your quest my friends. Go in peace and let god guide you safely.

William

Sally and Cornelius felt that their relationship with William had grown and they felt much closer to him. Despite the centuries that divided them, they were now able to see him and they could see first-hand his work in the tunnel beneath them.

They pondered for a moment about his writing and his comments about the treasures that lay there. It was now getting late into the evening, Cornelius and Sally were both tired from the day's events. Sally's ankles ached from walking on the uneven stone surfaces in the tunnel and Cornelius' eyes felt heavy. Blackfriars was completely silent except for the sound of the wind rushing through the orchard.

On reaching the first step of their wide gothic staircase in Blackfriars, their telephone rang, breaking the silence and Cornelius stopped.

'Who on earth would be ringing at this hour? It's almost midnight.' Cornelius barked.

Sally remained on the staircase as Cornelius walked to the telephone on the table in the vestibule.

'Hello.' Cornelius spoke as if he was asking a question.

'Hello Cornelius, this is Stephen Montrose.' Said the professor. 'I'm sorry for contacting you at this hour.' Continued the professor.

'That's ok, what is it you wanted?' Replied Cornelius slightly more pointedly. 'It's the professor.' He whispered to Sally, holding his hand over the telephone mouth peace.

Sally stepped down the two steps onto the vestibule floor and walked over to Cornelius.

'Like I said I'm sorry for calling you late into the evening but there is some method in my madness and I'll explain that when we meet. I've driven up to Northumberland and have checked into a hotel. I was wondering if you would like to meet with me tomorrow morning.' The professor sounded much friendlier than before.

'Yes of course, that would be absolutely fine.' Said Cornelius. 'You said earlier that you would like to meet in a public place?' Cornelius continued hoping to have his earlier concerns allayed.

'Yes, I'm so sorry if that alarmed you in any way.' Said the professor apologetically.

'Well yes it did a little.' Admitted Cornelius.

'There's a Garden Centre I drove passed earlier today called Peterson's. I wonder if that's far from you.' The professor asked.

'No it's not far from here, Sally and I have been there before. It has a nice coffee shop and restaurant if you would like to meet in there.' Cornelius offered the professor a suitable venue to meet his earlier terms.

'That will be fine, thank you, I will meet you there at eleven. Will that be ok for you?' The professor asked.

'That's perfect. How will we know who you are?' Asked Cornelius.

'I'll be wearing my deerstalker.' Joked the professor. 'No one else wears them these days. See you in the morning, goodnight' He concluded.

'Yes you're right.' Cornelius laughed. 'See you at eleven. Good night professor.'

Cornelius replaced the telephone handset and they both made their way up their staircase.

The next morning Cornelius and Sally drove into the car park of Peterson's and parked their car. It was not quite quarter to eleven and they realised they were too early. The car park was almost full and they made their way into the garden centre. They quickly located the restaurant and thought they might get some drinks before the professor arrived. They ordered coffee and walked in to locate a suitable seat that they thought would be acceptable to the professor.

Sally noticed the man wearing a deerstalker hat sat several tables away and they walked over to meet him. Her immediate impression of him was ironically, that of a retired academic. His clothing whilst smart, looked a little dated but nonetheless expensive. He was dressed in a tweed jacket that matched his hat and he had a colourful bow tie that gave him a mischievous look.

'Good morning Professor.' Said Sally smiling.

The professor rose from his table and removed his hat. He held out his hand to Cornelius and Sally.

'Good morning, it's a pleasure to meet you both.' Said the professor. 'Please call me Stephen.'

Sally reckoned that the professor was in his mid to late fifties. He was about five feet ten inches tall and had a bald head. What little hair he had was white, and was neatly trimmed around the sides and at the back of his head. He was a little over weight and had a large round face. Sally warmed to his smile and she felt he had friendly eyes.

'Thank you for meeting me here. I think I owe you an explanation to my recent, rather unfriendly behaviour.' Said the professor.

'We're all ears Stephen.' Replied Cornelius.

Professor Montrose wrapped both hands around his mug of coffee and began to relate his story to Sally and Cornelius.

'Firstly let me apologise for my behaviour; I needed to make sure that I could trust you and that you weren't one of those people.'

'Those people?' Interrupted Cornelius.

'Yes, those people. More about them in a moment. First I wanted to tell you about my research that I began about a year ago. I have been putting together a paper about the history of the Tudor monarchy and my research led me to some rather unusual anomalies.' The professor was continuing to outline his story but was interrupted by Cornelius again.

'Anomalies? What kind of anomalies?' Said Cornelius. Realising that he was not helping, he allowed the professor to continue. 'I'm sorry, you were saying Stephen.'

167

'It's ok no problem, I know that this must seem very unsettling for you both. I found some anomalies a few months ago concerning the reign of Henry VIII. Without wanting to go into any great detail, there are some irregularities and I explored this in much greater depth. The upshot raised some very startling questions.' The professor stopped short of giving any further details.

'So why did this make you so aloof when we first spoke?' Asked Cornelius.

'Yes I was coming to this. You mentioned that you had found some parchments written by a Dominican Monk. This lends itself perfectly to the work I was doing and why I decided to stop the research.' The professor was a little cryptic in his statement.

'Look I was wondering if you might like to come home with us and we'll show you the parchments we've found. Perhaps the parchments will add to your research and fill in some gaps for you.' Cornelius offered the professor the chance to view William's instructions and knew he was taking a small risk.

Cornelius knew however, that Stephen Montrose was a respected academic and was unlikely to pose either him or Sally any real danger.

'Thank you, that's very kind of you. I'd be delighted to come along and I appreciate your help. Perhaps I may be able to fill in a few gaps of your own.' Stephen responded.

Cornelius suggested that he follow them in his car and they headed off for Blackfriars. Stephen Montrose turned his car into the driveway behind Sally and Cornelius and he looked up at Blackfriars for the first time.

Cornelius welcomed the professor to their home and they invited him inside. Sally told Stephen that she would put on some coffee and Cornelius invited the professor into the dining room where the parchments were kept safely inside the box that Sally had kept her beloved Spode.

The professor was taken by the inner beauty of Blackfriars and complimented Cornelius on their work. He commented that in keeping much of the original architecture was worthy of particular praise. Cornelius raised an eyebrow at this comment and he wondered how he might know about the building's original look. He continued that in doing many years of research involving this period had taught him much about building design and even the materials that were commonly used.

Sally returned with the coffee and they all sat at the dining table. Cornelius removed the parchments from their box and the professor commenced to look them over. Cornelius also provided his own transcripts which he thought might help the professor. However, he told Sally and Cornelius that he preferred to read through the parchments first, then if he needed to, he would view Cornelius' translations.

Stephen accepted the first folder from Cornelius and he held it very carefully. He had the look of astonishment that was brought about not by the age of the document, but more because Stephen knew of its intrinsic value.

Stephen opened the delicate folder and was greedy for the information it contained. He noticed the date at the top of the parchment and he gasped with enthusiasm. He took out a pair of glasses from his tweed jacket and began reading. Cornelius and Sally sat and watched in silence as the Cambridge academic scanned the document from their friend William. After he'd finished reading he quickly looked over Cornelius' transcript and congratulated him on his etymology and near perfect accuracy. He told Cornelius that he was delighted with the parchment and that it contained so much information. He asked if he could read the second document and again, Sally and Cornelius watched as the professor absorbed the information like a hungry lion devouring its prey.

He scribbled furiously into a small notebook that he'd produced from his pocket. Cornelius asked him what the notebook was for and he explained that all the main points of his research were contained in there. Cornelius asked why he didn't use a computer or some form of electronic media for this, but Stephen was quick to reply that, like their friend William, he preferred to write everything in manuscript. The small notebook looked like it was made from leather and was stuffed with supplementary information on additional sheets of paper.

It was all held together neatly by an elastic strap that was there to prevent the additional pages from falling out.

He continued to cast his expert eye over the remaining parchments and wrote more information into the notebook. He sealed the leather strap around the fourth and last parchment folder and looked over the top of his reading glasses at Sally and Cornelius. They were eager to know his initial thoughts but the professor asked if he could have some paper so that he could illustrate it graphically for them. Cornelius asked if he would like to use their white message board that was on the wall in the kitchen.

'That would be perfect, thanks.' Said the professor as he headed eagerly for the kitchen.

Sally and Cornelius followed and took a seat at the kitchen table, so that the professor could begin his lesson. He took hold of a marker pen and asked them to cast their minds back to the sixteenth century - the year 1509 to be exact. The professor felt as happy and more excited than he had in years.

'Fill your coffee cups, because I have a very interesting tale to tell.' Stephen looked at his pair of history students who were now captivated by him. He took the lid off his pen and started to write on the white board.

'1509. This is the year that Henry VIII was crowned king of England.' Stephen spoke in a confident way that demonstrated his obvious, expert knowledge. 'These were dark times and Northern Europe was in a great deal of unrest following the King's unexpected accession to the throne from his late father King Henry VII.' Stephen continued his gripping tale.

'Henry wasn't expected to accede to the throne because that was preserved for his older brother, Arthur. This was why there wasn't much known about Henry in his earlier years. Yes, England was meant to have its King Arthur but within 4 months of becoming the Prince of Wales and being married to Catherine of Aragon, Prince Arthur died, and of course with it his right to the throne. This paved the way for Henry to become King and to eventually become married to his brother's former bride.

Ironically, the young King Henry required papal authority from Rome in order to marry Catherine. Of course, later, we know that Henry denounced all forms of Catholicism after he was not granted a divorce.' Stephen had Cornelius and Sally enthralled and they continued to sit silently, listening to Stephen.

'This led to a number of religious changes imposed by Henry VIII. In fact, he became obsessed by it; separating the Church of England from that of the Roman Catholic Church. He proclaimed himself to be the head of the Church of England and later as defender of the faith. Of course, at the time of his denunciation of Catholicism, he also set about the dissolution of the Catholic Monasteries in England and this was later legitimised by Parliament with the Act of Supremacy.' Stephen paused for a moment.

'This is where your friend William comes into the picture. William was a Dominican Monk and they are from the Catholic Order; known as the Order of Preachers. Part of the act dictated that unless a monastery was able to make two hundred pounds in a year, it was seen as unworthy and was to be closed, sometimes quite violently. His brothers at Newton House had been slain by the King's men and he was desperate to warn his brothers at Blackfriars. He was also desperate to avoid a similar fate and this is where William's, and now your tunnel, becomes a very important factor in the equation.'

'But why was it all carefully fitted out and lined in solid stone?' Cornelius challenged Stephen for an answer.

'That is a very good question. It is also something I'm keen to know myself but there are more important components to this puzzle, and I would like to impart those to you first if I may.'

Stephen was in full flow and wanted to pass on as much of his research as possible. Cornelius and Sally didn't need to speak, instead they nodded in agreement and allowed the professor to continue.

'We all know about Henry VIII and his six wives but this is where I have found an unusual anomaly. Henry acquired the throne from his father and we now know that it should have went to his older brother, Arthur. England was strong and Henry inherited a large amount of money from his father. He also had a strong army and he was to put this to use against France a little later into his reign. We know too that Henry was famous for his large frame and for being quite obese. However, in his youth Henry was rather athletic and had a rather insatiable sexual appetite; indeed, he had several mistresses, which we know resulted in a number of illegitimate children.'

'But what was the anomaly?' Interrupted Sally.

Stephen took out his pen again and listed the dates that Henry was married to his 6 wives on the white message board in the kitchen. He drew three columns and wrote the names of his wives, the dates they were married to Henry and what happened to each.

Catherine of Aragon	Married 1509 – 1533	Divorced
Anne Boleyn	Married 1533 – 1536	Executed
Jane Seymour	Married 1536 – 1537	Died
Anne of Cleves	Married 1540 – 1540	Divorced
Kathryn Howard	Married 1540 – 1542	Executed
Katherine Parr	Married 1543 – 1547	Widowed

'Henry was never without a wife, right up until 1537. Then suddenly, after the death of Jane in 1537, his marriages came to an abrupt end. History tells us that he wasn't married again until 1540, when he married Anne of Cleves, his fourth wife. There was no apparent reason for the three year break in his marriages. It would have been understandable if the King had been concentrating on a war or some other project, but there was simply a void. There is of course the Act of Supremacy and the dissolution of the Monasteries and this was something that kept parliament, and the royal household very busy. It is this that intrigued me when you called.'

'Why's that Stephen?' Cornelius stopped the professor's flow again.

'It's because something happened after the death of Jane Seymour. There seemed to be a great shift in power and an enormous change in royal influence. My research led me to a few conclusions but one very specific one which alluded to the commission of another royal crown. My interim findings, which were published, claimed that another Royal crown had existed and had been replaced around the time that Jane Seymour died. It appears that the new crown, that which is known today, differed in minute detail from the earlier one worn by Henry VIII.' Stephen's lesson to Sally and Cornelius held their imagination even tighter than it had earlier.

'It is at the time that I published my interim findings about the missing crown, that I received some extremely unwanted attention.' Stephen displayed a serious look.

'A group of 3 very unsavoury individuals presented themselves wanting to know more about the missing crown. When I refused to co-operate they became violent and I ended my research as quickly as I'd started it.'

'Who were these people? Didn't you report them to the police? Sally asked.

'Sally, please understand, these aren't the people one reports to the authorities. If my research and theories were proven to be correct, the crown would hold so much value that no person could even attempt to attach a realistic price to it. It would indeed be absolutely priceless.' Stephen paused again and searched Sally's and Cornelius' expressions for some hint of their thoughts.

Cornelius looked at Sally and his body language gave away his deep concerns. He immediately lost all thoughts about the crown and about William's claims about unimaginable treasures. He was now more concerned about the unsavoury group to which Stephen had just referred.

'Stephen I'm afraid I'm going to need more information about this unsavoury group. Who the hell were they and just how violent were they?' Cornelius demanded an immediate reply.

'I would say they would be about as violent as it was possible to be. That said, I haven't heard from them in weeks.' Stephen gave Cornelius an honest response that he was sure would provoke more questions.

'So how do you know they've given up on you? How do you know that they haven't been following you for all these weeks?' Cornelius wanted better answers from the Cambridge professor.

'Look, if this lot wanted to pursue their quest for missing Tudor treasures, they would have been in touch many more times by now. This is why I was a little hesitant to discuss my research with you at first. I thought they were back and I wanted to be sure I could trust you. Turns out I can.' Stephen concluded his statement hoping it had satisfied Sally and Cornelius. He quickly changed the subject to divert their attention away from the three men who'd threatened him.

'I wonder if I might be able to view the tunnel.' Stephen felt he'd earned the right to at least see it.

Cornelius and Sally were reasonably happy that they, and indeed the professor were not in any danger and they said they'd be delighted for him to see it and would appreciate his view of it.

Cornelius handed a spare safety helmet to the professor and they headed down the stone steps into the cellar. When Stephen entered the tunnel, he gasped in amazement. His eyes darted from side to side and his expert mind struggled to absorb all the information that was pouring in through his senses. Cornelius illuminated the tunnel with one of the portable devices and all three walked into the tunnel.

'What are these wooden supports for?' Asked Stephen, pointing to the first section of wooden beams. 'It looks like the whole tunnel is stone apart from these couple that have wooden supports. You don't think anything is behind them, do you?' Continued Stephen, his brain now in overdrive.

'No, we thought that at first. There are actually three wooden sections in the first part of the tunnel. We wondered why they might be there too, initially we thought that they were used because the stone was in short supply, but as we go further in you will realise that there must have been an abundance of stone.' Cornelius replied to Stephen but knew he had not answered his question.

'Given that it was an escape tunnel, my guess is that they would have removed the wooden supports to collapse the tunnel behind them, had they needed to use the tunnel as designed.' Stephen was quite sure he was right but hoped he hadn't sounded flippant in his reply.

'That would make sense, and it's clear we came to the right man.' Cornelius smiled and spoke to the professor while looking at Sally.

'What intrigues me more is the markings on this wooden support.' Stephen pointed to a small collection of markings near the bottom of one of the supports.

'Another reason why we came to you Stephen, we hadn't seen those before.' Admitted Sally. 'What do you think they are?'

Stephen asked Cornelius to point his torch to the area he'd pointed out and Stephen crouched down to get a better look. He took out his notebook and pencil and copied the markings.

'Do you know what they are? Asked Sally.

'Yes it's Latin. It says *Ecce Homo.*' Said Stephen as he stood up.

'Any idea what it means?' Cornelius frowned while looking for an answer from Stephen.

'Yes it means *Behold the Man.* Said Stephen. 'It was a phrase used by Pontius Pilate just before Jesus' crucifixion.

Chapter Eleven

'What do you think the markings were referring to? Asked Sally, appearing a little confused.

'I haven't the faintest idea Sally my dear. However, I will say this. People change the future every single day by their actions and deeds. But it's not often one gets the chance to change the past. It is moments like this that I love history so much.' Stated Stephen. 'Let's move on, shall we?'

The three explorers continued their way deeper into the tunnel. Cornelius and Sally pointed out each of the recesses where they'd found William's parchments and Stephen stopped briefly to view each of them. They continued further and, as they reached the latest recess they'd uncovered, Cornelius and Sally stopped.

'This is where we slow down Stephen, it's unexplored territory from here.' Cornelius explained that they would now need to start scanning to search for William's next stone marking.

Stephen felt cold and he could sense that the air quality in the tunnel was damp. However, he accepted that this would not necessarily be that unusual and he was too wrapped in the moment to worry about this. He started to scan the walls with Sally and Cornelius and was thrilled by the prospect of finding another parchment from William.

His excitement grew and he found it extraordinary that his research was now coming back to life; he felt that this was going to add a new dimension to his work. All thoughts about the threats he'd received from the three men paled into insignificance now.

Whilst walking slowly forward he carried out his own systematic sweep of the walls, moving his head up and down so as not to tire his eyes. Sally joined Stephen in scanning the left wall and Cornelius continued as he had before focussing on the right. Stephen was impressed by the lighting system that Cornelius had obtained and he paused for a moment to wonder how William and his brothers had coped by candle light.

Sally, Cornelius and Stephen walked for another twenty-five minutes. All three were growing tired by their search when Stephen inhaled sharply and dashed forward.

'I've found one, I've found one.' Stephen rushed his words out. He rubbed a finger around the contours of William's marking on the stone and looked at Cornelius and Sally. 'I can see now how excited you must have been when finding the other parchments. It is a truly wonderful feeling and I can't wait to see what your friend has to say.' Stephen found it hard to contain his enthusiasm.

Cornelius and Sally witnessed Stephen's outward expression of raw emotion and was equally eager to find out what William had to say. Cornelius joined Stephen at the stone and produced his hammer and masonry chisel.

'Ready when you are Stephen.' Cornelius placed the chisel into the old mortar. 'Here we go.'

Stephen took a step backwards allowing Cornelius to complete his familiar routine. Cornelius carefully chiselled at the mortar and it crumbled to the floor. He handed the hammer and chisel to Stephen and tugged at the stone; gradually he dislodged it and he lifted it free of its ancient site.

Cornelius invited Stephen to reach inside the recess and Stephen eagerly obliged. He moved his open hand around inside and found the folder. The leather felt soft and cold to Stephen and he removed it from the recess. He was wide-eyed with excitement and suggested that they return directly to the house to view William's parchment.

They hurried back along the tunnel towards Blackfriars. Stephen estimated that they were approximately 3 miles or so from the house and that it would take at least 45 minutes to complete the journey. They maintained a good pace on their return journey; Stephen was soon warm again and he congratulated himself on the exercise he was getting.

They raced up the stone steps to the cellar and hastily made their way to the dining room. Stephen placed the parchment down carefully and asked if he may have the honour in opening it. Sally and Cornelius were happy to allow Stephen this privilege. He carefully removed the leather strap and opened the folder to reveal William's fifth set of instructions. Stephen not only recognised the familiar handwriting of William but he was also familiar with the old English language he was seeing.

He asked Cornelius for some paper and he started to translate the parchment into meaningful information. All three looked over the transcript and absorbed it.

20th February 1542

Greetings my friends, You will see that we have made further progress with our masonry work and I must tell you that you are close to finding the end of the tunnel. There is only another 3 miles to travel. However, there is a more important milestone that you are reaching.

It will not be much further for you now until it can be revealed what lies within these walls. However, you will have work to do, before you can claim what is here.

The things that are here are too precious to unveil too easily and they can only be found with true wisdom. What lies in this tunnel can only be reached with information that will be held by my Abbot and

I. He and I will die before revealing this information and he will pass it on verbally to his successor. Thereafter, it is accepted that each of his successors will pass the information needed to the next.

To find the information you need, you must first find the Abbot or Friar who presides over Blackfriars. However, the information will not be released for 100 years from this date. This will be necessary to protect the lives of my brothers, the villagers, and their descendants for several generations to come.

Once again, my friends, continue with your quest and go in peace. May god guide you and protect you.

William

'Well there goes any hope of finding what's down here.' Sally said rather dejectedly.

'Not so.' Replied Stephen.

'Really, what makes you think that?' Cornelius joined the conversation and reminded Stephen that Blackfriars had probably not been a dwelling for the Monks for centuries but he was interested in the professor's thought process.

'The Order of the Dominican Monks had a number of secrets that were passed down from Abbot to Abbot. Some remain secret, some were lost forever throughout history. But some were documented.' Stephen spoke confidently and he had researched this in some detail before.

'But why would someone document something that was meant to be kept secret?' Cornelius interrupted and appeared confused.

'Some of their secrets had lost all their meaning and because they were deemed meaningless, they were simply documented, should they need to retrieve the information at a later date. I don't know much more than this, but given that Blackfriars is no longer a monastery, and probably hasn't been one for many years, and as you say possibly even centuries, I'm hoping that the information we need will be one of those secrets that was documented for becoming meaningless.' Stephen spoke deftly and once again, both Cornelius and Sally were impressed by Stephen's breadth of knowledge.

Stephen calculated that he was probably right and he knew that it was highly likely that his suspicions about this being documented by the Dominican Order of Monks, would be proven correct. He asked Sally and Cornelius if they would be happy for him to contact the Dominican

Order. Stephen felt that his knowledge had bought him respect from Cornelius and Sally and a great deal of credibility. He hoped that they would see him as an integral component to their team and allow him to obtain this information for them.

Cornelius and Sally said to him that they would be delighted and thanked him for his assistance.

'Who will you contact Stephen? I wouldn't have the first idea where to begin.' Cornelius enquired.

'The Dominican Order of Monks are a large fraternity. I have done research on their organisation before. If I dare call it an organisation. You see, the Dominicans have a long history dating right back to the thirteenth century. The English Province of the Order of Preachers, as it is known, was founded by St Dominic at the General Chapter of Bologna in 1221. They have a number of Priories now, the largest are in London, Oxford but also in Cambridge, which is where I centred much of my research.' Stephen paused and Cornelius seized the opportunity to ask another question.

'It's a pity there isn't one located around here, do you think there might be?'

'As a matter of fact, there's a Dominican Priory about 30 miles from here. I will drive over there first thing tomorrow morning. If you've no objections I will see if I can keep my room at the hotel for another couple of nights.'

Stephen paused and was interrupted again, this time by Sally.

'You'll do no such thing. You will settle your bill with them tomorrow morning, collect your belongings and stay with us. We have sufficient space here and we'd love to have you stay while we are investigating the tunnel.'

'Sally's right Stephen.' Cornelius was in full agreement with her. 'We'd love you to stay with us, please say you will.' Cornelius made a hearty plea to Stephen and hoped he would accept.

'Well I'd be absolutely delighted to stay, thank you, very much.'

Stephen was more excited than ever, and said to them that he would drive back to the hotel and get some rest. It's going to be a long day tomorrow. If you've no objections, I will drive back over in the morning to drop off my bags and then I will head straight over to the Priory.'

'Yes that sounds perfect.' Replied Cornelius. 'In the meantime, I am going to contact the office and see if I can get some leave.'

Stephen thanked then both again for their kind offer and told them that he would leave them to enjoy the remainder of their evening. Cornelius and Sally both stood by the door and waved to the professor as he drove off down their driveway.

The next Morning Stephen rose early. He was surprised that he'd slept so well and he reasoned that it was because he felt excited about Blackfriars. For the first time in weeks, he felt that he has purpose in his life again. Research *was* his life; History *was* his life and now he was able to combine both again in an unfamiliar but very exciting and pragmatic way. He arrived at Blackfriars as promised and was worried that, at 9am, he may be a little early. However, his concerns were quickly allayed as he stopped the car in the front of the large house and he saw the large oak front door open with Cornelius and Sally standing by to greet him.

'I was afraid that I might be too early but I wanted to get on the road to the priory. It's probably going to take me a good forty-five minutes to get there.' Stephen hoped for some agreement from Sally and Cornelius.

'That's fine Stephen. To be honest, I thought you might be here earlier.' Cornelius' response placated Stephen and he smiled.

'If I'd known that I would have been here at 6am.' Stephen laughed.

'In that case, you'd have found us both still fast asleep. Please come in and we'll show you to your quarters. We have put you in William's room.' Cornelius joked in return.

'Goodness, I am honoured indeed. I hope he won't mind.'

'Stephen I said last night that I was intending to get a few days away from the office.' Cornelius wondered if Stephen had remembered.

'That's right, were you successful?' Stephen asked, as he reached the top of the staircase.

'I was, and I'm coming with you to the priory.'

'That's great.' Stephen said. 'We can chat on the way across about some of the questions we might need to ask and I'm pleased that I will have some company. Are you both coming?'

'No I will be staying here.' Sally replied. 'This place doesn't run itself and I've plenty of jobs to keep me busy.'

'It's ok Sally, I doubt we'll be that long. I expect to be back by early afternoon. Possibly even lunchtime.'

'That's fine, I'll prepare some food for when you both get back.'

Cornelius and Stephen waved to Sally as they drove off in Stephen's car. Stephen told Cornelius that he'd made some enquiries at the hotel and had planned a route. They both chatted en route and had prepared their questions by the time they reached the priory. As Stephen had indicated, it was situated about thirty miles away and was west of Blackfriars, deep into Northumberland.

The roads were reasonably traffic free for the majority of the journey, particularly the latter part when they were deep into rural Northumberland. They saw the sign that pointed them towards the priory and they turned off the main road on to a single lane. Soon the tarmac lane became a dirt track and they began to wonder if they were going in the right direction until the old house came into view. There was a simple sign on the gate, 'The Order of Preachers', and there was an emblem which was a black and white shield bearing a cross. This was encircled by a scroll depicting the order's motto, LAVDARE BENEDICERE PREDICARE. This confirmed to them that they were in the right place and as they approached the gate, a small chapel came into view at the rear of the house.

The priory buildings comprised the chapel, and an old house that was not too dissimilar to Blackfriars thought Cornelius. There were several smaller out buildings off to the left and the gardens were all walled. The house looked old but it appeared to be in a reasonable state of repair. Like Blackfriars, it was double fronted but it had more modern windows. Cornelius thought that they were probably of 20th century design and had iron frames. The gardens were not perfectly kept, but they looked tidy and functional. Cornelius noticed two people who were tending the gardens. They both wore a white, hooded robe and a black cape that hung around their shoulders. Cornelius looked to Stephen and he stopped the car.

'Ok let's go.' Stephen said. 'In for a penny, in for a pound.'

They walked over to the men in the garden and asked if they could help them.

'Hello my name is Stephen Montrose, and this is my colleague Cornelius.'

'That's a wonderful name, Cornelius.' The taller of the two men replied. He put out his hand to greet them and introduced himself. 'My name is David and this is my colleague and brother, Ronald. How can we be of assistance?'

'We were hoping to meet with your head Friar, would we be able to speak with him?' Stephen asked.

'I will locate him for you, will I be able to tell him why you're seeking him?' Said David.

'I am a Professor from Cambridge University and Cornelius is my Research Associate. We are concluding some research about the Tudor dynasty and we hoped that your Priory could help us.' Stephen knew this was not strictly true, but he satisfied himself by remembering that he had still had full access to the University's library and other resources.

'Let me see if I can find him – his name is Friar James. Will you be good enough to wait here?' Asked David.

'Yes of course.' Replied Stephen. We'll enjoy the tranquillity of your garden while we wait.'

Stephen and Cornelius waited only a minute before David returned with Friar James. They introduced themselves to him and asked if he could provide them with some of his time.

'Would you like to come inside?' James said with a warm smile.

'Thank you. After you.' Cornelius thought James had a friendly face. He was a little shorter than himself, and a little larger around the waist line. Cornelius estimated that James would be about 50 years old, he had dark hair that was greying and he wore rimless spectacles. He was wearing a similar white robe and black cape like the others, denoting their allegiance to the English Province of the Order of Preachers.

'Would you like anything to drink?' James asked.

'I'm not too thirsty.' Replied Cornelius.

'We would both like some tea, Thank you James.' Stephen interrupted Cornelius. James invited them to sit at the large table in the centre of the room and left to prepare the tea. Once James had left the room, Stephen informed him that it would be considered bad manners to refuse an offer of hospitality. Cornelius apologised and realised that Stephen was probably right.

James returned to the room and poured the tea for them. He joined them and sat at the table.

'David tells me that you are a Cambridge Professor Stephen and you're conducting some research?' James look at Stephen directly.

'Yes. Actually, I'm retired now but still have access to the University's resources and they have been kind in letting me further my research.' Stephen wanted to be truthful with James and he knew that James would appreciate his honesty.

'And how can I be of assistance?' James continued to look directly at Stephen and he spoke formally.

'We have been conducting some work on the Tudor Dynasty and our findings have revealed some interesting documents. They are parchments that were written many centuries ago. We believe they might have been written by members of your Order and we thought that you may be interested in the information. Perhaps it may even provide some answers for you and fill in gaps in your historical scriptures.'

Stephen chose his words carefully. He knew that by freely offering information, James was more likely to be open in return. Stephen had explained to Cornelius on the journey to the priory that whilst their Scriptures were not necessarily secret, they were rather sacred to them.

'Do you have the parchments with you?' Asked James.

'No, I'm sorry I don't.' Replied Stephen. 'But we have a date from one of them and my research tells me that you may be able to link this to a date in your Book of Clandestine Concealment?' Stephen already knew that this was where the meaningless and unanswered secrets were documented.

'You seem to know your area of history very well Stephen. You should therefore, also know that this is where we keep our most sacred information.' James delivered a straight forward response.

'Yes I understand. This is why I came here. I am aware that most of the documented information is meaningless and we were hoping that we may be able to help one another. The information we have is probably in much greater detail than what is documented in your Scriptures. Indeed, we may even be able to work it all out for ourselves, but we thought this was the right thing to do.' Stephen gave an eloquent plea and he hoped that it would be met with a nod of agreement from James. He also knew that if James was to provide evidence of answers to their sacred Book of Clandestine Concealment, this would be viewed very favourably from the Order's higher authority.

'You seem to be an honest man.' Said James, then there was a long pause. 'Perhaps if you were to provide me with the date, I may be able to see if there is any corresponding information.

'That would be excellent. Thank you.' Said Stephen.

'Yes thank you very much.' Added Cornelius.

The Friar left the room and told them he would return with the Book. Stephen and Cornelius continued to sip their tea and it was at least ten minutes or so before they heard James whispering to one of the other members of the Order outside the room. Shortly afterwards, James walked back in and was holding the book. It was a reasonably modern book that had a hard back and James told them this was what they used for their teachings and that it also contained their Book of Clandestine Concealment.

'I have found some information but I am not sure it will be any use to you. I have found an entry that was made verbally in February 1542 and it was then documented in our Book of Clandestine Concealment a little over 100 years later.' James showed the entry to Stephen and Cornelius, it simply said:

William

There were also two symbols against his name. A Pine Tree and an Olive Branch.

'But what do you think this means?' Cornelius asked, looking at Stephen.

'It means we have to go to Cambridge!' Stephen said, looking up from the page. Stephen took his notebook from his pocket and added the symbols to it.

'Cambridge! But why?' Cornelius looked confused.

'He's right.' Said James. 'You can see that the entry in the Book also depicts a Portcullis at the end of the line.'

'This means that the entry is protected.' Stephen interrupted. 'The information we require to complete the full message is in another document. It will be in Cambridge, this is known throughout the Order of Preachers, English Province, as the House of Writers for its intellectual connections. It has strong links with the University and I will need to go there to complete it.

'Do you know where it is in Cambridge?' Cornelius asked, looking for an answer from Stephen.

'Yes I know exactly where it is.' Stephen said. 'The Cambridge House of Writers is also called Blackfriars.

Chapter Twelve

Stephen and Cornelius climbed back into the car and thanked James for his time and invaluable help. They waved to James and headed back to see Sally.

So, there's another Blackfriars? Cornelius said.

'Yes, interesting, isn't it?' Stephen replied, glancing over to Cornelius while steering. This is where all the key elements of scriptures bearing the Portcullis symbol are documented. It isn't far from where I live.'

'So did we have a wasted journey today?' Cornelius looked more confused.

'Indeed not. The information contained in the Master Book of Clandestine Concealment only contains the key to the information. It does not contain the full message. We will need to link it to the message we've just found to be able to understand it completely. The Pine tree and the Olive branch are also vital.'

'Won't it be difficult to get this information?' Cornelius enquired. 'Didn't you say that this was in the Master Book of Clandestine Concealment? Surely that will not be so easily accessible.'

'The information contained in it is equally meaningless without the other pieces of the jigsaw.'

Stephen smiled at Cornelius. 'And the man in Charge at the House of Writers is a personal friend of mine.'

Stephen and Cornelius arrived back at Blackfriars in time for lunch. Sally had prepared a light meal and both Stephen and Cornelius were hungry, and not just for food. They were hungry for information too.

'So how did it go? Asked Sally.

'It went very well, but we still don't have all the pieces of the puzzle.' Cornelius replied.

'Not yet we haven't, but we will have. I can promise you that.' Stephen took his notebook from his pocket and held it aloft. I am hoping that by tomorrow evening, everything we need to know will all be inside here.'

'You're not going to Cambridge, now are you?' Cornelius asked.

'First thing in the morning.' Stephen replied.

'Cambridge?' Sally interrupted. 'Will someone tell me what is going on?'

Cornelius relayed what he and Stephen had seen in the Book of Clandestine Concealment and what they'd discussed on the way home to Blackfriars.

'How long do you anticipate being down at Cambridge for? Cornelius had an ulterior motive for asking Stephen.

'I don't know, maybe a couple of days. If you've no objections, I will collect some more suitable clothing and return with it later in the week.' Stephen said.

'The reason why I asked was because I think we could all use a break.' Cornelius voiced his motive. 'Sally and I are a little tired and I could certainly do with a few days away. What do you think about a few days in the city darling? It will be good to catch up with the old gang.'

'I've got a better idea.' Sally said grabbing hold of Cornelius' hand. Let's go to France for a few days. I've been chatting to mum and dad this morning while you were out and they were saying that their place has been empty since they visited last month and we should go and have a few days there.'

'Sounds good to me.' Said Cornelius. 'It'll be great to see the old place again and then there's that great wine shop. You know the one, owned by Fabrice and Madeleine.'

'Yes it will be lovely to see them again. Please can we go darling?' Sally begged Cornelius but she knew that he secretly loved her parents' second home in Lille.

'Stephen, why don't you take a couple of extra days at home and we could meet up back here at the weekend?' Cornelius said to Stephen.

'Yes that sounds fine. I will take the opportunity to see my friend Friar Timothy at Cambridge and I will do some more research while I'm there.'

'Let me give you our address and telephone number at Lille in case you want to get in touch. It's 2321 Rue de Vouziers, St Mourine, Lille, France. The telephone number for us in Lille is 0033 235 897 1359.'

Stephen carefully added their names and the address and telephone number into the rear cover of his leather-bound notebook and placed it back in his pocket.

'Does everything go in that notebook?' Joked Cornelius.

'All the important stuff, yes.' Stephen smiled. 'I've given your address and telephone number a prime location inside the back cover.'

'I'm honoured – I think.' Laughed Cornelius.

The remainder of the afternoon, Sally arranged tickets from St Pancras in London on Eurostar. Meanwhile Cornelius arranged for flights into London and they both packed a small suitcase. Sally and Cornelius often travelled with a small amount of luggage into Lille as they had some clothing that they kept in their room there for their visits.

Stephen spent the remainder of the afternoon scrutinising his entries in his notebook. He wanted to ensure that all his notes were ordered properly and that they were meaningfully relevant to his research. Stephen, Cornelius or Sally didn't see any value in returning to the tunnel that afternoon, none of them were particularly struck on hiking another few miles. They thought it best to wait until they returned at the weekend when they were more refreshed and when Stephen had more information following his trip to Cambridge.

The following morning, they all had breakfast and prepared to set off. Stephen had offered to drive them to the airport before travelling on to Cambridge and they had accepted seeing it as an opportunity to discuss their plans for the weekend. Sally and Cornelius ensured that Blackfriars was secure and they sealed the end of the tunnel moving one of Cornelius' wine racks to cover the hole in the cellar wall. They also locked the trap door sealing the cellar for the duration of their temporary absence. On the way to the airport they chatted about Stephen's trip to Cambridge and what he had planned for the remainder of the week.

'Are you sure that your friend will be able to help us?' Sally asked.

'Yes he's a very good friend, he and I go back a few years.' Stephen reassured them both. 'I had hoped to visit him today but I'll give him a call this evening and hopefully arrange to pay him a visit in the morning.

Stephen pulled into the Airport and drove straight to the terminal drop off point.

'Please look after that notebook and make sure you come back at the weekend.' Cornelius said.

'I wouldn't miss our next trip into the tunnel for all the World.' Stephen said. 'You've made an old man very happy and I'm so excited about getting back. We've still got work to do but I feel so close to completing the research and I believe we've really got a chance to show history in a completely new light.'

Sally and Cornelius unloaded their bags from Stephen's car and they said they would see him at the weekend. They agreed to meet him on Saturday and thanked him again for his assistance and for his friendship. They shook hands with him and walked into the terminal. As they approached the revolving door they looked around to wave at Stephen but he had already driven off; they could see his car driving away from the airport complex and they continued inside.

Stephen arrived home early in the afternoon. Still excited at his new project, he allowed himself to smile and to be happy with his efforts. His research was starting to knit together and he started to think about the missing crown of King Henry VIII once again. Only a short time ago he hadn't even dared to think about the crown. Let alone the months of research and man-hours he thought he'd wasted.

Now he felt renewed and that his work had not be in vain. Instead it had been completely worthwhile and was about to reveal true value and make him revered in his field. He wasted no time and reached for the telephone to call Friar Timothy at Blackfriars Cambridge. It rang only twice and Stephen heard his friend make his familiar greeting.

'Timothy it's Stephen Montrose. How are you old friend?' Stephen knew that his friend would want to know how he'd been and why he hadn't been in touch for a few weeks.

'I was wondering when you were going to call me. I've been talking to a colleague of mine in Northumberland and he said you'd be in touch.' Timothy had humour in his voice and Stephen sensed this.

'Ah, I wondered if James might brief you about our visit to him. He was most helpful and I hoped that you will be of equal help.' Stephen said.

'And why should I do that?' Timothy teased him.

Stephen knew that Timothy was playing games with him and that he would get what he wanted.

'Because, you're my dearest friend, and we always help one another.' Stephen added his own humour to the conversation.

'True, true. Perhaps I could be persuaded to assist.' Timothy left a pause, then laughed loudly. 'Of course I'll help you old fool. 'When are you coming over?'

'I was hoping to come over in the morning. Would that be ok?' Stephen asked.

'Of course it is old friend. Can you make it for nine?

'Yes no problem. Stephen replied.

'Great, maybe we can have some breakfast.' Timothy offered his old friend breakfast and he always knew he loved his eggs on toast.

'You know I can't resist one of your legendary breakfasts. I'll see you at nine Timothy.'

The two men finished their call and Stephen unpacked his small bag. He took out his notebook that had been his companion for months now. He reviewed his notes from the last few days and smiled once more. His thoughts shifted to Sally and Cornelius. He was pleased that his new friends had contacted him and he hoped that they would be able to rest for the next few days.

Meanwhile, Sally and Cornelius arrived at Kings Cross Railway station in London. They made the short walk across the road to St Pancras to join the Eurostar Express that would transport them under the English Channel and deliver them to Lille. They soon found their platform and after a short wait they boarded their train for France.

Stephen Montrose woke early and drove the short journey to Blackfriars Priory in Cambridge. Blackfriars Priory at Cambridge is a large an imposing building. Once the family home of a prominent family, it was bequeathed to the Order of Preachers in the will of the Lady of the house. She left the property in the nineteen thirties after her son became a member of the Order. Stephen rang the doorbell and a young man answered. He introduced himself as Matthew and he said that Stephen needed no introduction, Friar Timothy had been expecting him.

Stephen entered the old room at the back of the large house that Timothy used as his office. The two old friends shook hands and Stephen noticed the large book on Timothy's desk. He recognised it as the Master Book of Clandestine Concealment and he returned his glance to his friend.

Timothy said that the book should wait, and that they should eat breakfast. Timothy asked Stephen to follow him into their dining room. The two men ate their breakfast and chatted for some time but Timothy could sense that Stephen was keen to view the scriptures in the Book on his desk.

'Let's go back to the office, shall we?' Timothy said.

'That would be great, and thank you for breakfast. It was as tasty as always.' Stephen thanked Timothy but now had his thoughts firmly fixed on what the book would tell him.

Both men sat in the office and Robert had already located the entry that was identified by the date, February 1542 and William's name.

The Cambridge University Professor looked at the brief information in the Book. He took out his notebook and entered the information that he'd been seeking directly beneath that which he'd seen in the Book at the Northumberland Priory. Stephen looked at Timothy and smiled broadly.

'Thank you Timothy, this is exactly what I was looking for. I need to run now but thank you again.'

'Glad I could help.' Timothy replied. 'Will I see you again old friend?'

'You will indeed.' Stephen shook hands with Timothy again and made his way out.

Stephen returned to his car and climbed in. He took out his notebook again, held it against his chest and he spoke out loud.

'We've got it.'

He reversed his car out of its slot and drove off towards his house. He checked his rear view mirror before pulling off and did not notice the car that pulled off behind and which started to follow him. It wasn't until he'd checked his rear view mirror again to make a right hand turn that he noticed the vehicle behind that was indicating to make the same turn.

Still, he thought little of the vehicle that was now close behind him. Stephen had far more important things on his mind now. His notebook was complete and contained everything he needed to finish his research. More importantly, he was now able to return to see Sally and Cornelius at Blackfriars in Northumberland and this would provide the physical evidence to support his theories. He thought it would probably also make Sally and Cornelius very rich and put them on the academic map in terms of historical finds.

Stephen continued to the end of the road until he came to the final junction where he needed to turn left. The car behind seemed impatient to Stephen and he became unnerved that it was very close behind him. He pulled out and continued to drive at the speed limit. The tree lined road was quiet; it was a little outside of Cambridge and reasonably rural. Stephen slowed to allow the car behind to pass him, which he reckoned what the driver of it clearly wanted to do. Stephen moved his car over to the left and the car sped past him. It pulled back in front of him and slowed. There were three men in the car and the man sitting in the back turned to look at Stephen. Stephen became more unnerved but the car sped ahead. With only a matter of two miles or so to his house, Stephen relaxed and continued to drive at the speed limit.

He turned off the main road and followed the side street as it wound through his estate. He remained a little anxious about the actions of the aggressive driver that he'd encountered a few moments earlier. He just wanted to get home again and to consolidate the findings he'd made that would conclude his research. He approached the driveway to his house and positioned his car in the centre of the road to make the right turn. He looked along the road and saw the same car that had followed him, it was parked at the side of the road about three houses away. The three men were still sat in the car and Stephen could see that all three were looking at him.

His nervousness returned immediately and he was certain that these men were the same that had threatened him a number of weeks ago. He quickly secured his car, got inside his house and locked the door. He thought for a moment about driving straight to the Police. Then he thought that he should call them and warn them that he was being followed. He peered out through the corner of his front room window and could see the car remained where it was. His subconscious tormented him and wreaked havoc on his nerves. Anxiety came in wave after wave and swept through his mind, paralysing him from any constructive thoughts. The men were still sat in the car; he considered calling the Police again and he looked over at his telephone.

Suddenly the car pulled off, it drove slowly passed his house and he could see the three men look over to his house, then it raced away at speed. Stephen was now deeply concerned and he was utterly convinced that they were the same men who had threatened him previously. He wondered how long he'd been followed. Were they waiting for him when he returned from Northumberland? Did they spot him in Cambridge by chance and follow him from there? Or worse still, had they been following him for the past few weeks? Perhaps they were trying to build a picture of his recent movements to find out more. If this was case, he grew increasingly anxious and was now concerned for the safety of Sally and Cornelius. While they were currently safe in France they would have to return at some point and they could return at any time in the next few days. Then there was the tunnel. These were all questions that raced around his mind and he thought again about contacting the Police. He paused to think about his next move.

He considered contacting Sally and Cornelius in France. He paused for thought again and wondered if that might worry them unduly. Perhaps they would be angry with him? What was more important than anything was his own safety and that he should contact the Police. He decided that this was the most sensible course of action. He had no evidence of any wrong doing and he was concerned that this might cause the Police to take no action. He decided that he should contact the Police but in fear of his immediate safety, he would drive to the Police station in town and report his concerns in person.

Stephen climbed back into his car and drove off towards Cambridge. He was more aware than usual and he checked every vehicle that passed him. Suddenly he saw the same car that had followed him parked at the side of the road. He couldn't help but stare at the men inside as he drove passed. He made eye contact with the driver and the car pulled out to follow him. He increased his speed and the car held back. He turned, heading towards the centre of Cambridge and checked in his mirror to see if they'd followed. He checked for a few seconds and thought that they must have driven passed the junction. His concerns returned when he saw the car turn and follow him. He checked his pocket for his notebook and was relieved to find it. He was growing more anxious by the moment and his thoughts stayed on his notebook. It contained everything. It had the address of Blackfriars in Northumberland – William's writings from over 450 years ago. His findings and worse still, it contained the key to exactly what they were looking for. Now it held the details of his friends in France and where they were.

He checked the mirror again and saw that the car remained in view. He had to protect the notebook at all costs. Before he went to the Police he decided to go to the Post Office and he would post it to someone he could trust. He didn't want to send it Sally and Cornelius as they might return to Blackfriars before it arrived in France. Moreover, it could also go missing and be lost forever. He couldn't send it to Sally and Cornelius at Blackfriars as the men that followed him might already know about Blackfriars.

He decided that he would send it on to his only living relative. He would send it to his nephew John. John

Huggett was the son of his only sibling, his sister Rita who had passed away a number of years earlier. He was never struck on John Huggett and often saw him as being a little ignorant. Still, this seemed to be the most sensible course of action; he would send it on with a note telling him to look after it, until he was able to drive over and collect it. He continued towards the post office which he knew was located on the way into town. The car remained in his rear-view mirror and he continued to monitor it. The post office was only a few moments away and he would be able to send the precious notebook to safety. He arrived and realised that there was no obvious place to park. Seeing this as an opportunity, he parked illegally on the road side. He watched as the car drove passed and continue along the road. However, he noticed that it had stopped but the men stayed inside.

He hurried inside the Post Office clutching the notebook in his right hand. He took out a pen and tore a blank page from the notebook. He wrote to his nephew, telling him that he was sending the book to him for safe keeping. He explained that he would collect it in a few days and hoped that he, his wife Helen and their daughter Tabitha were in good health.

Stephen was satisfied that the key to the information he needed for the tunnel at Blackfriars, and which he'd completed following his trip to the Cambridge Priory, was now firmly locked in his mind. With the notebook in the care of the Royal Mail he was content that if the men came to him, they would not be able to take anything from him. He grabbed a padded envelope from the post office shelf and wrote John's name and address on it. He handed it to the Cashier and asked for it to be sent recorded delivery, first class. Stephen paid the fee, collected the receipt bearing John Huggett's address and walked back to his car. He drove purposefully now and with only one thing in mind, getting safely to the Police Station where he could outline his story and his fears.

Stephen could see the car was still parked ahead of him. He ignored the car and focussed his attention of the road ahead and he tried to estimate how long it would take him to arrive. The men in the car had re-joined the road and were on his tail again; but this time he had the Registration number of the vehicle emblazoned on his mind and he would not allow himself to forget it. He guessed that he would be at the Police Station in a little over 3 minutes, this would be depending on traffic as he approached the centre of town.

The car continued to remain in his rear view mirror and he checked for it at irregular intervals. By the time he'd reached the Police Station the car dropped away from its pursuit and when Stephen arrived at the Station it had turned off down a side street. Stephen felt triumphant that he'd won this round of his battle with the 3 men. Nonetheless he remained extremely unnerved by the whole episode. He strode into the Police Station and presented himself to the desk officer. He briefly explained to the young Police Officer what had happened and he asked to see someone in authority. He waited for only a few moments and then a side door opened. A man presented himself in civilian clothes and introduced himself as Detective Constable Mark Patterson.

'Would you like to come through Professor?' Said the young detective.

'Yes, thank you.'

'I understand that you think you've been followed today, is that right?'

'It's not just today detective. I was first approached by these three men a number of weeks ago. They threatened me about some research I was conducting but when I ceased it, they disappeared and I didn't see them for weeks. I thought they'd given up pestering me but I'm afraid to say that they're back and they've been following me since this morning.' Stephen gave a full account of what had happened to him in the past few hours.

'Have they approached you today at all?' Asked the detective.

'No, not yet. But I know that they'll be paying me a visit tonight.' Stephen continued with his description of recent events. He provided the detective with the registration and details of the car, including the occupants and the detective agreed to follow it up.

Stephen also claimed that he was worried for the future safety of his friends Sally and Cornelius Galbraith. He gave the detective their name and address at address at Blackfriars. The detective asked him a number of questions about why he thought that he would be followed and why they would be showing so much interest in him. Stephen was reluctant to give the detective too much information but he wanted to ensure that he had sufficient information so as to provide him with as much help as he needed to give him protection.

Stephen's initial fears were confirmed when the detective told him that he would be unable to arrest the men unless they'd committee a crime. However, he would check up on the vehicle details and he would pay the men a visit. He would advise them that there was a complainant and he suspected that this would be sufficient for them to stop their pursuit of him. Stephen thanked the detective and returned to his car. He couldn't see the car that had been following him anywhere in sight and he drove off for home. Stephen continued to check for the car on his way home but he couldn't see it in either direction.

Later that evening Stephen remained very cautious. He'd spent the day peering through just about every one of his windows. He was not able to see anyone but now that it was dark, he became quite frightened. He consoled himself that he'd passed the details to the Police and that they would be conducting their enquiries. Stephen's thoughts were interrupted when the telephone rang.

'Hello is this Professor Montrose?' Said the voice of the man on the telephone.

'Yes, speaking.' Replied Stephen.

'Good evening sir, this is detective Jarvis from CID at Cambridgeshire Police.'

'Hello again, thanks for calling me back. Do you have information for me?' Asked Stephen.

'Well sir, we have conducted some initial inquiries and the registration details you gave us for the vehicle that followed you today does not exist.' Said the detective.

'What do you mean, does not exist?' Said Stephen who was now extremely concerned. He started to perspire and he could feel beads of cold perspiration forming on his brow.

'All I can say sir is that the vehicle registration does not exist. It never has, not even as write off.' Continued the detective. 'However, this causes us a little more concern and we'll be sending someone round first thing in the morning.'

'But what about tonight?' Asked Stephen.

'Don't worry sir, I don't think you have anything to worry about tonight. Besides, we will be sending periodic patrols around your estate throughout the evening.' Assured the detective in an authoritative and sincere voice.

This placated Stephen to some degree but he remained concerned and did not feel like sleeping that night. He lay awake for most of the evening, drifting in and out of sleep but he was relieved when he saw the sun rise and start to illuminate his bedroom. He thought about what he would do throughout the coming day. He was not due to return to Blackfriars for another two days and he considered contacting Sally and Cornelius. He thought about passing on his good news at the findings he'd made whilst in Cambridge but decided it may be best to wait until he saw them again.

Sally and Cornelius felt refreshed from their visit to Lille. They decided to return to Blackfriars a day earlier than planned and were excited about the prospect of seeing the tunnel. They were equally excited about meeting Stephen again and discovering what he'd learned from his visit to Blackfriars Priory in Cambridge. They were sure that he'd found what he needed and they were grateful that he'd left them to enjoy their break and not interrupt their peace.

They hoped that he had been able to do the same but they would call him when they arrived home. Their journey would take them the majority of the day and they didn't expect to make it home until early evening.

It was a few moments after 6pm in the evening when they finally arrived back at Blackfriars. The house was cold and dark. It reminded them of the time when they first set foot in Blackfriars all those months ago to view it with

Elizabeth from the estate agency. Sally went immediately into the kitchen to put on the central heating and Cornelius headed upstairs to empty their small travel case. It didn't take long for the heating to take effect and for Blackfriars to feel like home again.

They had only been in Blackfriars for about an hour and they decided that they would eat a light meal that evening. Cornelius had already viewed the entrance of the tunnel to ensure it was intact. They had almost finished eating when they heard the doorbell ring.

'Surely it can't be Stephen already. I thought we said we wouldn't be back home until the weekend?' Cornelius said.

'Haven't you called him yet?' Asked Sally.

'No I was going to ring him after eating.' Cornelius replied, heading towards the door.

Cornelius opened the large front door and he was surprised to see a Police Officer standing in front of him.

'Good evening sir, my name's PC Davison from Northumbria Police. I wonder if I could have a moment of your time.' The PC spoke very confidently and with an air of authority, whilst simultaneously holding his Police Warrant Card for Cornelius' benefit.

'Yes of course, would you like to come in Officer? My wife and I were just eating but we can chat in the living room if you like.' Cornelius offered.

'Only if you're sure it will not inconvenience you.' The PC looked for reassurance from Cornelius.

'No it's fine we're almost finished anyway. Darling it's the Police.' Cornelius shouted through to Sally who appeared at the doorway.

'Hello. What is going on? Asked Sally.

Sally and Cornelius showed the Officer through to their living room and asked him to sit down.

'How can we help you Officer?' Cornelius was keen to know why the Police Officer was there and wanted to know right away.

'Do you know a Professor Stephen Montrose?' Asked PC Davison.

'Yes he's a friend of ours and he's been helping us with some research. We're expecting him here this weekend in fact.' Cornelius replied and gave a puzzled and worried look to the Officer.

'I'm afraid I have some bad news; Professor Montrose has been found dead at his house in Cambridge.' The Officer delivered the news and immediately looked for a reaction from Cornelius and Sally.

Sally sank back into her chair. Cornelius reached over to her and grasped her hand.

'I'm, I'm dumbfounded.' Cornelius struggled to get his words out.

'What happened to him? Sally's voice sounded weak as she asked the question.

'More importantly, why have you come to tell us? Cornelius interrupted, demanding an answer.

'Yes sir, I was just coming to that. We're treating his death as suspicious but I'm sorry to report that it appears Professor Montrose has been murdered.' The Officer was about to continue but was stopped again by Cornelius.

'You already have our attention officer. Now tell me the reason why you are here.' Cornelius gripped Sally's hand tighter.

'The previous day he apparently presented himself to his local Police station in Cambridge and they contacted us yesterday. We have tried a number of times to reach you at home. To be honest with you, we were starting to get a little concerned.'

'Why were you concerned?' Cornelius's tone turned to one much more serious.

'We were concerned because Professor Montrose told the Police that you might be in danger.' Said the Police Officer.

'I knew it.' Cornelius spoke angrily. 'I just knew it was too good to be true.'

Cornelius explained to the Officer that Stephen had told them about some men that had previously threatened him. He went on to outline about the research that he'd been conducting and how they'd come to know him. Cornelius concluded by asking if they had made any arrests yet.

'I must be honest with you sir, no arrests have been made yet.'

'There is no way we are staying here until these people are caught.' Cornelius told the officer. 'Will you be able to provide us with some protection tonight until we can find somewhere to stay?'

'Yes sir, that is why I'm here, we'll provide two police officers who will be here as a show of force. We'll also provide regular patrols tonight. Do you have somewhere else you can go tomorrow?' Asked the PC.

'Yes.' Said Sally. We'll go right back where we came from this morning.

'And that's where we are staying until you find these people.' Added Cornelius.

That evening, with the Police standing guard outside Blackfriars, Cornelius contacted his office to advise he'd be away for longer. They also arranged for tickets on Eurostar and flights into London for first thing in the morning.

The following morning, Sally and Cornelius flew back into London and transferred directly to St Pancras Station. Sally and Cornelius boarded the Eurostar Express bound for Lille and located their seats. With Blackfriars locked up and their tunnel completely hidden from view with racking and other items, they looked at one another; going over their last few months adventures, they tried to work out how they could have found themselves in this position. Then they remembered Stephen and they couldn't believe they wouldn't be seeing their friend again.

The express train started to move and they watched as the sights of London slowly started to pass by. Cornelius and Sally wondered when and if they might ever be able to return.

Act Three – An Unlikely Partnership
Chapter Thirteen

On his first morning in Her Majesty's Prison Fulton on the outer reaches of Peterborough, Robert Easton awoke with strange feeling. He thought to himself that he should be feeling angry and upset but he was experiencing an inner strength that he had not felt before. Not only did he feel strong and able to deal with his terrible ordeal but he also had a deep-rooted determination to overcome it.

His prison cell was plainly furnished with one set of bunk beds, a toilet and a small table with a chair. The walls were clean and freshly painted white, and a large steel door separated the room's occupants from the corridor and other cells. A small window was directly opposite the door that had toughened safety glass and ventilation panels either side, built into the wall.

Robert put on his freshly starched prison uniform and followed the others down to the communal ablutions. He tried to remain aware of what was going on around him, knowing it was immensely important to make a good impression and to send out the right message to the other inmates. A weak person would quickly become a victim, and he was determined that was not going to happen to him. He quickly washed and shaved and returned to his cell to await the call for his floor to make their way to breakfast. While he waited, a Prison Officer appeared at the door to inform him that the Governor would be seeing him later that afternoon.

'Make sure you are here at 3pm, the Governor is a real stickler for being prompt and you don't want to make a bad start, OK Easton.' Said the Officer.

'Yes I will be ready, do you know what sort of things he will be asking me.' Replied Robert.

'It's just an informal interview to find out more about you that's all. It's prison policy that everyone receives one of these, so don't get any ideas that you're receiving special treatment.'

'I didn't, I was merely curious.' Said Robert dispassionately. Robert wanted to correct the Officer but thought better of it.

'Afterwards you will be allocated to a place of work and don't expect any favours there either.'

Robert was about to reply with a sarcastic comment but his cell mate returned in timely fashion. The Officer smiled acerbically and walked off along the landing.

Robert was placed in a cell with an old lag that went by the name of Reefer. Tony Reefton, like Robert, was a 'lifer' and was 8 years into his sentence. A tall man, Robert guessed that he would be a little over 6 feet 2 inches but was lean without an ounce of body fat. He had a craggy and weathered complexion that Robert thought must have come from his rough background.

It was an unwritten prison rule that the inmates never spoke of their crimes but Robert quickly learned that Reefer was inside for armed robbery. The two 'cellies' were roughly the same age and it didn't take them long to form a good relationship. The buzzer sounded in their cell to notify them that they may proceed to the Canteen.

Reefer sighed audibly. 'Thank god for that, I'm starving man.' He said.

Robert however, wasn't particularly hungry nor was he keen to mix with the other inmates just at the moment. Although, he knew that breakfast was an important meal and he should take every opportunity to retain his strength.

'OK Reefer, lead the way. Show me what I've been missing all these years.' Said Robert.

Reefer gave Robert a cynical glance and replied 'Don't worry Rob mate, you'll be sick to the back teeth of breakfast by next week. And you haven't tasted the tea time slop yet.' Reefer's dryness appealed to Robert's sense of humour. He chuckled to himself, then his paranoia reminded him where he was and he wasn't permitted pleasing thoughts.

They arrived at the servery and queued for their morning meal. Robert viewed the sitting area and watched the other inmates as they ate. The tables and the servery were partitioned by a safety glass screen. There were about 20 tables in the large room each with six chairs. Approximately 40 men were sat eating, some had just sat down and others were finishing. One man looked up at him from his fried breakfast and Robert quickly looked away. He was aware that he was starting to stare and expected to receive unwelcome attention had he been caught doing so. He returned his attention to Reefer who stood immediately ahead of him in the short queue.

'Dave, it's Matey's first day today, do him a favour and don't give him any of your scrambled eggs,' laughed Reefer. Robert's gaze once again returned to the sitting area, this time to search for a place to sit.

'Do yourself a favour mate,' said the inmate behind the servery. 'Don't go staring at people in here. In fact, don't do it anywhere in here, you're liable to upset someone.'

Robert explained that he was trying to find a space to sit down before getting served. He sensed that he was making a wrong impression already and it may be best to accept the advice offered to him and say nothing more. Experience had taught him that this particular episode would probably be forgotten very quickly.

Robert followed Reefer to a table where two other prisoners were seated.

'Rob I want you to meet two of the biggest creeps in this place,' said Reefer. 'This is Jono and Ticker. Jono works in the store room looking after the floor cleaning machine. And you'll find Ticker in the laundry facility most days, usually skiving as well the lazy bastard.'

'Hey less of the lazy,' answered Ticker. 'Don't listen to him Rob mate, it's nice to meet you.' Continued Ticker as he reached over the table and offered his hand to Robert. Robert shook hands with both men and listened as all three made general whinges about the food, the Prison Officers and most other things. He laughed at their comments, all the time studying his two new acquaintances.

He guessed that both men were of similar age, estimating that they would be in their late twenties. Jono had a rough exterior with black hair and dark skin. He had obviously shaved that morning by the fresh cuts on his face but he still had a blue tinge around his chin suggesting that he needed to either try again or use a new blade. Quite stocky in build, he presented a very strong and masculine appearance. Ticker had light brown hair and a fairer complexion. He was much slimmer than Jono and displayed a quicker intellect than both other men.

'How did you come by your nick name Ticker?' Said Robert.

'It's because he's the most precise bloke you'll ever come across.' Interrupted Reefer. Robert had wrongly assumed that his name had been connected to a heart defect. However, Ticker's appropriate pseudonym came from his every action which was carried out with the accuracy of an atomic time piece.

'Annoys the shit out of us,' announced Jono. 'But you'll get used to it.'

'What's wrong with that? You'll thank me for it one day, you'll see, mark my words.' Responded Ticker with his strong Birmingham drawn accent.

'Yeah of course you will Ticker, we'll thank you for getting us all in the shit for making us look late all the time.' Jono mocked him but gave the impression that all three were good friends.

Robert and Reefer finished their breakfast and all four men made their way back to their cells.

'We'll catch up with you later Rob.' Said Ticker as they turned their separate ways down the corridor. Robert felt very pleased that he had made friends with Jono and Ticker and he was equally satisfied with his cell mate. Collectively all three had something positive to offer Robert and he was very keen to exploit their friendship. Jono's tough appearance would keep the other lags off his back, Ticker's work place and intellect may, after all, come in useful to him. Then there was the street wise Reefer whose knowledge of the prison and ways of bucking the system may prove the most useful of all.

Robert lay on his bunk and kept thinking about the murderer who was still out there. He imagined him sitting at home or in the pub, even enjoying a holiday, all this made his hatred grow towards him. He thought to himself that he mustn't think this way, it was wasteful and damaging. He must channel this negative energy and discipline himself into adopting a more positive and constructive outlook. However, no matter what thoughts had run around his head since his imprisonment, one thought remained constant. Somehow, he knew that he would not be serving his full sentence. This worried him immensely and why would he be thinking in this way. More to the point, how devastated would he be if his worst fears were in fact realised and he remained incarcerated there for years.

'You're not asleep there are you kid,' came the voice from the top bunk.

'No,' said Robert. 'I was just thinking that's all.'

'Well don't get too deep in thought will you, we're back out again in a minute. Unfortunately, it's not enough that we have to rot in here, because they make us work while we're rotting.'

'Where do we have to go, I haven't been given anywhere to work yet?' Robert thought that he must have sounded nervous - and he was. He wasn't especially nervous about any one thing in particular but generally, he felt uneasy about the unknown. The buzzer sounded and Reefer climbed down from his bunk.

'Come on mate.' Reefer walked out of the cell closely followed by Robert. 'We just have to wait in the communal area, then we'll be allocated our duties.' Reefer spoke as if he poked fun at the system. Several men were already gathered there and more were arriving.

'This is the communal area, what the screws call the recreation facility.' Reefer briefed.

The Recreation area was a large room and had a high ceiling. It was very basically furnished with a few tables and chairs and had several adjoining doors down both sides. The room extended into a corridor where three telephones were positioned on the wall. Robert scanned the large room and observed the gathering men who formed into smaller component groups. Three men chatted by the wall exchanging views on sport, then Robert turned to analyse a different group.

His eyes met with those of the same man who had glared at him during breakfast earlier. Again, he quickly looked away and re-focussed on Reefer who had now been joined by Ticker and Jono. This time he suspected that he may not have got away with it. He felt the presence of someone approaching from behind and his suspicion was confirmed when Jono glanced over his shoulder at the man closing in on him.

Robert did nothing until he could see the man's head almost resting on his left shoulder.

'Is there something wrong with your face?' The man spoke with an aggressive Scottish accent. Robert turned to face him.

'What you talking about?' Robert tried to sound as rough as his well-groomed exterior would allow.

'It's just that every time I look round, you're staring. Well your card is marked you little piece of shit.' The man continued looking for a response in Robert. His fixed gaze was broken by Jono who had now joined the altercation.

'Piss off Muir, he's new here and doesn't need a wanker like you making things worse.' Jono was uncompromising with his response and spoke equally as aggressive.

'Just want the little twat to know that I'll pull his head off if he doesn't stop staring.'

'Alright Muir, just leave it will ya.' Reefer arbitrated.

Muir scowled cruelly at Robert and returned to his group.

'Don't worry about him Rob, his bark is worse than his bite.' Jono tried unsuccessfully to reassure him.

Muir was not a large man maybe an inch or so shorter than Robert but he was strong and athletically built and had a reputation for being a hard hitter. His neck and both arms were tattooed and he had deep set, menacing eyes.

'Best thing you can do Rob is stay well away from him,' Said Ticker adding his support. 'He'll find someone else to bother before too long.'

'Don't be too sure Ticker, he's got a screw loose that one.' Replied Reefer, looking in the general direction of Muir and his friends.

'If you ask me I don't think he's got a single screw fully tightened.' Robert was careful to ensure that only those in his immediate vicinity heard this remark.

'Yes Rob but be careful what you say in this place,' advised Ticker. 'For example, don't let anyone hear you say Muir and Screw together in the same sentence. They might put two and two together and come up with...'

'Five.' Interrupted Robert.

'No, I was going to say a good kicking.'

A Prison Officer walked passed them holding a clip board. 'Right, listen in,' shouted the Officer. 'Abbot, Browne and Carlton, toilets and showers. Church and Davidson exercise yard. Dawson, wait here because the Governor said he'll see you now and not this afternoon.'

'Hang on I'll just check my diary.' Came a voice from the back.

'Shut it Dawson.' Replied the Officer, pouring scorn on Dawson's unwanted comments. 'Easton, same for you wait here.' The Officer continued alphabetically through the list of names.

Reefer winced as he was paired alongside Muir for the morning's duties. Meanwhile, Robert was escorted along a series of corridors and up three flights of stairs to the Governor's office.

For the remainder of the day Robert was led through a series of administrative procedures. Form filling, listening to rules and regulations and of course the rights of a prisoner. The day dragged on and Robert did not see Reefer until later that afternoon.

When Robert was returned to his cell Reefer was already back.

'So you're a fully paid up member of Fulton now are you.' Laughed Reefer.

'You wouldn't believe it man, I've got forms and rules coming out my ears. I can't remember half of it, there was so much.' Said Robert as he lay down on his bunk, mentally exhausted. 'And they've put me in the Library Stock Room. They said that my clerical skills would be kept sharp there. I suppose I should be grateful really'

Reefer laughed at his remark but more so at the system's undoubted victory over Robert and said. 'Oh, I can believe it.' Then he changed his voice to a more sombre tone. 'Rob you know I was placed with Muir today.'

'Yeah why.' Said Rob raising his head from his pillow.

'Muir has got a real problem with you man. He's gone on and on for most of the day about what he going to do to you.'

'Didn't you try and tell him to wind his neck in and just forget it.'

'Yeah of course, but he just won't let it go. All I can say is just mind how you go. All you have to do is stay within eyeshot of a screw.'

'Come on Reefer, that's easier said than done.' Robert offered a response but he had other things on his mind now.

The next day started in very much the same way as the previous one for Robert. He made his way down to the ablutions with Reefer. He was still very much aware that Muir was going to be on his case and he was waiting for him to show up. He quickly finished and headed back to his cell, pleased that he had not seen Muir. However, that was short lived as Robert and Reefer walked towards breakfast they were joined by Muir.

'Hello Easton, did you miss me when you were cleaning your teeth this morning.' Make the most of them cos I'm going to knock the bastards down your throat. I wasn't at the ablutions because I didn't shave this morning. I'm saving my razor blades for a special occasion.' Muir was determined to unnerve Robert.

'Don't you ever stop?' Said Reefer. 'Give it a rest will ya'

Robert stopped suddenly making Muir walk into him. He turned to face Muir and looked down at him.

'*What* is your problem?' Robert spoke firmly and in a manner that shocked Muir. 'Why don't you get back in your box and leave me alone.'

Muir was enraged at Robert's confident words. He leapt forward at him but he was immediately restrained and pulled away by Jono who had rounded the corner at precisely the right moment.

'Leave it Muir, you're not making yourself any friends, and besides, you've got nothing to prove to anyone here.' Jono tried a psychological approach that didn't have the planned effect.

'Your time will come Easton.' Muir taunted Robert one more time before walking off.

After breakfast Robert was taken to his new place of work. He was led through three doors and into a final corridor to the Library Stock Room. While he waited for the Officer to unlock the door for him he was able to glance at the prison main exit through a barred window. He found it frustrating and torturous to be given duties this close, but yet so far from freedom. His duties were relatively basic and Robert knew he'd find this work very simple indeed. Still, he was content that he could come here to be alone for a while and to have something to occupy his mind.

The next few days passed fairly quickly for Robert. He quickly fell into a routine which he remembered had been the advice from the Governor. Things never changed from one day to the next and unfortunately, the problems with Muir also continued. He would exchange the odd glare with him but so far he had been able to follow Reefer's advice and stay close to an officer when they were close to one another.

Muir's chance came three days later when Robert was stood in the doorway of Ticker's cell. He was facing the inside of the room and was chatting to Ticker when Muir ran from behind him and launched him into the Cell. Robert was knocked to the floor and Muir used the opportunity to kick Robert three times in his Ribs and back as he lay on the floor. Robert searched frantically for the strength and courage to get to his feet. He could see his TA Sergeant Major in his mind's eye and his inner strength took over.

Robert jumped to his feet still reeling from the latest blow to his back. He selected his spot and punched

Muir squarely in the centre of his face. The sound of Muir's nose breaking echoed outside the room and the force on the impact sent him sprawling into the corner of the cell.

Muir climbed to his feet and produced a kitchen knife from his pocket. He stared angrily at Robert.

'Put it away man.' Said Ticker.

'You stay out of this.' Said Muir, with blood now streaming from his nose. He wiped away the excess blood from around his mouth with his hand, 'You're going to get it. You're really going to get it man. I've got nothing to lose.'

Reefer and Jono appeared at the doorway. 'Nobody's getting anything today Muir.' Said Jono. 'Why don't you go and wipe that shit off your face?'

Muir walked quickly out of the room. Robert was still shaking, not from the shock of seeing Muir's knife but from his own courage.

Reefer escorted his cellmate to their own cell and Robert lay down. He held his left side as delayed pain started to develop from the blows he's received there. However, he was more concerned that his private war with Muir had now reached a new level.

He stared straight up and his mind began to focus on one thing only.

'Reefer,' he said. 'I'm getting out of here.'

'What?' Replied Reefer incredulously.

'I'm getting out of here, I'm going to escape and I'm going to need your help.'

Chapter Fourteen

Robert awoke early having hardly slept at all throughout the previous evening. He wasn't particularly excited nor did he feel especially content, but for the first time since he arrived in prison he had something worthwhile to concentrate on.

He struggled to understand why he was taking such drastic action particularly as he had been so level-headed throughout his entire life. This was surely the most ridiculous course of action he had ever considered and it held so many appalling consequences. How would he survive, where would he live and would he spend the remainder of his life looking over his shoulder? Surely, escape would be an admission of guilt and his appeal would be lodged before too long.

These were all questions that he knew deserved consideration but the events of the last few days had made him feel that freedom was more important.

Between brief periods of sleep he had spent the last few hours discounting various ideas before Reefer had awoken. He wanted to be able to present Reefer with plans that would sound at least slightly plausible, so as not to have his scheme dismissed immediately.

'Are you awake,' said Robert. There was a momentary pause before Reefer gave a reply.

'I am now.' Reefer tilted his head to one side a waited for Robert to reiterate his bold statement from the night before.

'Thought any more about what I said to you last night?' Enquired Robert, angling for at least some acknowledgement to his comments from the night before.

'Not really, but then you were only joking, weren't you?' Stated Reefer, who was not asking but telling him.

'I've never been more serious about anything in my entire life.' Robert climbed off his bed and reached for his shirt.

'Reefer I really mean this; I can't stay in here I'll go mad. Don't tell me that no one has ever escaped before and don't tell me it's impossible.' Robert wanted to sound convincing.

'Listen to yourself, this is not a film or something from a comic book, it's real. This is real life and the sooner you face up to it the better.'

'I know that you think I'm making a terrible mistake, but I'm doing this and I need you help. Don't worry I'm not about to implicate you but I'm doing this with your help or without it. But I would sooner have your help, you know this place better than anyone.' Robert made a passionate plea to Reefer, hoping that he could win his seal of approval before they went for breakfast.

Both men walked down to wash and shave. They exchanged no words at all, only to acknowledge others as they walked. Silently they walked back to their cell; Reefer followed Robert through the door and pushed it closed.

'Right, if you're going to do this, you're doing it on my terms. There's going to be no rushing and looking for any opportunity that comes up, we will plan it and you'll stick to it.

'Thanks mate, it means a lot to me that you're on board with this.'

'Don't get any ideas about me going over with you. Once you're out of here you're on your own.' Reefer made it perfectly clear to Robert that he would be playing absolutely no part in the escape at all. Of course, he was going to make sure it happened and he would help where possible, but he would be serving his full sentence where the Crown Court had initially intended.

'I have a couple of ideas that I would like you to sound out if that's ok.' Said Robert, thinking that now would be as good a time a time as any to discuss his initial plans with Reefer.

'Let's go to breakfast Rob mate, I want to test the water out on Ticker and Jono first ok?' Reefer buttoned up his shirt and leant against the wall waiting for their call to breakfast.

Robert was in fact *counting* on Jono and Ticker's support. Although, one thing still bothered Robert. He was fully aware that once he had gone over the wall, his silent accomplices would almost certainly come under the spotlight. He knew that none of them would break this unwritten code of prisoners conduct and remind Robert of their sacrifice. But following the escape of a prisoner, surely the first people they would be interviewing would be his cell mate and those that were closest to him.

The breakfast buzzer sounded and the two men walked off along the landing. Robert and Reefer had just begun eating when they were joined by Ticker and Jono.

'Mind if we join you?' Said Jono sarcastically.

'Yeh, you'd better sit down. Especially after you hear what Rob has to say.' Stated Reefer, as he prepared the others for Robert's revelation.

'Is it about Muir?' Said Ticker who sat up in his chair attentively.

'No much worse than that,' replied Reefer, lowering his voice and stooping over the table. Ticker and Jono both closed in to listen to what Reefer had to say.

'I think this may be better coming from me don't you think.' Interrupted Robert. 'I've done some thinking over the past couple of days and I don't intend being here much longer.'

'I think Muir has the same idea.' Joked Jono.

'I'm serious Jono, and Muir is just one of the reasons why I'm getting out of here.'

'Ok you've got my attention,' said Jono apologetically. 'You're going to need some help.'

'And you're going to need an expertly prepared plan,' added Ticker. Robert was pleased with the response he was receiving from Ticker and Jono, as well as the enthusiasm they were showing. 'Have you given any thought to how you're going to do this?' Continued Ticker.

'I've done nothing else but think for the past few hours. Don't worry I've already discounted tunnels and sheets knotted together. I do have a couple of ideas but they're pretty much half-baked at the moment. I want to do this properly, but if that means getting you all into trouble then I'll leave it.'

Ticker looked at Jono and Reefer. 'Don't know about you guys but I'm all for it. You've got my support Rob.'

'Right listen, let's sort out some rules here,' said Reefer. 'No one else knows about this and that's how we're going to keep it. We'll all go away now and do some thinking. We'll meet up later and see what we've got.' The others agreed with Reefer and got up from the table. Robert walked out of the canteen and was confronted by Muir.

'Ah I remember you, you're that dead man whose days are numbered here.' Said Muir as he knocked into Robert on his way past.

Reefer glanced over his shoulder at Robert and said, 'if only he knew just how right he is.'

The whole day was long and difficult for Robert. He knew that this was going to be difficult enough without Muir making things worse. He spent the day discarding ridiculous ideas but one idea kept returning to him. He was starting to form the basis of a plan that maybe, just maybe had potential. He knew one thing for certain; any plan would benefit immensely from an expertly executed diversion.

Later, when he was returned to his cell, he was greeted by Reefer who had arrived back before him. 'So Houdini, have you come up with anything yet?' Asked Reefer, trying to make light of the serious subject in hand.

'I'm not in the mood for jokes Reefer.' Responded Robert who displayed a less than content facade.

'I've had a good think today and I have an idea brewing. I'm not saying this is it but I feel fairly confident that I'm on the right lines. If I go through it with you will you give me your honest opinion?'

'I'll play devil's advocate for you, that might be more help.' Reefer sensed that Robert was eager for his help and therefore sounded more positive. Robert stood resting his forearms on the foot of the top bunk and commenced his initial briefing to Reefer. He imagined himself giving a set of commands to a section of soldiers and this helped with his confidence.

'Firstly we're going to need a diversion,' commenced Robert.

'*We*,' said Reefer. 'Sorry, carry on I know this is a… a team effort.'

'The sort of diversion I'm looking for needs a tactic that will tie up at least three screws.'

'Good thinking,' said Reefer, 'taking three screws out of the equation will leave them very light on the ground.'

'That's the idea,' assured Robert smiling for the first time since he arrived back at their cell. 'One of us is going to have to go to hospital for the day.'

'I like where you're going with this, can it be me?' I could just with a day out.' Said Reefer.

'The thing is, just feigning injury and going to hospital is not going to be quite enough. We're going to need a few rumours of a planned breakout first, and the rumours need to fall on the right ears.' Robert gave Reefer an intense look and Reefer instantly knew what he meant.

'You want the screws to think that *I'm* going over the wall, but you want them to find out by accident, right?'

'Spot on.' Said Robert.

'I like your style man. Normally, for a hospital visit you will get a couple of screws at least.'

'Yes but I'm anticipating at least three this way, and possibly at least one more left here to co-ordinate the visit in case anything goes awry.' Robert was beginning to sound convincing and Reefer was impressed in the way in which he was delivering his plan.

'Hang on, have you thought about the Police? One sniff of a breakout and they'll be there in numbers at the hospital.' Reefer put his devil's advocate role into operation.

'That's a risk we'll have to take, but my money's on the Screws wanting to deal with this internally.' Robert paused for a few seconds. 'At the very least it'll tie up two screws, your words. Look I've studied the Governor and he'll see canvassing for help from the Police as a sign of weakness.'

'Ok, leave it to me, I can think of a way to get into hospital for the day, and I know just the guy to start a rumour.' Assured Reefer.

'Who's that? Enquired Robert.

'Everson, he's up for parole in a couple of weeks. One loose word in his direction and he'll squeal in seconds.

Can you imagine the brownie points he'll win with the Parole Board?' Explained Reefer.

'Nice one, it's yours mate. Thanks, Reefer.'

'Don't mention it. Now what about the rest of the plan?'

'What do you mean?' Asked Robert.

'Oh, well there's the small matter of what you're going to do when you get on the other side of the wall, like money.' Said Reefer, sarcastically.

'I have enough money in the bank to keep me going for a long time.'

'Yes, and are you just going to nip into your local bank and ask them to unfreeze your account, are you? You can forget what you've got stashed in there man, you'll never get access to that.'

Robert felt stupid for not realising that, let alone saying it.

'However, I might be able to help you there actually?'

'Really, how?'

'Well I've got something put away for a rainy day. I've got four grand in used notes hidden and I could do with it collecting before they go out of circulation. I'll give you a grand to get you started if you make sure the rest gets to my old lady.'

'Reefer, I don't know what to say.'

''Thanks will be fine.''

'But how do you know you can trust me?' Asked Robert, uncertain if he had just asked a leading question.

'I can't trust you. But my guess is that you would do the same for me, am I right?'

'Yes I suppose you are. Thanks Reefer, I won't let you down.'

'I know you won't. And besides, if you did I'd find you and break both your legs and pull all your teeth out.' Both men laughed. 'Anyway, is that your escape plan or is there more?'

'Yes, that's where Ticker comes in. As soon as we get down for some "R and R" we'll discuss that then.'

'You know, if I'm going to make it into hospital, it's got to be convincing.'

'How convincing?' Replied Robert.

'The only way to get into hospital is for treatment that you can't receive here. Usually an X-ray on a broken bone or something like that.'

'Bloody hell Reefer, I don't want you going over-board.'

'Well I might have to, literally. But a tumble down the stairs won't do me any harm. After all I'm guaranteed an afternoon being pampered by nurses, and who knows, I might even get to raise a Health & Safety case against the Prison.' Reefer was at last demonstrating an enthusiasm that until now had been redundant.

'Come on let's go and meet the others, before you scare me to death with what you're planning to do to yourself.' Said Robert.

Robert and Reefer made their way down to the communal area where they found their two friends sat at a table. Several prisoners were in the room, some occupied tables whilst others stood around in small groups chatting to one another. It wasn't particularly noisy but there was sufficient background noise for the four conspirators to enjoy a relatively private conversation. Jono held a pack of playing cards which he started to deal when they both sat down.

'Don't ask what we're playing just tell us what you've got so far.' Instructed Jono.

'We haven't done that bad actually. We've got a good diversion which should keep three screws busy for an afternoon.' Reefer continued to explain how they intended to dilute the prison staff on the afternoon of the escape.

248

'When do you have in mind?' Ticker paused briefly. 'For 'E' Day I mean.' Enquired Ticker.

'Well this is where it all links together.' Said Robert, selecting two cards from his hand at complete random and placing them down on the table.

'Next Wednesday morning, the Government appointed Inspector of Prisons will be visiting Fulton.'

'Don't remind me,' said Ticker. 'We've had to order more floor cleaning solution so we can blitz the floors all Monday and Tuesday.'

'Precisely,' replied Robert. The one thing they *wouldn't* want to break down on Tuesday morning would be the electric floor cleaner right. The word is that the Governor is out to make a huge impression with this guy. So Ticker, tell me what it would take to warrant a site visit by the repair guy?'

'It would probably take the guy who looks after the cleaning machine, to pour some cleaning fluid into a part of the machine where it shouldn't be poured.' Ticker offered his recommendation and thought that it would be well-received.

'The rest should be plain sailing,' assured Robert. 'All we'll need is a little luck.'

"Yeh, but we're not having everything riding on good fortune Rob; that would be dangerous and we can't leave anything to chance,' said Ticker.

'Yes I know that, but I need to make sure that the repair man can't fix the machine on site. I'm gambling on him having to go away for a replacement part.'

'That shouldn't be too much problem,' ensured Ticker. 'The prison has a contract with the company that says any machine must be either repaired or replaced. There's no way they'll fix it after I've finished with it, they'll have to go and get a replacement. And I know for certain that the guy doesn't carry spare machines around with him, they're too big. But it's their policy that they have to come and try to repair it first.

'Ok, and when he leaves the prison, he has to walk right past the Library stock room.' Robert commenced briefing the crucial part of the plan. Now I've studied this. Nine times out of ten, official prison visitors are allowed to leave unescorted. The last door is remotely controlled and covered by a camera linked to the Control Room. With screws low on the ground I'm banking that the repair guy will be alone.'

'Yeh, but how you going to get through the door?' Enquired Jono.

'The camera points to the door, right. The repair man would have been escorted to the last door but one. The Control Room are going to be looking for the man wearing the same coat and the back of his head will be facing the camera. The Library Stock Room door is well before the camera so when he walks past my open door, I simply ask him for help with a heavy box and as soon as he's in the room, bang. I've got enough Sellotape in there to wrap him up for Christmas.'

'Yes very good Rob,' said Jono. 'But what about the keys for his van, they've got to be handed in when he arrives.'

'That's ok,' replied Reefer. 'They're not allowed to be at the gate office, they're in the Control Room, and he'll have picked them up by then, they'll be in his pocket. Anyway, when do I take my tumble?'

'Probably Monday night might be best. We have to rely on you being in hospital on Tuesday morning.' Said Robert.

'Sounds perfect,' said Jono. 'The hospital will more than likely be the General on the other side of town. It must be all of thirty minutes to drive and you'll be there for the best part of the morning. By the way, where do I fit in? I'm beginning to feel like a fifth wheel around here.' Jono placed one of his cards on the table.

'Reefer and I were just talking about that before. We're going to need a rumour starting that Reefer is planning an escape. We thought that Everson should hear it by accident and if anyone is going to be believed it's you.' Robert ensured that Jono understood exactly what he needed to know. 'The thing is, you're going to have to start the rumour now, that'll give them time to think about it. By next Tuesday morning they'll be convinced and we think that three screws will be going to Hospital with him.'

'Crikey, you have thought of everything, haven't you?' Said Ticker.

'So, next Tuesday it is then,' concluded Robert.

With that the three men ended their card game and stood up. Ticker spotted Everson in the corner of the room. He nudged Jono and signalled with his eyes that his target was in the perfect place. The two men walked over to Everson and stood chatting. Robert and Reefer looked on as their two accomplices put the first part of the plan into operation.

Chapter Fifteen

DC Jim Craven unlocked the car that was parked in the multi-storey car park on the edge of town. He and Paul Bretherton had been making some enquiries about a local fish dealer who had been suspected of making fraudulent declarations to the Tax Office. They had both admitted earlier that it was difficult to find the motivation for this kind of work.

This was largely down to the fact that they had recently wrapped up the, rather more important, murder investigation. Paul would like to have thought that he had brought that whole case to a successful conclusion, but something troubled him. His intuition was telling him that something wasn't quite right. He had decided to opt for early retirement some time ago, and that was approaching in the next few weeks.

He had explored several ideas concerning his future employment in recent months, but one idea kept returning to his mind. He climbed into the passenger side of the car and fastened his safety belt.

'Jim, you know I've been playing around with this idea about starting a detective agency when I leave the Force.'

'I know you've given it a lot of thought recently. Is that what you've decided on then?'

'Well yes and no really. My gratuity will pay the mortgage off. The pension will help pay the bills and the wife is in full-time employment. I should really take a back seat now, I've done my hard work and I could do without all the stress that this lot brings. But I feel that there's still something I need to finish.'

'You're not still thinking about Easton, are you?' Asked Jim.

'Come on Jim, you must be just a little unsure that there's something that we've missed.'

'Paul the Chief Super will go bananas if he finds out you've been making further enquiries into the murder. Besides, we've spoken to both Lamb and to Prevett, you must know that the right man is banged up.'

Paul recalled his brief conversation with Lamb. In the days leading to the trial, he had been told by Lamb's girlfriend that they had driven in the opposite direction of the garage when they left the pub, and returned directly to his parent's house where they stayed until she had left to go home. And then there was Prevett, a trusted family friend for years who had come to the rescue of his friend after his accident.

'Maybe you're right Jim, but it would certainly put my mind at rest if I were to put this to bed during my gardening leave.'

'Haven't you got any courses lined up for your resettlement into civvy street?'

'Nothing planned no, and if I'm taking up this line of work I hope I won't need any courses either, I've just about finished a twenty-year training course.' Laughed Paul.

On Monday evening Robert Easton stood on the inside of his cell with his fists clenched and eyes closed tight. He and Reefer had planned to the last detail when and how he should take his fall. He was waiting for his friend to tumble down the metal staircase along the corridor and couldn't bear to watch. Guilt ran around his head, passing on the feeling to every cell of his body. Reefer was doing this for *him*, but knowing that this was a vital link in the plan did nothing to make his remorse subside.

He heard a commotion and knew that he had done it. The cell door swung open and Ticker stood looking at him. His expression confirmed to Robert that Reefer had carried out the selfless act.

Robert and Ticker rushed to the stairs and down towards where Reefer Lay. Jono was at the bottom where he had waited until Reefer had fallen. Reefer was conscious which pleased Robert but he was clearly in immense pain. Blood seeped through the sleeve of his shirt but Reefer concentrated on the more obvious pain that he was feeling in his shin. He gripped his leg with both hands tightly.

Robert still did not know whether this was real or fake but now that the onlookers had been joined by two prison officers he knew he would have to wait for more information from the prison nurse and doctor when he arrived. Reefer was helped to his feet and was taken away, supported by two officers.

Robert was more bothered if Jono's information to Everson had been received and passed on in the way that they had intended. They would have to wait now. The three men stood chatting at the foot of the stairs and the assembled crowd started to disperse back to their evening's activities.

'There's no turning back now Rob!' Said Jono.

'Yes I know, let's just hope that they won't send him straight to hospital tonight for an X-ray.'

'I doubt it, they'll probably pack his leg in ice around where he's complaining of pain and see if it's better tomorrow. That's when Reefer's acting will come into play and the doc sends him for a precautionary X-ray.'

'Have you heard anything from Everson yet?' Asked Robert.

'No, not a sniff, that's been worrying me because it should have got around by now and we should have heard something.' Stated Jono.

'Do you think we should try again?' Said Ticker.

'No, definitely not. Everson's not stupid and he might smell a rat, and the last thing we want now is unwanted attention on us.' Replied Jono.

'You're right Jono.' Said Robert. 'We gave it a try and should leave it alone now. Ticker, how's the floor cleaner?'

'I fixed that about an hour ago.'

'What do you mean, you fixed it.' Asked Robert anxiously.

'You know what I mean.' Said Ticker.

'You had me worried for a minute, thanks mate. Right is everyone happy about tomorrow. Ticker, as soon as you start tomorrow, let the guards know that the machine is out of action.' Said Robert.

'Yep don't worry, the repair guy is normally here within the hour and with the Governor on the screws back you can bet he'll be here prompt. My guess is he'll be here around half ten. That means he'll be passing your store about 15 minutes later... just be ready.' Robert and Jono were impressed by Ticker's precision and hoped it wouldn't let them down.

'Good, he's got to pass me anyway so I'll know when he's inside.' Said Robert. The buzzer sounded, signifying that all prisoners should return to their cells. 'Right, I'll see you two at breakfast.'

The three men dispersed and returned to their cells. Robert lay on his bed alone and wondered about Reefer. He was unsure whether he would be returned to his cell or would spend the night in the hospital infirmary. Robert went over his plan in his head several times and satisfied himself that he could do no more than wait.

Everything that had been done could not be undone and everything that lay ahead was now down to him and his friends. He started to speculate about what he was to do when he got out. He hadn't dared think too much about that until now although Reefer had mentioned it several times. Robert remembered him saying that getting out was probably the easy part. Getting away from the prison and into society while the heat was still on, was harder still. But staying out was the hardest part of all.

Robert felt his eyes become tired and he started to drift off to sleep. He wasn't quite asleep when the cell door opened and Reefer hobbled in, flanked by two prison officers. Robert and Reefer never spoke until the door was firmly closed.

'What's happening man?' Asked Robert.

'Don't know could be bad news.'

'Why what happened?'

'My leg is bruised but the nurse couldn't find any swelling. She wouldn't call the doctor out and I had to use that injury as it was the one place giving me the most pain.' Said Reefer.

'So now what?'

'I've got to go back in to see her tomorrow morning.'

'And if you don't go to hospital, what then?

'Stop worrying Rob, I think I will swing it with her tomorrow. Besides this part of the plan is not essential is it. If I don't go into hospital I will still have screws with me at the infirmary. And if I do go, then that's just a bonus.

Reefer spent the next hour or so trying to placate Robert. Robert stared up at Reefer's crutches standing against the wall and wished Reefer a pleasant and pain free night.

The next morning Reefer hobbled to breakfast on his crutches escorted by Robert. They had to wait sometime before they were joined by Jono and Ticker for what Robert hoped would be the last time.

'Well I suppose that this should be goodbye then.' Whispered Ticker.

'Yes let's hope so.' Replied Robert.

'You will understand if we don't shake hands, won't you.' Said Jono.

'Yes don't worry, I understand, but I do want to thank you all for helping out. If I do go over is there anything I can do for any of you?'

'Yes,' said Reefer. 'Don't come back. Oh, and there's something else mate.' Reefer handed him a piece of paper. 'Everything you need to know about what we discussed is on there. Exact directions to it and my brother's phone number. When you've got it, give him a call and give him what we agreed. He'll make sure it gets to my old lady. Just promise me that if you get caught, make sure you eat the note I've just given you ok?'

Robert smiled and pressed his lips together graciously but his feelings soon diminished when he noticed that Muir was staring directly at him from another table. Muir was smiling which unnerved Robert.

'Don't look now but Muir is staring right at me and smiling. He's the last thing I want today.'

'Rob mate, I've done nothing else so far, why don't you let me handle him.' Said Jono. 'Best of luck mate.'

'Where you going?' Enquired Robert. Jono never replied but just winked at Robert and walked towards Muir.

As he drew level with him, Jono unleashed a mighty punch straight at Muir's face that sent him sprawling over his chair and into a table behind him. Two prison officers that had been talking by the entrance rushed to the two men who were now throwing blows in each other's direction.

'You will have to write and thank Jono, that's something else for the screws to deal with this morning.' Said Reefer.

Robert felt humbled by Jono's actions and the three men stood and walked towards the door. Ticker and Reefer gave Robert a reassuring but inconspicuous pat in the small of the back as they left the room.

'Thanks for everything.' Whispered Robert, and he walked off to the Library.

Robert was escorted to the penultimate security door and allowed through to the Library Stock Room. He opened the door and moved from the bright, naturally lit corridor into his approved work area. The room had no windows and was dark. He pressed down on the switch and filled the room in light bringing the furniture immediately into view. Two filing cabinets stood directly opposite the door which contained the Library's basic and antiquated stock rotation system. A single desk occupied the space to the left of the door, and the remaining space was filled with shelving that stored the hundreds of books that had been acquired over the years.

Robert sat at the desk and went through his plan again and tried to work out roughly what time to expect the repair man. All thoughts about having additional screws tied up with other things was the furthest thing from his mind right now. He glanced at the clock on the wall and calculated that the repair man should be there in ninety minutes or so. He made an attempt at some work, thinking that this would help pass the time. He sat at his desk knowing that he could expect a visit from a prison officer in an hour or so but he ensured that the door was left fully ajar. The last thing he needed was to miss the repair man on the way in to see Ticker. At least then he could time him and knowing Ticker, he would be closer to the fifteen minutes it normally took him than at any time in the past.

Robert found himself consciously watching for the minute hand to move. His mind had started to play tricks on him and he had to restrain his imagination from running wild. He reprimanded himself for allowing his sub-conscious to invade his sanity, he had to continue functioning. He still hadn't allowed himself to consider what lay on the outside of the prison. How long could he drive before he had to dump the van? Would it be best to abandon it in a residential area or somewhere more remote? And what if it needed fuel? All questions that remained unanswered but he knew needed consideration.

Robert's thoughts were interrupted by the outside door opening. Suddenly he was aware that his heart was beating faster than ever before. He wondered how the repair man could be so early. It seemed an eternity for Robert as he sat waiting for the person to walk passed the door. A prison officer appeared around the door and spoke to Robert.

'Everything alright in here?' Asked the Prison officer. 'Feeling a little claustrophobic?'

'Sorry, I don't understand.' Answered Robert.

'The door Easton.' Said the officer as he smiled at Robert.

"Oh, sorry, No I...I just wanted some natural light that's all.' The officer shook his head and walked on to the next security door.

Robert chastised himself again, first for even thinking that it could have been the repair man that early, but more importantly for acting so strangely. He identified that acting was going to have to play a big part in his life in the next few days and weeks, perhaps longer. He returned to his work and continued for what he believed was a good hour. He decided he would treat himself to one more glance at the clock. Ten fifteen.

He was concerned now; he hadn't had his visit yet to check on him. His mind started to wander again and he started to ask himself what would happen if he received his visit at the same time the repair man was scheduled to leave. What then?

The time passed and Robert grew more and more anxious. Ten thirty came and went. Ten forty, ten forty-five and still nothing. At Ten fifty-three Robert, had started to perspire but he was startled by the inner door opening. He heard voices but he recognised one tone above the others.

Reefer, with officers at both sides and one behind, struggled passed his door on his crutches. For a second the two men were afforded a brief smile at one another and Reefer went out of sight. Robert wished that he could embrace his friend and thank him for everything, but he knew Reefer was already aware of his complete gratitude. He heard one of the officers speak as the outer door was opened.

'We've been watching you all weekend Reefton. So don't get any bright ideas at the hospital, and when the hospital find nothing wrong, your arse is ours.' Grunted the officer as the door was closed and remotely locked behind him.

Robert felt humbled once more that his friends had helped him. Jono's words to Everson clearly had worked just as they planned. And not only had he got three officers away to hospital with Reefer; now he had further officers busy sorting out that morning's fight.

He looked at the clock again, ten fifty-six. He heard the outside door unlocking again and two men walked passed his door. One officer, and one wearing civilian clothing that was carrying a tool box.

Chapter Sixteen

Robert remained in his chair and never moved. Briefly, he went over the events of the last few weeks and how his life had changed, probably irreversibly. From a respected position with an active social life to an escaped convict that had been found guilty of murder.

He was so wrapped up in his feelings that he forgot to make a mental note of the time that the repair man had passed. He couldn't believe that his plan was actually in operation and more importantly, on track. The man that had walked passed his door was there because *he* had put him there. He estimated that the repair man had been in the prison for approximately 5 minutes. He was confident that Ticker would hang onto him for the full fifteen minutes, and if he couldn't he would certainly make sure that he tried to stall him with small talk of no particular relevance. As the time passed, Robert became more and more anxious. His palms felt hot and they began to perspire; he found himself drying them on his prison issue trousers. He was becoming increasingly uncomfortable and fumbled with a pencil, all the time staring into the empty corridor.

He heard the inner security door unlock and swing open followed by footsteps down towards his room. Robert leapt to his feet and made for the door to attract he man's attention. A prison officer stood in front of him suddenly Robert realised that this was his periodic visit that he had awaited earlier. He couldn't believe that things had gone so well and now his plans were about to come crashing down before him.

Robert watched as the officer moved a pen up and down a list that was attached to a clip board.

'Easton, Library Stock Room. Time, eleven zero five. Any problems Easton?' The office spoke while staring into his clip board. Robert wanted him to leave and as quickly as possible. However, he was afraid that he may make this look obvious.

'Yes everything is good thanks, no problems.'

'Right, I'll leave you to it then Easton.' Robert was relieved that the visit was a short one but the officer didn't leave immediately. He stood in the doorway facing outwards with his back to Robert and flicked through a selection of other pages that were on his clip board. Occasionally he mumbled things to himself before going to the next page. Robert grew more and more tense. As the minutes passed by, the prison officer continued to flick through pages of information. Robert had taken the initiative to return to his desk to give the impression that he was continuing with his work, oblivious to the officer stood in the door way.

Still he remained there and the time went by. Robert was watching the clock convinced that it was beginning to speed up. To Robert, it seemed an eternity for the officer to leave and walk back down the corridor from the direction that he had come. Robert heard the door close and he tried to relax a little but neither his body nor his mind would allow any such relaxation and he remained as tense as ever. He found himself beginning to question his own sanity. Here he was staring at a piece of paper that held absolutely no interest or significance to him whatsoever. He stood from his desk and walked towards the open door.

Robert hadn't quite reached the door when the inner security door opened once more. There were a few brief distant words that Robert was unable to make out. The door closed and a single set of footsteps walked down the corridor. Robert's chest tightened and he was aware that his brow was starting to perspire. The man grew ever closer and Robert knew that he had to be prepared to seize this opportunity. He was conscious that this was the most important component of the plan and this could be the one thing that might prevent his liberation.

The man drew level with the door and Robert's words leapt from him.

'Excuse me, can you please help me with this box? It's full of books and I just need to move it into the corner out of the way.'

'Yes mate, no problem.' The man replied, ignorant of the fact that he was to become the kingpin in a master plan that would see a man escape. Robert quickly surveyed the man and noticed that he was in his mid-forties, slightly over-weight and an inch or so shorter than himself.

He accepted that he couldn't waste any additional time and as soon as the man had started to lower his side of the heavy box, Robert let go of his end of the box. The box fell heavily to the floor and the man stumbled backwards. Robert pounced knowing that this may be the only opportunity he would receive. It took little more than a single punch to his face and the man was sent sprawling towards the wall opposite the door. He wrenched at the zip fastener on the man's waterproof coat almost tearing it from his body and threw it behind him across the room. He reached for a roll of clear tape and dived on the man, quickly wrapping the tape around his mouth and several times behind his head before finally snapping the tape. Robert did not gain any satisfaction at all from seeing the man hurt and in pain. In fact he would have preferred to reach out and help him rather than continue to lash together his feet and hands with the remains of the roll of tape. He stopped for a moment and looked compassionately at the man on the floor.

'Please forgive me?' Said Robert. 'I am not a bad or a violent man, but I must get out of here. I am innocent and until only a few weeks ago I led a normal and free life. I hope you understand.' The man gave Robert a wide eyed frightened stare and nodded nervously in agreement.

With that Robert put on the man's blue coat and checked the pocket for the keys to his van. They weren't in any of the pockets but sensing Robert's quest, the man rolled his eyes towards his own left trouser pocket and nodded. Robert retrieved the keys and gave the man a gracious look that expressed his gratitude. He took two long deep breaths and walked confidently into the corridor and towards the outer door.

He knew the drill for the outer door having rehearsed it on many occasions from the stock room with official prison visitors and officers coming and going. He stood by the door standing firmly looking directly at the door and not allowing a single glance to either side. Robert estimated that it took between three and five seconds for the door to buzz and signify that the door may be pushed open.

Robert waited anxiously, praying that a prison officer would not be coming in the opposite direction. Robert thought that it was much longer than he had anticipated. The waiting was prolonged but the noise eventually came and he gently pushed his way into the yard; he entered a part of the prison he hadn't believed possible to venture to until now.

Time was a principal factor, and at this moment it was both with and against him. He had to be swift and yet he also had to be seen to be perfectly calm and walk to his van coolly and not like a man who had just escaped from a modern prison.

It was at that moment that Robert realised that he had left the tool box with the man in his stock room. He hesitated for a brief second and then he decided that no matter what happened now he was not going to get through that door again unnoticed. The tool box would have to stay where it was. It was of no use to him, and he gambled that the officers in the Control Room who had opened the door remotely, would have paid little attention to his lack of tools.

He made directly for the solitary van sat in the prison yard, opened the door in and climbed inside. He was breathing deeply whilst fumbling through the small set of keys to find the right one for the ignition.

He knew that he was already passed the point of no return but still he thought he wouldn't start the engine until he was correctly seated and had secured his safety belt. Had his nerves not been in complete turmoil he knew that under normal circumstances he would have laughed at himself obeying the laws of the road, whilst breaking out of prison. However, he also knew that these were not normal circumstances, for anyone, let alone him.

He started the van and concentrated on the gate directly in front of him. The officer in charge of this gate swung it open and waved at Robert. As he drove passed him Robert lifted his hand as a thanking gesture and made sure that his hand obscured his face as he passed. Robert didn't expect that the prison officer would recognise him anyway, but he wanted to give himself the best possible chance of escape and the smallest of errors now would see him back inside having to face the likes of Muir for a long time to come. Beyond the inner gate lay a twenty metre straight stretch of tarmac that led to the outer gate.

He drove carefully and waited patiently at the last obstacle that separated him from the outside. Robert looked into the wing mirror and saw the same officer that had opened the first gate walking towards the van on the driver's side. Robert didn't know the procedure for the last gate and he could only hope that the officer was walking to open the outer gate. He prayed that he would walk straight passed his window and on to the gate. Robert was pleased to see the officer flicking through a large set of keys that were attached to his trousers by a chain. He realised that he was preoccupied with his keys and was probably searching for the right key to quickly open the gate. Robert's heart sank low when the officer stopped and tapped on the side window with the keys. Robert remained facing forwards and opened the window leaving it one quarter open. He turned to look up at the officer and put his hand to his forehead to protect his eyes from the sun like a poorly executed naval salute. Robert knew however, that the sun was not quite in his eyes, but he wasn't concerned by that at that particular moment.

'Don't worry, I'll sign you out.' The officer spoke quickly as he headed off towards the gate.

'Thanks mate.' Replied Robert, who quickly realised that he had needed to get out of the van and sign out in the exit gate office. Still, he had been spared that potential stumbling block. He watched as the outer gate swung open and gave Robert his first glimpse of the outside world for several weeks.

The officer waved Robert forward and once again Robert raised a grateful hand. He felt several emotions flood through his body as he drove off. He was enormously frightened of how he was going to manage the next few vital hours. He was elated at finally escaping and he was sad at the prospect of not being able to thank his friends properly.

He hoped that he would be successful in his quest for the truth and that he may eventually prove his innocence. He even thought about the probability of finding the real killer, something that he had not considered until that time.

He washed all those thoughts away knowing that he must concentrate now on the immediate future and consolidating his freedom. He estimated that he would have approximately five or ten minutes at the most before the man in the stock room would be found. He calculated that he would have an additional ten minutes or so for the message to reach the control room and a call to the Police to go out. So maybe twenty minutes to make his initial bid to melt into the background of society. He knew that the nearest and largest town would help him to blend in quicker. The country side would be swarming with police with the latest heat seeking devices attached to helicopters which during darkness would spot him from a great distance.

He checked his speedometer and quickly assessed that at an average speed of 60 miles per hour he could expect to cover a distance of twenty miles or so in the time that he had allotted himself. As he approached a junction he quickly scanned the road signs looking for a major road that would not only lead him to a large town but also enable him to travel faster.

He turned left onto the busy road that led into Peterborough centre. He recognized that that would be busy enough for him to lose the van in a crowded car park and he ought to be able to make it in about fifteen minutes. His mind was in overtime making calculations and reassessing various situations that could arise.

He sped towards Peterborough aware that the unfortunate, rightful driver of the van was possibly being discovered right at that moment. The traffic was fairly thick and this slowed him slightly. He wished that he could pass the row of vehicles that had assembled in front of him but he knew that would only serve to attract unnecessary attention.

He approached the outskirts of the town and saw a traffic island ahead. He knew that he was now on the outer ring road that encircled the town. He headed for the town centre, constantly checking his time. He still had at least 5 minutes or so of free time which would enable him

274

to find a car park. He decided to search for a multi-storey car park that would help him to hide the small van more effectively and make it much more difficult to locate. He knew that he needed every minute he possibly could.

The traffic grew thicker as he entered the centre of Peterborough, Robert encountered a seemingly endless supply of traffic lights and pedestrian crossings. In the distance, he saw what he was looking for and drove into the entrance of a multi-storey car park and retrieved a ticket from the machine at the barrier. He managed to locate a free slot on the third floor and he parked neatly between two large cars. Not sure if he would find anything of use to him, Robert checked the glove compartment before he left his initial mode of escape for the last time. The man's wallet lay neatly before him and Robert couldn't believe his luck. He remembered that Reefer had mentioned something about this some time ago. Of course, any sane person would be unlikely to take money and credit cards into a prison, Robert thought. He opened it and found thirty-five pounds in notes. He hated himself for stealing the money but he knew that, were he to prove his innocence he would be delighted to return the money at a more convenient moment. He did not remove the man's credit cards, instead he placed the man's wallet back into the glove box and placed the keys under the visor.

Robert realised that he had to act swiftly, and he also knew that he had to return to his house to collect some clothes and other essential belongings. He knew however, that the police were sure to be watching his property before too long.

Standing in the damp, urine soaked concrete stair case of the car park, Robert pondered for a moment and thought about his next move. To escape overseas would be the immediate and most obvious solution, but the authorities still held his passport. Either way, if he were to survive he needed cash and quickly, therefore following his visit home he was going to need to go in search of Reefers cash. He checked the piece of paper in his pocket and made his way down the steps and walked briskly to the Railway Station to buy a ticket for the eighty or so miles journey to his village. Robert walked into the Station and stopped for a second to get his bearings. He stood still and looked around. A Newsagents Kiosk was positioned immediately to his left. A whole series of travel information was in front of him along the length of the wall and the Ticket office was to his right. Several people were there, going about their business oblivious to Robert's presence. He knew that if he were to purchase his own ticket, there would be a chance the man who sold him his ticket would be questioned and he may remember Robert's appearance and the destination of his journey.

Robert decided to buy a ticket for the station before his own stop. Should the Police check for Tickets sold, they were sure to only check for those sold to his own village. Robert approached an elderly lady and adjusted his voice to a very hoarse whisper.

'Excuse me, I am having trouble buying my ticket. I have an extremely sore throat and the man can't hear me behind the glass screen, can you help me please?' Asked Robert, holding out money for the lady.

'Of course I can. Would you like me to buy it for you?' Enquired the lady.

"Yes, thank you, I need a single ticket to Lower Mittley.' Spoke Robert, his voice beginning to show signs of weakness. His throat became genuinely sore. The lady took the money from him and walked off to the ticket booth.

Robert looked around again and tried not to look at the transaction that was going on between the lady and the man behind the screen. Both were talking and the lady had turned to face Robert pointing in his direction. Robert felt very uneasy but he realised that she was probably trying to explain his predicament. Still he turned away and walked to the board to check which platform he would be needing and how long he would have to wait. He was having to rely on the large clock situated high on the wall of the Station foyer as his own watch was securely locked away at the prison.

'There you are, and there's your change.' Said the lady who stood behind him as she handed him his ticket.

'Thank you,' said Robert. 'You've been very kind.' The lady smiled and walked off.

Robert checked the time of the next train once more, but this time he was interrupted by sirens outside. Two police patrol cars raced passed Peterborough Station.

Chapter Seventeen

Robert didn't have to wait long in the dusty waiting room. The four-carriage commuter train arrived and he walked out onto the platform waiting for it to come to a complete stop. The first carriage he found was almost empty. He quickly located an empty set of seats that surrounded a table and he sat by the window facing forwards. He took the piece of paper from his pocket and studied it again. Robert cursed Reefer for selecting a hiding place for his money so far away in Portsmouth. Still, he knew he had over a hundred pounds in cash at his house. He always kept an amount hidden away in case of emergencies and that would see him through to Portsmouth. It was going to be the laying in wait outside his house for the right moment to enter that was irritating Robert now.

The train gathered speed and he watched the scenery rush by. The train ran parallel to a road and he saw the hustle and bustle of everyday life that everyone was accustomed to. Robert however, appreciated it much more now. Particularly now that he was no longer a member of society, in any way at all. Sensing this, Robert began to feel an outcast and that he had been abandoned by the system that until recently he had belonged to. He had been accepted by society, but now he was in an invidious position. He belonged in prison, that was where society wanted him to be, yet he didn't belong there at all.

Confused, he reprimanded himself and walked to the end of the carriage and checked his route again.

He had three stops to make before he had to change trains at Cambridge and then four more before he would arrive. He went over his plan again to leave the train one stop before his village and wait until darkness. He was certain that there would be a police presence at his station, and every member of the police would have his full description emblazoned in their minds.

Robert finally arrived at Lower Mittley station shortly after 4pm. He knew that he couldn't spend another four hours or so until darkness fell, without attracting some unwanted interest. Therefore, he left the station immediately and decided to make his way to a quiet public footpath that he knew linked Lower Mittley with his own village of Elston. Used by dog walkers, this would provide him with the perfect cover as it led along the side of a river and through several meadows.

Having only just left the small station car park Robert rounded the corner and came to a brisk halt. His heart thumped and he struggled to breathe, only two car lengths away DS Paul Bretherton was unlocking his car. Robert didn't want to stop and immediately turn around, that would give him away at once. He was aware that he had hesitated briefly but he must continue forward. Paul Bretherton glanced momentarily in Robert's direction but climbed into his car. Robert continued to move forward but without the help of his muscles. He was so terrified that he wondered if it was his momentum that carried him forwards. He considered his good fortune for a moment as he walked passed DS Bretherton's door having no courage at all to look inside. Maybe, Paul Bretherton didn't recognize him, he hadn't seen him and perhaps he didn't even know about his escape yet.

Robert continued along the footpath and looked for the quickest route that would take him out of sight of the car. He located a side street on the other side of the road. He ran into the road without looking in any direction, completely focussed on the corner ahead of him. Fortuitously, no traffic came in either direction however, Robert was aware that Paul Bretherton's car was pulling away and coming towards him. Robert leapt onto the pavement and the car drove passed him. He watched as Paul Bretherton disappeared around a bend in the road. Robert stopped for a moment to compose himself. Drawing in breath sharply to fill his lungs with much needed oxygen, he continued quickly in the direction of the bend.

Robert hurried towards the small side road that would lead him to the secluded public footpath. Away from the road he now allowed his thoughts to wander. His mind darted from one thought to another. He wondered for a moment about getting back into his house, he thought about his work colleagues and now he was thinking about his friends in prison that had helped him in his bid for freedom.

He remembered the note book that he had found and he decided that he might retrieve it from his house too. Now his thoughts returned to John Huggett, why he'd had the note book in his possession and if it held any significance. He felt that it may perhaps hold some information that would identify someone with whom he had a feud and that would help to prove his innocence. Robert continued along the lonely pathway, resolute in his immediate quest to gain access to his house and retrieve the items he needed. Spare clothing, cash and the notebook were at the top of his list and he could not hope to continue with his quest of proving his innocence without these items; he began to form a number of different methodologies in his mind of how he could gain access to his home unnoticed.

He tried to make sense of the irony. He had just escaped from a high security prison, and now he was planning to break into his own home.

Paul Bretherton returned to Radley Street Police Station and he wanted to clear some documentation that had been accumulating on his desk for several days. He reminded himself that was the part of the job that distressed him most and, if anything, this was one of the one things that would make him retire from the Force above everything else.

He sat at his desk and tried to arrange the large amount of case literature and sort it into some order before he started to add his notes. The CID office door opened and the Custody Sergeant stood in the doorway, looking directly at Paul Bretherton.

'Have you seen the Chief Super? Asked the Custody Sergeant.

'No I've only just got back in the door?' Answered Paul, trying to intimate that he was preoccupied with work.

'He's been after you for the last half an hour.'

'He knows how to use a radio doesn't he?' Said Paul, flippantly.

The uniformed sergeant felt chastised.

'You might need to pop up to see him. Have you heard about the escape at Peterborough?' The sergeant asked.

'No. What escape?

'I'm amazed you haven't heard. Has your radio been turned off or something? Robert Easton broke out of prison earlier and hasn't been seen since. We've got uniform on it already.'

'Holy shit.' Exclaimed Paul, he didn't need to hear anymore. He thanked his colleague and raced passed him.

Paul Bretherton knocked on the Chief Superintendent's open door and didn't wait to be invited in.

'Is it true boss?' Asked Paul.

'Yes I'm afraid it is.' Replied the Chief Superintendent.

Chief Superintendent Alastair Molyneux had been with the Police Force for 30 years. He was 52 years old and he had a dark complexion with dark brown hair that had only recently started to show signs of going grey. He was six feet tall, slim and rather athletically built for his age. His square jawline depicted a man that was strong with an assured sense of confidence about himself. There was no doubt that Alastair Molyneux had been spotted very early in his career as one of the Elite who would be groomed for hierarchy and greater things by his earlier superiors. He had recently transferred to Radley Street from the Metropolitan Police on promotion and was well-respected by his Officers and staff.

'I want you to co-ordinate the search using Radley Street as the base. We've asked for support from two other forces and they are standing by waiting for the call.' Alastair continued.

'Yes no problem, I'll get Jim Craven onto it straight away but I might go down to the prison first. I might get some good information from his cell mate there which will get us started.' Said Paul, hoping that his superior would agree.

'Yes good idea. I'll remain here and start to formulate a press release, Division will want to see that go out before the end of the day.'

'In the mean time, I'll get someone down to his house. It's going to be dark soon and I wouldn't mind a chat with some of his neighbours.' Paul explained his thought process to Chief Superintendent Molyneux and was pleased to see a reassuring nod of agreement from his boss.

Paul excused himself from the Chief Superintendent and raced down to his office to find his trusted colleague, DC Jim Craven. He pushed open the door to the CID main office and found him already waiting. Paul walked over to his DC and noticed his own reflection in the window as walked across the room, indicating to him that darkness was already starting to fall outside and time was going to be critical in the next few hours.

Robert Easton grew more anxious as he approached the end of the footpath. He was only two hundred yards from his house but he was aware that police activity would be intense now and he could expect patrols in his vicinity at any time. He knew he had to act fast and be away from his home as soon as possible. With darkness almost upon him, Robert walked from the footpath over a small stone bridge which led to a brook and into a children's play area. No one was around and any dog walkers or children would have left the area over an hour ago.

He continued through the park and he could see the rear of his house on slightly raised ground above him. Like four others, Robert's rear garden was on a slight rise and looked out over the park. He clambered up the hill towards his rear fence. He felt cold and the day's events started to flood back into his mind. He recalled waking up in a prison earlier that morning. He had taken the bold step of escaping from prison and was now a fugitive on the run. He knew he should be planning his next few hours and how he would maintain his freedom over the next few days. However, the only thought Robert could muster was not letting down his friends in prison by returning there.

He cleared these thoughts from his mind and returned his mind to thoughts of planning and staying vigilant. He exploited the darkness but continued to scan the area immediately around him and reached his fence. He climbed onto a rock to gain a good foothold and he peered over his fence into his garden. There was very little activity and he could hear nothing other than distant traffic.

Realising that he had little else to lose he hauled himself up the fence and then over the top dropping onto the flower bed on the other side. He moved quickly and stealthily to the house and retrieved a spare key that he always kept under the small paving slab at the side of his patio. He unlocked the back door and entered his cold dark house. It was difficult for him to navigate his way around in the extremely low visibility despite it being his own familiar abode.

He resisted the temptation not to put on any lights, not even to use a small flashlight as this might give away his presence. He thought it mildly ironic that he felt like an intruder in his own home, but he made haste in finding the things he needed. He grabbed a small back pack, placed some clean warm clothes into it along with every bit of cash he could find. He changed into his own clothes and thought about collecting his mobile telephone. He held it for a moment then he laid it down where he had found it. He had thoughts of the Police using this a method to locate him; Robert was becoming more resourceful and this grew with his confidence. He located the most suitable coat that he felt would give him some degree of concealment and disguise, let alone warmth. He zipped himself into his coat and quickly loaded his back pack around his shoulders and secured it in place. He went into his kitchen to find a small torch in one of his drawers.

Lying next to the torch was the small leather notebook he'd found under John Huggett. He picked it up and thought about the evening when he'd found it and the eventful journey that he'd had since. He placed it into his inside pocket and headed for his back door that would lead him back out into the cold darkness.

He locked his door and returned his key to its original hiding place and leapt over his fence walking quickly off into the darkness.

DS Paul Bretherton stood in front of the detectives and selection of uniformed Police Officers that had gathered in Radley Street CID for Paul's briefing. He stood by the large briefing board that held the key information he needed to impart to the group of officers that had already broken themselves into smaller teams.

'OK listen up.' Paul raised his voice over the small conversations that were taking place. 'This is what we've got to go on so far.' Paul pointed to the notice board to his left.

'You all know why we're here. This is the latest photo we have of Robert Easton.' Paul pointed to the police photograph taken of Robert at the time of his arrest.

'There are many places that he could go to, but for now we are going to concentrate on relatives and of course his own home.' Paul looked over to the four uniformed officers in the room and said I want you to start with his house.' DC Craven handed a list of addresses that he'd prepared for Robert's relatives and his home to the four officers.

Paul shifted his attention to DC Jim Craven.

'You and I will start with a visit to prison. I want formal interviews with every one of Easton's associates, particularly his Cell mate.'

'Already sorted.' Responded Jim Craven. 'I got in touch with them earlier and they're expecting us any time tonight.'

'Good work Jim, thanks for that.' Paul showed his appreciation to his senior detective. 'We'll get uniform to make the calls to division to get the neighbouring forces engaged. If we can have them out here first thing in the morning, we should be in a better position to give them more information.'

Paul knew that he would be better placed to formulate and coordinate a more methodical search with more time to prepare. He also felt that he stood a reasonably good chance of success that night. He had the British Transport Police alerted, all the railway stations and bus depots alerted too. He hoped that Robert Easton would make a mistake at some point and that they would be ready to recapture him quickly.

Paul Bretherton and Jim Craven drove into the holding area of Peterborough Prison and the large gates closed behind them. The secondary gates were opened for them from the control office to their left and they were signalled to proceed through by a prison officer that was standing to their left. They parked up and headed for the control room that they'd just passed. DC Craven showed his warrant card to the prison officer and he asked them to follow him through the corridor and inside to the interview suite.

Paul and Jim waited for their first interviewee, and Reefer was shown in escorted by two prison officers. Prisoner Tony Reefton took a seat opposite Paul and Jim and one of the officers remained in the room standing by the door.

Paul was acutely aware that he was addressing a convicted criminal and there was no need for pleasantries. However, Paul knew that manners normally worked in these situations and sometimes made the difference between success and failure.

'Hello my name is Detective Sergeant Paul Bretherton and this is my colleague Detective Constable Jim Craven. First of I wanted to thank you for talking to us.'

'Yes I imagine you would be grateful, given how late it is.' Said Reefer rudely.

'Did you have more pressing things to do this evening?' interrupted the prison officer who was stood behind him.

Paul looked up at the prison officer but chose not to comment on his unhelpful remark. Paul returned his attention to Reefer and explained to him about the dangers that Robert could be exposed to. He went to say that he was likely to be arrested that evening anyway and every available resource was being deployed to find him. However, information he might be able to provide would save everyone a great deal of time and it would probably save Robert from possibly freezing to death somewhere.

'Did Robert Easton give you any indication about his plans to escape?' Paul asked.

'Look mate.' Replied Reefer, you know only too well that I had an idea he wanted to be out, but how the hell am I expected to guess which way he'd go when he got over the wall?' Reefer knew that the two detectives would know that he would be aware of Robert's wishes. Moreover, he knew they wouldn't be expecting much in the way of information that would lead to his eventual re-capture.

'Have you any idea where he might be heading? We are concerned about his safety more than anything else at the moment. We have a man who knows everyone is going to be after him. He'll be frightened and he could be a real danger to himself.' Paul gave an impassioned plea hoping that Reefer might see some sense and help them to bring him back to safety.

Reefer remained quiet and stared down at the floor. There was a long pause and Reefer said nothing, giving no indication that he wanted to cooperate. Then he raised his head again and looked at Paul.

'If I do say where I think he might have gone, what would be in it for me, and how can you make sure that Rob wouldn't know I told you anything?' Reefer felt like he was becoming a super-grass.

Paul and Jim both shifted in their seats and knew they were winning the 'hearts and minds' battle with Reefer.

Reefer however, sat motionless and smiled. He knew that by now, Robert would be well on his way to Portsmouth.

'If you want my best guess, He'll go straight to the nearest whore house, get his rocks off and then head home for a good rest.' Reefer knew that his information would not be well received.

'Let's go Jim, we're wasting our time here.' Paul looked at Jim Craven and stood up.

'Thanks mate, we'll be on our way now.' Paul, glanced over to the prison officer and indicated that they wanted to leave.

Robert Easton was cold but grateful of his warm coat with a fleece-lined hood that was now secured around his head and ears. It was only a few moments since he had been on the same secluded footpath that ran parallel with the river. However, the temperature was now markedly cooler than it was then. He hurried along the footpath and wondered to himself if he would be too late to risk travelling by train. This was by far his most preferred method of travel as it would be the fastest and most direct route for him to get to Portsmouth. He was mindful of course, that the British Transport Police would probably be involved in the search and it was this that was causing him the most concern.

Undeterred by his fears, he continued along the footpath and tried to make sense of the thoughts that were riding roughshod over his logic. As he approached the end of the pathway, he sensed that something was wrong. He caught sight of two police officers walking towards the small railway station. A short tree-lined pathway separated Robert from the two officers who were walking away from him. Robert stopped for a moment and was satisfied that he wouldn't be seen on the unlit pathway. The officers continued and Robert decided to wait until they had walked a little further.

He knew that it would be unwise to return back in the direction of his house. He also calculated that if the police would carry out checks at the railway station, it would only be a matter of time until they made the link between the station and his house and would therefore be checking the path that he was on. He decided to wait for a few more moments and then continue to the road that led to the railway. He didn't wait long and then he emerged from the pathway through a gap in a stone wall. He looked to his right and saw the two officers still walking and he noticed that they would only be a few moments from the railway station.

Robert turned left and walked quickly in the opposite direction of the two officers. He was troubled by his inability to use the railway system – this offered him the most obvious and direct route. Now Robert was analysing the alternative methods of getting into the city as soon as possible. He thought it strange, if not a little ironic, that he wanted to head back in the general direction of Fulton Prison. However, he'd already concluded that the city would give him the best chance of finding somewhere warm to sleep. Equally, he felt that the higher concentration of people would provide a greater degree of concealment, giving him more chance of finding a safe passage to Portsmouth.

Robert stopped for a moment and turned around. He could see the railway station in the distance and he stared at the cars that were parked there. Parallel to the parked cars was a small rank of taxi cabs and he congratulated himself again on his resourcefulness.

He was motionless and waited, ready to seize his opportunity when it arose. He waited for about ten minutes before he noticed a taxi draw up to the station and drop off a passenger. The cab did not wait in the queue. Instead it drove straight out of the station and headed in Robert's direction. He calculated that it would take no more than a few seconds to reach him and waited for his moment to step out into the road. The taxi drew closer and Robert emerged from the shadow of the wall and raised his right hand to gesture his requirement to the driver. Robert noticed that the car started to brake and it drew level with him. The driver looked over to Robert and he climbed into the back seat.

Robert paused for a moment before issuing the driver with his intended destination. He wondered whether the driver would know that an escaped prisoner was at large in the area and if so, whether he would recognise him.

'Hi how's it going?' Robert said.

'Good thanks.' Replied the driver. 'Where to?'

'Can you take me into Peterborough please? I'm off to the Crystal Rooms.' Robert expected the driver to know this venue, because of its popularity with a good bar and restaurant.

Robert glanced at the Red Lion as he drove passed and wondered for a moment if John Huggett's friends would be inside. A few moments later he approached John Huggett's garage. He gave a baleful stare which remained fixed on the sign above the garage showroom as he drove passed. The taxi cab continued out of Lower Mittley on the quiet rural road and headed towards Peterborough.

Paul Bretherton sat in his dimly lit office. It was late at night and all the other staff that were involved in the search for Robert Easton had gone home for the evening. Only dedicated night shift staff were working and they were all out in patrol cars helping with the main effort which was the recapture of a convicted murderer.

Paul was exploiting everything at his disposal and he was putting every piece of his vast experience to use. Paul was troubled because his mind was engaged in two entirely separate pieces of Police work. Not only was he working on how to recapture Robert, but his sub-conscious was now in a struggle with his mind that was raising questions about Robert Easton's guilt.

Paul struggled to come to terms with his thoughts. Whilst he hadn't been completely satisfied that Robert Easton was guilty at the time of the investigation, he knew that he had the motive, intent and the murder weapon was at his house. Whilst most detectives would have been delighted with the result and the conviction, something worried Paul. He couldn't fathom why a previously robust and good citizen with plenty to live for, would waste his life by taking John Huggett's. Why would he choose to escape and what was it he would be seeking once free? Was he trying to find the information he needed to prove his innocence? These and other questions raced around his mind.

Paul's face contorted as he took a sip of cold coffee from the mug on his desk. He put the mug back onto its coaster and pushed it away to arm's length. He was tempted to turn on the Police crime database. The Home Office Large Major Enquiry System (HOLMES) was a tool that helped police to link crimes but he was acutely aware that it had its flaws. Paul's experience taught him that the system was only as good as the information that was fed into it. Of course, this was the problem and he was mindful that sufficient information was rarely loaded into it.

Whilst he was happy that his team had used HOLMES during the investigation into John Huggett's murder, he wasn't certain as to the degree in which it was employed. He turned on the monitor and CPU for the system and waited for it to go through its set-up process.

Paul walked out of his office and made himself fresh coffee as HOLMES finalised its configuration.

He returned to his desk, placed his warm coffee onto the coaster and pulled it across the desk nearer to him. He searched in the drawer to his right for his log in details and password. He recalled that he always scowled when he was reminded why he shouldn't keep his personal log in details where others could find them. He entered them into the system and he started to navigate his way around the database. He searched the index for information that would yield anything that would lend itself to his case.

The taxi cab drew up to the kerb outside the Crystal Rooms restaurant and Robert paid the driver. Still, uncertain if he'd been recognised by the driver, he had decided to be dropped off at the popular restaurant so that if the driver went to the Police, this would buy him at least a little time. Robert had no intention of entering the restaurant and he certainly didn't feel hungry, despite not having eaten for a number of hours. Robert's true destination was another half a mile or so away. He secured his back pack over his shoulders again zipped up his coat to its fullest extent and started walking quickly towards the City Bus Depot.

Robert knew that long distance coaches operated from there and he hoped that there might be an overnight coach that would take him into London. Robert just wanted to be away from the general area and saw this as his best opportunity. It didn't take him long to make the short journey and he slowed as he approached the bus depot. He carefully scanned for any signs of Police activity and, content that there was none, he made his way into the passenger reception area. He could see through the window of the reception area into the large depot that a number of large white coaches stood in neat rows.

Three people were sat in the waiting area and a young woman was busy typing at a keyboard behind a tall counter. Robert checked the wall-mounted TV screen for information about coach departures. He checked his watch and saw that it was approaching 9.30pm. He quickly established that he was going to be left with two options. Wait until 10pm and board the coach bound for Birmingham, or he could wait until 11pm for the coach that would be leaving direct for London.

Robert knew that he couldn't risk waiting a full ninety minutes and so he approached the counter and asked the young, dark-haired woman if he could buy a ticket for Birmingham. Robert paid in cash and asked which bus it would be that he would be boarding. Robert wanted to board now and secure his place on the bus rather than sitting in the open waiting area. The young woman however, told Robert that it would not be ready for boarding for another twenty minutes or so and that he would need to wait until the bus had pulled forward to its boarding point.

'You will be getting on at boarding point 'D2.' Said the young woman. 'It's right outside the side door.' She said, pointing at the door that led directly to boarding point D2.

Robert thanked her and said that he would return in a few moments. He could not wait in the reception area and felt that it would be better if he left the station and return when the coach was ready to leave. He crossed over a dual-carriageway and headed for a patch of waste ground that he'd noticed earlier. He found a rubbish skip that was positioned ideally for him to stand behind which gave him an excellent vantage point from which to view the entrance to the bus depot.

Robert removed his back pack, placing it at his feet and he stood in the darkness with his eyes fixed on the large bus depot entrance. He checked his watch again. He watched intently for signs of Police activity and knew that he only had approximately fifteen minutes to wait before the bus would make its way forward to the boarding point. He was satisfied that he could not be seen from the road and this placated him. Robert calculated that he would make his move in approximately eighteen minutes so that he would be sure not to miss it and that he would have to be in the depot for no more than a few minutes.

He allowed himself some time to gather his thoughts and he tried to regulate his breathing. Robert knew that he was in good shape but he reckoned that his heart rate had been raised now for too long and he wanted to try to lower it to a normal level again. He checked his watch that he'd collected from his house and saw that it wouldn't be too much longer for him to wait. Traffic continued in both directions on the dual-carriageway in and out of the city; he felt satisfied that there was no police activity, at least not here and, more importantly, not at the bus depot.

He checked his watch again, more minutes passed and he looked up to see a large police minibus carrying a number of Police Officers inside. The vehicle slowed as it passed the bus depot and Robert quickly lowered his head so that he was only just able to peer over the top of the rubbish skip. The police van picked up speed again, commensurate with Robert's heart rate and continued on towards the city.

Robert remained in his half-crouched position for a few more seconds and chose not to stand up fully just yet. His heart rate was starting to recover again when he felt a sharp pain in the centre of his back. He quickly realised that someone was directly behind him and his heart rate raced to sprinting pace again.

'What you got in the bag?' Came the voice of a young man. 'I'm taking it and if you make one move I'm going shove this blade as far as it will go – RIGHT?' Shouted the young man.

Robert now knew it wasn't the police and for a moment he was relieved until the reality of the situation dawned on him and that he was being mugged instead.

'Look there's nothing in there. A sleeping bag and a torch mate. But you're welcome to it, just don't do anything stupid, take it.' Robert said.

Robert felt the blade of the knife sticking into his coat and it was now pressing hard against his back. He fretted about the valuable time that the young thug was wasting and he thought about his belongings, including the notebook that the thug wanted to take from him.

Time was slipping away and Robert could see the coach moving forward inside the depot to its boarding point. The people that he'd seen sitting in the waiting room started to board the coach.

Robert began to lose his feeling of fear. Instead, he grew angrier as more time passed. He slowly turned so that he could just see where his attacker was standing. He prepared himself, taking in one deep breath and launched his elbow rearwards straight into his assailant's throat sending the young man reeling backwards. Clutching his throat, the young thug dropped his knife and Robert seized his opportunity. He launched two more forceful punches to his head and the young man ran off. Robert didn't shake as he felt he would have done only a few weeks earlier. Instead he felt a rush of adrenaline wash over him and he felt seven feet tall. He allowed himself to feel sorry for the young man whom he'd just taught a lesson. Then his thoughts returned back to the bus depot.

Robert was not worried that the young man might return but he thought it would be wise to dispose of the knife. He quickly wiped the handle and blade against his coat, not knowing what the young thug had done with it that evening and he threw it into the skip.

Robert then picked up his bag and ran towards the bus depot. He barely looked for traffic as he darted across the dual-carriage way and into the bus depot. The driver was preparing to depart when Robert raced in front of it with his arm raised. The driver opened the door and Robert leapt onto the coach. He quickly showed the driver his ticket and he found a seat towards the rear of the coach. He sat down and sucked in hard for air, wondering if his luck would ever change. Still, he reminded himself that he'd successfully boarded the coach and he forgot about his altercation with the young man who'd just tried to mug him.

Robert placed his bag on the empty seat next to him and rested his head against the window.

Paul Bretherton took another large gulp of his coffee and started to enter information into the database. He entered every piece of information he had into every field of the HOLMES database, including dates of the murder, the weapon that was used and how the murder took place. He put in the name of John Huggett's garage that was still trading under his father's good name. He set the program query running and sat back in his chair and waited to see if it returned any links. He hoped for any information that would show a link to another crime.

The results returned a nil response and Paul sighed. This time he narrowed his search and tried to show results of all murders and suspicious deaths that had taken place in the last eighteen months in the area. Another nil response was returned. Paul sighed again.

Paul continued entering every piece of his available information into the Police database and in all permutations, he could imagine.

Meanwhile Robert's coach was starting to pull out of the depot and Robert looked out of his window, first at the young woman in the reception area who'd just served him. Then at the dual-carriage way as it came into view as the bus slowly emerged from the depot. He was still looking out of his window when the coach jolted suddenly; the passengers were all thrown forward in their seats and the bus came to an abrupt stop.

Robert looked to the front of the bus and immediately noticed the blue flashing lights of the Police Van that was blocking the bus exit from the depot. A nervous pain shot through Robert and he cursed his luck once more. His heart thumped hard, he grabbed his bag and held it tightly. He sat motionless for a few moments and wondered what the Police's next move would be.

Robert still didn't know if they would board the coach or if they would simply allow the coach to drive on. He prayed for the latter but started to plan an escape route should he need it. The Police remained in front of the coach, he could see at least three Officers talking to one another in front of the coach. He could see that the driver was growing impatient and he opened the coach door to speak to the officers. Robert expected the worst but still, he hoped for the best.

To his horror, one of the Officers boarded the coach and spoke to the driver who was still in his seat. The officer said that he could leave the depot in a few moments but he just wanted to carry out a routine check. The officer looked down the coach at the few people who were on board. The officer apologised and said that they could be on their way in just a moment. The Officer then looked directly at Robert sitting towards the back of the coach. His stare remained fixed on Robert and he reached for his radio.

Robert knew that his time was almost up and that his brief spell as a fugitive was about to come to an abrupt end. He quickly looked around him and explored his immediate surroundings. The Police Officer was now striding purposefully down the coach towards Robert and more Officers were boarding the coach. Robert lurched towards the emergency exit on the opposite side of the coach and pushed his whole-body weight against the bar on the exit door. It swung open and Robert fell through and crashed onto the floor of the bus depot.

He ran towards the rear of the depot and he could hear raised voices behind him as the Officers gave their chase. He headed towards a row of coaches at the rear of the large indoor depot and disappeared between two of the parked coaches. He raced out from between the coaches and emerged at the rear of the depot. He could see a fire door to his right and he sprinted for it.

He could hear the Officers behind him but he didn't waste any time in looking backwards. His plan now was to keep moving as quickly as possible. If they caught him then at least he had tried his hardest to escape. He continued running for the fire escape and he raised a foot at the opening mechanism and kicked the door open. The cold air hit him and he raced for the fence at the back of the yard at the depot. A number of containers were positioned along the rear fence but they were quite high. Then he spotted a large refuse container and he headed for it. He quickly hooked his back pack over his shoulders and leapt onto the bin. In one movement, he launched at the high interwoven wire fence and dropped over to the other side. By now the Officer that was immediately behind him was also on top of the bin. He was being joined by other officers and Robert allowed himself to turn around briefly. He had made a little ground on the Officer in pursuit and then he raced away as fast as he could.

He found himself in a small business park and he was immediately aware that the road he was on probably led back to the dual-carriageway where the remaining officers would be waiting. He came to a junction with two possible routes. A turn to the right would lead back to the main road and probably to the Police. He ran to his left and deeper into the business park. A number of large warehouses were scattered around the park on both sides of the small road on which he was now running.

He could hear the shouts of the officers behind him and he could sense the sound of a fast-moving vehicle that had turned into the business park. He became aware of the blue flashing lights of the Police van behind him and he darted to his right and into the premises of an insurance company. He raced across the small car park and down the side of the large office building. When he reached the rear of the building he was faced by another fence only this one was much too high to climb over and it was topped by razor-wire. He turned to look at the building which was his last remaining hope of escape. He climbed onto a window sill and shimmied along to a drain pipe. He leapt onto it and proceeded to haul himself up the wall. The first Police Officer was now directly beneath him.

'Stop – NOW.' Screamed the officer.

Robert continued to climb and the Officer was now joined by his colleagues. Robert maintained his ascent and didn't stop to communicate with the Officers. He continued upwards and the Officers continued to shout at Robert as he rose further up the building. The Police van had now appeared and all its occupants were gathering below.

Robert was now approaching the top of the building and one of the officers had climbed onto the same sill that Robert had only a few moments before.

Robert felt that his recapture might be imminent but still he climbed upwards. He thought that there might be another route off the building. He was sure that the Police would have every exit covered now but he felt that perhaps he might be able to clear the tall fence at the rear of the building from the roof.

Robert was cold and afraid. He didn't even want to think of what his heart rate was. He reached the top of the drain pipe and looked down. He froze for a moment and knew that if he fell now he would suffer serious injuries at best but the fall would more than likely kill him. He gritted his teeth reached out for the top of the flat roof. There was a large overhang and Robert knew that he would have only one chance and there would be no way he could return to the safety of the drain pipe once he'd committed himself. Robert put one hand, then the other one on the roof and dangled for a moment. He had to summon all his remaining strength to haul himself onto the roof.

Robert reached the top and rolled onto his back. He looked to the sky and sucked in hard for oxygen. He looked over the side of the building and he couldn't believe that he'd climbed so high. The Police Officer who had given chase had now given up his pursuit and had climbed back down to safety. Robert climbed to his feet and looked around quickly for another possible route off the building.

He couldn't see any other way and he ran to the rear edge of the building. He looked at the fence and guessed it would take an Olympic athlete all his strength to make the jump. There were trees at the other side of the fence but even if he made it he could not guarantee a safe landing.

He sat for a moment and listened to the Officers below.

'Stay where you are. The building is totally surrounded by Police and there is no chance of escape.' Shouted one of the officers.

Robert gave no reply but he sat and gathered his thoughts. He remained in place, checking periodically over the edge of the roof to see if anyone was making an attempt to climb up to him.

Robert felt his chances of escape starting to ebb away. His energy levels were sapped. Lactic acid started to build up in his muscles and he started to ache. He lay down again and thought about his next move. He stood up again and looked over at the fence. He knew that it would take an extremely fast run up but that would give him no guarantee of clearing the razor wire.

Robert sat down again and went over his options. He concluded that there were really only two. Wait here until he was eventually recaptured or risk his life and make the jump. He sat down again and returned to his thoughts. He heard more sirens approaching from the dual-carriage way and he knew that more officers would be on site soon.

He noticed that the sirens were from a fire tender that had entered the business park. It was being followed by another Police van and a Police patrol car.

Blue flashing lights now filled the immediate area and the fire tender was being positioned. Fire fighters were deploying a large extendable ladder towards the roof of the building. Two uniformed officers were on the ladder and behind them was a plain clothed officer. The ladder reached the top of the building and the officers stepped out onto the roof, followed by Paul Bretherton.

Robert raced to the rear edge of the building and the Officers shouted for him to stop.

'Stay where you are.' Shouted Robert. I'll make the jump; I swear to god I'll do it.' Robert started to walk backwards to make room for his run up.

'Robert stand still. I think you might be innocent.' Shouted Paul.

Chapter Eighteen

Robert stared at Paul Bretherton and wasn't sure if he'd heard him correctly.

'What did you just say to me?' Robert demanded an answer and held his stare in Paul's direction.

'Robert stay calm, I know you've had a traumatic experience.' Replied Paul who was sure that his comments wouldn't have helped.

'Traumatic?' Replied Robert. 'Traumatic? You could put it that way. How come it has taken this long to work it out?'

'Robert I know what you've been through but there is some new evidence that has come to light.' Paul knew that Robert was going to take a while to come to terms with the events of the last few weeks.

Anything he told him now was probably going to be met with more questions and Paul anticipated this. However, Paul had a little more bad news for Robert before they could proceed with proving his innocence.

'Robert, I know what you've been through this past few weeks and you have many questions. Officer please can you put the cuffs on him. Sadly, I'm afraid that, innocent or not, it's still illegal to escape from prison and I'm going to need to re-arrest you. You understand that I needed to have you restrained in case the news sent you over the edge.' Paul laughed.

'So what happens now?' Robert asked, still in shock from his ordeal.

'Now Robert, I take you down to Radley Street and get you cleaned up. We've got a great deal of paperwork to get through. Then there's the prison, you've upset a lot of people today Robert.' Paul joked with Robert but there was a serious tone to his statement.

'I really don't care.' Replied Robert. 'Just promise me you won't be taking me back to prison tonight.'

'No. You'll be a guest a Radley Street tonight Robert.' Smiled Paul.

'You are joking, aren't you?' I'm afraid not Robert. And sadly, I'm afraid I will need to return you to prison first thing in the morning. We've got much to do tomorrow and you'll will be in front of the Prison Board in the next forty-eight hours or so, if not sooner.' Paul said.

Paul led Robert to the waiting patrol car and protected his head with his hand as he guided him into the back of the car.

'Cheers, lads. Good work tonight.' Paul thanked the officers and fire fighters for their efforts in recapturing Robert Easton and then he climbed into the back of the car next to him.

311

Back at Radley Street Paul reminded Robert that there were formalities to attend to and that it may take a couple of days to resolve. He would need to be returned there and the Prison Board would be sitting in judgement on him

Robert, however, was more interested in the new evidence that had come to light. Moreover, he wanted to know why he had to go back to prison again.

'I came across the new evidence tonight when I was going through the national crimes database. It turns out that our friend John Huggett had an uncle who was murdered a couple of years ago. The database didn't reveal any connection back then but it has since been updated and we can confirm that John Huggett's uncle was murdered by a gang of three men. When I contacted the station that made the arrest I was lucky enough to find an officer involved in the investigation on duty. We spoke for a while and it looks like these men were after some kind of information from his uncle. He told police there was a notebook that he posted to John Huggett and we're convinced that this is what they wanted when they murdered Huggett.' Paul could see that Robert was bursting to speak and he paused to allow him to say what he clearly needed to impart.

'I don't believe it. I found a notebook at the scene of the accident.' Robert blurted the information out as quickly as he could. He was sure now that this would be crucial to the investigation but not only that, it would almost certainly prove his innocence.

'Do you still have the notebook?'

'It's in my bag next to me.' Robert quickly searched through his back pack and produced the notebook.

He placed it on the desk in front of Paul Bretherton and Paul smiled broadly.

'This is perfect – well done Robert. How did you know that this was going to be crucial evidence?' Asked Paul.

'Well I didn't really.' Robert offered his reply. 'I had completely forgotten all about it at the time of the accident. If I'd known, it would have been this important at the time of my arrest I would have remembered. When I went over the wall I had to go home and collect some things and that's when I remembered it. Something told me that I should keep it safe.'

'Well I'm pleased you did. I've already alerted your solicitor and I believe the barrister who defended you will be preparing his appeal and would be presenting this first thing in the morning.'

Paul gave an honest response but reminded Paul that he was still under arrest at the moment and it would be best if he slept for now as they had a long day tomorrow.

Robert slept better than he had in weeks despite being in a prison cell at Radley Street Police Station. By the time he had awoken, Paul was already back at the station and was making phone calls prior to the day's meetings that he would be setting up for Robert.

He was also keen to set his team to work on a murder investigation that was now reopened. Robert stretched and he exhaled a sigh of great relief. He was still a little shaken from the night before and he was ravenously hungry.

Fortunately, Paul appeared at his cell door at that moment and had some breakfast waiting for him. He asked Robert to eat for now while he went through some paperwork. He reminded Robert that he was still under arrest and would be returned to prison. He advised him that he could be there for a number of days before an appeal could be lodged with the Crown Court.

'Why do I have to go back to prison and why do I have to go back to court if you think I'm innocent?' Robert demanded and answer.

'Well two reasons really. Firstly, your barrister Mr Silkin QC, will be wanting to lodge your appeal. This is likely to take only a few days and with the new evidence you can expect a very speedy decision.' Paul offered a response.

'And the second reason?' Robert was quick to remind Paul that he'd told him there was a second reason for his attendance in court.

314

'The second reason is what I went over with you last night. You see, escaping from prison is a crime in itself and this is what we need to address.' Paul went on to describe what the process would entail.

'I have already spoken with your brief James Wilbert and he says that Mr Silkin will be asking the judge to consider a sentence of time already served.'

Robert remembered the young solicitor from his trial and he knew exactly what the term 'time already served' meant, but despite feeling pleased and relieved, he felt cheated that the last few weeks had been taken away from him. However, he kept reminding himself that he was lucky that Paul had taken the time to work on his case and he felt sure he would be thanking him in the next few days for that.

'I've been on the phone to the Prison this morning and the Crime Prosecution Service. I've told them that you're back in custody. I've also spoken with James Wilbert and he'll be along shortly.' Paul said.

'OK no problem. Have you any idea what he'll need from me?' Enquired Robert.

'Yes he'll need you to go over a few points with him. He'll be accompanying you and I on our way back to the Prison at about eleven o'clock.' Paul replied.

James Wilbert arrived at Radley Street a little after ten o'clock and asked the Reception desk constable if he may speak with DS Bretherton. Paul quickly appeared and escorted the young brief through to his office. Paul Bretherton went over the new evidence with James Wilbert and then he took him straight to the cell to see Robert. Robert rose out of his chair when he saw James Wilbert enter the cell.

'I'm pleased to see you again James.' Said Robert, looking James directly in the eye and he offered his hand.

'It's good to see you too.' Replied James. 'Although I wasn't expecting to see you again this quickly.' James said whilst wearing a somewhat wry smile.

'What will be happening in the next few days after I'm returned to prison? Robert asked.

'As I'm sure the good DS here has already explained, you are still technically a convicted criminal and still on the run. I will be presenting the fresh evidence this morning to the prison board but we still have to go through this process. Later this week Mr Silkin and I will be formally lodging an appeal on your behalf to have the conviction overturned.

'Does that mean by lunchtime I will be back in prison again?' Robert hadn't dared think about that until now.

Paul explained to Robert that he would still be escorting him to the prison along with one of his uniformed officers. He outlined that they would need to be there until the formalities has been dealt with.

The three men sat in Fulton Prison reception area. Robert sat motionless and went over the last two days in his head. He wasn't sure if it all had actually taken place. There was so much information and so much trauma that his mind became swamped with fear, anxiety and elation. He felt ambivalent although he was powerless to stop the horrific elements of his experiences that were manifesting themselves as vivid images in his head.

He was rescued from his thoughts by a Prison Officer who had presented himself at the door.

'The cell is ready now.' Uttered the middle-aged prison officer who was pristinely dressed in his prison officer's uniform.

Paul and James briefly went over some of the protocols again that they'd explained in the car to him on their way to the prison. All three men stood up and Robert was led back into the prison.

James Wilbert said that he would be speaking to him again in the next few hours. Robert was told that he would remain in solitary confinement and would not be allowed to return to his original cell – this was normal prison protocol following an event such as this. He was separated from his belongings and he was told that they would be retained along with those that were already at the prison. Robert was led down a corridor that he had not seen before. He noticed that a Royal Crest bearing the words Dieu Et Mon Droit, which Robert knew meant 'God and My Right. This was attached to the wall and Robert studied it as he passed by.

James Wilbert visited Robert in his new cell briefly and said that he would be returning later or tomorrow to represent him at the prison board which would be convened as a matter of urgency. Soon after, Paul and James returned to Paul's office in Radley Street in the Police patrol car that was driven by the uniformed officer who had taken them to the prison. James Wilbert explained that he had all he needed and would be lodging the appeal once he and Mr Silkin had prepared everything they needed.

'Will you be needing the notebook, only I've retained this as part of the new investigation?' Paul asked, holding aloft.

'No I shouldn't expect so.' Replied James. 'We'll be in touch if we need it but I think we've got enough.' James' reply satisfied Paul and he placed the notebook back onto the desk.

James excused himself and said, he'd be in touch once they had a firm date for the appeal.

Paul sat down and started to go through the pages in the notebook. He wondered about Robert for a moment and how he would be feeling. He had an overwhelming sense of responsibility for him but he satisfied himself that his work the previous evening would be enough to free him. He expected that his ordeal would be over in a short time, in a few days he would be collecting him from prison and reuniting him with his belongings.

Robert lay in his cell and looked up at the ceiling. For the first time in weeks he was able to have time to himself to properly absorb what had happened to him. He tried to compartmentalise all the events in his life leading up to this moment since he ran down John Huggett. He wanted to box up every single second of it and lock it away forever. He was grateful that he was able to apply rational thought to his circumstances without having to worry about other prisoners or from being recaptured by the police. However, despite feeling that he was close to the end of his ordeal, he knew that he still had one hurdle to clear.

The hardest thing for Robert now would be having to wait for James Wilbert and Mr Silkin to build the case for his appeal. Once again he would be putting his life in the hands of his legal counsel but this time he felt more confident of a favourable outcome. As the days went by, Robert thought about his friends Reefer, Jono and Ticker and if they knew he had been recaptured. He expected that they would know but he felt frustrated that he couldn't speak to them. He wanted so much to talk to them and to thank them for what they did to help him.

Of course, there would be teasing and Robert would be subjected to friendly ridicule from his friends but

Robert wanted that. He wanted to apologise to Reefer too for not fulfilling his contract in getting Reefer's money to his wife. Robert decided that this would be one of his priorities when he was eventually released. Then his thoughts returned to Paul. He hoped that he would be looking after the notebook and he was excited about seeing it again. He knew that technically it didn't belong to him but it seemed to have suddenly become important to him and he wanted to know it was safe.

Three further days passed by and Robert remained in lawful custody at Fulton Prison in Peterborough. He had gone over every detail of his ordeal, from the accident to the trial and from his escape to his recapture. His thoughts now however, were firmly fixed on his appeal and how long it was going to take to prepare. Robert didn't like that he had to wait and not know when things would start to move for him. It was the not knowing he hated most of all. James had told him to be patient but the waiting was torturing him.

Robert had been incarcerated now for 4 days since his recapture and he lay on his bed going over dates and timings that he considered may come in useful for him when the formal appeal was finally convened. He could hear voices approaching his cell and he could recognise the voice of one of the prison officers. Robert sat upright on his bed waited for the door to open. The prison officer told Robert that he had a visitor and he prayed that it would be James Wilbert.

'Your brief has arrived and he's waiting to see you.' Said the prison officer.

'That's brilliant.' Replied Robert standing up and adjusting his clothing.

'Follow me then. He hasn't got all day.' Said the prison officer.

Robert followed the prison officer out of his cell and the officer waited for Robert to pass through and he closed the door of his cell behind him. They walked down the corridor and into an interview suite.

When Robert walked into the room he could see James Wilbert sitting at a table. James stood up and walked over to Robert offering his hand to him. They shook hands and James asked him to join him at the table.

'It's good to see you again Robert.' Said James. 'How have you been coping this past few days?' James asked.

'I've been fine, thank you, although I was beginning to wonder when and if I would ever see you again.' Robert replied, feeling that he may have sounded a little rude.

'Yes, sorry about the delay. You will appreciate that these things take time and trying to secure a date for an appeal at Crown Court is not a speedy process.' James gave an honest and frank reply.

'What... do you mean that you have a date already fixed?' Asked Robert, hopeful of a positive response.

'Yes we have a date set for a week on Friday but there's much more than that. We've also had the murder weapon re-examined and we have confirmed that there is DNA from both victims, Mr Huggett and his uncle. This proves beyond doubt that it is the murder weapon and this fresh evidence will almost certainly demonstrate your innocence.' James Wilbert delivered the pleasing news to Robert.

'I know I'm innocent, but will this be enough to get me pardoned?' Asked Robert.

'We'll probably ask your employers to confirm you were at work when Professor Montrose was murdered. This isn't necessarily essential to your case but it will help. Collectively, this will prove your innocence beyond all doubt but if you would like my opinion, the murder weapon alone suggests that your murdering both men is so mathematically remote, it's not worthy of consideration.' James hoped that this would be sufficient to satisfy Robert.

'In the meantime, we will be contacting your office again and hopefully they will give us everything we need to conclude it all in your favour.'

'What about my escape? Didn't you say that this was itself a crime?' Robert enquired, attempting to have all his questions answered before James left again.

'Yes, we are hopeful that this will be dealt with in the same session. Courts are on the clock most of the time and they are always trying to save money one way or another. This will be a 'no-brainer' for them and I expect it all to be wrapped up together.' James concluded his comments and started to place the documents he'd brought back into his folder.

'I need to be getting back now as I would like to speak to your office and I need to brief Mr Silkin before close of play today. Is there anything else you need to know about before I go?' Asked James, as he zipped up his folder.

'No, you've answered everything for me. Thank you for coming to see me. Will you be here next Friday?'

'No, you will be taken to the court and Mr Silkin and I will be there when you arrive.' James offered his hand and Robert showed his appreciation to his brief by gripping his hand tightly and looking directly at him.

For Robert, the next few days just melted into one another. Time dragged for him yet by the time the day of his appeal arrived, he felt that it had flown over. He waited in his cell and was dressed ready for the proceedings that were about to unfold in Crown Court.

One of the prison officers who would be escorting him to the court opened the cell door. Robert stood up and adjusted his shirt collar. He stood still and waited for the officer's instructions. The officer gestured to Robert to follow him and Robert duly obeyed. He thought for a second about looking back as he left hoping that this would be last time he saw the inside of a prison cell. However, he intentionally did not look back. Instead, he looked forward and walked purposefully out of the cell and down the corridor. Robert intended that this would be the beginning of a new chapter in his life and wanted no reminder of his last few terrible weeks.

The journey to the court was fairly quick and the prisoner transfer vehicle was able to negotiate the light traffic easily. Robert was escorted from the vehicle and he noticed several windows that looked out over the internal courtyard and one large door. He was led into the court through the large door and down a corridor and through another door which had its opening mechanism controlled from the other side by a police officer.

Robert was taken to a room that adjoined the court and he remembered it from when he had been there during his trial. He was told to wait and he sat between the two officers who would be escorting him when proceedings were to commence.

The Court Usher appeared at the door after a few moments and he was led up the small flight of steps and into the dock. Robert sat down and looked around the courtroom. He saw James Wilbert and Mr Silkin who both nodded to him as they caught eye contact. There was no prosecution in attendance and the seats where the jury had sat during his trial remained empty; he remembered James telling him that there would be no jury needed for his Appeal. He watched as members of the general public were filing in to view proceedings. The Court Usher and Clerk were in position and then they were all asked to rise as the Judge entered the Court. Robert stood flanked by the two officers and he looked around the room again. He felt tense despite James' previous encouraging words about the new evidence. He looked up at the gallery again and sensed that they were waiting for the drama to commence.

The judge sat down and Robert was asked to sit again and everyone else took their seats. Mr Silkin remained standing and addressed the Judge, Mr Justice Parsons.

'My lord, this is the Appeal hearing for my client Mr Robert Anthony Easton. Please may I deliver a brief opening statement my lord?' Mr Silkin asked.

'Proceed.' Mr Justice Parsons nodded in acknowledgement of the respect Mr Silkin had shown to him.

'I'm very much obliged my lord. Mr Easton, as my lord will know, has served a number of weeks at Her Majesty's pleasure in Fulton Prison. He was convicted of the murder of John Huggett and was sentenced to life imprisonment. I shall be presenting fresh evidence to the Court my lord which has since come to light and which demonstrates that my client cannot have carried out the crime. If it pleases the court I will also be seeking my lord's judgement in the matter concerning his recent escape from prison.' Mr Silkin delivered his opening remarks and looked up at the judge, seeking approval that he might be allowed to continue.

Judge Parsons signalled to the experienced Barrister that he may continue.

'Thank you my lord. My client, Mr Easton, was originally convicted on flimsy evidence and despite there being motive and intent, albeit equally flimsy, this was enough for the jury to convict him. Had it not been for his finger prints found on the murder weapon, it is highly doubtful that the jury would have been able to convict him. Mr Easton found the weapon outside his home. He was forced to pick it up after he found it blocking his driveway when he was trying to park his car.' Mr Silkin paused briefly and looked up at the judge.

'My lord, if it pleases the Court, I would like to call my only witness, Detective Sergeant Bretherton from Radley Street Police Station.' Mr Silkin once again looked to the judge for approval.

'Please call Detective Sergeant Bretherton.' The Court Usher announced.

A door opened and Paul Bretherton walked into the Court Room and took his place in the witness box. Paul was familiar with the procedures of the court and knew how to conduct himself whilst in the stand. Having been there many times throughout his career, Paul was accustomed to the standard protocols and he was 'au fait' with the unusual jargon sometimes used by those in the legal profession.

'Please state your name.' Asked the Court Usher.

'Detective Sergeant Paul Bretherton.'

The Usher handed Paul a copy of the Bible. 'Please take the bible in your right hand. Do you swear that the evidence you shall give to be the truth, the whole truth and nothing but the truth?'

'I do.'

'Detective Sergeant Bretherton, thank you for appearing today. I understand that you were at the scene when Robert Easton was apprehended on the roof of the building.'

'Yes, yes I was.'

'At the time, I understand that you said to Mr Easton that you thought he was innocent. Is that correct?' Mr Silkin was aware that his line of questioning might suggest that he was perhaps trying to discredit the Detective. However, he and Paul both knew that his method of questioning would see a swift end to the Appeal and Paul not only knew this, he was happy with it. This would see an end to Robert Easton's ordeal and it would finally confirm his suspicions.

'Yes, that's correct.' Replied Paul.

'Why did you think that he was innocent detective?'

'Even at the time of his initial arrest, despite the damning evidence against him, there was always some doubt in my mind. When he escaped from prison I continued with my investigation. On the evening of Robert Easton's re-arrest, I was using the HOLMES 2 database and this was when I made a crucial link.'

'For the benefit of the court, please can you explain what the HOLMES 2 database is?'

'Yes, my apologies, this is more commonly known as the national crimes database and it allows access for different Police Forces to retrieve information about crimes across the country. It stands for the Home Office Large Major Enquiry System.'

Paul started to explain how he discovered the connection between John Huggett and another man who had been murdered several months before, his uncle, Professor Stephen Montrose.

Paul went on to describe his findings to Mr Silkin. He explained that in the hours after his re-arrest, he had the murder weapon re-examined and this is what led him to his conclusions.

Mr Silkin made his final comments and summed up every piece of evidence that he, his junior counsel and Paul Bretherton had prepared. He delivered it to Judge Parsons and explained that his Appeal was drawn up and that this demonstrates beyond any doubt that his client was truly an innocent man.

'I've listened to the evidence and to your eloquent plea Counsel.' The judge began the formal part of his response that would lead to his binding judgement.

'I'm much obliged my lord.'

'The law is what it is. It is in place to protect and to serve all citizens. The judicial process is as robust and firm as it is needed and upheld. However, in your case it failed to find the true perpetrators of a heinous crime.'

Robert swallowed hard as the Judge continued to make his statement.

'Whilst this crime remains unsolved, it is clear that you were not responsible for it. It is the decision of this court that you receive a full pardon.'

Robert swallowed hard again and his palms began to perspire and he realised that he was no longer a convicted murderer. Judge Parsons continued with his judgement.

'However, this is not the end of the matter. There is another crime that has taken place and this is where the law and judicial system must be upheld. The crime of escaping from prison is a serious offence and despite your innocence, you must be punished for this offence. My judgement in this case is that you are sentenced to time already served. You are free to go.' The judge concluded his statement and banged his gavel. He rose from his seat and the Court was asked to rise as he left the Court Room.

Robert looked over to his legal representatives, Mr Silkin and James Wilbert and he signalled his thanks to them both. He then started to walk towards the same door from where he'd entered. He saw Paul Bretherton standing there and he continued to walk towards him. Paul raised his arms and embraced Robert.

'Come on, let's get you home. I've already got all your belongings in my car outside.'

Chapter Nineteen

Paul Bretherton drove up the driveway of Robert Easton's house. Robert thanked Paul for taking him home and he asked him if he'd like to come in. Robert walked into the cold house and Paul walked immediately into the living room and turned on his gas fire. Robert sat at his kitchen table and Paul turned on his electric kettle.

'I'm guessing you're going to need a really sweet cup of coffee?' Asked Paul.

'You got that right. I'm afraid I don't have any milk but I really don't care. Just make it hot and sweet please.' Robert said.

'Not a problem, I think I'll make myself one while I'm at it. Paul replied.

'Fill your boots, you deserve it. I never thought I'd end up saying this, after you first arrested me. But I owe you so much and I just hope I get the chance to show my appreciation one day.' Robert spoke compassionately.

'How about a beer in the Red Lion one day?' Paul asked.

'How about several. And tonight.' Robert said.

Paul laughed but told Robert that he needed to rest and said that their evening at the Red Lion would have to wait for now.

'I've applied for early retirement from the Force and I wanted you to know.' Paul said.

'Why did you do that?' Asked Robert.

'I've been thinking about it for a long time Robert, the events of the past few weeks have kind of sealed it for me. I don't want you to think that you were the cause, but you certainly helped in my decision making process.' Paul explained.

'As long as I'm not to blame for anything, I would hate to think that...'

Paul interrupted Robert.

'You've no need to worry Robert, I am not in any trouble. And as I said, I've been thinking about this for a long time now. My pension is waiting for me and I'm going to use my gratuity to help set me up in business as a private detective. I only have a short time left at work. I have several week's accumulated leave which I'm planning to take in the next few days and I wondered if you might like to help me?' Asked Paul.

'Me, but how can I help you?' Robert gave Paul a puzzled look.

'You strike me as a resourceful man Robert and I like those qualities. You seem to have a knack of thinking on your feet.' Paul continued.

'You can thank the British military for that Paul.' Robert replied.

'Yes, I thought you were going to say that.

Paul produced the notebook from his pocket and he placed it on Robert's kitchen table in front of him.

Robert looked at the book and he took hold of it. Paul asked Robert if he would like to see what it contained.

'I've had this locked in my office drawer for that last couple of weeks and I was hoping that you might want to explore its contents with me. Robert opened the book and slid it over the table so that they both could read it together.

Robert wondered if Paul would be looking for different things in the book. He sensed that Paul would be making mental notes about information that would lead to the real killers of Professor Montrose and Steven Huggett. Robert however, was becoming more and more intrigued by what he was reading and it soon became clear to him that the notebook had had the same effect on Paul.

'Are you finding this as interesting as me?' Robert asked.

'Yes I am. In fact, it's had me quite captivated for the past few days.' Replied Paul. 'I'm wondering what the anomaly is that the Professor found.'

Robert and Paul continued to flick through the pages of the notebook together. Every turn of every page held Robert's imagination as it had for Paul and his interest grew. Whilst they couldn't understand all the information, they could certainly follow what Professor Montrose was alluding to. They continued through the notebook and then started to read about the Tunnel that Sally and Cornelius had uncovered. There was an address for Blackfriars House in Northumberland and it explained briefly about the house owners Sally and Cornelius. Paul stopped for a moment and made a hand-written note of the address and the telephone number.

'I'll give them a call in a while, they're bound to know more information about the Professor and possibly even John Huggett.' Paul said. He went on to explain that he wanted to wait for Robert's release but that they should perhaps pay them a visit at some point.

Both Paul and Robert's excitement grew as they got deeper into Professor Montrose's research. They were captivated by the scriptures that had been left by William and about the treasures he referred to.

Paul could wait no longer and said that he wanted to call the Galbraiths now. He explained to Robert that it would be important to speak to them and that he should go to see them. Paul asked Robert if he would like to accompany him. Whilst it was a little unusual, under the circumstances he felt that it would be fine. Whilst Paul wouldn't be visiting as part of an official Police investigation, he was keen to view the tunnel for himself.

Paul picked up Robert's telephone and dialled the number for Sally and Cornelius Galbraith at Blackfriars House. Paul looked at Robert as he waited for a dialling tone. He pressed his forefinger into the handset cradle, ending the call, and he dialled the number again. He ended the call again and dialled the number a third time.

'Problem?' Asked Robert.

'Yes, it's a dead line.' Paul replied.

He checked the number in the Professor's notebook and dialled the number a fourth time.

'That's that then!' Exclaimed Paul.

'What's what? Enquired Robert.

'We're off to Northumberland. Something is not quite right. I doubt the Professor would note the number down incorrectly, and I cannot understand why the line's dead.' Paul said.

'Perhaps they changed it.' Robert offered a solution to Paul.

'Perhaps.' Paul paused for a moment. 'No. Why would they just change their telephone number?'

'There could be any number of reasons why they would change it. However, I'm starting to wonder myself now.' Robert said. 'When were you thinking about going up to Northumberland?' Asked Robert.

'I'll pick you up first thing in the morning.' Is 8am too early for you?' Paul asked, expecting him to be surprised.

'I'll be ready for 7.30.' Replied Robert.

Paul smiled at Robert. Robert offered his hand to the detective. He looked at him in the eyes and shook his hand.

'Thank you again for what you've done. I couldn't have survived in that place.'

'It's my pleasure Rob. You don't mind if I call you Rob, do you?' Paul asked.

'No in fact I prefer it. I was going to tell you that but you've beat me to it.' Robert said.

'I'll see you in the morning Rob.'

'I'll be ready. Hey are we going to be staying overnight up there?' Asked Robert, wondering if he should pack a small bag.

'That's a good point. We'd better pack for a couple of days.' Paul gave Robert the answer he was looking for and he headed for the door.

Robert woke early the next morning. He hadn't set his alarm as he knew he would be awake in plenty of time. He looked over to his small overnight bag that he'd packed the evening before. He shaved and showered, then walked downstairs to make himself a cooked breakfast. This was something he normally saved for weekends but he'd visited his local supermarket the evening before and decided to treat himself following his horrendous ordeal.

As he approached the bottom of his stairs he could see headlights moving in the window of his front door. Robert opened the door and could see Paul climbing out of his car.

'Morning Rob.' Said Paul as he walked up his driveway to Robert's front door.

'It's not even 7 o'clock yet.' Said Robert, tilting his left wrist towards him and looking at the empty space on his wrist.

'Yep. Couldn't sleep. Too excited I think.' Paul offered Robert an explanation.

'Well you'd better come in; I've not had breakfast yet. I've got plenty of eggs and bacon. Would you like any breakfast?' Robert asked.

'Rob, you read my mind.' Paul said, smiling at his new friend.

Paul sat at Robert's kitchen table as Robert cooked them both some breakfast.

'Rob, would you mind if I had another look at the Professor's notebook. I just wanted to go over a few things before we left?'

'Yes no problem it's in my backpack behind you. What you looking for?'

'Nothing in particular.' Paul said. 'But I was lying in bed last night and I was wondering about the symbols that the professor was referring to. It really didn't make any sense and I was wondering if you had given it any thought?'

'I was rather hoping that you were going to help *me* out with that.' Robert said, implying that he needed Paul's investigative prowess.

'I was trying to find some information about this Book of Clandestine Concealment too but could find absolutely no reference to it anywhere.' Paul was hoping for at least a little help from Robert but was disappointed again.

'It seems that it's so secret it doesn't even exist!' Robert concluded. 'But it must exist or the Professor wouldn't have made reference to it.'

'It's just the symbols he was referring to, appear key to his research. I'm hoping that the Galbraiths will be able to shed some light on it.'

'Yes I'm looking forward to meeting them, very much.' Added Paul.

Robert and Paul continued to chat while they ate breakfast and then decided it was time to depart. Robert locked up his house and climbed into the passenger seat of Paul's car.

Robert was excited about his journey North with Paul. Following his recent incarceration, he appreciated the countryside and the colours that adorned the scenery. He took in the wonderful views of the fields and the trees that appeared as silhouettes on the morning horizon.

He took out the Professor's notebook and he started to flick through the pages. He chatted with Paul about the startling information that the notebook had revealed to them and they were eager to view Blackfriars with their own eyes. However, there was still work to do and they hoped that the Galbraiths would help them. Not only were they keen to see what the professor had been referring to in his research but they were also keen to talk with the Galbraiths about the gang that had killed him.

Paul and Robert held their own reasons for ensuring that these men were brought to justice. Robert wanted it so that he could have some closure about his recent ordeal and that he may move on with his life. Paul however, had his own professionalism in mind and wanted justice so that he could restore and maintain his personal integrity; not that anyone in the Force had doubted it for a moment. Robert studied the page that held the information that the Professor had found from Fr Timothy in Cambridge.

The instructions in the Professor's notebook were simple. The Pine Tree and the Oliver Branch symbols are vital to locating the last piece of information that will reveal the site of what the professor was looking for. Robert explained to Paul that it should be simple enough to find.

'It says that the information is held on the internal west wall of St Oswald's Church in the Village of Plashetts in the northern reaches of Northumberland. Apparently, we will need to locate the Oliver Branch and Pine Tree which has been embedded into a stone in the wall.' Robert went over the instructions again with Paul.

'I wonder if the Monk had put the final piece of the jigsaw in the Church as an act of rebellion to the establishment of the day.' Enquired Paul.

'What do you mean?' Asked Robert.

'It's just that The Order of Preachers are a Catholic order and you can bet that the Church in Plashetts is probably Church of England.' Paul outlined his theory to Robert.

'That's a good point.' Added Robert.

'It would seem poetic justice and perhaps even a little mischievous victory for the Monks.' Concluded Paul.

Robert continued to read through the notes and he asked Paul if they might be able to go to the Church to see the clue for themselves.

'You bet we will.' Replied Paul. 'That's our first stop after we've paid a visit to the Galbraiths at Blackfriars.'

Robert and Paul continued on their journey to Northumberland. They discussed the notebook and they tried to guess at what they would find when they reached Blackfriars. They each tried to imagine the house and its immediate surroundings, curious as to its proximity to other residences.

As lunchtime approached, Robert and Paul approached the northern reaches of Northumberland. Robert checked the route that he and Paul had pre-prepared and he gave Paul his estimation that they should be seeing Blackfriars at any moment.

They both scanned the area intensely and were thrilled at the prospect of meeting the Galbraiths in their home.

'Look. Over there.' Shouted Robert. 'That's gotta be it.' Robert pointed to his two o'clock position and Paul quickly surveyed the area where Robert was pointing.

'That's it alright.' Paul replied. If that's not a 16th Century building, nothing is.'

Paul drove another two hundred yards and he turned into the driveway of Blackfriars house. Both men were utterly captivated by the old building. They tried to absorb the features of the old monastery dwelling and its surroundings. They remained silent until they drew up to the front of the house. They wondered if the occupants might have noticed their approach and guessed that they wouldn't have many visitors.

They exited the car and headed to the large front door. Paul commented that it seemed eerily quiet but proceeded to bang the iron door knocker heavily against its housing. The sound resonated throughout the building and Paul stood back away from the door waiting for the occupants to answer their call.

They both waited for a few seconds and listened intently for the sound of footsteps or for any other indication that people approached the door and were about to open it. It was only a few more seconds and they concluded that either no one was at home, or they hadn't heard the knock.

'I think it's safe to say that if they were at home they would have heard the knock.' Robert said flippantly.

They waited a little longer then decided to walk round to the rear of the property. Again, they received no reply from their knocks at the back door. Robert peered through the kitchen window and Paul cupped his hands and looked through the window into the dining room. Not able to see any movement they decided they would return a little later in the afternoon. For now, Paul suggested that they find some suitable accommodation for the evening. Robert checked the map again and suggested they continue in the same direction as they had been travelling and there was a small town only a few moments away.

After about 4 miles, Robert and Paul found the small town and they looked for a public house or inn. It only took a few moments before the Travellers Rest Inn came into view. They drove into the small car park at the rear of the Inn and wandered into the bar area.

'We're looking for a couple of rooms for tonight, do you have any vacancies?' Paul enquired, looking at the middle-aged woman behind the bar.

'Yes, that wouldn't be a problem, would you like two singles?' Asked the woman.

'Thank you yes.' Replied Paul.

'We were wondering if you were serving lunch yet too.' Asked Robert.

'Yes we are. The menus are on each of the tables, would you like something to drink while you decide?'

Yes, I'll have a lemonade please.' Said Paul.

'Make that two please.' Echoed Robert.

I was wondering if you've heard of a village called Plashetts.' Asked Paul. 'Only it's supposed to be fairly close to here, only a few miles away, but I can't see it on the map.'

'Can't say I have, sorry. Hang on I'll ask my husband he'll probably know.' Replied the Inn Landlady. She shouted through to her husband who was in a room behind the bar.

'Simon. Have you heard of a village called... sorry what was it called again?'

'Plashetts.' Interrupted Paul.

'Plashetts?' Answered the Landlord, as he walked in from the room behind the bar. 'Yes, I've heard of it.' He continued.

I was wondering if the place actually existed. I've been scanning this map for ages and I can't see it anywhere.' Robert said.

'Well, it kind of does and it doesn't.' Said the Landlord.

'What do you mean?' Asked Paul wearing a puzzled expression.

'It's just I hope you weren't planning on visiting it, that's all.'

'Why not?' Asked Robert.

'Because it's under about 300 million gallons of water. It was flooded and submerged when the reservoir was built.' Continued the Landlord.

'The reservoir?' Asked Paul.

'Yes, Kielder Reservoir. The people of Plashetts were bought out as part of the Reservoir project and the whole place was consumed when the reservoir was filled. It was about 30 years ago now. I think there are a couple of farms down there too.'

The landlord's words stayed with Robert and Paul for a while and there was a long pause while Robert and Paul looked at one another. They searched for a response in one another but it was Paul who finally broke the silence.

'Are you joking with me?' Asked Paul.

'No. The place was flooded when I was a young boy. I watched with my dad over the days and weeks as the water level grew higher. There was a lot of controversy over it at the time, but like my dad said, they had to build the reservoir somewhere and this was the perfect place.'

'Have you any idea how deep the village is?' Robert asked with an inquisitive expression that suggested he was plotting an idea.

'They reckon it's about 100 feet or so.' Answered the landlord. 'Why are you asking?'

'Yes. Why are you asking?' interrupted Paul.

'It's just that it sounds like the perfect place to go SCUBA diving. Wouldn't you say Paul?' Stated Robert who was now looking at Paul with a wry smile.

'You're not seriously thinking about going down there are you?' Asked Paul.

'No.' Robert answered and then paused for a moment. 'Not yet anyway. All my SCUBA gear is at home.' Robert continued and then searched for a reaction from Paul.

'Is there any end to your talents Rob?' Paul asked humorously.

'I've been SCUBA diving for years, it's probably my next biggest hobby, to that of keeping fit.'

'Surely you'll not be able to see a thing.' Enquired Robert.

'You'd be surprised.' Interrupted the landlord. 'I'm told it's supposed to be very clear and it's a very popular venue for divers. We get quite a few staying here and they come from all over to see the submerged buildings.'

'Either way, we still have a little work to do yet. We still need to speak with the Galbraiths.' Paul reminded Robert that they came here to meet Sally and Cornelius Galbraith and that he should wait until they had been to see them before he became too excited about diving.

Robert agreed but he explained to Paul that it might not be as ridiculous an idea as he was perhaps thinking. They both continued to chat more about Robert's proposal as they ate their meal. Robert outlined to Paul that he had been diving for many years. He explained that there were 5 recognised grades of diving standards and that he was at the fourth stage as an Advanced Diver. In reaching this level of diving expertise, Robert described to Paul that he had already been certified to plan his own dives and he had done so at a number of different sites and in different circumstances. He articulated to Paul that he'd had experience of using small crafts from which to dive and he'd also had experience of simple navigation. Of course, this wouldn't be needed for such a dive and locating the site of the village ought to be relatively easy.

Paul reminded Robert that whilst finding the site might be easy, locating the symbols and the monk William's final clue, may not be so straight forward. Both men continued to discuss the intricacies of the dive throughout the afternoon and early evening. They passed the time until they felt that, if Cornelius and Sally had been out for the day, now they would be back at home and this would be the best time to call.

Robert and Paul drove the short distance back to Blackfriars and they went over what they wanted to discuss with the Galbraiths one more time. Dusk had already descended over Blackfriars and as they entered the driveway, Paul and Robert looked for lights inside the building. They were now sure that with the limited remaining daylight, any occupants would almost certainly require to have some lights on inside.

Paul stopped his car at the front of Blackfriars and neither could see any lights inside the building nor indeed any evidence that they were at home. Still, Paul knocked on the large front door but he already knew that he was unlikely to receive any reply. Both men saw no reason to remain and they decided to return to their accommodation for the evening.

Back at the inn, they ordered drinks at the bar and located a table where they could discuss their next move. Robert retrieved the professor's notebook from his jacket pocket and they went over the professor's research in a little more detail. Unclear as to the Galbraith's whereabouts, and whether they should try again and return to Blackfriars the next morning, they continued to look through the book.

Paul wanted to go over the notebook in more detail and with a little more method. He felt that they may have missed something important and the investigator in him was telling him to start again at the beginning of the book.

Robert was more impatient. Paul found it mildly frustrating that Robert flicked through the pages with no appearance of any method at all.

'I'm sure that the professor wouldn't necessarily leave any clues as to the whereabouts of the Galbraiths in his notebook. After all, it contains all the key points of his research, so why would it.' Asked Robert, aware that he was perhaps irritating Paul to some degree.

'You need to start thinking like the professor Rob.' Said Paul, wondering if Rob understood what he was talking about. 'The professor would want to keep all relevant points together in his notebook. If he considered that the Galbraith's would be away from home and that they were key to his research, it would be in the book.' Paul continued.

'What about the address on the inside rear cover? I'm sure I saw a telephone number with it.' Said Robert as he quickly opened up the rear cover of the book to reveal the address he'd remembered seeing the day before.

'Give me the number.' Paul demanded as he took his telephone from his pocket.

'Are you going to ring them now?' Enquired Paul.

'Yes. At least we will know for sure if that's where they are.

'It has their name on the rear cover so they will have been there at some point in the past.' Robert said.

'What's the number and I'll give it a go?' Asked Paul. 'Don't worry, I'm not going to spook them, I just want to know they're there.'

'Ok the country code is 0033 and the number is 235 897 1359.'

Paul repeated the numbers back to Robert as he pressed them into his mobile telephone. Paul and Robert looked at one another as Paul waited for the ringing tone.

'It's ringing.' Paul said. The two men continued to look at one another and Paul waited for someone to answer. One ring, two rings, and third ring and no one came to the phone.

'It looks like there's no one at ...' Paul stopped talking.

'Hello.' Said the voice of the English-speaking man.

Paul immediately hung up.

'It was him, I'm sure of it.' Paul stated.

'Why didn't you speak to him?' Asked Robert.

'Like I said, I didn't want to spook him. There's every chance they're there in hiding and the last thing I want is them fleeing after hearing the voice of an English guy, asking questions.' Paul was direct in his reply.

'Ok, makes sense. So, what now?' Asked Robert.

Paul picked up the professor's notebook and looked at the inside rear cover.

'Now Rob old friend, we go to 2321 Rue de Vousiers, St Mourine in Lille, Northern France.'

Act Four – The French Connection

Chapter Twenty

The train carrying Robert and Paul trundled through the outer suburbs of the city towards central London. It had slowed significantly and now cantered along the tracks in an audibly symmetrical pattern. Several passengers had already risen from their seats and waited by the doors at the end of their coach. Other passengers were starting to prepare to alight the train and were beginning to collect their belongings. As the large passenger train approached Kings Cross Railway Station, Robert and Paul arose from their seats and collected their small holdalls from the overhead compartment.

Fully stopped, the doors of the train opened simultaneously and the passengers alighted onto the platform, heading for the exits. Some left the station, some turned right at the end of the intercity platforms seeking connections and some carried on ahead towards the London Underground and onto their final destinations.

Robert and Paul exited the station and made the short walk across the road to St Pancras Station. As they waited for a gap in the traffic Robert looked around him at the large buildings and at the many people that were going about their business.

A large and majestic station, St Pancras is the gateway to the continent from London via the Channel Tunnel. It is also the starting point for the Orient Express which Robert pointed out to Paul as they approached the station. They made their way up the flight of steps and into the upper section of the station, passing the meeting place statue, known to many as 'The Lovers' statue. Robert and Paul continued their way around the upper part of St Pancras, passed the Renaissance Hotel and found a small outlet to drink coffee while they watched the elevated large screen to indicate when they would be allowed to board.

The station was busy and Robert used the time to reflect on his recent experiences and he watched as the many commuters darted about the station in different directions, each with their own sense of purpose.

'You look like you're in a world of your own Rob.' Said Paul.

'You're not far wrong Paul. To be honest, I can't believe I'm sitting here. It seems like five minutes since I had a relatively hum-drum existence. Of course, I never realised that at the time, but now I feel like I'm on some kind of big adventure.' Robert replied.

'Perhaps you are Rob but I guess that's life.'

'Life!' Robert chuckled. 'And what is life, but a mystery between two secrets.'

'That's a good way to put it Rob.' Said Paul as he glanced back up at the large departures screen. 'I think that's us Rob, it says we can board.'

'Yep, Gate Two.' Robert confirmed.

Robert and Paul each took one more gulp from their plastic coffee cups and picked up their bags. They headed for Gate Two where they found their train. They made their way along the platform; more and more people joined them who, like Robert and Paul, searched for their nominated carriages. Robert and Paul finally arrived at Coach E and checked their tickets and allocated seat numbers once more. Once on board they secured their bags and located their seats opposite one another.

As the train pulled off from the platform, Robert and Paul watched as the familiar sights of London went by. They listened to the wheels on the tracks that echoed in the same audible symmetrical pattern that they'd heard when approaching King's Cross a short time earlier.

After only a few minutes the Eurostar Express started to pick up speed and they soon started to see more and more greenery as they left the City and entered the countryside. Another twenty minutes or so and the countryside had replaced walls of concrete which stayed in view for a few moments. Then there was darkness and they entered the Channel Tunnel. Robert didn't feel like small talk at this point. He explained to Paul that he'd had enough of walls and closed in spaces to last him a life time and preferred to sleep through this part of the journey. He closed his eyes and tried to rest.

Robert was awoken by the daylight that flashed at him as the train left the tunnel. Robert hadn't been to France for many years but the French countryside didn't seem too much different to that of England's. It wasn't until he noticed the occasional trading estate and factory buildings that displayed French names that he accepted that he and Paul were in France. They both looked out of the window and watched at the everyday life that went by.

It was only a short hop to Lille Paul reminded Robert. At that moment, the passengers were all notified of this by the audible message that sounded throughout the train.

'Mesdames et Messieurs, nous allons bientôt arriver à Lille.'

'Ladies and Gentlemen we will soon be arriving in Lille.' Repeated the announcement.

Robert and Paul could feel the Eurostar Express starting to lose speed and they remained in their seats until it became obvious to them that they were pulling into Lille station. Once the platform appeared next to the train they stood up and collected their bags from the luggage compartment at the end of their coach. They were among a small number of people who had risen from their seats, most of the passengers remained seated for the onward journey to Paris.

Robert and Paul exited the train and strode purposefully off towards the 'Sortie' signs indicating the exits. Outside the station they found a French taxi cab. The driver opened the back of the car and they placed their bags inside and climbed into the back seat.

'Bonjour Monsieur, Je voudrais aller à cette adresse.' Paul said, handing a small piece of paper to the cab driver.

'Oui monsieur.' Replied the driver, who studied the piece of paper before handing it back to Paul.

'I'm impressed.' Said Robert. 'I didn't know you spoke French.'

'I don't.' Said Paul, smiling at him. 'I was studying my French phrasebook while you slept on the journey through the tunnel. This is about the extent of my French vocabulary.'

Their journey took them through the town and onto a dual carriageway. After approximately fifteen minutes, the taxi turned into a street and stopped next to a house. Robert looked up at the number on the stone gatepost – 2321.

'Rue de Vousier.' Said the driver.

'Merci.' Replied Paul and he paid the driver the cab fare.

Once they had collected their bags, the car pulled away behind them and Robert and Paul looked up at the house. The property was reasonably small but it was detached from the neighbouring houses. It was painted completely white and it was adorned with white window shutters at all the windows. There was an iron gate flanked by two stone pillars and there was a small flight of steps leading up to the mahogany stained wooden front door. There was a window to the right of the front door and two further windows on the first floor. The roof had red tiles and it was topped by a red chimney. Robert and Paul could see that the property was well-maintained and was in excellent condition. They walked up the steps and Paul rang the doorbell. They looked at one another while they waited and after a few seconds they both heard footsteps that echoed down the wooden hallway.

The door opened and Sally Galbraith stood before them.

'Bonjour messieurs. Puis-je vous aider?' Sally asked if she could help them.

'I'm sorry to trouble you.' Replied Paul. 'My name is Paul Bretherton and this is my friend and colleague, Robert Easton. I'm sorry but I don't speak any French. We are trying to find Cornelius and Sally Galbraith'

'What can I do for you?' Asked Sally.

'Please don't be alarmed.' Paul immediately tried to reassure Sally and produced his Police Warrant Card. I am a Police Officer from England and I am trying to find information about the murder of Professor Stephen Montrose.'

'How did you find us here?' Asked Cornelius in a slightly raised voice and who'd approached from behind Sally.

'We're not here in an official capacity.' Paul offered this as a response but he felt that he needed to explain more in order to placate them fully. 'Robert here was originally convicted of the murder of Professor Montrose's nephew but he has since received a full pardon.'

'That's all very well, but it still hasn't answered my question about how you found us here?' Repeated Cornelius.

'Perhaps this will answer your question.' Robert produced the Professor's notebook and held it in front of him.

'My god.' Said Sally. 'Is that Professor Montrose's notebook?' Sally walked forward and reached out to accept it from Robert. She took hold of it and showed it to Cornelius.

'I haven't seen this for a couple of years. How did you come by it? Asked Cornelius as he handed the notebook back to Robert.

'I found it at the scene of an accident a few months ago.' Replied Robert. 'We were hoping that you may be able to help us find the killers of the Professor.'

'We believe that they are almost certainly responsible for the death of his nephew John Huggett too.' Paul interrupted.

'They?' Sally questioned.

'Yes we believe there were three men who had been following the Professor and we wanted to get as much information as possible.' Answered Paul.

Robert re-joined the conversation. 'But then after my release, we started to look into Professor Montrose's notes and we found some very interesting facts.

'Would you both like to come in?' Asked Cornelius.

'Thank you, we'd love to.' Paul said.

Paul and Robert followed Sally and Cornelius into the house, along the hallway and into their kitchen. The house seemed larger on the inside and it extended further back than Robert and Paul had first thought. Sally made coffee for Robert and Paul and invited them to sit at the kitchen table.

'You've no idea how pleased we are to see that the Professor's notebook is safe.' Said Sally.

'And we're equally eager to find the real killers of the Professor.' Said Cornelius. 'That's one of the reasons we've been living here for the past couple of years. We've been following the investigation and the Police have kept us informed but they've found nothing yet. And by the way, you've no idea just how fascinating those interesting facts in the notebook actually are.'

'We've attempted to further the Professor's research but it's been hard going having to work from here.' Sally said. 'We've enlisted the help of a local historian here. Her name is Louisa and she's something of an expert in the Tudor Dynasty.'

'I imagine you'll want to get back to Blackfriars – it would be easier to continue with the research from home. It looks like a lovely place.' Robert said.

'You've been to Blackfriars?' Asked Cornelius.

'How does the place look?' Enquired Sally with a more excited tone than Cornelius.

'It looks to be in good shape and it's a very nice house.' Paul said.

'It's our home and we want to go back.' Said Cornelius. 'But the thought of those three men you speak of and who are still at large scares us.'

'Well it's this that they're after.' Paul said, lifting the Professor's notebook from the table.

'Yes, and I understand it contains the key to finding what we and the Professor were looking for.' Cornelius said.

'Can we see what it is please?' Asked Sally.

'Yes of course.' Said Paul. 'However, I'm afraid that this is not the final piece of the jigsaw.'

'What do you mean?' Asked Cornelius.

'Do you want to tell them, or shall I?' Said Paul, whilst glancing to Robert.

'Tell us what?' Asked Sally.

'Rob and I aren't sure exactly how much you know about the Professor's research or indeed about the visit to the Order of Preachers?' Paul Asked.

'The Professor and I visited the Order together in Northumberland. Sally and I know just about everything except what the Professor found at Blackfriars in Cambridge. We were going to visit there ourselves but we haven't dared venture out of France. Besides, the Order are very secretive and I doubt we would have got anywhere with them. The only reason the professor was successful was because of his close friendship with the head Friar there.' Cornelius offered a full account of his and Sally's understanding of the Order of Preachers.

Paul turned to the page where the Professor had detailed his findings at Blackfriars, Cambridge. He

361

reminded Sally and Cornelius of the Olive Branch and Pine Tree symbols and that they would be key to the final clue they needed.

'Yes, yes, we know all that. But what did the book of Clandestine Concealment yield for us?' Cornelius asked.

'Basically, it said we would find the information we needed on the internal west wall of St Oswald's Church in Plashetts Northumberland.' Paul stated.

'So, what's the problem? We go to the Church in Plashetts and find the information, right? Cornelius offered the solution to Robert and Paul but he held a puzzled expression for them. 'Wait a minute, you're not saying it's been demolished, are you?' Cornelius continued.

'No, it's there alright.' Paul said. 'It's just that it is sitting at the bottom of Kielder Reservoir.'

'You're joking me right.' Cornelius added.

'That's what we said when we found out.' Said Robert.

'Well we'll just have to borrow some SCUBA gear and go down to find it, won't we?' Said Sally.

'We?' Said Cornelius. I'm not sure we should be going back there just yet.'

'Darling, we've been here long enough. I don't want us to be here any longer. We're prisoners here and

362

we shouldn't have to live this way. Please let's go back. Please.' Pleaded Sally.

Cornelius knew that Sally was right. Despite thinking that he was Sally's protector, deep down he also wanted to return to England and to their home, Blackfriars.

'She's right Cornelius.' Said Paul. 'You can trust the Police and you can be assured that every force in the land will be looking for these men. I think it's time you went home and finished the professor's research.'

Darling, why don't we chat about this later? I'm sure Robert and Paul will want to rest after their journey. Perhaps you'd like to have dinner with us tonight? Sally asked.

'Wow yes that would be lovely. Thank you.' Replied Paul. 'We just need to sort ourselves out some accommodation. Do you know any good hotels in the area?

'Yes there are plenty.' Said Cornelius. 'But Sally and I would like you to stay with us.'

'Yes we'd love to have you stay with us, we've room for you both.' Agreed Sally. Darling, can we invite Louisa over this evening for dinner tonight too? It will be good for her to meet Robert and Paul.'

'Good idea, I'll give her a call. Shall we say 7pm?'

'Yes that'll be perfect. It will give you two a chance to freshen up. You must be hungry?' Asked Sally.

'Starving.' Added Robert. 'And can I just say how much I, I mean we, appreciate your hospitality. It's really very kind of you.'

It's really no problem. We're delighted to have you stay and we're looking forward to chatting about the professor's research. We've so much to talk about and so many gaps to fill in.' Cornelius made Paul and Robert feel at home. 'You'll probably want to know more about the tunnel too.'

'Yes, indeed we do. We were so excited about seeing it when we visited Blackfriars. You can't imagine how disappointed we were when we found out you weren't there. Robert said.

Cornelius asked Robert and Paul if they'd like to go and freshen up. He showed them to their room and gave them a guided tour of the upstairs so they could navigate their way around.

After they'd been showered and unpacked, Robert and Paul made their way down to the kitchen and they could hear people talking. They wandered in and were met by Cornelius.

'Hi fellas. Sally and I would like you to meet a good friend of ours. Louisa, this is Paul and Robert from England.'

Cornelius and Sally had met Louisa soon after arriving in France following their hasty exit from England.

They had met her by pure chance in the local library when they were trying to expand on the Professor's research. When they noticed, Louisa reading a book that had been written by the Professor, they struck up a conversation. In a very short time, only a matter of days, Louisa, Sally and Cornelius had become great friends and Louisa had become immersed in their research and had developed an insatiable appetite for helping them. Louisa and Sally had become very close and would often go shopping together and even went to Paris together on a number of occasions for shopping excursions and to the theatre.

'Good evening.' Said Paul, rather formally. 'I'm very pleased to make your acquaintance.' Paul offered his hand to Louisa and she shook his hand firmly.

'Pleased to meet with you Paul.' Louisa said in near perfect English.

'You speak very good English.' Paul said.

Then Louisa turned to face Robert. They held their gaze on one another for a moment longer than would be considered polite. Then Robert offered his hand to Louisa in an attempt to resolve the awkwardness.

'Hello my name is Robert. It's very nice to meet you.' Robert introduced himself, while fixing his gaze on Louisa once more.

They shook hands and Robert felt a bolt of electricity shoot through him as they touched hands for the first time. Louisa had a natural beauty about her. She was 5 feet 4 inches tall, had auburn hair which had a natural waive and fell to her shoulders. Her fringe hung low, almost covering her beautiful brown eyes. Robert could see immediately that she was slim, with a good figure.

Louisa was born in the Lille area and had grown up there. She was 28 years old and a school teacher in the local school where she taught English and History. She had studied English and Medieval History at University in Paris before moving back to Lille. She was single, and despite her having a few brief relationships in the past 5 years or so, she had never found the right man for her and felt that she never would. She wanted to find someone with not only good looks, but someone who shared her love of history and of the outdoors. She craved adventure; her and Sally had often talked about the man who would fit the bill and fulfil her dreams.

'I'm Louisa, it's very nice to meet you Robert.'

'You speak very good English Louisa. Have you lived in the UK at any time in the past?' Asked Robert.

'No, I studied English in school and I have only visited England on a few occasions and each time, only briefly.'

Robert and Louisa continued to chat with one another and became oblivious to Sally, Cornelius and Paul.

'What brings you to France Robert?' Asked Louisa, demonstrating a clear interest in everything Robert had to say.

'I'm here with Paul on, I suppose on what you could call business.'

Sally interjected at this point.

'Louisa you'll be very interested to see what Paul and Robert have brought with them.'

'Oh really, what is that?' Enquired Louisa.

'They have the notebook that belonged to Professor Montrose.'

'Mon Dieu.' Exclaimed Louisa, forgetting her English for a brief moment. 'I have only heard about this and cannot believe that you have it. Cornelius and Sally thought that it was lost. How did you come by it?'

Robert and Paul went through the events of the last few weeks, between them relating everything to Louisa from the accident that injured John Huggett, his subsequent murder and to Robert's wrongful imprisonment.

Louisa was saddened by Robert's ordeal and she offered her sympathy to him, exclaiming that it must have been quite harrowing for him. Nevertheless, she was delighted to see the notebook. She explained that she had been assisting Sally and Cornelius for some time with their research and Sally added that Louisa was something of an authority on Tudor history.

'I once had the pleasure of meeting Professor Montrose at a history seminar. I read some of his work when I was studying too and I am so pleased that you have brought the book with you.'

Louisa displayed genuine interest and gratitude towards Robert and Paul. She also displayed genuine interest in Robert and she hoped that her initial excellent impression of him was mutual.

There was no doubt about that and the others could sense it too. Sally watched for a moment as Louisa and Robert chatted. Louisa had become a close friend to her over the past few months and whilst she felt she should be prepared to protect her feelings, she felt happy that she had found someone with whom she could relax.

Sally and Cornelius liked Robert and Paul; there was a genuine sincerity about them both and Sally had always relied on her excellent judge of character. Over the years she felt she could see a person's true values through their eyes and expressions.

She was certain that Robert had many virtues and she was in no doubt that he was a very attractive man. She would never admit this to Cornelius with whom she was in love with and adored. However, she saw much good in Robert and she hoped that something may develop in between him and Louisa. Sally thought for a moment about how she might act as a catalyst in that process and became inwardly angry with herself, for thinking such a thing. If anything was to develop between Robert and Louisa, she would welcome it, but she would not be responsible for it.

'May I see the book please Robert?' Asked Louisa, in an accent that Robert hung on.

'Yes certainly.' Said Robert, racing to get the notebook from the table so that he was able to hand it to her personally.

'Why don't you sit here Louisa, and Robert you can sit here next to Louisa to help her navigate through the pages?' Sally was angry with herself again but then dispelled all those thoughts and smiled as Robert and Louisa hitched their chairs closer together and closed the gap between their shoulders until they were almost touching.

Louisa placed the book on the table and Robert took it in both hands and opened it for her. They started to flick through the pages and Robert outlined what he knew about it. Louisa expertly filled in the gaps from her own knowledge, gradually taking over the conversation. Robert became captivated by her obvious understanding of the Professor's notes. Her friendship with Sally and Cornelius had provided her with the information about William and the tunnel. This, coupled with the professor's notes and her own research, collectively gave them a much greater understanding.

Louisa wondered about the Professor's findings in Cambridge and asked if the details were contained in his notes.

'This is where things go slightly awry Louisa.' Cornelius said. The information we needed is in the notebook but sadly there is still more to discover.'

'I don't understand, what do you mean by this?' Replied Louisa.

Robert leapt to answer Louisa's question.

'The answer is in the notebook here.' Robert turned to the page in the Professor's notes that detailed his findings from his visit to Blackfriars Priory in Cambridge.

'The Professor found that the last piece of the jigsaw is inscribed in the walls of St Oswald's Church in the village of Plashetts in Northumberland.' Robert spoke carefully and precisely so that Louisa could take in the place names.

'Plashetts? That is an unusual name. It is so exciting, when do you plan to visit?' Asked Louisa.

'Well there is a little more to it and things are a little more complicated I'm afraid to say.' Said Paul.

'How are they complicated? I do not see any complexities, like Robert says, this is last piece of the jigsaw.' Replied Louisa simplistically.

'Plashetts village was lost when a huge reservoir was created about 30 years ago. The village is now under water.' Paul gave her the news that he thought might answer her question.

'Oh I see.' Replied Louisa. She stayed silent for a moment and then spoke again. 'I still don't see the problem and certainly cannot see any complications. Perhaps we may need some additional towels to dry ourselves. Or are you saying that the church is no longer there?'

'No, it's still there. It's just that it's at least 100 feet under the surface of the water. It will require a specialist dive team to find the information we need.' Paul said. 'Robert is qualified to dive to that depth, but he cannot go alone.'

'Then I should bring my SCUBA gear with me and Robert and I will dive together.' Louisa said, looking at Robert.

'You can dive?' Asked Robert.

'I have been diving for many years Robert. My father first interested me in diving when I was 15 years old and I have been qualified to dive for many years.'

The others looked surprised at Louisa's revelation and that someone so slightly built could be involved in such a strenuous and masculine activity.

'I'm impressed.' Robert said.

They all sat for dinner that evening and discussed their options. Paul was intent on returning to the UK as soon as possible and wanted them to concentrate their efforts in finishing the research. He hoped that if they returned to Blackfriars, this may draw the gang of 3 men from hiding and bring them into the open. Of course, he didn't want to draw the others into danger and this was a concern for him.

Robert, Sally, Cornelius and Louisa were all in agreement and all felt that they should return. They continued to discuss their options and made their plans for returning. They all chatted late into the evening until they decided to meet again to continue discussing it the next morning.

Sally called a cab for Louisa and when it arrived Robert said that he would see Louisa safely inside. Robert held the cab door open for her and Louisa kissed him on both cheeks.

'Goodnight Robert.' Said Louisa. 'It was very nice to meet you.'

'Night Louisa. It was lovely to meet you too. I'll look forward to seeing you in the morning.' Robert replied.

Robert waved to Louisa as the cab drove off, not sure if Louisa had seen him standing. Louisa meanwhile, sat in the cab and smiled to herself.

Chapter Twenty One

The following morning, Robert woke early but he felt refreshed after sleeping well. He looked over to Paul who slept in a single bed at the opposite end of the room. Paul was already awake and was sat up making notes in a small book.

'How did you sleep?' Paul asked.

'Not bad thanks, and you?'

'OK thanks Rob. I'm just making some notes that I want to pass onto the Police when we get back. I want to go back to Blackfriars more than anyone but I think it will be wise to alert the Police as to our plans. As soon as we're back in the UK, I will get in touch with the office and they'll notify Northumbria of our plans.' Paul highlighted to Rob his strategy and hoped he would understand why he wanted to take this course of action.

'That's a good idea Paul. Do you think the 3 men will try to follow us?'

'I have no idea Rob, but I'm not taking any chances,'

'Thanks for that. I'm glad you're here and I bet Sally and Cornelius are too.' Robert said.

There was a knock at their bedroom door and it quickly opened. Cornelius entered and said that he'd heard them chatting.

'Sally and I were wondering if you two would like some breakfast before we make a start.' Asked Cornelius.

'That'd be great. Thanks, Cornelius.' Robert said.

'We'll be down soon, just want to have a quick shower.' Added Paul.

Downstairs, Cornelius and Sally continued their own discussion that they'd had in bed before going to sleep. They had gone over their plans again and again and Cornelius had asked every possible question he could. When Paul and Robert joined them at the kitchen table for breakfast they continued to discuss the pros and cons.

Paul was quick to allay Cornelius' fears and this placated Cornelius enormously. Robert remained a little quiet but he had thoughts of Louisa on his mind, and wondered when the French beauty he'd met the night before would be arriving.

They all ate breakfast and as they were finishing, the telephone rang. Sally rose from the table to answer the telephone that was attached to the wall in the kitchen.

'Bonjour.' Sally said. There was a short pause while Sally listened to the person who had just called. 'Oh good morning Louisa, how are you this morning?'

Sally reverted to her native tongue as she knew Louisa preferred to talk to her in English. Despite being quite fluent, Louisa always liked to speak in English so that she could practise her conversational language skills. However, she had another reason which was that she did not want to appear rude to Cornelius who had never learned more than the very basics of French.

'Oh I see, I hope it's all ok. I'll ask him if you like, I'm sure he'll be delighted to help.' Sally held the telephone to her chest and looked over to Robert. 'Robert, Louisa has been looking at her SCUBA diving equipment and she is a little worried that one of her valves on her oxygen tanks may be faulty. She wondered if you might like to take a look at it for her.' Asked Sally, who wore a half smile aimed in Cornelius' direction.

'Yes I'd love to. Is she bringing the tank over here?' Asked Robert innocently, hoping that he would be asked to go to her house.

'No I'll drive you over there.' Sally replied.

'That would be great.' Robert said quickly.

'Louisa, we'll be across in about 30 minutes if that's ok.' I'll bring Rob over myself.'

Sally ended the call with Louisa and asked Robert when he would be ready.

'I'm ready when you are.' Robert replied.

'If it's ok, Paul and I will stay here making some arrangements for the trip back to England.' Cornelius said.

'Yes that's fine darling. Do you think we will be able to get back this week?' Asked Sally.

'I was hoping that we might go back in a couple of days. I was hoping that we might travel on Saturday. How does that sound to you honey?' Asked Cornelius.

'It sounds wonderful darling. Thank you, I can't wait to see the old place again. I'm so excited and it's been too long.'

Sally and Robert climbed into Sally's car and drove the few miles to Louisa's house. Robert's heart pumped a little faster on the journey and when they arrived at Louisa's house, it had raced to a much faster pace.

The house was very quaint Robert felt. It was beautifully designed and despite looking small, it was extremely clean and looked almost new. It was built from red bricks and had a beautiful wooden door painted in high gloss red paint. The small garden looked very well-tended and Robert thought it looked exactly like the property one would expect a school teacher to own.

Sally drew the car to stop outside Louisa's house but she did not turn off the engine. She looked over to Robert and asked him to just go up and knock.

'Won't you be coming in too?' Robert asked.

'No I have to pop into town to pick up some things. It's ok, Louisa's expecting you.' Sally suspected that Robert felt uneasy about going into Louisa's house alone.

'Ok, I'll see you later, Sally. Thanks for dropping me off. Will you be returning after your trip into town?' Robert wondered if Sally would be returning so that she could take him back.

'No I wasn't planning to, but I will if you want me to. Tell you what, why don't you get Louisa to call me if you need a lift back, but I'm sure she will bring you back over.'

Robert thanked Sally again and got out of her car. He made his way up the garden path that was flanked by neatly prepared borders containing colourful shrubs. He knocked twice on the red door and waited. His heart was beating so quickly that he didn't notice Sally driving away behind him.

Louisa opened the door and she smiled sweetly at Robert. Robert sensed that Louisa was as equally pleased to see him as he was to see her and this had an immediate calming effect on him.

'It's very good to see you again Robert, and thank you for coming over to my rescue.' Louisa said in her now familiar French accent.

'Please call me Rob, and if I may say, it is very good to see you too Louisa. You have a lovely home.'

'Please come in. Can I offer you anything to drink?' Louisa asked.

Robert thought about Louisa's offer for a moment. He tried to figure out what the French would drink in the morning when visiting someone. He didn't want to embarrass Louisa by asking for tea, if this was something that the French rarely drank. However, Louisa came to Robert's assistance and she asked him if he would like coffee.

'That would be great, thanks Louisa. May I have it with milk but without sugar? Thank you.'

'Yes of course. So how are you this morning?'

'I'm great thanks.' Said Robert. 'I slept well and Paul hardly snored at all.' Said Robert, smiling at Louisa, hoping that she understood his attempt at mild humour.

'I'm pleased you slept well and I'm pleased that Paul had clear sinuses last night.'

Robert followed Louisa through to her small kitchen. Inside the kitchen, there was a small table against one wall and the units looked fresh and clean. The work tops looked pristine and everything had its place. Robert was impressed by Louisa's tidiness and he had always felt that this reflected on the person. A neat and clean house represented a person whose life was ordered and functional. This was one of the things that his military training had taught him.

'I was very impressed that you liked SCUBA diving. I hope you don't mind me saying, but there are not many women in the UK who enjoy it.'

'I've loved it for years.' Louisa responded. 'I'm pleased that we have something in common Rob.'

'Me too.' Said Robert. 'Sally said that you'd had problems with one of your tanks.'

'Yes Rob, would you mind looking at it for me? If you'd like to follow me into my garage, you can take a look while the water is boiling for your coffee.'

'Lead the way.' Robert said.

Robert followed Louisa into her garage and she took him to a cabinet that housed her SCUBA equipment.

'It is this tank Rob. I think the valve is perhaps faulty.'

'Let me take a look.' Robert said reassuringly.

Robert took hold of the cylinder and he tried to operate the valve. He opened and closed the valve a number of times and eventually it released and the remnants of oxygen that was contained in the tank escaped through the valve.

'There you are. That seems to have shifted it. I have had this problem before with my own tanks. When they are stored away under pressure for a length of time, the pins inside the valves tend to stick.'

'Do you think it will be ok now?' Asked Louisa.

'Yes I think so, but it may be worthwhile having it checked when you have it filled next.' Robert tried to reassure Louisa and he was careful to recommend having her equipment checked properly before using it again.

'I think the water will be boiled now.' Louisa said. 'Let's go and have some coffee, shall we?'

Louisa thanked Robert for his help and she led the way back inside the house.

'I was very excited to hear about the Church that is under the water in the reservoir. Wouldn't that be wonderful to go and see it?' Louisa asked.

'Yes, but I suspect that the others have some reservations about making the dive. I was wondering if we should try to convince them that you and I should make the dive together.' Robert asked, hoping for a positive response from Louisa.

'Rob I would love to come. I have dedicated much of my life to history. To be a part of this research seems like a dream come true for me.'

'I don't think that the others will take much convincing. You seem to be the most qualified of us all. You know the history of the Tudors; you've met the Professor and know his research well. And to top it all, you're a qualified diver. You seem to fit the bill perfectly.' Robert said. 'Perhaps we can go across this evening and chat to the others about it. How does that sound?' Asked Robert

'Oh I was rather hoping that you would like to have dinner this evening. I would like to show you the sights of my town.'

Robert's heart almost leapt out of his body.

'Wow, I don't know what to say. I'd be delighted to have dinner with you what a lovely idea.' Robert was truly broadsided but he was so happy. He was flattered and could not believe his luck. He considered Louisa to be quite incredible. She was beautiful, sexy, intelligent, friendly and loving. She seemed almost too good to be true and Robert was completely smitten.

'Perhaps we could drive back to see Sally, Cornelius and Paul and discuss arrangements with them about returning to the UK. Then later, we get dressed and you and I could have dinner this evening.' Louisa hoped Robert would like her suggestions; she would not be disappointed.

'I love that idea. I'm looking forward to getting back to the UK and to continuing with the research. But I have to say that I am looking forward to us having dinner together most of all.'

'What a lovely thing to say Rob. Thank you.'

Robert and Louisa chatted for another hour or so. They were not short of things to say and they found endless topics of discussion. As they chatted they learned more and more about one another. They realised they had so many common interests, they even had similar ideals.

'Shall we take a drive over to see the others now?' Louisa asked.

'Yes I'm ready when you are Louisa. I have to say, I'm quite excited about going back up to Northumberland and seeing this tunnel that Cornelius and Sally have uncovered.'

'Yes me too, I'm also excited about getting my diving gear out again. It'll be fun for you and I to see this village that has been under water all this time. I wonder what the visibility is like.'

'According to a man who lives in the local area, it is a popular diving site for recreational divers, so I'm hoping that the visibility should be quite good.'

Robert and Louisa drove the short distance to Sally and Cornelius' house on the other side of the town. Robert used the opportunity to compliment Louisa's town. He remarked on its natural beauty and that it had been largely untouched by commercialism. He commented that it must be the perfect place to live, being so close to a wonderful city such as Paris, but just far enough away to be able to enjoy the peace and tranquillity that it held. This pleased Louisa enormously; she was happy that Robert had recognised this and she was fiercely proud of her beloved Lille.

When they arrived back at Rue de Vousiers, Sally's car was already parked up, having returned from her shopping excursion some time earlier. Louisa and Robert made their way up the small flight of steps and Louisa knocked briefly on the front door before opening it and walking inside. This was something that Cornelius and Sally had previously insisted upon and that Louisa was always to make herself at home there. It had taken some time for Louisa to become accustomed to this but now she accepted their hospitality as normal.

'Hey you two. Have you had a good day?' Asked Sally, curious as to how Louisa and Robert had dealt with their first time alone together.

'We've had a… how should I put it… a very fruitful meeting.' Said Louisa whilst smiling at Sally.

'Oh. That sounds very promising.' Replied Sally, smiling equally as much to Louisa.

Robert seemed to be innocently unaware of what Sally and Louisa were up to. However, it was quite clear to Cornelius and Paul that Sally and Louisa were communicating in a language all of their own.

'Yes. Rob was able to fix my faulty breathing apparatus. It was a sticky valve. Hopefully I will be able to use my tanks now in Northumberland.' Louisa scanned for a response in the others, wondering if they would agree.

'Sadly we won't be able to take your gear over or indeed, under the channel. Robert explained to the others about the international shipping laws on taking dangerous good such as pressurised containers across borders. 'You can use mine – I have a spare set of tanks.'

'Thanks that would be great, I will just bring my suit and mask.' Louisa said.

Paul said that he and Cornelius had been discussing their entry back into the UK and when they should go.

'I'm pleased you've decided to come Louisa, I was thinking that you might need to be persuaded.' Paul said.

'Yes, we're delighted that you want to come with us. Paul and I were almost at the point of drawing straws as to who would be having a crash course in diving. Are you sure you won't mind Louisa?' Cornelius added, aware that he was asking Louisa to do something he felt he should be doing.

'Are you two joking? I wouldn't miss this trip for all the World. When can we leave?' Louisa was pleased that she wouldn't have to convince the others that she should go. She was doubly pleased as her skills as an accomplished diver made her feel valued and part of the team.

'I think we should leave tomorrow morning. Paul and I have been checking the trains and there is a Eurostar with spare seats leaving tomorrow at 10am.' Cornelius looked up for a response from Sally.

'Let's start packing then.' Sally gave Cornelius the answer he was looking for. 'I'll make dinner for about 7pm tonight then we can have some rest.

'Don't worry about dinner for Rob and I. I promised to take him into Lille to show him the sights and we will find somewhere in the town for dinner this evening.' Louisa said whilst trying not to sound too obvious.

Sally looked at them both and smiled.

Chapter Twenty Two

Robert's taxi drew up outside Louisa's house and he felt as nervous as he had the first time he arrived there. He fretted that he wouldn't be dressed appropriately, having not brought many changes of clothes. He felt that he might be too casual, or indeed that he was not sufficiently casual enough.

He paid the cab fare and walked up Louisa's pathway. Before he had the chance to knock the front door opened and Louisa greeted Robert with a large smile.

'I've been watching for you coming and saw your cab arrive.' Louisa said, glancing to one side, giving away her eagerness at seeing him again.

Robert felt immediately at ease and he wondered how she always had this ability to do that. All his fears of being inappropriately dressed had been dispelled by Louisa and he felt totally at ease.

'You look great.' Robert said, wondering if he'd been too forward.

Louisa wore denim jeans, which also pleased Robert as this is what he'd been forced to wear. He wondered whether Louisa had perhaps done this purposefully, thinking Robert might have travelled light. She wore a lilac blouse and Robert was truly smitten with what stood in front of him.

'You don't look bad yourself Rob.' Louisa said, making him feel yet more comfortable. 'In fact you look quite handsome.' Louisa said, smiling sweetly at him.

'Are we ready to go? Asked Robert.

'Yes, I won't be a moment, honey.' Said Louisa as she disappeared inside the house. 'Please come in.' Louisa continued as she walked along her entrance hallway.

Robert loved her choice of words. He chose to wait in the hallway for Louisa to return. She returned only a few seconds later and told Robert that she was ready to go. Robert repeated his earlier compliment to Louisa and she thanked him again.

Louisa told Robert that she'd ordered them a cab and that it would collect them from the small bar at the end of the road in an hour to take them into town.

'I thought it would be a good idea to have a small drink before we went into town. I hope you didn't mind me taking the liberty to order the cab from there.' Louisa asked.

'Not at all, what a fabulous idea. Thanks Louisa.' Said Robert.

Robert and Louisa walked along the road and chatted while they walked the short distance.

'I must say it's really good of you to invite me out with you tonight.' Robert said, hoping that he would live up to Louisa's expectations throughout the evening.

'I'm loving it already.' Said Louisa.

'I was wondering if you might like to tell me more about you.' Asked Robert

'I think you know quite a lot already.' Joked Louisa. 'But yes of course, what would you like to know about me?'

'Well you have such a lovely name and I was wondering what your surname is?'

'Ahh, how nice of you to say. My family name is Arnoult. This is a fairly popular surname in France.'

'Yes I think I may have heard it before. My family name is Easton.'

'Oh like the famous singer Sheena yes? Louisa's comment made Robert smile.

Robert felt at ease once more and again, he revelled at Louisa's ability to do this. They continued to chat as they wandered along Louisa's road. Robert glanced at the houses as he chatted to Louisa. He equated the street to that of a typical English one, only the houses seemed more individual, but they were all well-maintained and there was absolutely no litter, anywhere. Robert joked with Louisa about this and she agreed that this was something that she didn't like about England. However, she loved it and its heritage which she described was how she came to research and become somewhat of an authority on the Tudor dynasty.

When they reached the small bar, Robert held the door open for Louisa and invited her to go in first while he waited. This was something that she had not witnessed for a long time and she adored this quality in Robert. Inside he quickly regained ground so that he could reach the bar slightly ahead of her.

'What can I get you to drink Louisa?'

'Oh, please may I have a small glass of red wine?'

'Je voudrais deux petite vin rouge, si vous plait.' Robert tried out his very basic conversational French. It was not perfect but the man behind the bar understood his request and was pleased that the man who was clearly English had made an attempt to speak his language. Louisa also appreciated his efforts and she told Robert that he had done very well.

'You seem to have many talents Robert.' Louisa said, grinning at him.

'I'm afraid my French is rather weak to say the least. But I find it's very rude of the English who often expect foreign people to speak English in their own country. This has always irritated me and I find it embarrassing to be English sometimes.'

'Perhaps you will let me teach you some French Rob. I would be delighted to help you learn if that is what you would like to do.' Louisa was impressed by Robert's description of his own countrymen. Louisa loved England and the one and only gripe she had was when they generally didn't try to speak other languages. Only very few people she knew, like her friend Sally and to some degree Cornelius had made some effort. Now that Robert had made this observation she was even happier with him.

Louisa and Robert found a small booth and sat down together. Louisa hitched herself closer to Robert as she had when they'd first met at Sally and Cornelius' house. She took out a small notepad from her handbag and she began to write a few basic rules on the French language. While Louisa made her basic list of French vocabulary rules, Robert looked at the way her hair fell onto her shoulders. Occasionally he would glance at her notes and then his gaze would return to her face and eyes. Aware that she had noticed him staring, he quickly returned his attention to her writing.

Louisa smiled inwardly and knew that Robert had been looking at her. She was truly flattered and delighted by Robert's attention, but didn't say so.

Meanwhile, Cornelius, Sally and Paul prepared for their journey back to England the following day. They arranged for 5 single tickets to take them from Lille through the Channel Tunnel and into St Pancras in London. Thereafter, they would travel north, stopping so that Paul could collect his car and more clothing. They would also stop over at Robert's and collect his SCUBA diving equipment so that he and Louisa could make the dive down to St Cuthbert's Church in Plashetts.

Sally had prepared them some dinner and they chatted over their plans while they ate. They agreed that they would stay at Blackfriars as there was more than enough space for all of them. Paul highlighted to Sally and Cornelius that he was excited about seeing their tunnel for the first time and it would be interesting to see where they had found William's parchments. Paul still had the murder investigation firmly implanted in his mind, but he was allowing himself this period of excitement that was enveloping them all at the moment.

Louisa and Robert had travelled into Lille and Louisa had selected one of her favourite restaurants for them to eat while they continued to get to know one another. The next few hours also held enormous excitement for Louisa and Robert but they were momentarily enwrapped with their growing relationship to provide any thought for what the coming days would bring. Louisa was surprised at herself; only a short time ago she would have been taken over with enthusiasm for what has been forefront in her mind for a number of years now.

However, Robert was sat in front of her now and at this moment, despite only meeting him a short time ago, she was the happiest she'd been for as long as she could remember. Robert had similar emotions and he was still counting his blessings after his recent ordeal that he'd communicated to Louisa.

Louisa had been very forward leaning throughout his recount of events over his recent weeks. Robert had also described to the enthralled Louisa, his earlier years in the British Army and his time on the support team for the Special Air Service. The time seemed to rush by for them both and they were surprised to see that it was already 10 pm. They decided that they should be getting back and they booked a cab to take them both directly to Louisa's and Robert would make the short journey onto Sally and Cornelius' house in the same cab.

They arrived a short time later and Robert asked the driver to wait while he saw Louisa to her door. Louisa was once again impressed by Robert's manners.

'I hope that you've had a good time tonight and that I wasn't too much of a bore for you.' Robert asked.

Louisa took a step closer to Robert and leant forward to indicate to Robert that it was time to kiss her on the cheek as he remembered was customary for the French. As Robert leaned forward to kiss Louisa on the right cheek, she moved to face him. With their eyes firmly connected, they were only one or two inches from one another. Slowly they both moved forward and kissed one another passionately on the lips.

'Does that answer your question Robert?' Whispered Louisa.

Robert reopened his eyes again.

'Yes it does. Thank you Louisa, I had the best time ever and I think you are absolutely incredible.'

'I can't wait to see you tomorrow honey.' Louisa said those words to Robert again that meant so much to him.

Robert felt that he'd known Louisa for years and waved to her from the cab as it pulled away.

The following morning Robert awoke early again as he had the previous day. He looked over to Paul who was already awake.

'Morning Paul. Today's the day then.' Robert spoke quietly so as not to wake the others in the house.

'Morning Rob. Yes, today's the day.' Paul replied.

'What time are we due to leave?' Asked Robert. 'Is it on the 10am train you mentioned yesterday?

'Yes. It's just gone 7.30 and if you'd not awoken by 8am I was going to have to wake you. We have a cab booked for 9.15 to get us to the station. I think Sally is collecting Louisa at 8.15 and bringing her over here.'

Robert immediately remembered his evening with Louisa. He lay back down and looked up at the ceiling. He was feeling very pleased with himself and tried to recall every part of the evening. He quickly showered and dressed and walked downstairs. He wandered into the kitchen where he heard Sally and Cornelius chatting.

'Good morning Rob.' Said Sally. 'How was your evening? Asked Sally, having gone to bed before Robert had returned.

'It was great thanks.' Replied Robert, not knowing if Sally was referring to their meal or to his relationship with Louisa. Robert suspected however, that it was very much the latter.

'I'm going over to collect her soon. Would you like some breakfast before we set off? Asked Sally.

'Oh yes, please. I'm ravenous.' Replied Robert.

Cornelius wished Robert a good morning and said he'd cook him eggs and bacon while Sally went over for Louisa.

'Sally and I like Louisa a lot. She's a good friend of ours. I think you already know that she's very fond of you Rob. We don't want to pry or to preach at you Rob but all we ask is that you look after her feelings.' Cornelius made a genuine but passionate plea to his and Sally's new friend. 'If it's any consolation to you, we hope you two hit it off, we really like you too Rob mate.'

Robert thanked Cornelius for his honesty and said he would tread carefully and would act as a true gentleman at all times.

'I can't promise to keep my hands off her when we get under Kielder Reservoir though.' Robert's joke was well-received and Cornelius laughed.

A few moments later Paul joined them in the kitchen and after a few more moments Sally returned with Louisa. Robert raced to the door and asked if he could help with Louisa's luggage.

'Morning Louisa.' Said Robert. 'How are you feeling this morning?'

'Morning handsome.' Replied Louisa, as she walked up to Robert and kissed him on the cheek.

Robert tried to hide his embarrassment from Sally but she came to his rescue.

'It's ok Robert, Louisa told me that you'd both had a really lovely evening.' Said Sally, whilst winking at Robert.

Robert felt at ease again and he walked round to the rear of the car to retrieve Louisa's bag. He followed Louisa and Sally into the house and joined everyone in the kitchen.

'I guess we're all set to go.' Said Cornelius. Then he turned to look at Sally. 'I've ordered a cab honey; it should be here in the next ten to fifteen minutes.'

''Is everything locked up?' Sally asked.

'Yes I've just about finished that. I'll turn off the heating and power when we leave, then it's just the front door.' Cornelius pointed to the pair of suitcases that stood in the corner of the kitchen close to the door.

'That's everything we arrived here with. It seems mildly ironic that we're going home with the pretty much what we came with.' Cornelius sounded quite matter of fact but he sensed that Sally was more reticent and he decided that he should be a little more tactful.

Robert came to Cornelius' rescue and suggested to the others that they might want to collect all the luggage and place it near the front door while they waited for the taxi cab. Paul and Louisa agreed and they helped Robert start to move the luggage. They left Cornelius and Sally to finish their final items on their check list that they'd hastily prepared the night before.

Cornelius hugged Sally while Paul, Robert and Louisa carefully stacked the luggage at the front door. He reassured her that this was the right decision and that this time they would return to Blackfriars and put an end to the ordeal that had driven them from their home. Then they could start where they'd left off and try for the family that they'd dreamed of.

'We've got some unfinished business with a guy called William first.' Said Sally whilst smiling at Cornelius. 'Come on darling, let's get the place locked up and go home.'

Cornelius could see that Sally's eyes were filled with tears. He wiped away a small tear that had formed and ran down her face. He kissed her gently on the cheek and told her that everything was going to be ok.

'The cab's here.' Louisa shouted from the door.

'It's early.' Said Sally. 'Well no time like the present. Let's get going.' Sally gave Cornelius a reassuring smile and he was reminded why he loved her so much.

Robert and Paul loaded the luggage into the small minibus while Cornelius and Sally locked the door. They all climbed aboard the minibus and Louisa huddled up close to Robert. She took hold of his hand and placed her head onto his shoulder. Cornelius and Sally took their seats and looked up at the house as the cab drove away.

They arrived at Lille station in ample time and decided to have coffee at one of the large station's cafes while they waited. After their coffee, they decided to wait on the platform for the train's arrival. The station felt cold to them and there was a stench of spent diesel that clung to the air. The imminent arrival of the train attracted more people to the platform. A number of small groups started to form and people who were travelling together made conversation with one another. When the Eurostar Express arrived, Robert, Louisa, Paul, Cornelius and Sally watched as the train slowed and they searched for their coach. Once the train had fully stopped they walked towards the front of the train and boarded coach B. Paul, Cornelius and

Robert loaded all the luggage into the compartment at the end of the coach while Sally and Louisa located their seats.

Robert was pleased to see that Louisa was seated and she signalled to him that she had saved the seat next to her for the journey into the UK. Sally checked her small bag to ensure that she had replaced hers and Cornelius' passports that had been checked on entering the platform and they all waited for the train to move. As it started to roll, Sally grabbed Cornelius' hand and he gave hers a reassuring squeeze. The train cantered from the station and started to gather speed. Once away from the suburbs of Lille, the powerful engines of the Eurostar Express roared into life and it was soon at full speed, racing towards the tunnel that would lead them back into the UK.

Louisa watched the French countryside rush by and she felt happy. Not that she was leaving France or because she was going to England, but she felt a strong sense of purpose and that she was doing something meaningful and exciting. More to the point, she was doing it with a group of people that she liked and with whom she felt at ease with. She was with Robert too and despite knowing him for a very short time, she felt she had been with him for much longer.

Robert flicked through a French newspaper that someone had left wedged between the seats. He made an attempt to understand the words and felt he was doing reasonably well but knew he had much to learn about the French language. He noticed many of the words were similar to their English counterparts and some even had the same spelling. Louisa watched Robert as he struggled his way through the article he was reading. She felt it amusing as she watched him but she also felt so much affection for this man whom she met a short time ago. Robert noticed Louisa watching him trying to read the article and he smiled at her. He put the newspaper down, took hold of Louisa's hand and they both returned their gaze to the passing countryside.

The train continued to hurtle through Northern France and all five of them returned to their individual thoughts. Paul whose career with the Police Force was in its terminal stages, wondered about the gang of men who remained on the run and how he might assist the Police with their investigation into the two murders that had taken place. His thoughts dwelled on what was contained in the Professor's notebook and how it might be used to draw the gang back into the open.

Sally and Cornelius were thinking about Blackfriars, the home that they'd left behind and to which they were now returning. They wondered about the condition of the house and its furnishings. However, their thoughts were more centred on the tunnel that lay beneath Blackfriars and which wound its way off under the Northumberland landscape. They thought about William and what secrets he may be about to reveal but their thoughts also kept returning to the three men who had killed their friend Professor Montrose - and his nephew

John Huggett. Robert and Louisa thought about little else than one another and their blossoming relationship.

After a few more moments, the countryside was replaced by sections of concrete walls which darted passed the windows at great speed. Then there was darkness and the train entered the Channel Tunnel. Louisa closed her eyes and rested her head against Robert's shoulder.

When Louisa woke again she glanced at the window and noticed that they had exited the tunnel and were approaching the city of London. The suburbs drifted past the window and she was aware of Robert's reassuring arm around her.

'Hello sleepy head.' Robert said, as Louisa battled to regain her full senses.

After a few seconds, she regained her full awareness and she remembered the man who sat embracing her. She smiled warmly at Robert.

'Hello, have I been sleeping long?' Louisa said.

'Almost the whole way back since we left France. I hope you feel ok after your sleep, you must have needed it.' Louisa warmed to Robert's words.

'Are we in London yet?' Asked Louisa.

'Yes, these are the suburbs of South London, we should be arriving in about ten or fifteen minutes.'

Robert's estimate was confirmed by an announcement to all the passengers and that they should remember to collect all their personal belongings before leaving the train. Sally and Cornelius were preparing all their hand luggage and Paul had already done this and was ready to leave. Louisa asked Robert to retrieve her small bag from the overhead compartment and she packed away a book into her bag that she did not get the opportunity to read.

As the train slowed, Robert looked out of the window to see the huge imposing sight of Kings Cross that sat adjacent to St Pancras station. He signalled to the others that they were close to arriving at the station. The Eurostar pulled into St Pancras and slowed to a gentle stop.

Louisa stepped from the train and became immediately aware of the magnificent architecture of St Pancras. She cricked her neck slowly backwards to look up at the huge domed ceiling. Louisa was impressed by the size of the structure and she commented to the others about how humbling it was.

They all made the short walk across the busy road and between the black cabs on the taxi rank and into Kings Cross railway station. Louisa noticed that it was not as resplendent as St Pancras; nevertheless, it too left her feeling humbled by its size.

The journey North by train to Robert's would take them only a short time and they had decided to all stop there to allow Robert to collect his SCUBA gear. Thereafter they would all travel on to Northumberland using Robert's and Paul's cars. Robert felt excited about showing Sally and Cornelius his home. However, it was Louisa that he was most keen to impress. Robert felt it strange that he was not concerned about showing Louisa his home. In the past he would have been reluctant to show someone for whom he held so many feelings his house without first having ensured it was immaculately prepared. However, Robert had never held these feelings for anyone else before and was not remotely concerned about inviting Louisa into his home. He simply knew that she would be impressed and that she would accept it as she found it. Robert somehow sensed that she would be happier that she'd been invited into Robert's house than she would be with its condition.

Robert was right. As they exited the taxi cab with their luggage, Robert watched for Louisa's reaction as she looked upon his home for the first time. Louisa had tried to veil her outward expression, but she felt that she might have failed. Robert watched as she smiled when she saw his home. Robert's house was not particularly striking, nor did it stand out from the other properties in the immediate vicinity. It was modest and well kept; it appeared to be in good condition and Louisa smiled. Not because of its individual qualities, but because she knew that this would be exactly the house that belonged to this man. This man that had captured her heart and with whom she felt completely relaxed and comfortable.

Sally assessed Robert's house in the same way that an estate agent would when making an initial valuation. Whilst not as grand or as unusual as Blackfriars, it was a very modern, medium sized detached property comprising one large window downstairs and a blue front door at the right-hand side at the front of the house. The upstairs had two smaller windows and the roof and guttering looked to be in excellent condition. There was a garage at the right-hand side of the house which was at the top of a slightly inclined driveway leading to a blue garage door. The garage was separated from the house by a small external passageway that led to the rear of the house and garden.

'You have a lovely home Robert.' Sally exclaimed.

'Thank you Sally. It's nothing quite as beautiful or unique as yours but it's home.' Replied Robert.

'Don't they say that an Englishman's home is his castle?' Louisa showed her approval of Robert's humble but well-presented house; she gave him a reassuring embrace, placed her arms around his waist and rested her head against his arm. 'I love your house Robert, it is beautiful. I am so pleased that I have seen it.'

'So are we going to get a guided tour?' Asked Sally.

'There's no time for that.' Remarked Paul, hoping his comment had been received light heartedly. 'We've got to get our skates on if we're to make it up to Blackfriars before nightfall.'

'You're right Paul.' Said Cornelius. 'Let's get the SCUBA gear together and we'll collect your car.'

Robert invited Louisa and the others into his house and he brought all his SCUBA equipment into his front room. He and Louisa rummaged through it to ensure they had arranged what they needed. Robert suggested that they probably need only one tank each and they prepared weight belts and the other associated items of equipment that they would require for the dive at Kielder Water.

Cornelius, Sally and Paul watched as Robert and Louisa went through their checks like a pair of seasoned SCUBA diving professionals and Sally noticed how good they looked together while making their preparations.

Once completed, Cornelius took out the Professor's notebook from his pocket and he held it aloft in front of his four friends. He was afraid that his next comments would sound a little melodramatic, but he felt they should be said and that the words were appropriate.

'Tonight we go home and we uncover secrets that have lain for nearly 500 years.'

Act Five – A Helping Hand from William

Chapter Twenty Three

Two cars headed to Northumberland. Robert drove his own car that contained all the SCUBA gear that he and Louisa would need for the dive at Kielder Reservoir. Louisa sat by his side. Robert was pleased that he had Louisa with him and pointed out sights to her they drove. Louisa was equally delighted to be in the car with Robert and to be together with him brought a lasting smile to her face. Whilst she enjoyed the company of her friends, she'd craved more time alone with Robert since they'd met and she was loving their journey together.

Meanwhile, Cornelius and Sally were being driven by Paul and they chatted about the latest findings of Professor Montrose in his notebook. Cornelius pointed out that Louisa and Robert would soon be searching for an Olive Branch and a Pine Tree and that they would hopefully resurface from their dive with the final piece to the ultimate jigsaw puzzle.

'I'm so excited about getting back to Blackfriars. I can't believe we have been away for so long.' Cornelius' comments pleased Sally and she allowed herself to dream about their home again.

Sally had tried not to think about Blackfriars and the happy life that she and Cornelius had left behind. When they first escaped to France, Sally had thought about Blackfriars frequently and she'd soon learned to stop thinking about it as it made her more upset each time.

'You've no idea how pleased I am too; nothing will tear me away from there again. It's our home and we belong there.' Sally spoke forcefully and she knew that Cornelius would never try to counter argue when she was in this determined frame of mind.

'If I may say I'm looking forward to it too.' Added Paul. 'I have only seen the external parts of your home and it will be good to see the inside. Let alone the tunnel.'

'And you'll be very welcome there Paul.' Concluded Sally.

Robert's eyes were becoming tired. He knew they couldn't be far away from Northumberland now and he was looking forward to stretching his legs. He rubbed his eyes then quickly tried to refocus on the road ahead.

'Robert, you look so tired!' Louisa said, concerned that he had driven so many miles without a break. 'Wouldn't you like to stop and have a rest for a while? Maybe you would like some coffee to help you feel more alert.'

'No I'm fine Louisa, thank you. We can't have too much further to travel now; we passed the Pennines some time ago so we must be approaching Northumberland any moment.'

'As long as you are ok to drive honey. I don't want you falling asleep at the wheel.' Louisa smiled to Robert and hoped that he'd accepted her comments in the light-hearted way they were meant.

Robert wound the window down slightly to get a little air, then he looked up again at Paul's car ahead of him. He noticed that he was indicating to leave the motorway and he turned on his left-hand indicator to follow.

Robert suddenly felt more alert. He wondered whether it was the fresh air that had reinvigorated him, or whether it was the fact that he knew they were getting close to their destination. Whatever the reason, he was now excited at the prospect at seeing Blackfriars again and was equally excited for Louisa who would be seeing it for the first time in her life.

Dusk had fell. The sky was quite clear, but for a few clouds that were lit by the moon. Paul steered his car along the winding country roads that were guarded by high hedgerows. He wanted to remember the route but he was pleased to listen to Cornelius' directions. Cornelius and Sally scanned the road ahead, all the time searching for familiar sights that they remembered. Sally noticed that the sights that were known to her were becoming more frequent.

She knew she was getting closer to their home and her heart raced faster and faster. Suddenly she noticed the familiar dry stone wall that signified to her that they were only moments away. Sally closed her eyes for only a few seconds. When she reopened them, Blackfriars was in view. The house appeared darkened and was sat silhouetted against a beautiful backdrop of a moonlight sky.

Cornelius reached over and took hold of Sally's hand.

'We're home honey.' Cornelius didn't need to say anything else to sally. He looked over to her and saw that tears filled her eyes.

'Thank you darling.' Sally struggled to get her words out. 'Thank you for bringing me home again.'

Paul turned into the drive way and drove slowly up to the house. Blackfriars looked as majestic and mysterious as it always had to Sally and Cornelius. Sally almost sensed that the house was pleased to see them too. She looked up at the bowed walls and beautiful features. She had a strong sense of guilt that they'd left it behind all those months and years ago. Paul pulled his car to the front of the house and stopped it, leaving room for Robert and Louisa.

Robert turned into the drive way that led to Blackfriars. Louisa had only seen one photograph of Blackfriars but now she was seeing it with her own eyes for the first time. She was utterly captivated. Robert looked over to Louisa who stared at the house without blinking.

She had been told about Blackfriars by Sally on a number of occasions and she'd had its beauty described to her. From Sally's descriptions, she'd been able to visualise how the house really looked and the photograph was not good quality. However, seeing it for real was an amazing experience for her. Louisa saw the house in a different way to how some would see it. Her knowledge of history and in particular her knowledge of the House of Tudor dynasty made her appreciate its real value and place in history. She tried to imagine how it would have looked when William knew it as his home and how his brothers would have tended to it all those centuries ago.

Robert stopped the car and Louisa leapt out and ran to Sally.

'Sally it's beautiful. It's really beautiful. I'm so pleased to finally see it.' Louisa's raw emotion was too much for Sally and she reached out to hug her friend, tears still in her eyes.

'So, are we going to go inside?' Asked Paul.

'You bet we are.' Answered Cornelius.

'Darling, are you ready to go inside?' Asked Cornelius.

'Try and stop me.' Sally quickly followed Cornelius to the door. He unlocked it and pushed the large door open.

The house felt cold and a little dank Cornelius thought. He was not entirely surprised at this but he told the others that he would turn on the water and heating. He reassured Sally that once Blackfriars had warmed up, it would feel like home again and that it wouldn't take too long.

Cornelius was right. As soon the as the house started to warm through, the cold soon disappeared and was replaced by a soothing warmth that was starting to envelop the whole interior of the house. The dank atmosphere started to abate and whilst there was a little dust, Sally was surprised by the general condition to the house. She couldn't believe that she was finally home and that it was exactly as she remembered it.

She'd gone over this moment in her mind for so long and now that she was finally back at Blackfriars, she couldn't take it all in quick enough. She wanted to see so much of the house and raced around looking at everything as quickly as possible. Cornelius remained in a more practical mood and proceeded to show Paul, Louisa and Robert to their rooms so that they could unpack and refresh themselves following their long journey. However, the tunnel remained first and foremost in all their minds.

Cornelius asked the others if they'd like to accompany him down into the cellar to view the tunnel. He anticipated that they would be keen to see it for the first time. However, for Cornelius and Sally it held so much more intrigue and they wanted to ensure that their secret had remained untouched and more importantly, that it remained intact. Louisa and Sally had agreed to prepare a simple evening meal for them all, after hastily collecting some items from a supermarket en route. Everyone was in total agreement however, they wanted to see the tunnel and that they should do this without delay.

Cornelius gathered together some protective clothing and suggested that they all put it on before entering the cellar. He unlocked the trap door and turned on the cellar lights.

As Cornelius walked slowly down the cold steps, he could sense that the atmosphere was still but it appeared dry and that removed one of the worries he had as to what he might find. Further worries were removed when he looked over at the racking that he'd placed against the wall to see that it completely veiled the tunnel's entrance.

Paul, Robert and Louisa looked all around the cellar impatiently, searching for clues about where the tunnel might be. Sally and Cornelius walked over to the racking against the wall and stood looking at it for a moment, before lifting it at the ends to start moving it.

Robert quickly leapt to Cornelius' side to help him move the rack away from the wall. Paul wondered about the ease at which they moved the rack and how this would have prevented anyone from gaining access. He considered this carefully, concluding that if anyone had knowledge of the tunnel's existence then no amount of protection would have prevented them getting through. This was clearly a simple veil to shield the tunnel from potential intruders who may have broken in to steal items of value, not to look behind racking on the slim chance of finding something of much greater value.

Cornelius entered in the tunnel first and asked the others to wait while he ventured inside to turn on the first set of portable lighting units. He wanted to ensure that Sally and the others would be completely safe before entering. He also wanted to prepare the tunnel so that their first impressions of it would be one that they would all remember. Sally, Louisa, Robert and Paul all waited in eager anticipation for Cornelius to return. With the exception of Sally, who knew what treasures the tunnel held, they all had their own mental images of what the tunnel would look like when they eventually walked in. They all had their own expectations too and their own reasons for wanting to see inside.

Cornelius appeared back at the entrance and he greeted them all with a smile. He looked over to Sally and told her that it was as beautiful and as mysterious as ever. He took hold of Sally's hand and invited them to follow them into the tunnel.

Paul entered the tunnel and Robert took hold of Louisa's hand and they followed the others inside. They walked carefully down the stone steps that William had prepared for them all those centuries ago. When they reached the bottom of the steps they looked ahead to see the tunnel in its true splendour.

Sally and Cornelius stood looking ahead of them. They were as captivated as they had been when they first entered it. The stone walls and floor appeared to be in as good condition as they remembered and possibly as it was when it was built by William and his brothers. It was intact and it was completely dry.

Louisa was beside herself with excitement and looked down the tunnel with awe. When Sally told her about the tunnel she didn't want to believe it at first but she knew her friends would not have lied to her about it. However, the mental image of the tunnel that she'd formed in her mind over many months was entirely different to what she was seeing. It was far more robust and permanent. It had much more character and a more professional finish than what she'd expected.

Robert and Paul too, gasped in amazement at what they were witnessing. They all had so many questions but Cornelius wanted them to press on a little further before they closed the tunnel again for the evening. Cornelius took them to the first recess where they'd found William's first parchment. They all eagerly looked inside and then Cornelius suggested they all go back up again.

'Let's not get too far in tonight. There's more to see but we're all tired and I think we should have some food and rest.' Cornelius said.

'I agree. We've got a long day ahead of us tomorrow and we'll need a good night's sleep.' Replied Robert. Louisa and I will need to go up to Kielder to see if we can find anything about Plashetts and the location of it in relation to the surface.'

They all headed for the entrance to the tunnel again but Louisa, still in awe of what lay in front of her, remained for a few more seconds to savour what she was witnessing. She imagined William walking along the tunnel and placing his carefully prepared parchments into their recesses. She tried to imagine what life would have been like for them and that only her friends had been in the tunnel since it was sealed. Finally, she turned and hurried to catch up with the others.

Sally and Louisa prepared an evening meal and they all ate around the kitchen table. Blackfriars was now enveloped by darkness and an eerie silence surrounded it. Sally was pleased that her friends were all there with them but she still felt uneasy. She had no idea if the men that were responsible for the Professor's and his nephew's murders knew they were back in the UK. Moreover, she didn't know if they knew about Blackfriars or indeed if they knew that they were in possession of the professor's notebook.

She discussed this with the others and they tried to allay her fears. Paul said that he would be speaking to Northumbria Police as soon as he could to inform them that they had returned to Blackfriars.

Sally thanked them all but said that she was tired and needed some sleep. Cornelius and Paul both agreed but Robert and Louisa remained at the kitchen table and said they were staying up a little while longer.

'We'd just like to go through the professor's notes one more time before we sleep. Tomorrow we'd like to go over to the local dive centre to get some information about Kielder.' Robert said.

'OK but don't be late you two, we've got a long day tomorrow.' Sally said, smiling at Louisa.

'We won't Sally. Good night and try to sleep well, everything is going to be alright.' Louisa said.

Robert and Louisa listened as Sally made her way up the staircase. Then they turned to face one another.

'It's so good to have some time alone with you Robert.'

'You've no idea how happy I am at the moment.' He replied. 'You look absolutely stunning and can't take my eyes off you.'

They stared at one another, their eyes were fixed one each other and darted back and forth as they followed one another's eye movements. They moved closer together and kissed gently on the lips.

'I feel like you've taken my heart Robert. Please be careful with it my darling.'

'I will treasure it always.' He replied.

The next morning Cornelius and Sally woke late. They made their way down stairs and made breakfast for the others. They heard a car approaching in the driveway and looked at one another wondering who it could be. Cornelius looked over to Sally and saw that she wore a concerned expression. He told her not to be afraid.

'It's daylight honey, I'm sure it's probably someone who wants directions or something.' Cornelius said.

'Nevertheless, I don't want you going out alone, please will you get Robert and Paul up? Please go now darling, I'm afraid.' Sally looked serious and Cornelius agreed that it might be best to get the others up. He was about to race up stairs but he feared that whoever it was, they were just outside the house.

They heard a car door closing directly outside the front of the house and they both rushed into the lounge to look out of the window. They saw that Robert was helping Louisa out of the car and they both walked towards the house.

Sally rushed to the front door and opened it.

'You two scared the living daylights out of us, where have you been?' Sally appeared frightened to them and Louisa apologised.

'I'm sorry Sally, we didn't mean to startle you. We just wanted to go along to the local dive centre. We've got some information about Kielder.' Louisa said.

'We've managed to find out where Plashetts is too.' Added Robert.

'Well you'd better come in both of you. You had us worried for a moment.' Sally felt guilty for making them worry. 'Let's have some breakfast and you can show us what you've found out about Kielder.'

They all gathered around the breakfast table and heard about what they'd learned about Plashetts and Kielder Water.

'We can't believe it.' Robert said. It's a really popular dive site and the buildings, including the church are supposed to be in excellent condition.' Robert said excitedly.

'What's more, is that we don't even need a boat.' Added Louisa. 'We can enter the water from the North-Eastern end of the reservoir and it's only a short swim. Apparently, the church is clearly marked with buoys.

'When do you think you will be ready to make the dive?' Asked Sally, wondering if they may require a couple of days to make their preparations.

'Later this morning.' Answered Louisa. 'We already have our equipment; we took it to the dive centre in the car with us.'

Cornelius laughed at Louisa's answer.

'Always the adventurer eh Louisa?' Cornelius joked.

'No time like the present.' She replied.

Louisa was clearly eager to commence the dive. Robert was equally keen and his body language suggested that he wanted to leave the house and head for Kielder as soon as possible.

'Don't you have to check your equipment or make any plans for the dive?' Cornelius asked.

'Yes we always need to do that when we dive and we've done both.' Robert replied.

'We have all the information we require. We have bought new underwater lights and we have a map of the village of Plashetts.' Louisa said. 'Clear the table and we'll show you a plan of the village and the dive site.'

Louisa unrolled the plan view of Plashetts which showed St Oswald's church and where it is entered by divers.

'You can see the doorway here. This is where Robert and I will enter the church. Then we will need to proceed carefully until we reach the internal west wall which is opposite the doorway.' Louisa pointed out their route on the map to the others.

Robert watched as she described how she and Robert would need to equalise the pressure in their ears on their journey down to the bottom of the reservoir. Robert was impressed by Louisa and he was so pleased to see that she appeared very confident and animated. She seemed to be so excited and happy and this pleased him.

'Did you know too that the word reservoir is derived from a French word meaning storehouse?' Louisa pointed this fact out to the others which they found amusing.

'So are you lot ready to leave or not?' Robert asked.

'We haven't even had breakfast yet, and you two aren't going anywhere until you've had something to eat' Sally replied.

'Isn't it supposed to be dangerous to go diving on a full stomach?' Paul enquired.

'An old wive's tale Paul.' Louisa replied. 'We're both starving. Let's eat and then let's get going.' She continued.

Ok let's have breakie and then we'll head off. I've had the battery on charge for our 4x4, hopefully I'll be able to crank up the old girl and we can all go in that.' Cornelius offered.

'Sounds good, now where's those sausages that I can smell?' Robert asked.

After they had eaten, Cornelius left and returned to the front of the house in his and Sally's 4x4 truck. Robert started to move the SCUBA equipment into the back from his car and they all climbed in.

Armed with their map and their instructions on how to get to the dive site, they drove off down the driveway and turned right heading for Kielder Reservoir. As they drove away, a car appeared in Cornelius' rear view mirror.

Chapter Twenty Four

Cornelius drove along the winding Northumberland road and whilst he was aware that a car was behind, he paid little attention to it. He was more excited about reaching Kielder Reservoir, as were the others.

For Louisa and Robert, the journey held so much excitement. They each hadn't done any diving for a number of months now and they both loved it so much. Moreover, it was the excitement of what the dive would reveal about the tunnel and their search for the final clue, but perhaps more than anything, they were with each other.

The car that was behind, and which had momentarily driven rather close to the back of Cornelius' car, had since pulled back to a safe distance but still it followed. The car had three occupants and maintained its distance behind, changing it speeds to match Cornelius'.

After approximately 15 miles, Cornelius saw the first sign post for Kielder Reservoir and reckoned that they would be there in another 15 minutes or so. It was a crisp morning and the sky was quite clear. Only some cirrus clouds were scattered thinly in the distance and the temperature was only about 10 degrees C. Cornelius wondered if the water would be too cold for a dive.

'Are you sure that you two are ready for this dive?' Cornelius looked for more reassurance from Robert that they were indeed, as fully prepared for the dive as they'd reported. He'd not accounted for the fact that both Robert and Louisa were outdoor types and that for them, the dive was a routine exercise that presented no real challenges.

Another ten miles or so later, Cornelius advised them all that Kielder was only a few moments away. The car with the three occupants remained a safe distance behind, but behind nonetheless. Cornelius, whilst unconsciously aware it was in his rear-view mirror, remained oblivious to any significance of it having followed them since they left Blackfriars. Cornelius reached the top of a hill and as he steered his car over the apex, Kielder Reservoir appeared in view.

Louisa gasped at the size of the man-made structure. It looked beautiful she thought and marvelled at the way it fitted into the surrounding hillocks and in the way, it hugged the natural contours of the surrounding hills and landscape. Its surface shimmered peacefully and Louisa thought that it looked utterly resplendent.

'I'm so pleased to see the reservoir for the first time.' Louisa said. 'It looks truly beautiful.'

'I agree.' Said Sally. 'What a magnificent sight, and right on our doorstep.'

Robert's mind started to analyse the technical aspects of their dive. He went through the mental checklist that he'd always used as a trusted method to ensure he hadn't forgotten anything. As Kielder drew nearer, Louisa joined Robert in her own version of mental preparations for the dive that was now imminent.

Cornelius followed the signs for the Visitor Centre and he pulled into the empty car park. The car that had been following continued on and disappeared slowly around a bend in the road. Paul and Robert checked the map of Kielder and judged that the entrance point they needed was further round the reservoir. They pulled back onto the road and continued for approximately two more miles passing the car that had been following which was parked in a layby.

Robert pointed out that they should be approaching their dive site just around the next corner.

'There it is, next right.' Said Paul.

Ahead they could all see the turning to the right that Paul had pointed out. It was a tarmac surfaced road but had no road markings. It led right to the water's edge then disappeared beneath the surface of Kielder. Paul pointed out that the road had previously been one of the roads that led to the Village of Plashetts and now it was used as a jetty for yachting enthusiasts and for divers when entering the water.

Cornelius pulled to the side of the small road only a few metres from the edge of Kielder Water. They all exited the car and Robert opened the back of the 4x4.

Louisa joined him and they both arranged their SCUBA into the order in which they would be donning it. Louisa and Robert changed into their wet suits inside the rear of Cornelius' and Sally's car, emerging ready for their trip down to the bottom of Kielder and to St Oswald's church.

Robert and Louisa went over their checks once more time then checked that one another's equipment was properly functional and that their weight belts were secured correctly.

'OK, here we go.' Louisa exclaimed.

'Please be careful you two.' Sally made a genuine plea to both her good friends and she gripped Cornelius' hand tightly.

Louisa and Robert made the short walk down the road and began to wade into the water. It felt a little cold to Robert and Louisa but not uncomfortably cold. Robert stopped and he attached a tether cord to Louisa's belt so that they could not become separated once they'd submerged. They attached their face masks and began breathing from their SCUBA equipment. The others watched as Robert and Louisa walked further and further until they had disappeared beneath the surface.

Robert and Louisa turned on their powerful lamps and started to swim out and further down following the road surface that became deeper and deeper. Every ten or twelve feet, they would stop and pop their ears to equalise the pressure, each time relieving the build-up of pressure that became uncomfortable for them.

As they went deeper they were surprised and encouraged by the clarity of the water. Their lights were powerful but they were still delighted that they could see so well. According to their dive instructions, for St Oswald's church in Plashetts, divers should follow the road down to a distance of about 50 feet. Then a stone wall would lead them to their left and eventually to the ropes that were attached to buoys on the surface. They should then be able to see the top of the church which would be sat a little deeper at around 75 – 80 feet.

As they approached the stone wall they scanned around looking for the ropes that were attached to the floating buoys. Louisa spotted the ropes ahead of her and she tugged at the tether to attract Robert's attention to her. She pointed in the direction of the ropes indicating that they were probably only a few yards from being able to see the church. They continued to scan the area beyond the wall and they moved further down a slight slope.

They had moved about 30 feet then Robert and Louisa caught a glimpse of St Oswald's Church. It lay further down the slope and sat at the bottom. As they grew closer, the building became clearer to them. The church was a small building with a small spire at one side. The walls looked grey and the windows were missing, either broken by the weight of the water or probably removed before the reservoir was filled Robert thought. The building was largely intact which surprised and pleased Robert. It was clearly visible to them both and it became clearer as they swam closer to it. It sat in front of a backdrop of darker water that gradually disappeared into complete darkness.

Robert and Louisa were only inches apart from one another but they remained tethered. As they approached the doorway of St Oswald's, Robert looked over to Louisa and he signalled to her that he would lead the way inside the church. He made a circle with his thumb and middle finger to signify that all was good. Once he received the same signal in return from Louisa he was satisfied that he could proceed ahead of her.

Robert pointed his lamp inside the church and the area ahead of him was illuminated. Once he was safely inside he looked behind him and saw that Louisa was following. The church was small inside and Robert quickly assessed that when it was in use, it would probably have accommodated no more than 50 people at most. The pews had all been removed and the floor of the church was covered in a layer of silt and some water borne vegetation. Over to their right they could see that the end of the church where the altar would have been situated was raised by two steps and the wall behind had a stone cross that was still visible and pronounced from the wall.

The water inside the church was still and only moved when Robert and Louisa disturbed it. They swam carefully over to the wall that was opposite the doorway and they started to scan for the symbols that they were looking for.

Despite a number of stones that bore wording, some more legible than others, nothing appeared obvious to them. Robert began a systematic search of the wall. Using his powerful torch, he scanned the surface of the stones in a sweeping motion. Louisa followed with her own torch to help illuminate the same areas of stonework. It occurred to Robert that they might find it difficult to locate what they were looking for. A further thought occurred to him that the symbols or words may have been eroded.

Robert was continuing to search when Louisa tugged at the tether. She had moved a few feet away to Robert's right and she held her hand against the wall. Robert moved his torch to wear her hand was and he watched as Louisa's fingers ran over the outline of a pine tree. The symbol was little over 6 inches high and it was still beautifully formed. She tugged at Robert's torch a little further to the right and there was the oak leaf in clear form a few inches away. Robert patted Louisa on the back and she responded by making the circle symbol with her thumb and middle finger to indicate that all was indeed good.

Beneath the symbols was the letter 'W' confirming for them that they had struck the jackpot. This was the work of William and it had been etched into the wall of the church for over 450 years. The last 30 of those years under the waters of Kielder. Further wording became visible to them under the pine tree and oak leaf symbols. The words

427

'Ecce Homo' which meant little to Robert but everything to Louisa. Beneath that was one more piece of information. It was simply a pair of gull-like wings.

Louisa tugged at the tether once more and she gave a 'thumbs up' signal to Robert meaning that they should return to the surface immediately. Robert took hold of Louisa's arm and they swam quickly through the Church doorway and headed for the surface. When they reached the surface Louisa quickly removed her mask. Robert did the same.

'What's wrong? Are you ok honey?' Robert was worried that Louisa might have been in difficulty and that is why he had raced to get Louisa back up.

'Darling I'm fine.' Said Louisa grinning and almost laughing with delight.

'You had me worried for a moment.'

'There is nothing to worry about honey, I know what these symbols mean. I know what it all means.' Louisa was finding it difficult to contain her excitement. She grabbed Robert's arm.

'Come on we must swim back and tell the others what we've found.' Louisa started to swim back to the shore line.

Robert held a puzzled look but raced after Louisa. He was finding it difficult to keep pace with her but they both eventually reached the side and the clambered awkwardly out of the reservoir and back to the others that were still waiting. Louisa almost fell trying to race towards the others whilst trying to remove her flippers and calling for Robert to be quick.

Sally asked what was wrong as Louisa raced towards her.

'Nothing is wrong Sally. Nothing at all. I know what the symbols mean. I know what they mean.' Louisa was clearly out of breath but she almost laughed the words of her mouth.

Cornelius looked to Robert and he asked him what he's seen.

'Well there was the Pine Tree, the Oak Leaf, a letter 'W', the words 'Ecce Homo' and another symbol that looked like wings. And that's it.' Robert looked as confused as the others and then they all looked to Louisa for an explanation.

Louisa removed her diving mask from the top of her head and shook her hair.

'We need to return to the tunnel and as soon as possible.' Louisa said.

'But why, what does it all mean Louisa?' Sally demanded a response from her friend.

'We have all the information we need and we must go back but all I will say for now is that the gull-like wings that Robert was referring to are the coat of arms of the Seymour family. Jane Seymour's family.'

Robert and Louisa took off their wet suits and changed back into their clothes. Meanwhile, Sally, Cornelius and Paul were keen to know more about the dive and the information that Robert and Louisa and uncovered.

Cornelius drove out of the car park and headed back towards Blackfriars. As the car gathered speed, the others all sat in mutinous collaboration, wanting to know more from their friends.

'So what can you tell us about the Gull-wing coat of arms? What is so special about it? Sally enquired.

'There is nothing really special about the Gull-wings.' Stated Louisa. They simply identify the person who is maybe key to everything. That person, as I said, is Jane Seymour.'

'What is so important about her?' Asked Cornelius.

'Well as we know from our history books she was the third wife of Henry VIII.'

Louisa continued to explain that Jane Seymour was the beloved 3rd wife of Henry VIII.

'She was his favourite for a number of reasons. Notably for providing Henry with a son and heir. Moreover, Jane Seymour was ironically a devout Roman Catholic. Her family's coat of arms were the gull-like wings that Robert and I saw in St Oswald's. When we return to Blackfriars, I will hopefully be able to shed more light on it for you. I will use the professor's notebook to fill in some of the gaps.' Louisa was clearly enthused about what they were involved with. 'My only regret is that the dear Professor is not here with us.'

The journey back to Blackfriars seemed to take less time and Cornelius turned his car into driveway of Blackfriars. They drove up and stopped the car at the front of the house.

Chapter Twenty Five

Inside Blackfriars Louisa asked Sally to bring the parchments and the Professor's notebook. They all gathered around the table in the dining room and Louisa took out some paper and started to illustrate what she thought the information might mean.

She took out the Professor's notebook and started to explain, first about the symbols. Louisa knew what the symbols meant but she supported her comments with notes from his book. She said that the oak Leaf symbol means peace, concordance and reconciliation. The pine tree symbol means death and eternal life thereafter.

'I think that now might be the right time to go into the tunnel.' Said Sally. 'We should maybe look for another of William's parchments.'

'Do you think there might be more?' Louisa asked.

'We have not gone all the way into the tunnel yet, so there's every chance there will be more.' Added Cornelius.

'And as you know Louisa, we did leave in rather a hurry.' Said Sally.

'Then I think we should waste no more time. Please let's return to the tunnel and see what William has for us.' Louisa said eagerly.

The others agreed and Cornelius went to collect the protective clothing they would need. Dressed, they headed down the stone steps, each with a renewed sense of excitement and enthusiasm. Cornelius turned on the first set of portable lighting units and with their passage way illuminated, they set off on the long walk to the last recess that Cornelius, Sally and the Professor had found.

They walked carefully along the illuminated tunnel. Louisa walked with the same sense of enthusiasm that the Late Professor had when he was last there. She was totally absorbed by the experience and her knowledge of history gave her an added dimension to her senses that she felt the others perhaps were not as fortunate to possess. By the time they'd reached the final recess they were tired but their curiosity gave them a boost of energy. They needed this to overcome their fatigue and to compensate for the poor air quality.

As he'd done in the past, Cornelius made the point that they were now in unchartered territory and they should not only tread carefully, but they needed to slow their progress so that they didn't miss another of William's clues. Sally explained to Louisa, Robert and Paul what it was they should all be looking for. Cornelius added that the 'W' to signify William's mark would possibly be at head height but they needed to scan the entire wall, and at both sides.

Louisa, Sally and Paul started their search on the left wall and Robert and Cornelius on the right. They all walked slowly and deliberately in their exploration and pursuit of William's mark. Louisa was methodical in her examination of the wall. She was determined that if William had left his next mark on this side of the wall, she would not miss it. Indeed, all five examined the stones conscientiously and precisely, paying particular attention to any stone that had an usual surface or looked like it may have been tampered with.

Paul guessed that they must have walked for almost 4 miles but it was hard for him to judge the distance they'd covered accurately as he'd had no landscape to compare with, only a narrow tunnel and possibly the time it had taken them. Of course, now that they were walking slowly, it would be even more difficult to gauge.

Robert's eyes were beginning to tire and he stopped for a moment to wipe away the fatigue from around them. As he pressed the thumb and fore-finger of his right hand into the bridge of his nose he heard Louisa gasp sharply. He turned to see that she was pointing towards a stone.

'It's William's marking. I've found one of William's stones. I can't believe it.' Louisa was thrilled that she'd located one of William's marks that would hopefully lead to another of his parchments.

Robert and Paul ran to her side. Paul tried to see what the marking looked like and Robert put his arm around her to congratulate her on her find. Louisa turned and threw her arms around him. Cornelius stood ready with his tools to remove the stone from its housing. Louisa stepped aside for him to and he began to chip away carefully at the mortar, with Louisa remaining fixated on the stone.

Once Cornelius had dislodged the stone he removed it and invited Louisa to look inside. She was so thrilled to have the chance to do this and thanked Cornelius. She looked inside to see the end of a leather folder sitting in an internal recess. She reached inside and took hold of it. She carefully removed it and held it in her hands. It felt very cold to her and she paused for a moment to think about William the Dominican Order monk who was the last person to hold it more than 450 years ago. She looked up to Robert and the others and asked if they could go back now to view its contents.

They started on their long walk back to Blackfriars, a journey that Cornelius knew would take a considerable amount of time to complete. They all strode purposefully in the direction of Blackfriars and Louisa clung tightly to the folder that she'd retrieved from its hiding place. She reckoned to herself that she was possibly the most excited of them all and her knowledge of history perhaps made this so. The walk back was beginning to take its toll on them and they were all tired. They agreed that this would be the last visit to the tunnel today but they still had the excitement of opening and deciphering William's latest parchment.

When they reached the cellar again, Robert helped Cornelius replace the racking against the wall and they returned upstairs. Louisa placed the folder containing the parchment on the dining room table and they all gathered around. Aware of its precious contents, Sally noticed that Louisa handled it with the same care as the Professor had when he'd found the previous parchment. She carefully loosened the leather strap and opened the folder. Louisa gently guided the parchment from its folder and rested it on the table. Like the Professor, Louisa needed little assistance in translating the document into readable English.

The others were impressed by Louisa, but it was mainly Robert, who looked on in silent admiration; the new lady in his life commenced translating William's work onto a fresh piece of paper. He reminded himself that not only was she demonstrating huge knowledge, but she was translating an old English document into modern English which was her second language. When she'd completed her translation, she laid the paper on the table and asked the others if they'd like her to narrate what William had to say.

They all nodded eagerly, impatient as to what information William would be passing on to them. Louisa started to read out the transcript to the others, it was short but for Louisa it was extremely meaningful and informative.

20ᵗʰ March 1542

Greetings my friends,

In my last instructions, I wrote about an important milestone that you will be reaching soon. However, I said that you will have work to do to reach it and claim what lies therein.

I only have one more set of instructions for you and if you are indeed to claim what is here, you will have proven worthy to have completed the work.

You will need to look for peace, concordance and reconciliation. You will also need to understand death and eternal life thereafter. Between these two ideals you will find true salvation. You will also find a treasure that is too precious for one man to possess and the understanding of true love.

Once again my friends, please go in peace and may god guide you and protect you.

William

When she'd finished reading she looked up from her notes and grinned.

'Isn't this truly amazing?' Louisa said, whilst looking for a response from the others. 'I am so pleased that William has been so helpful.'

Cornelius, whilst pleased for Louisa and with her obvious enthusiasm, held a puzzled expression. He wondered if the others felt as perplexed as he did. Cornelius examined the expressions of the others and noticed that they too were perhaps not on Louisa's wavelength.

'Louisa I'm not sure if I am speaking for the others but I don't think I'm operating on the same frequency as you.' Cornelius finally opted to talk of his bewilderment.

'I'm a little mystified too.' Said Robert. 'You are obviously very knowledgeable but please will you enlighten us.'

Louisa laughed at Robert's remark and told them all to make themselves comfortable while she tried to explain. They all took their places at the table and Louisa remained standing.

William said that we should look for peace, concordance and reconciliation right.' Louisa started with her explanation.

'Yes but how do we find it? I don't understand.' Sally said.

'If you remember, I told you that the meaning of the olive branch symbol was peace, concordance and reconciliation. I also told you that the Pine tree signifies death and eternal life thereafter.' Louisa said.

Cornelius and the others all moved in the seats; he sat forward and rested his arms on the table. Louisa knew that she held their attention now.

'So we look for the symbols then?' Paul's tone suggested he wanted an answer.

'Yes indeed.' Said Louisa. 'However, there is more. William said that we would only find true salvation *between* these two ideals, we may need to search for something in addition to them. I think this is why William had us go to St Oswald's church in Plashetts. I think we need to visit the tunnel again, however, I suspect that what we are seeking may be even further in.'

'I think you're right.' Confirmed Robert.

'So do I but I'm not sure my legs will carry me that far again today.' Joked Sally. 'Perhaps we should all get some rest. Why don't we cook a nice meal for dinner tonight and talk through what we need, and then go back in tomorrow morning.'

Louisa was very eager to get back into the tunnel but she was expecting Sally and the others to say this and she was still a little disappointed.

Cornelius noticed this and he asked Louisa if she'd like to go down into the cellar and choose a couple of bottles of her favourite wine to accompany dinner.

'What a great idea, do you mind if I help you select them?' Asked Robert.

Louisa was pleased by Robert's question.

'Yes shall we go down now?' Asked Louisa. 'What will we be eating and I will try to pick something suitable?'

Sally knew that Louisa liked her own recipe for beef stroganoff and she suggested this to her. Louisa smiled and she grabbed Robert's hand and led him down into the cellar.

'I've been so impressed with you today Louisa. There seems to be no end to your talents.' Robert offered this as a means to make her smile.

'I've been impressed by you too Robert, my handsome man.' Louisa reached out to Robert and they hugged one another. Then they released their grasp and looked into each other's eyes. They kissed passionately and held their lips together for longer than they ever had before.

'Shall we find some wine my handsome prince before they start complaining?'

'Yes, although I'll let you decide honey. You seem to have a remarkably good instinct and know what will be appropriate.'

Robert and Louisa returned upstairs to join the others. Louisa was excited about going back into the tunnel the following morning but she was now more settled and looked forward to the prospect of eating dinner with her friends. She poured everyone some wine and she walked over to Robert. She raised her glass to his.

'To us darling man.' Louisa said.

'To us.' Replied Robert.

As Sally and Cornelius prepared dinner, Louisa went over the previous transcripts that Cornelius, Sally and more recently the professor had found. She examined them again, concerned that she may have missed something important. Once she was satisfied that her theories were valid and consistent with those of the professor, she was content. Dinner arrived and they all ate around the table. Cornelius and Sally felt more at home now and were eager to continue with the professor's work and return to the tunnel. Louisa had similar feelings but she knew she was tired and needed some sleep. Robert too was excited about what William had in store for them tomorrow and Paul remained in investigator mode, curious about what all this meant and why two people had already died over it.

Once they'd finished eating they agreed to finish the wine in the lounge. Cornelius brought more from the cellar and they chatted about the tunnel. They chatted too about William and the adventure he had led them on. With all the wine finished they agreed to enter the tunnel again after breakfast.

As the sun rose over Northumberland it illuminated the eastern gable end of Blackfriars. Louisa's eyes flickered open and her first thoughts were of Robert. She smiled and gathered the duvet up around her neck and ears. Then her thoughts returned to the tunnel and her excitement at what the day would bring began to grow inside her. Today was a special day for Louisa and she looked forward to seeing her friends at breakfast and to exploring the tunnel after what William had passed on to them.

The other occupants of Blackfriars also started to awaken as the daylight started to come through their windows. One by one they made their way down stairs and into the kitchen where Sally had started to prepare some items for breakfast. They slowly gathered around the table in Sally's kitchen and Cornelius was the last to arrive. Louisa found it odd that they were discussing a number of things but seemed to skirt around the topic she really wanted to talk about. When she brought it into the discussion however, the others eagerly grasped the opportunity to carry on with it. This relieved Louisa and she rushed out to collect the parchments and notebook that Sally had in the dining room and she reminded the others that in terms of history, they were making bold steps and should be proud that they were a part of it.

Louisa went over the professor's notes again with them and then she narrated the last transcript that she'd translated from William's parchment the night before. Robert watched Louisa as she concentrated on the paper and he felt so close to her. She rested her left elbow on the table had her left-hand resting against her right shoulder. Robert watched as she kept brushing her hair behind her right ear with her other hand as she read from the transcript that was laying on the table in front of her.

'I fear we will have a long walk this morning.' Louisa said. 'However, it is a very interesting project. I hope you have all slept well.'

'Yes I agree that it will be a long hike for us.' Cornelius replied. 'William certainly made sure we had plenty of exercise.'

'I wonder how far this tunnel actually goes. Have you actually been to the end of it yet?' Asked Paul.

'No not yet.' Sally said. 'Every time we go in we find another of William's parchments and we're usually too excited to get it back home than proceed further in.'

'Well we'll be going further than ever before this morning, so make sure you've had enough breakfast. As soon as you've eaten, we'll get ready to go in again.' Cornelius said.

'I'm ready to go when you are.' Said Robert.

'Me too.' Added Louisa.

Sally cleared away the small selection of dishes, plates and cups from the kitchen table and put on her walking boots.

'I'm ready too.' Sally said.

The friends all made their way down the steps into the cellar and Cornelius handed out the protective clothing and accessories that he's purchased from the DIY store before he and Sally had fled to France. Robert helped Louisa fasten the head adjustment strap on her protective helmet and they all declared their readiness to Cornelius.

They all started to walk along the beginning section of the tunnel and Louisa led the way. She knew that the walk to William's last parchment was a long way and the information he provided was little for the lay person to understand, but with the additional clues now uncovered, it would be easier for them to make sense of what they were and what his words meant.

Cornelius switched on the lighting units to illuminate their route down the tunnel and they continued walking. Cornelius was armed with his hammer and chisel and all were armed with knowledge of the symbols they needed to search for. Louisa had the Professor's note book with her so she could refer to it if needed and record her findings after his.

They walked at pace through the tunnel but were careful not to trip on the uneven surface of the stone floor. They passed the time on the walk discussing the size of the symbols they might find and where they would be situated. Cornelius was sure that they would be further into the tunnel than they had so far ventured. Whilst on previous visits they had been looking for the letter 'W's only, he was certain that he had not come across any unusual symbols. The only other clue he had seen was 'ecce homo', the symbol that the Professor had found before they'd fled to France.

This had intrigued Louisa and it was one of the only things that did not make sense to her. The oak leaf and the pine tree had meaning to her but she felt that the words 'ecce homo' had no place. She knew what they meant but she considered them to be out of context.

The tunnel felt cold to them but it was dry and the air quality was reasonably good they thought. They continued to progress their way along the tunnel, aware that they had a significant distance ahead of them. Louisa was completely enwrapped by the occasion and revelled in the excitement she was experiencing. The others too were excited as to what the information that William had provided would reveal.

'Did anyone hear that?' Asked sally.

'Hear what?' replied Cornelius.

'I could have sworn I heard voices.' She said.

'Where were they coming from?' Enquired Paul.

'I don't know if they were ahead or behind.' She said. 'It's really too hard to say.'

'Are you sure you weren't hearing things?' Cornelius said to her.

'There they go again. Did you hear them?' Sally repeated. 'I think they were coming from behind.'

'I definitely heard them.' Robert said. 'And I'm sure they were behind us.'

They all stopped and looked behind. Trying to see back up the tunnel towards Blackfriars was difficult as the lighting units were pointing directly at them. They stood motionless and silently trying to see or hear something.

Suddenly shapes appeared in front of the last lighting unit and the outline of three men came into view.

Chapter Twenty Six

Cornelius, Sally, Paul, Louisa and Robert stood still and stared down the tunnel at the approaching men. Sally felt a shiver run through her and she knew that these men were not here with good news. There was only one way into the tunnel so they would have had to have broken into Blackfriars and the Police would not have done that.

The men continued to approach and they all stared at them in disbelief. Robert stood in front of Louisa and Cornelius in front of Sally. They started to move backwards further into the tunnel retreating from the men's unrelenting advance. Cornelius, Sally, Paul, Robert and Louisa retreated backwards faster and started to turn to make their escape.

'Stand still.' Said one of the men in a forceful manner whilst continuing to stride forwards quickly. 'There's no place to run to so stay where you are.'

The three men advanced further and stopped a few feet from them. The man who'd spoke was in the centre and slightly in front on the other two. He had a bald head and was largely built. Cornelius thought that he looked to be in his mid-thirties and dressed in smart but casual clothing. The other two men were both a little older and dressed similarly and were clearly subordinate to the man in the centre.

'There's no way out of here. Other than back down the way we've just come. You see we've been here before. We noticed that you have removed from whatever was in those alcoves but that's not what we're here for. What we want is in the notebook.'

Cornelius and the others turned to look behind again to see if they could make their escape.

'I've told you, there's no point in running away.' Said the man, who was almost laughing. 'Like I said, there's nothing down there but a dead end. Now where's the notebook?'

'What if we haven't got it?' Asked Cornelius.

'Well that's easy, we kill you all and then we ransack the house looking for it.'

'And if we do have it? Asked Cornelius.

'Then you give it to us and you get to continue breathing. Sound like a good deal?'

'Give him the book Louisa.' Said Robert whilst staring at the man.

'But what about the Professor's work and all the information it holds.' Answered Louisa.

'Why do you think we want it? Now where is it, I won't ask you again.' Said the man whose tone turned more aggressive and sinister.

448

'Give him the book Louisa.' Said Sally. 'We have no choice to hand it over. Please don't try to be brave. Think about what he said, you have Robert now. Just give it to him.'

Louisa took the Professor's notebook from her pocket and held it in both hands. She looked at it one more time and handed it the large man.

'Now it's time to fulfil your part of the bargain. Leave us alone, you've got what you wanted.' I just hope you know what to do with it and what value it holds.' Cornelius was quick to inform them that what they had was very valuable. He hoped that they would be pleased to have taken such a prized and valued item and they would indeed leave them unharmed.

'Yes this is all we wanted. Don't try to follow us.' Said the large man.

They all turned and started to walk away quickly. Back down the tunnel towards Blackfriars. Cornelius hugged Sally and Louisa flung her arms around Robert.

'We're all lucky to be alive.' Paul said. 'I think we should make our way out of the tunnel as quickly as possible. There's no telling what they might try to do.'

The others agreed. With the three men, out of sight, they started to hurry back towards Blackfriars, still severely shaken by their ordeal and still in fear of their lives.

The three men continued to race towards the house and soon they reached the wooden support beams. The large man picked up a sledge hammer that they'd left there on their way into the tunnel and he started hammering at foot of the beam. Gradually it started to weaken and he continued to pummel it with huge blows. Cornelius and the others could hear the blows of the hammer echoing down the tunnel.

The man continued to hit the wooden beam and it started to give in to the blows. The two other men with him noticed it starting to collapse and they began to make their way ahead and out of the collapsing structure.

'Wait. We're not done yet.' He shouted at the men. 'I want this collapsed properly before we leave. No one goes anywhere until this comes down and they're sealed in behind us.' He growled at the other two men.

The man gave two more large blows of the hammer and suddenly the ceiling started to creak under the huge weight of the earth over the tunnel. First stones fell and then what was above the stones groaned under its own weight, having being held in place by William and his brother's engineering over 450 years ago. The men ran as fast as they could and the ceiling behind them came crashing down.

Then the remaining entrance section to the tunnel completely collapsed and all three men were crushed under hundreds of tons of earth and stone. They all died instantly and lay consumed in the tunnel, along with the professor's notebook.

Robert grabbed at his ears when the tunnel collapsed as a pressure wave hurtled down the tunnel at them.

'That didn't sound good.' Cornelius said.

They all ran towards the roar that they'd heard, petrified at what they would find. Their hearts all raced and they were now terrified that they'd be trapped. Sally started to go into shock and Cornelius stopped to hold and reassure her that they would soon be out and into the open air again. Soon they reached the collapse and their worst fears were realised.

A huge mound of earth filled the tunnel from ceiling to floor in front of them. They stared in disbelief and wondered if they should start to dig.

Robert walked to the collapsed area and looked up and down.

'I think this could be all the way back to the house.' We are going to need to find another way out.' Robert said calmly.

'But you heard what the man said, it's a dead end. We can't escape that way.' Sally said and was becoming hysterical.

Louisa, Paul and Cornelius tried to calm her and reassure her that there would be another way out.

'William has been our friend; he has led us here and he will lead us out. I'm sure of it. Let's go back into the tunnel and see if he will help us.' Louisa implored.

'Louisa's right honey. Let's walk back and let's have William show us the way out.' Cornelius tried to divert her attention.

They all walked back into the tunnel unaware if the men had survived the collapse or not, Sally started to recognise that she had been in mild shock and she started to regulate her own breathing. They continued to walk further into the tunnel, aware that they would have a long walk. Not only to where they had been but further, to the end of the tunnel and hopefully to their escape.

They travelled along faster than they had ever before. The portable lighting units remained strong and showed them the way. Cornelius and Robert checked to see that they had their torches with them, in case the units failed.

Soon enough they arrived back at the spot where they had been confronted by the three men. Now they slowed slightly and looked for clues from William that might show them the way out. Louisa was sure that the information provided by William in the last parchment was probably the last clue and that any further clues would surely be instructions on how to escape. They searched in vain and began to realise that William might not have left clues for an escape.

Still they searched for any sign of William's that might lead them to safety. They scanned walls as they had before, and on many occasions. However, this time they scanned them more intently and closely than ever before. The mood was sombre and the tunnel that had once been a friendly place filled with excitement and intrigue, suddenly had a cold and sinister edge.

Robert was about to suggest that they give up looking and head for the end of the tunnel at speed. He was afraid that Sally might go back into shock and he was afraid for Louisa's safety too, this beautiful and shiny thing that had swept into his life, was too valuable for him to lose.

However, his thoughts of running to the end of the tunnel were interrupted by Louisa who stopped dead in her tracks. She was looking at a stone at the bottom of the right-hand wall. Into it was etched a beautifully designed and crystal clear Olive branch.

'My god. It's the olive branch. It's the olive branch.' Louisa repeated.

They all rallied around Louisa and examined the symbol on the stone for themselves. Cornelius was pleased because it gave something else for Sally to focus upon and he watched her as she became more wrapped up in what Louisa had found. Louisa studied the stone in more detail and she could see that the mason who had etched the symbol into the stone had done it with exquisite detail. It was no more than 4 inches in length and carved beautifully. Louisa tried to work out why William would want to place the stone with the symbol at the bottom of the wall. It made sense to her that he would not wish to make it obvious that it was there, unless one was looking for it and he had achieved that. The symbol was small enough to miss, but clear enough to find, if someone was looking for it.

'Remember what William said in the parchment, we must look between the two ideals he told us about which we know are denoted by the symbols. So, we must look further along the wall for the pine tree symbol.' Louisa explained.

They all concentrated their efforts on finding the pine tree and started to look along the wall. They split their search pattern into three different heights and continued walking slowly. Sally and Louisa scanned the bottom row, Paul and Robert searched the rows around waist level and Cornelius looked at head height. Nothing appeared immediately and they continued with their search pattern. They walked for another few feet and Sally was the first to see it.

'The pine tree, it's here.' Shouted Sally. 'It's looks beautiful.'

There was no doubt at all that this was the work of the same man who had crafted the oak leaf. It was the same size as the oak leaf and finished in the same intricate detail.

'So what now?' Asked Paul.

'William told us that we had to look between the ideals, or symbols as we now know. So, that is what we must do.' Answered Louisa.

'But that could be anywhere across this whole section of wall.' Said Cornelius. 'There must be about thirty feet of wall in between them.'

'May I suggest that we count the number of stones between the symbols and start at the centre stone?' Louisa talked with a sense of purpose and she was making sense to the others.

They all started counting to ensure that they agreed on the correct number of stones.

'Twenty-five.' Said Robert, who was first to finish.

'Twenty-five.' Said Paul.

'Yes, agreed. Twenty-five.' said Louisa.

'So that means the stone we're looking for is number thirteen, right?' Asked Sally.

'I guess so.' Replied Louisa.

They all counted again and found the stone. Cornelius marked it with his chisel so as not to lose it.

'Are you sure that this is it?' Asked Cornelius. 'There are no markings on it at all.'

'I'm just going with my instinct Cornelius, and hopefully with William's helping hand.' Said Louisa.

'Ok, in for a penny, as they say.' Said Cornelius, and he started to chisel away at the mortar.

He found it more difficult having to chisel at a stone at the bottom of the wall, but he persevered and was able to remove the stone, after a great deal of levering. Robert helped him to pull the stone clear of the wall. Cornelius looked into the recess to find nothing but earth. He cleared away as much as he could with the chisel and found nothing. There was no recess behind and nothing but earth.

'What now? Do we keep going in deeper, or do we start with the stones at either side of this one?' Asked Cornelius.

'Neither.' Said Paul. 'Turn around everyone and take a look at this.'

Paul was looking at a stone which was approximately at shoulder height. It was etched beautifully with a pair of gull wings.

'This is it. This has to be it.' Said Louisa. 'How come we didn't see it before?'

'Maybe it was because we were looking one the other wall.' Joked Cornelius.

Sally gave him a friendly slap on the arm for his attempt at sarcasm.

'This is the gull wing that I was telling you about. It was on the wall in St Oswald's Church under the reservoir and this is the Seymour family crest.'

Cornelius moved over to the stone and placed his hammer and chisel against the mortar underneath the stone, ready to start removing it.

'Please be careful Cornelius.' Said Louisa. 'Please try not to damage the stone. It's too beautiful to destroy.'

Cornelius started to hammer away at the mortar and gradually the stone became loose. Robert helped Cornelius again to free the stone and they both lifted it clear of its housing.

Cornelius shone his torch inside the recess. He peered inside for a moment and then stepped back.

'I think you need to look inside.' Cornelius said.

Robert handed his torch to Louisa and she looked into the expanse behind the wall.

'What can you see?' Asked Sally, eager to know what was there.

'It's a chamber.' Said Louisa.

Louisa stood back and allowed the others to look for themselves at what she and Cornelius had seen. One by one, they took their turn to look inside.

'What do you think it is?' Asked Sally.

'I'm almost too afraid to say.' Answered Louisa.

'What do you mean?' Asked Sally.

'I think it may be a burial chamber.' Said Louisa.

'A burial chamber.' Said Sally. 'Do you think this is where William is laid to rest?' She continued excitedly.

Louisa remained silent and shook her head.

'I think we need to get inside and see more, don't you?' Asked Robert.

Louisa and Sally stood back and watched as Robert, Cornelius and Paul removed the surrounding stones to make an access to the chamber behind the wall. Occasionally as they continued, Louisa would shine her torch inside, hoping to catch a glimpse of something that she'd not seen.

After twenty minutes or so, they had made a large hole in the wall and were able to climb through into the chamber.

The chamber was approximately fifteen feet square and a little over 7 feet high. It was finished in beautiful stonework, and of much higher quality than the walls of the tunnel.

'My god, look at this.' Said Cornelius who had been first to climb into the chamber. On the left wall of the chamber was an open recess.

Inside the recess was a golden crown, beautifully adorned in jewels.

Louisa asked them to be careful and not to touch it in case it was damaged.

'Do you think it is the Kings crown?' Asked Robert.

'No.' Said Louisa. 'This is the crown of a queen. I think it is the crown of Henry VIII's third wife, Jane Seymour. More importantly, and quite unbelievably, I think she is buried right underneath us.' Louisa pointed to the gull wing marking on the floor. The others looked down to see the gull wing and dates, 1508 – 1537.

'Jane died in 1537 and must be buried here.' Said Louisa.

'Look there's another parchment folder behind the crown.' Said Robert.

'William must have put it here before the chamber was sealed.' Cornelius said.

Robert reached in to retrieve it and was careful not to move the crown which was situated on a slightly raised piece of perfectly flat stone.

'I don't understand.' Said sally. 'Jane Seymour is supposed to be buried in St Georges Chapel, isn't she?' Asked Sally.

'Yes that's right.' Said Louisa. 'This is what history will have us know and what the anomaly that the Professor was talking about.'

Louisa carefully opened the parchment folder and removed the document that was inside.

'I don't have any paper with me but I will try to translate what I can from it.'

They walked back into the tunnel where the lighting units offered some better light. Robert held the torch over the document so she could see more clearly.

'It's from William.' Louisa said.

She started to read the parchment to the others.

'Greetings my friends. This is a sacred chamber and it is important that you respect the peace that this

place represents. Underneath this chamber lies the remains of Jane Seymour, the Queen Consort and wife of Henry Tudor.

The King had visited Blackfriars previously. He was not content with the progress being made by his men on the dissolution of the monasteries and he came himself to demonstrate his power and to show his strength. However, Blackfriars was granted a reprieve from him when he saw our work and the escape tunnel. After his return to London, he reported his findings to his new wife Jane.

Jane was the love of his life and she was a devout Catholic. Henry VIII doted on her and she was the only one of his three wives to produce a son and heir. When she died shortly after child birth, his orders were to have her body moved here. His wishes were for her to rest in peace and to have her body protected by my brothers and I, the Monks of the English Province of the Order of Preachers.

He had a crown commissioned in her honour and this resides here with her. Do as you will with the treasure but always preserve the sacred tomb of the Queen.

Go in peace my friends. God has led you here and now god will go with you and lead you to peace and fulfilment. Return to Blackfriars, or go forth further into the tunnel to find my mark and your freedom. William.'

'I don't know what to say.' Said Sally. 'That was beautiful.'

'It was beautiful indeed.' Commented Louisa. 'It seemed interesting that William commented that Jane Seymour was the only one of his three wives when of course, we now know there were six. She was the only one of his six wives to receive a queen's funeral and this all makes sense to me now.

The professor found that there was an enormous shift in the Tudor dynasty after the death of Jane. There was a three-year gap when Henry did not want to marry. His attitude towards Catholicism changed and now we have seen the biggest change of all. His wife that we thought lay next to him in St Georges' Chapel at Windsor, in fact, is right under our feet near Blackfriars. The Latin words 'ecce homo' meaning behold the man are clearly the respect that the Order of Preachers have for Henry Tudor.

'What about the crown?' Asked Robert.

'The crown is priceless.' Said Louisa. 'And no one could even start to place a value on it, without considerable thought. But let's just say that I think we should take it with us, collect the parchments and advertise the existence of the crown. I believe it will make Cornelius and Sally, very rich indeed.' Exclaimed Louisa.

'It will make us all wealthy.' Cornelius was quick to correct Louisa, and reminded her that this was a joint effort and that any rewards should be split evenly.

'But how will we prove its true value and history without the professor's notes?' asked Paul.

'This is history Paul and we have every piece of provenance that anyone would ever need in the parchments.' Answered Louisa.

'And in the tunnel, of course.' Reminded Sally.

Louisa smiled at her friend and embraced her. Then they all left the chamber and headed for the end of the tunnel. Robert held the Crown of Jane Seymour carefully in his hands knowing that it was last held by the great king himself and Louisa held the final parchment as they moved quickly along the dimly lit tunnel. They walked as quickly as they dared unsure as to what would be at the end.

William had already told them they were almost at the end in his previous parchment but still they rushed ahead.

A few moments later they came to a sudden stop and, as the three men had told them earlier, there was no way out, only another stone wall.

There was no telling how deep under the surface they were. And they all looked around frantically looking for some clue that would lead to their escape.

'We need to look for a 'W'.' Shouted Louisa hastily. 'There must be a letter 'W', this will be the sign that William has left for us. Look for a 'W'. She repeated again.

'Here it is.' Shouted Sally. 'Here it is, right in the centre of the wall.'

Sally was pointing to the wall at the very end of the tunnel.

Cornelius moved quickly forward started to remove the mortar from the Stonework. However, this time he was much more aggressive and careless. He pounded at the Mortar, and when the stone started to move he kicked at it. The stone shot through the wall and landed at the other side, echoing in the dark chamber behind as it fell.

'This has got to be it.' He said in a raised and forceful tone.

Cornelius, Robert and Paul, launched further blows with the chisel and they kicked at it until they were able to climb through the space they had made.

Robert climbed through first and shone his torch around. There was another small chamber but directly ahead was a set of stone steps that led upwards. The others followed Robert into the chamber and Sally commented that this chamber was exactly like the other under Blackfriars. They raced up the steps to find another wall.

On the wall at the top of the steps was another stone which had one more etching and which they all knew immediately was the way out. The stone was large and had been crafted like the others.

It simply said, *'Go in peace. William.'*

Sally started to cry and wished that she could see William to thank him. Louisa consoled her friend with another embrace.

Again, Cornelius removed the mortar from one side of the stone and Robert took over the chisel and he attacked the remaining pieces of mortar.

They took away the stone and those around it to reveal earth and clay. They dug at it furiously until it fell away and in front of them. There was only about 6 inches or so of mud, and clay to get through and it took moments to reveal an opening into a cave like structure. Natural daylight poured into the chamber containing the stone steps and they climbed through.

They made their way into the cave and looked back at the small hole they'd clambered through and could see that it was half covered in earth and foliage.

They decided to seal it as best they could and headed the thirty feet or so up the gradual incline to daylight and safety.

Sally flung her arms around Cornelius and sobbed uncontrollably, her emotions ran amok with her. They made their way back towards Blackfriars which was so far away that it was not even visible. It took at least fifteen minutes of walking before the beautiful old property came into view in the distance.

They continued walking until they reached the house. The car belonging to the men that had confronted them earlier was still parked in the driveway in front of Blackfriars. Paul was the first to enter the house, closely followed by Robert and Cornelius. They walked straight to the cellar eager to know what had become of the men, and the tunnel entrance.

As they walked down the steps of the tunnel entrance they could see no further. Tons of earth filled the tunnel from floor to ceiling and it was clear to them that the men were inside the tunnel and would have had no chance of escape.

The men returned upstairs and Paul said that he would need to call the Police to notify them of the men's probable deaths. And of course, that he had probably found the men responsible for the murder of John Huggett and his uncle, Professor Montrose.

Sally and Cornelius invited the others into the kitchen and they all sat and gathered their thoughts. They sat in silence for a few moments before Sally spoke.

'Thank you all. Thank you for bringing Cornelius and I home.'

'You're welcome.' Said Robert. 'Thank you for introducing me to the most beautiful and perfect woman in the World.'

Robert asked Sally and Cornelius what their plans were now.

'We are going to do what we came here to do.' Said Cornelius. Once those men are removed and the tunnel is made safe, we're going to start the family we always wanted. Oh, and I may need to go back to work.' Cornelius laughed. 'What about you two?'

'Well if Robert would like to come, I want him to come and stay with me in France.' Said Louisa.

'And I'm going to say thank you and accept.' Said Robert smiling and looking at Cornelius.

Robert reached over to Louisa and took her hold of her hand.

'What about you old friend?' asked Robert while looking at Paul Bretherton.

'Me?' Said Paul. 'I'm going to clear up here, go home, have a long soak in the bath and retire from the Force properly. Then I'm going to start up my Private Investigation business. And if you'll allow me Cornelius, I'd like to call it Blackfriars Investigations.'

'I like the sound of that.' Replied Cornelius.

They all relaxed in the kitchen of Blackfriars and drank coffee that Sally had prepared. A few moments later, two Police cars from Northumbria Police pulled into Blackfriars' driveway.

Exactly one year to the day later.

Louisa and Robert were having breakfast in their home in Lille, and the telephone rang.

'Louisa its Sally.' Said the voice at the end of the telephone. 'Cornelius has something to tell you both.'

'Hello you two, what is it? Do you have the news we've been waiting for?'

'Yes.' Said Cornelius. 'A boy, eight pounds and seven ounces. Behold the young man, William Cornelius Galbraith.'

Epilogue

September 1542

It should have been an average day for the Monks of Blackfriars and for the local people from the nearby village. Today, however, was not going to be an average day for them, nor indeed for William. Today heralded a milestone in the whole meaning of William's life. Not only that but it would signify an end to what had been a rotten period in the history of the Order of Preachers.

Horsemen could be heard approaching from a distance and as they drew nearer, William and his brothers could see that there were many of them. With them rode the King of England, Henry Tudor. William had been expecting the King and his Men's arrival.

'Is it completed?' Asked one of the King's horsemen.

'It is Sire.' Answered William, directing his reply to the King.

The horseman was referring to the tunnel that the king had previously seen and ordered completing to the highest of standards. A carriage carried the body of Jane Seymour, following her death about 5 years previously.

The King's men carried the Queen Consort's body carefully into Blackfriars and down into the tunnel. Henry

Tudor followed, holding the crown of his former Queen; William and his brothers walked quietly behind the King.

On arrival at the Chamber, Jane Seymour was laid in her final resting place and the King placed the crown in the recess that had been prepared.

William placed a parchment contained in a leather bound folder behind the crown and they all retreated back into the tunnel.

Later that day, William placed the last Stone into the wall of the chamber and said a prayer for Jane Seymour; the only wife of Henry Tudor to have a crown commissioned for her and the only one to have given him a son and heir, Edward VI.

THE END

19906084R00275

Printed in Great Britain
by Amazon